DEATH OR GLORY

CIAPHAS CAIN IS back, this time weaving a tale of his early life as a commissar in the armies of the Imperial Guard. Even this early in his career, Cain was displaying the virtues that made him the man he is today (hiding, running, trying to avoid danger whilst being thrust into it). Serving his formative years with the 12th Field Artillery, Cain travels to the beleaguered world of Perlia in an attempt to stop the battle-hungry orks from gaining a foothold on this Imperial world.

But that's as far as Cain's luck hold out. Shot down over enemy lines, Cain and his repugnant aide Jurgen find themselves right in the heart of ork territory. Surely Cain has to finally act like the hero with thousands of lumbering green berserkers between him and safety? Gathering together all the human survivors he can find, Cain makes for freedom, but how can he possibly come out of this one looking like a hero?

More Sandy Mitchell from the Black Library

• CIAPHAS CAIN •

FOR THE EMPEROR
CAVES OF ICE
THE TRAITOR'S HAND

• BLOOD ON THE REIK •

DEATH'S MESSENGER
DEATH'S CITY

TITLES IN THE NEW

Louisa M. Alcott: *Little Women*
Elizabeth Allen: *Deitz and Denny*
Margery Allingham: *The Tiger in the Smoke*
Michael Antony: *The Year in San Fernando*
Enid Bagnold: *National Velvet*
H. Mortimer Batten: *The Singing Forest*
Nina Bawden: *On the Run*
Phyllis Bentley: *The Adventures of Tom Leigh*
Paul Berna: *Flood Warning*
Pierre Boulle: *The Bridge on the River Kwai*
D. K. Broster: *The Flight of the Heron; The Gleam in the North; The Dark Mile*
F. Hodgson Burnett: *The Secret Garden*
Helen Bush: *Mary Anning's Treasures*
A. Calder-Marshall: *The Man from Devil's Island*
John Caldwell: *Desperate Voyage*
Albert Camus: *The Outsider*
Richard Church: *The Cave; Over the Bridge*
Colette: *My Mother's House*
Lettice Cooper: *The Twig of Cypress*
Meindert deJong: *The Wheel on the School*
Eleanor Doorly: *The Radium Woman; The Microbe Man; The Insect Man*
Gerald Durrell: *Three Singles to Adventure; The Drunken Forest; Encounters with Animals*
Elizabeth Enright: *Thimble Summer; The Saturdays*
C. S. Forester: *The General*
Eve Garnett: *The Family from One End Street; Further A ntures of the Family from One End Street; Holiday at the Dew Drop Inn*
G. M. Glaskin: *A Waltz through the Hills*
Rumer Godden: *Black Narcissus*
Margery Godfrey: *South for Gold*
Grey Owl: *Sajo and her Beaver People*
G. and W. Grossmith: *The Diary of a Nobody*
René Guillot: *Kpo the Leopard*
Erik Haugaard: *The Little Fishes*
John Hersey: *A Single Pebble*
Georgette Heyer: *Regency Buck*
Geoffrey Household: *Rogue Male; A Rough Shoot*
Fred Hoyle: *The Black Cloud*
Irene Hunt: *Across Five Aprils*
Henry James: *Washington Square*
Josephine Kamm: *Young Mother; Out of Step*
John Knowles: *A Separate Peace*
Marghanita Laski: *Little Boy Lost*
D. H. Lawrence: *Sea and Sardinia*
Harper Lee: *To Kill a Mockingbird*
Doris Lessing: *The Grass is Singing*
C. Day Lewis: *The Otterbury Incident*
Lorna Lewis: *Leonardo the Inventor*
Martin Lindsay: *The Epic of Captain Scott*
Jack London: *The Call of the Wild; White Fang*
Carson McCullers: *The Member of the Wedding*
Lee McGiffen: *On the Trail to Sacramento*

For my grandmother, Lillian Wright, whose enthusiasm for all things science fictional infected me at an early age, and who would have been delighted to know I'd grow up to earn my living writing the stuff.

A BLACK LIBRARY PUBLICATION

First published in Great Britain in 2006 by
BL Publishing,
Games Workshop Ltd.,
Willow Road, Nottingham,
NG7 2WS, UK.

10 9 8 7 6 5 4 3 2 1

Cover illustration by Clint Langley.

A CIP record for this book is available from the British Library.

ISBN 13: 978 1 84416 287 1
ISBN 10: 1 84416 287 7

Distributed in the US by Simon & Schuster
1230 Avenue of the Americas, New York, NY 10020, US.

Printed and bound in Great Britain by
Bookmarque, Surrey, UK.

IT IS THE 41st millennium. For more than a hundred centuries the Emperor has sat immobile on the Golden Throne of Earth. He is the master of mankind by the will of the gods, and master of a million worlds by the might of his inexhaustible armies. He is a rotting carcass writhing invisibly with power from the Dark Age of Technology. He is the Carrion Lord of the Imperium for whom a thousand souls are sacrificed every day, so that he may never truly die.

YET EVEN IN his deathless state, the Emperor continues his eternal vigilance. Mighty battlefleets cross the daemon-infested miasma of the warp, the only route between distant stars, their way lit by the Astronomican, the psychic manifestation of the Emperor's will. Vast armies give battle in his name on uncounted worlds. Greatest amongst his soldiers are the Adeptus Astartes, the Space Marines, bio-engineered super-warriors. Their comrades in arms are legion: the Imperial Guard and countless planetary defence forces, the ever-vigilant Inquisition and the tech-priests of the Adeptus Mechanicus to name only a few. But for all their multitudes, they are barely enough to hold off the ever-present threat from aliens, heretics, mutants – and worse.

TO BE A man in such times is to be one amongst untold billions. It is to live in the cruellest and most bloody regime imaginable. These are the tales of those times. Forget the power of technology and science, for so much has been forgotten, never to be re-learned. Forget the promise of progress and understanding, for in the grim dark future there is only war. There is no peace amongst the stars, only an eternity of carnage and slaughter, and the laughter of thirsting gods.

Editorial Note:

With the exception of a few short fragments, all the extracts from the Cain Archive, which I have so far prepared for dissemination among the gratifyingly high number of my Inquisitorial colleagues who have expressed an interest in reading them have come from a relatively short period of his long and eventful career: from the commencement of his attachment to the Valhallan 597th in 931 M41 to an incident in 937 M41, roughly a third of the way through his service with that regiment. Of the shorter extracts, three concern his first assignment, to the 12th Valhallan field artillery, and the remaining one his period of service as an independent commissar attached at brigade level in the year 928. Of Cain's subsequent activities as the Commissarial liaison officer to the Lord General's staff and a tutor of commissar cadets at the schola progenium following his official retirement, not to mention his intermittent involvement in inquisitorial affairs at my behest in the years following our first meeting on Gravalax, nothing has so far been said beyond occasional allusions in the disseminated portions of his memoirs.

It was with this consideration in mind that I decided, with the present volume to return the narrative to its beginning, so to speak. The circumstances of Cain's arrival among the 12th Field Artillery early in 919 M41 and his subsequent baptism of fire against the tyranid horde threatening the mining colony on Desolatia has already been covered in one of the shorter extracts, as has his participation in the subsequent campaign to cleanse Keffia of the infestation of genestealers preceding the splinter fleet concerned; anyone wishing to read a fuller, and somewhat less candid, account of these activities is referred to the early chapters of his published memoirs, To Serve the Emperor: A Commissar's Life. *In either event, there seems little point in repeating them here.*

Though these incidents laid the foundation stones of the heroic reputation which, true to form, he continues to insist throughout the memoir that he doesn't really deserve, it was his activities during the first Siege of Perlia which truly consolidated it, and it is therefore that campaign which I have chosen to concentrate on in the latest extract.

Astute readers, with access to the right Inquisitorial records and the appropriate security clearances, will probably be able to deduce another reason for my interest in what to the rest of the galaxy seemed little more than the routine cleansing of an ork incursion from an isolated Imperial backwater. Cain's actions in this campaign were to have unforeseen repercussions both for him and for the Imperium at large. A dozen years later, in his first reluctant activities as a clandestine agent of the Inquisition, and almost seven decades after that, when the thirteenth Black Crusade cast its baleful shadow across the entire segmentum and he found himself having to defend Perlia for the second time. The latter incident still lay a year or more in his future at the point this memoir was written, however, so all references to the siege refer only to the first one, and any implications of hindsight are mine alone.

As usual, I have broken Cain's somewhat unstructured account into chapters for ease of reading, and interpolated material from other sources where I felt it necessary to place his typically self-centred narrative in a wider context. Apart from this, and the occasional footnote, I have left him to tell his own story in his habitually slapdash fashion.

Amberley Vail, Ordo Xenos

ONE

IF I'VE LEARNED one thing in the course of my long and discreditable career, apart from the fact that the more blatant the lie the more likely it is to be believed, it's that an enemy should never be underestimated. A mistake I made a few times in my younger days, I have to admit, but I was always a fast learner where keeping my skin in one piece was concerned; which accounts for the fact that, not withstanding the odd augmetic or two, most of it's still where it belongs.

Of course back in the twenties[1] I was far more naïve, having managed to emerge from a couple of

1. *I assume he means the years 920-929 here, since, due to his somewhat obscure origins, he had only an approximate idea of his chronological age. Not to mention the fact that his innumerable journeys through the warp confused the matter even further. Time spent in that peculiar realm having, at best, only a tangential relationship to its passage in the galaxy at large.*

early scrapes with the beginnings of the reputation for heroism which has followed me around like Jurgen's body odour ever since, and a fine conceit of myself I had as a result you may be sure.

So picture me then in the relatively carefree days of my youth, cocky and overconfident, and still basking in the kudos of having single-handedly saved Keffia from the insidious genestealers who had almost succeeded in undermining our glorious crusade to eradicate them from that remarkably pleasant agriworld. (In actual fact, several Guardsmen and a couple of Arbites had accompanied me,[1] but the newsies hadn't let that inconvenient fact stand in the way of a good story.)

In the manner of all good things the war had finally come to an end, or to be more precise petered out to the point where the locals could clean up their own mess with the aid of a long overdue inquisitor[2] and a couple of squads of Deathwatch Astartes, and the 12th Field Artillery were being pulled out for reassignment along with everyone else.

'So where the hell is Perlia anyway?' I asked, raising my voice above the growling of the Trojans

---

1. *The officers concerned were actually local law enforcers rather than Arbites personnel, but like many seasoned travellers Cain often uses 'Arbites' as a generic term for all such functionaries. Given the number of worlds he visited, and the bewildering variety of local nomenclature encountered throughout the galaxy, he can hardly be blamed for this, although he tends to be more precise about the distinction in the instances where he had contact with actual members of the Arbites itself.*

2. *I had been delayed longer than expected dealing with the space hulk* Dolorous Tidings, *which had more than lived up to its name.*

hauling our limbered-up Earthshakers out onto the apron of the main cargo pad of Keffia's premier starport. By which I mean that it had a proper rockcrete landing field, and some rudimentary repair and maintenance facilities for the shuttles that grounded there. Most of the others were little more than cleared fields, where the shuttles from the grain barges in orbit could simply load up and depart again without undue ceremony. No wonder the 'stealers had found the planet so easy to infiltrate.

Lieutenant Divas, the colonel's subaltern, and the closest thing I had to a friend in the battery, shrugged, his fringe falling into his eyes as usual.

'Somewhere to spinward I think.' If he was going to say anything else he was forced to give up at that point, as a heavy-lift cargo hauler screamed in overhead, its landing thrusters kicking in at the last possible moment, and dropped to the rockcrete with an impact that resonated right up my spine through the soles of my boots. Clearly the pilot wasn't about to take our victory for granted just yet, coming in as though the landing zone was still potentially hot; and given the number of cultists and hybrids still at large, I couldn't altogether blame him for that.[1] I shrugged in return, as the howling of the engines died away to a level where my voice might just be audible.

---

1. *It was to take another year or so before the infestation was completely cleansed, but by this point the problem had diminished to a level where a large-scale Guard presence was no longer required, particularly with an ork* Waaargh *gaining momentum elsewhere in the sector.*

'I'm sure the colonel will fill us in when he gets back,' I bellowed, and turned away, already dismissing the matter from my mind, content to let Divas deal with the tedious job of supervising the stowage of our precious artillery pieces on his own. He nodded, absurdly eager as always, positively looking forward to the next war.

'I hear they've got a bit of an ork problem,' he yelled back. Well that didn't sound so bad. Never having encountered the greenskins before I was sure they couldn't be nearly as intimidating as the genestealers or the tyranid horde I'd already faced and bested. After all, the popular image of them was of uncouth, slow-witted barbarians, which meant that, if anything, they were considered a bit of a joke, at least by those fortunate enough not to have actually faced them in the flesh, so I plastered a self-confident grin on my face and left him to it.

Wynetha[1] had taken a few day's leave to see me off, and I could think of far better ways of spending my last evening on Keffia than watching sweaty gunners lug heavy objects about.

In the event, the night passed more than pleasantly, and I found myself stifling a yawn at several points in the briefing the following day. The windows of the conference room had been left wide open to admit a breeze, sharp with the chill of approaching autumn, and I found

---

1. *Sergeant Phu, one of the local law enforcers present at Cain's encounter with the genestealers. His account of the incident in question, elsewhere in the archive, makes it abundantly clear that her relationship with him was far more than merely professional.*

myself unusually grateful for its assistance in keeping my eyes open. All the battery commanders[1] were present, trying to look interested, while Colonel Mostrue, our commanding officer, regurgitated the information that had been passed on to him and the rest of the regimental commanders by the Lord General or someone equally exalted. In later years I was to be privy to the higher level briefings myself, of course, and find them a great deal more candid, not to mention worrying, but back then I still took a lot of what I was told at face value.

'Are we boring you, commissar?' Mostrue asked acidly, turning his ice-blue eyes in my direction. He'd never quite believed my hastily improvised explanation for being the inadvertent hero of Desolatia, when my perfectly natural attempt to make a run for it before the 'nids arrived had simply succeeded in luring an unsuspected flanking attack into the killing zone of our guns. Mostrue was too canny to let his doubts about my character show openly. Instead he tried to needle me at every opportunity, no doubt hoping I'd let something slip to confirm his suspicions. As usual I refused to respond,

---

1. The 12th, being an artillery regiment, was split into batteries, each roughly equivalent in administrative terms to a company in a line unit. Cain is typically vague about their disposition, but each appears to have consisted of around half a dozen Earthshakers, together with the support vehicles and personnel required for their proper functioning. The regiment also possessed a number of Hydras for air defence, but whether they formed a battery in their own right or were distributed among the others isn't clear from his account, and to be honest I can't be bothered to look it up in the official records. Cain seems to have been assigned specifically to the command battery rather than at regimental level, at least initially, but to have assumed overall commissarial authority for the regiment as a whole soon after his arrival. Presumably any other commissars attached to the 12th had failed to survive the tyranid onslaught on Desolatia.

meeting the challenge head-on, as though I considered it nothing more than light-hearted banter.

'Far from it,' I assured him, allowing a visible yawn to get out in the process. 'Bit of a late night, that's all, lot of paperwork to get through before we pull out.' Both of which were true statements, and if he chose to link them in his mind and draw the wrong conclusions that was hardly my fault. In fact, I had delegated most of the routine stuff to Jurgen, my malodorous and indefatigable aide, and was confident that he would deal with it in his usual meticulous fashion.

Despite his unprepossessing appearance, complete lack of social skills, and an all-pervading body odour that could fell a grox, Jurgen had turned out to be the ideal aide, at least in my case. For one thing, he was doggedly literal in following orders, unimaginative enough to simply accept whatever I told him without question, which meant that he had soon become an indispensable buffer between me and some of the more onerous aspects of my job. For another, he had turned out to have an almost preternatural talent for scrounging, which made my life a great deal more comfortable than it might otherwise have been (and probably his own as well, although I was careful not to enquire about that). At the time, neither of us was aware of his greatest asset, nor would be until our fateful encounter with Amberley on Gravalax a decade or so later,[1] but I was to

---

1. I realised almost at once that Jurgen was a blank, one of those incredibly rare individuals with the innate ability to disrupt psychic or warp spawned sorcery. Or, to be more accurate, my psyker Rakel did, making the fact immediately obvious by becoming even more incoherent than usual and passing out on the spot.

benefit from that as well on a number of occasions without ever realising the fact.

'Then I suppose we should be grateful that you could spare the time to join us at all,' Mostrue replied, not sounding in the least bit grateful, despite his words.

'You know me,' I said, nodding as though the colonel had paid me a compliment, and pouring myself a fresh mug of recaff. 'Duty first.' Given the Valhallans' love of low temperatures I'd taken to making sure there was a hot drink waiting for me whenever I had to sit through a meeting with the regiment's senior command staff.

'Quite,' Mostrue said dryly, turning back to the portable hololith. A star map appeared, the Keffia system easily identifiable in one corner from the cluster of contact icons marking the positions of the Imperial armada assembling in orbit. There seemed to be rather more ships there than I remembered, and I remarked on the fact.

Mostrue nodded, thinly masking his displeasure at being interrupted. 'That's correct. Our transport vessels and their escorts have been joined by a battle group from the sector fleet.' I sipped my recaff, which had suddenly become unpalatably bitter, a flutter of apprehension beginning to make itself felt in the pit of my stomach: that meant we would be on our way to a major war zone by the sound of things. I tried to quiet the nagging sense of foreboding. Even if that were the case, we would still be deployed well behind the front lines, far from the main bulk of the enemy forces. That was why I'd gone to so much trouble to secure a posting to an artillery unit in the first place, so that I could stay well away from the fighting, and by and large it had worked. The exceptions had been terrifying, of course, but I'd come out of those incidents hailed as a hero, and there was no reason to suspect that my luck wouldn't continue to hold on Perlia, wherever that was. I tried to remain calm, and sound insouciant.

'Sounds like a big operation then,' I interjected, more for the pleasure of putting Mostrue off his stride again than anything else.

'It is.' The colonel nodded, as though the remark had made sense. 'And it's still only one flotilla among many. Reinforcements are being brought in from all over the sector.'

The palms of my hands began to itch in earnest. This was beginning to sound more serious by the moment. Mostrue did something to the hololith, centring an otherwise unremarkable system a couple of subsectors away. Noticing that it was indeed to spinward, Divas grinned at me, and I nodded an acknowledgement. 'And this is where most of them are going. Perlia.'

'It doesn't look particularly remarkable,' I said.

Mostrue shook his head. 'That's because it isn't,' he replied dryly. 'Apart from the fact that it's been targeted by this.'

The picture in the hololith changed abruptly, eliciting a couple of startled intakes of breath from among the cluster of officers around it. A couple, older than the rest, flinched, reflexively reaching for their side arms before composing themselves.

'An ork,' I said. I'd seen holos of them before, and even a couple of preserved corpses at the schola progenium, but this one seemed particularly impressive. I assumed (wrongly as things were to turn out) that Mostrue was projecting it a little larger than life size for dramatic effect. It was as heavily muscled as most of its kind, more so if that were possible, and wore a ramshackle suit of armour apparently assembled from random pieces of scrap. It carried a crude form of bolter, large enough to be hefted by a member of the Astartes, in one vast misshapen hand as though it were no more than a pistol, and a huge axe in the other. Small red eyes glared hatred from under the thing's overhanging brow.

'Not just any ork,' Mostrue said. 'According to the lord general, this is their leader, Gargash Korbul. He's united the greenskins of several tribes, and declared *waaargh*[1] against the Imperial worlds right across the subsector.' He pronounced the ork word with noticeable distaste, and, as I was subsequently to discover, not nearly enough volume or saliva to get the true flavour of it. After giving us a moment longer to absorb the full ghastliness of the greenskin warlord, he switched the image back to the star map. 'So far they've struck here, here, and here.' Systems helpfully turned green with ork contact icons as he pointed. 'For the most part these incursions have been contained, however, at least for the time being. The

---

1. *When a particularly able or charismatic leader emerges among the greenskins, a* Waaargh *is the inevitable result. It's hard to translate the orkish term precisely, since it has a number of connotations, but the main ones are essentially a combination of migration and a destructive rampage, both of which seem instinctive activities among the species.*

critical system is this one, Perlia, where the bulk of the Imperial industrial capacity is. If they take that, they'll have all the resources they need to roll right across the subsector.'

'Then we'd better make sure they don't get it,' I said, summing up the mood of the meeting. Mostrue nodded.

'It sounds quite simple when you put it like that,' he said. His ice-blue eyes rested on mine for a moment, and I suppressed a shiver, which wasn't entirely due to the iceworlders' preference for wide-open windows. 'Let's just hope your confidence isn't misplaced.'

Editorial Note:

Since, as usual, Cain doesn't bother to put anything he describes into a wider context, this seems as good a point as any to interpolate an overview of the situation he was to find himself so unexpectedly thrust into. The book it comes from covers the main points as well as most popular accounts of the First Siege: readers wanting more detail are referred to Broedenour's thirty-seven volume work Waaargh! and Peace: The Siege of Perlia and its Neighbouring Systems. *(Had the author of this magisterial work not been tragically killed by a toppling library stack before its completion it would undoubtedly be regarded as the definitive work on the subject. As it is, it remains an unsurpassed work of reference for anyone interested in the minutiae of the first nine weeks of the two-year campaign.)*

From *Green Skins and Black Hearts: The Ork Invasion of Perlia* by Hismyonie Kallis, 927 M41

THOUGH THE GREENSKINS had struck almost without warning, their crude starships errupting from the warp in four systems almost simultaneously, they were to face far stronger resistance than they expected. The gunboats of the local Space Defence Forces took a heavy toll in every case, weakening the attacks on Savia, Metrium and Sodallagain[1] to the point where the local Planetary Defence Forces were able to keep the savage invaders who made it to the surface of these worlds effectively contained until Naval and Imperial Guard units arrived to turn the tide.

It was a different story on Perlia, however, where the vast majority of the ork forces were deployed. Despite the gallantry of the heroes manning them, the system defences were overwhelmed in short order, allowing the brutish greenskins to establish several beachheads across the face of the planet. With Imperial Guard reinforcements still several months away, the high command of the PDF reluctantly abandoned the eastern continent entirely, withdrawing what forces they could save to bolster the defence of the more densely populated and industrialised western hemisphere. Despite their best efforts to evacuate the region, roughly twelve million civilians and an untold number of PDF stragglers were left to the mercy of the orks,

1. *A remote system apparently named by a very bored explorator some time in M23.*

who, typically for their degenerate kind, had none to offer.

Of the suffering and privations these martyrs were to endure, and the heroic acts of resistance many were to carry out over the long weeks that followed, much has been written since. Their stoicism was to be rewarded, however, as deliverance was nearer at hand than anyone could possibly have dared to hope in those dark and desperate times. For among the first of the Guard reinforcements to arrive was Ciaphas Cain, the man whose inspirational leadership was to turn the tide more than any other factor in the whole war...

TWO

WELL, THE COLONEL spoke truer than he knew, of course, but having no inkling of that at the time, I dismissed it as just another fruitless attempt to get under my skin and forgot all about it, determined to make the best of our time aboard the *Hand of Vengeance* – a typically sturdy troopship which had already survived Emperor knew how many centuries of chugging back and forth through the warp, delivering supplies and cannon fodder to innumerable war zones. Though I'd never encountered a living greenskin by that point, I'd sat through enough lectures at the schola to believe I had a reasonably good idea of what they were like, and the 12th had been in action against them frequently enough for some of the older hands to have personal stories of their own. True to form, however, few of them felt like socialising with the regimental commissar, and the ones who did take the time to share their experiences struck me as exaggerating, no doubt with the intention of trying to disconcert me. That they were telling no more than the truth, or at least embroidering it no more than old soldiers usually do, I was to find out for myself soon enough.

'They can't be as tough as all that,' I said to Divas, on what was supposed to be our last evening in transit, over a hand of tarot in the stateroom which had been assigned to me. I didn't feel much like socialising by that point, as I'm sure you'll appreciate, but the familiar activity helped keep the thought of what we'd be facing in a few hours time at bay. 'You wiped the floor with them on Desolatia before I turned up.'[1]

'That's true.' He nodded, debating visibly with himself whether to draw another card, and deciding to stick. 'Of course the 12th never saw them close to, but they folded soon enough.'

'I'm sure you played your part,' I said, preparing to prove the old adage about a fool and his money yet again. Standing a long way back from the battlefront, lobbing high explosive death at the enemy from a safe distance, still struck me as the ideal way of passing a war, and despite the fluttering of apprehension in the pit of my stomach the rational part of my mind had no doubt that this campaign would prove as uneventful as most of my service with the 12th Field Artillery had been. Divas nodded.

'Of course we did,' he said, 'but I can't help envying some of the line regiments. They really got stuck in

---

1. The 12th, along with a couple of other Valhallan regiments, had been engaged in mopping up an ork raiding party when Cain first joined them, although by the time he did so the operation was all but over.

against the greenies.' They were chewed to bits by the tyranids shortly afterwards, of course, but that was beside the point. Divas was a Valhallan after all, which meant he relished the prospect of killing orks above pretty much anything else[1], so I nodded in understanding as I laid my cards on the table.

'My hand, I think.' I reached out to take the pot, comfortably beating his pair of ecclesiarchs.

'Not so fast.' The third player in our discreet little gathering smiled at me, perfect white teeth gleaming in a dark brown face framed by hair the colour of space, which rippled with highlights as she moved. 'Three inquisitors and the Emperor.' She scooped up the little heap of coins, grinning triumphantly, revealing an impressive amount of cleavage down the unbuttoned neck of her uniform shirt as she leaned across the table. Despite losing a fair amount of money, I smiled in return. I couldn't help it, she was just that kind of a girl.

I'd met Karrie Straun on the first day of our voyage, when she'd been dispatched to make sure our vehicles and artillery pieces had been properly stowed in the hold, and it hadn't taken us long to hit it off: she was gratifyingly impressed by the stories she'd heard about me, and I, as you might expect, was pleasantly surprised by the sight of a pretty face in these incongruous surroundings. One thing led to another, and despite the risk of discovery (which we were both young and foolish enough to find vaguely exciting)

---

1. Ever since their homeworld was invaded by orks, with a conspicuous lack of success it must be said, the Valhallans have detested the greenskins more than any other of the Emperor's enemies.

we had spent as much time alone together as we could contrive.[1] Had she not been due back on duty in less than an hour, I have no doubt we'd have found far more interesting ways of passing my last evening on board than fleecing Divas.

'Never mind, Cai.' She grinned, knowing how much the familiar form of my given name irked me. Divas used it all the time, of course, but he was an idiot with all the sensitivity of an ork, and had never noticed how much I disliked it. 'Unlucky at cards...' Before she could complete the quotation she broke off, a faint expression of puzzlement crossing her perfectly formed features. 'That's odd.'

'What is?' I asked, the palms of my hands beginning to itch as they often did when something looked like going horribly wrong.

Karrie cocked her head as though listening to something. 'I don't know. The engines are fluctuating.'

I was prepared to take her word for it. She was a third generation crew member, who'd grown up in the corridors of the ship, and was no doubt as attuned to the subtle sounds and vibrations of that environment as I'd been to the depths of the underhive.[2]

---

1. *Technically their liaison wasn't against regulations, as the Navy has its own commissars assigned to it, but if it had become known, both their careers would undoubtedly have received something of a setback. That Cain was prepared to take such a risk is another pointer to his relative youth and inexperience. By the time I made his acquaintance he was considerably more circumspect.*

2. *This is one of many allusions to his early life, which he apparently spent on a hiveworld somewhere; although which one, and the circumstances in which he left it for the schola progenium, remain obscure.*

Her expression grew grave. 'Better hang on to something.'

Almost before she'd finished speaking a new voice cut in, harsh and mechanical, echoing from the voxcasters placed throughout the ship.

'Prepare for transition to the materium. All crew to their posts. Emergency transition in–'

I never heard how soon the event was expected. Abruptly, something vast and malevolent seemed to sink its talons into the centre of my being, turning me inside out. I stumbled and fell, banging my shin painfully against the leg of the table. I staggered to my feet again, trying to ignore the nagging pain still flaring behind my temples.

'What the hell was that?' Divas asked, not unreasonably under the circumstances. Karrie shuddered, looking more disconcerted than I'd ever seen her in the few weeks we'd shared one another's company.

'The transition,' she said, clearly hanging on to her last meal with some difficulty. She pulled her jacket on. 'I've got to go.'

'I'm coming too,' I said, buckling the belt with my chainsword and laspistol round my waist, and looking for my uniform cap. 'If something's going on I should be with the regiment.' Before Mostrue had the chance to volunteer me for some mortally dangerous attempt to set things to rights.

'Me too,' Divas said, taking his lead from me as usual.

'That didn't feel like any transition I've ever been through before,' I said. 'What caused it?'

'I've no idea.' Karrie was beginning to recover now, and led the way out of my stateroom, glancing back over her shoulder to talk to us as she did so. 'The only time I ever felt anything like that...' She broke off, clearly unwilling to complete the thought.

'What?' Divas asked. Karrie shook her head.

'The navigator died. The wards failed, and a daemon materialised on the control deck. But that couldn't have happened; the alarms would have gone off.'

'Commissar?' There was no mistaking the owner of that voice, Jurgen's distinctive odour preceding it as always. He emerged from the cabin next to mine, his habitual expression of vague bafflement obscurely reassuring. 'Is something wrong?'

'Very,' I said. The corridor was beginning to fill with agitated officers from the other Guard regiments aboard. I caught a glimpse of a Chatachan major, towering over the rest of us, forging through the press with the ease of a Space Marine surrounded by ordinary mortals, a pasty and worried looking commissar trailing at his heels.

Confused and angry voices echoed in the confined space. Getting through that lot was going to be a nightmare.

'This way.' Karrie led us through a maintenance hatch I'd barely noticed before, gaining access with a short catechism to a speaker grille beside it which seemed to recognise her voice.[1] As it swung closed behind us, cutting off the tumult in the corridor, I found myself in a dimly lit passageway, considerably

---

1. *From which we can infer that Cain's new friend was either of surprisingly high rank for her apparent age, or knew the ship well enough to be able to circumvent its security systems. Given that she, and apparently her parents, were born and brought up aboard it, the latter seems the most likely.*

narrower than the one we'd just left, its walls lined with colour-coded pipes shrouded for the most part in dust.

'Where are we?' Divas asked.

'Conduit twenty-three,' Karrie told him, as though that meant anything to any of us, and led the way at a rapid trot which set up interesting oscillations in her uniform. 'We'll make better time in here.' She was evidently looking for something, because after a couple of minutes she stopped abruptly and I collided with her, taken by surprise, but not so much so that I didn't enjoy the experience.

'What are we waiting for?' Divas asked, looking almost as confused as Jurgen. By way of an answer, Karrie picked up the handset of a vox line and punched out a code on its numeral pad.

'I'm trying to find out what's going on,' Karrie said. As she spoke I felt a faint tremor through the deck plates under my feet, and if anything the expression of concern on her face intensified. 'That doesn't sound good.'

'Commissar?' Jurgen directed my attention to a small data lectern standing in a nearby niche, beneath an icon of the Omnissiah, no doubt for the use of any enginseers carrying out routine maintenance on whatever vital systems were currently surrounding us. 'Could you find out anything from that?'

'Maybe,' I said. I'm no tech-priest, of course, but like anyone else I'd been taught the basic rituals of data retrieval at the schola, so it seemed worth a try. While Karrie began a hushed and urgent conversation with whoever was on the other end of the vox line, I muttered the catechism of activation and slapped the power rune. The hololith came to life, projecting a rotating image of the Adeptus Mechanicus cogwheel, and I entered my commissarial override code, hoping that it would prove as effective with naval equipment as it did with its Imperial Guard equivalent.

'It seems to be working,' Divas observed, just quietly enough to disrupt my concentration. 'What are you looking for?'

'Frakked if I know,' I snapped, shutting him up, and turning back to the keypad.

Jurgen pointed to one of the icons encrusting the cogwheel.'That looks like a picture of the ship,' he offered helpfully, underlining the point with a waft of halitosis. None of the others looked remotely familiar, so I selected it, and a three-dimensional image of the *Hand of Vengeance* appeared, rotating slowly, flickering slightly in the fashion of all such devices. A couple of points on its hull were coloured red, stark crimson blemishes, which penetrated a deck or two beneath the skin like ugly wounds. As we stared at it, trying to understand the information we were getting, another appeared, and almost simultaneously I felt that faint vibration through the deck plates once more.

'What does that mean?' Divas asked. The palms of my hands tingled again. Nothing good, of that I was sure.

'We're taking damage.' Karrie replaced the voxline, her expression strained. 'The ork fleet was waiting for us.'

'How could they know?' Divas asked. 'We made the transit by accident, didn't we?'

'Apparently not.' Karrie's voice was clipped and decisive. 'The Navigator's down, due to some massive psychic shock, and ours isn't the only one. Nearly half the flotilla's been knocked back into the materium well outside the deployment zone, and the greenies are using us for target practice. Luckily some of the warships came through too, or we'd be floating scrap by now.'

'How could they do that?' Divas asked, his face white. Karrie shrugged.

'Who cares?' I said, my mind already racing. 'We have to rejoin the regiment, and get the shuttles away.' I reached for my commbead, hoping Mostrue would have had the common sense to begin embarking the gunners. 'If we can't get the artillery planetside we might just as well have stayed on Keffia.' The guns were the least of my worries, of course, but seeing them safe would be the best excuse for getting off the ship as quickly as possible. With any luck the greenskins would be so busy blowing up the starships they wouldn't have much attention or ammunition to spare for the relatively miniscule shuttles. A moment later my hand fell away again. The commbead, along with practically everything else that might have been useful to us in this unexpected crisis, was sitting back in my quarters.

'You're right, of course.' Divas nodded, apparently taking fresh heart from my words. 'What's the quickest way back to the hangar bay?'

'Down here.' Karrie indicated the route we should follow, and switched off the lectern, no doubt hoping we'd memorised it. Having grown up in a hive, the three-dimensional maze had imprinted itself on my subconscious almost as soon as I'd glanced at it, so I was sure my innate sense of direction would be enough to see me safe to our destination if we lost contact with our guide. Divas looked a little more dubious, but tagged along, keeping as far away from Jurgen as he reasonably could. 'I'll take you as far as the portside access corridor, after that you're on your own. I've got to get to my post.'

'Understood,' I said, breaking into a run again as she began to lead us through the belly of the ship. In truth we could only have been moving for a handful of minutes, but the jolt of adrenaline and the uncomfortable sensation of waiting for the next tremor in the deck plating, wondering if the enemy weapons would strike close enough to kill us next time, seemed to stretch the moment interminably. At length, however, Karrie pointed to another hatch apparently identical to the one by which we'd entered this strange, hidden realm behind the corridors we'd become so familiar with over the past few weeks.

'Through here,' she said, pressing a rune beside the portal, and it hissed open. Once again, a babble of agitated voices and the clanging of boot soles against deckplates assailed my ears. The volume was noticeably lower, however, so presumably most of the Guardsmen aboard had managed to rejoin their units, and the vast majority of the crew was at their posts.

As we emerged into the corridor itself I hesitated for a second, Jurgen at my side, in an attempt to orientate myself. I had a pretty good idea of where we were, and a moment later I recognised a landmark, the vivid scarlet icon of an emergency lifepod, one of hundreds placed at strategic positions around the hull. The identification number told me we were on deck seventy-four, section twelve, only a few hundred metres from the hold where our Earthshakers had been stored.

'You should find your way from here easily enough,' Karrie said as a couple of Guardsmen hurried past, Catachans without a doubt, their heavily muscled torsos betraying their world of origin as clearly as their uniforms. I was about to reply when the deck seemed to twist beneath my feet, with a shriek of rending metal, and the ceiling suddenly became a great deal closer. The lights went out abruptly, to be replaced a moment later by dull red luminators which strobed like a panicked heartbeat. Sirens began to wail, sounding curiously attenuated.

'What the hell was that?' Divas shouted, over a dull roaring sound which reminded me of a distant wastefall[1] echoing though the underhive. I shook my head, momentarily dazed, and tried to clamber up again. Somehow the task seemed harder than it should, as though I was fighting against a strong wind. As I regained my feet I began to realise that this was precisely what was happening.

'Hull breach!' Karrie was running down the corridor even as she flung the words back over her shoulder, the wind tugging at her as she did so, making her unfastened jacket and long, dark hair flutter like banners. 'Hurry, before the deck seals!'

---

1. A torrent of liquid dropping from the upper levels of a hive, sometimes for several kilometres.

The rest of us needed no further urging, you can be sure, stumbling after her as fast as we could. Some tens of metres away, to my horrified dismay, heavy steel doors began to slide across the passageway, sealing it off, and condemning us all to an agonising death. It was like running in a dream, where the more effort you put into forcing your limbs to move, the slower they become, the object you're striving to reach receding with every step.

'Come on, sir! Nearly there!' Jurgen held out a grime-encrusted hand, which I took gratefully, lagging as I was further and further behind the others. My commissarial greatcoat was catching the rush of air like a sail, slowing me down even more. I began to curse the impulse to arm myself before leaving my stateroom, although I was to be grateful enough for it before too long, since the tightly buckled weapon belt prevented me from shrugging the encumbering garment off. We weren't going to make it, I could tell, the thick slabs of metal moving closer and closer together as I watched...

Abruptly their progress halted, and I caught a glimpse of the two Catachan troopers straining to keep them apart, their overdeveloped muscles bulging with the effort. No ordinary men could have managed it, but the natives of that hellish jungle world are made of unusually stern stuff, and to my delighted astonishment they seemed to be prevailing. Faces contorted with stress, they shouted encouragement as our battered quartet neared safety at last.

'Cai!' Divas hesitated on the threshold, turning back to stretch out a hand towards Jurgen and myself, urging us on, and incidentally blocking the gap as he did so. Karrie slipped past him, her slight frame a distinct advantage under the circumstances. 'Come on!'

'Get in there!' I shouted in return, barging him through, desperate to get to safety. Knocked off balance by my frantic charge, he stumbled into the Catachans.

Slight as the impact of that collision was, it was enough. Among the strongest specimens of humanity they may have been, but even their mighty muscles couldn't tolerate the strain of keeping that heavy portal open for long. As their concentration wavered they were finally overwhelmed, the frantically whining servos gaining the upper hand at last. I had a final glimpse of Karrie's horrified face as the slabs of metal clashed together, then Jurgen and I were hopelessly trapped, seconds away from death.

Editorial Note:

The ambush of the relieving fleet in the outer system was the first indication the Imperial forces had that Korbul possessed a grasp of tactics considerably more sophisticated than most of his kind; indeed the trap was sprung with a precision which would have done credit to an Imperial task force. As to the question of how it was achieved, the following document should prove highly illuminating.

Extract from the transcript of the evidence of Inquisitor Ghengis Singleton of the Ordo Xenos to the Admiralty Commission of Enquiry into the losses sustained in the so-called Siege of Perlia, recorded 449 924 M41.

Admiral Benjamin Bowe (Chairman): *You mean the greenskins have psykers too?*

(General consternation, audible intakes of breath, and invocations of the Holy Name.)

Inquisitor Singleton: *That appears to be the case, yes. Instances have been recorded by all three ordos of the Inquisition, although detailed investigation of the phenomenon has generally been regarded as my own purview. Where greater knowledge of such unholy matters is required for a thorough analysis, the Ordo Hereticus has generally proven helpful, however.*[1]

Admiral Bowe: *How common are these abominations among the orks?*

Inquisitor Singleton: *Incredibly rare, far more so than among most other races we know about, including humans.*

(General expressions of relief.)

Admiral Bowe: *But extremely powerful, it would seem.*

Inquisitor Singleton: *That would depend on the individual, just as it does with other races.*

Admiral Bowe: *But to knock out a dozen navigators with a single blow…*

Inquisitor Singleton: *Would indeed require an exceptionally powerful adept, or, more likely, several lesser individuals working in concert. We know that the orks have an innate tendency to group action under stress, and it seems reasonable to assume that the same thing would apply to their psykers.*

Commissar Andersen Trevellyan (Commissariat observer): *In other words, you're guessing.*

---

1. *Something of a diplomatic simplification, I feel, having had personal dealings with witch hunters myself on a couple of occasions, but we'll let that pass…*

Inquisitor Singleton: *Drawing conclusions from previous observation of the species. Our colleagues in the Ordo Hereticus, whose understanding of matters related to warpcraft far exceeds my own, generally concur with this hypothesis.*

The Honorable Gianello Marcheisi (Navis Nobilitae observer): *There is also a tendency for such abilities to be amplified by direct exposure to the warp, is that not so?*

Inquisitor Singleton: *Such is my understanding, yes. But such a course would be unthinkably dangerous. The use of psychic abilities in the warp, unshielded, would attract the attention of powers and entities of almost incalculable might and malevolence.*

Navigator Marcheisi: *Nevertheless. (Activates hololith.) I would draw your attention to this sensor contact, recorded by several of the surviving vessels just prior to their sudden transition to the materium. An ork vessel lurking in the warp, is it not?*

Admiral Bowe: *We have considered this matter already. The vessel is clearly a hulk, a severely damaged Brute-class assault ship, with barely enough engine power left to maintain its position against the warp currents. Life support aboard is insufficient to sustain its crew for more than a few hours.*

Inquisitor Singleton: *A full crew, perhaps, but a handful of weirdboyz?*

Admiral Bowe: *You must forgive me, inquisitor, I'm unfamiliar with the word.*

Inquisitor Singleton: *An ork term for their equivalent of psykers. Could this ship have sustained a small group of them for a protracted period?*

Admiral Bowe: *I presume so. Your point being?*

Navigator Marcheisi: *Name of the Emperor, are you always so dense? It's perfectly obvious what he's suggesting!*

Inquisitor Singleton: *This vessel was probably stationed where it was, on the most likely warp current to be bringing reinforcements, with a complement of ork psykers. Their powers boosted by direct contact with the warp, they were able to unleash a psychic attack intended to disable the Navigators of the approaching ships, and force them back into the materium where the ambushing force was waiting.*

Admiral Bowe: *Emperor on Earth! How likely are we to encounter this tactic again?*

Inquisitor Singleton: *Given that the psykers in question would undoubtedly have been consumed by the warp entities attracted by the flare of energy within a matter of moments, I would say that all depends on how many weirdboyz your adversaries have at their disposal, and how expendable their warlord considers them to be.*

THREE

My feelings at that moment, as I was left goggling at my reflection in those damnable shutters, can only be imagined. Certainly I have no wish to recall them now. Anger at Divas's well-meaning obtuseness, which had led to our present position, would undoubtedly have predominated, had there been room for any emotion in my heart other than bowel freezing terror. Glancing around in blind panic, I met Jurgen's imperturbable gaze, and his habitual phlegmatism began to have a curiously calming effect on me. As usual he seemed to be under the impression that I had everything under control, and for some reason the notion of losing face in front of my aide began to seem almost as bad as the prospect of imminent death. If these really were my final moments, I thought, at least I would meet them with as much dignity as I could manage under the circumstances.

'What do we do now, sir?' he asked, the rapidly thinning air attenuating his voice as well as his odour, which was at least one dubious benefit of our position. As my gaze skittered over his shoulder, a large black rectangle on the wall of the corridor caught my eye, and I puzzled at it for a moment, oxygen starvation already beginning to slow my thoughts. I could recall nothing there that might account for it. Perhaps an open maintenance hatch, like the one we'd entered the corridor by–

'Run for it!' I gasped, the coin dropping at last, and forcing my limbs into a drunken stagger. The panel wasn't black at all, it was red, the same colour as the emergency lighting: the beacon marking the position of the lifepod I'd idly noticed a few moments before. The gale, which had buffeted us ever since the torpedo strike,[1] had moderated to a light breeze by now and the last few traces of air would be gone in moments. Needing no further urging, Jurgen fell in beside me.

In all honesty, I don't think either of us could have made it over that short, interminable distance without the support of the other. If you've ever seen a couple of inebriates holding each other up as they progress erratically down the boulevard, you'll have a good idea of the spectacle we must have made. Fortunately, as I've said before, the rapidly thinning air had taken Jurgen's body odour with it, or close physical proximity to him would have made the prospect of asphyxiation seem rather more attractive as an alternative. As it was, I tried not to think too much about

---

1. *Cain is clearly writing with hindsight here, since there would be no indication at the time of how the damage had been inflicted.*

his habitual lack of personal hygiene, which was quite easy given that most of my brain seemed to be shutting down, all my thoughts becoming focused on putting one foot in front of the other and forcing my labouring lungs to take one more increasingly tenuous breath.

Abruptly we slammed into the bulkhead, and I blinked the brown fog swirling across my vision away as best I could. The red panel was right in front of me, flickering like a badly tuned pictcaster, and I groped for the large handle recessed into the wall, tugging at it with all the strength I could muster.

If I'd had the breath to spare, or any at all by that point, I don't doubt that I would have screamed with frustration. In my weakened condition I could barely budge it. I tried to call out to Jurgen to help me, but an eerie silence had descended about us, and I felt the last of the air in my lungs errupt from my body in a chest-rattling belch. In a handful of moments it would all be over.[1]

Fortunately, Jurgen had realised what I was trying to do, and his grubby hands closed over mine, his bitten nails contrasting oddly with my own neat black gloves. Our combined weight was sufficient to shift

---

1. Contrary to the more lurid examples of popular drama, the human body can survive exposure to hard vacuum for several minutes before unconsciousness, followed shortly by brain damage and death from oxygen starvation, sets in. It helps if the blood has been well oxygenated by hyperventilation beforehand, of course, which given the state of panic Cain was apparently in at the time seems more than likely. Indeed, many naval veterans claim to have survived decompression during combat more than once, and I've experienced a similar situation myself on a couple of occasions, albeit assisted by augmetic enhancements.

the lever at last, and it descended smoothly, dropping to the horizontal almost at once. Immediately, a hatch in the wall slid aside, and the two of us tumbled through it with rather more haste than dignity, ending up in a tangled heap at the bottom of a short flight of uncomfortably hard metal steps. Blessed light, the normal yellowish white of properly functioning luminators, washed over us, revealing an open space about the size of a cargo module. I couldn't make out much more at the time, as it seemed to be full of crash webbing, which obscured my view of the walls and the further end.

Fighting my way free of my aide's encumbering limbs, I staggered upright, and smacked the palm of my hand against a prominent activation rune on the wall.

A metal hatch descended smoothly behind us, cutting off our view of the steps we had so precipitously descended, and a dull roaring sound gradually became audible in the fabric of the shelter we'd found.

Abruptly, my labouring lungs found something to inhale and I felt my chest inflating. After the desperate privations we'd suffered, the sensation was intoxicating, and I found myself laughing wildly as the rush of oxygen hit my synapses.

'We made it!' I cried, my voice still attenuated to little more than a bat squeak, while Jurgen hauled himself upright, a broad grin across his face.

'That we did,' he agreed. Then the familiar expression of puzzlement slowly eclipsed it. 'So what do we do now?'

'Well we can't go back out there,' I pointed out reasonably. Things were beginning to look up, so far as I could see. It seemed we had found a safe refuge, where I could rest for a while, try and find out what was going on, and decide how to put the best gloss I could on what had happened. It wouldn't take much to make Divas believe that I'd seen the doors about to close and heroically pushed him to safety, heedless of the almost certain cost of my own life...

'Emergency pressurisation complete,' a mechanical voice intoned through the ringing in my ears. 'Launch sequence running. Launch in ten seconds.'

'What?' I could hardly believe what I was hearing. Just when I'd thought we were safe from harm, it seemed we were about to be spat out into the middle of a space battle. 'Abort launch! Abort!'

'Launch in five seconds,' the voice persisted, with the single-mindedness of all cogitator systems. It seemed verbal control hadn't been installed, or if it had been there was no time to work out how to activate it. I lunged for the nearest set of crash webbing.

'Jurgen!' I yelled. 'Get strapped in!'

We just made it in time, before what felt like a very large boot kicked me in the fundament, and the world went spinning.

FOUR

Since that occasion I've been in rather more space battles than I care to contemplate, but I have to say that the Siege of Perlia stands out in my memory more vividly than most. Partly, of course, that's because in the majority of cases I've either been watching the progress of the action in a hololith somewhere, which induces a certain detatchment into the proceedings, or I've been otherwise engaged in hand-to-hand combat with enemy boarders (or to be more accurate trying to avoid them) which leaves little or no time to worry about what's going on in the rest of the fleet. Mainly, I suspect, it was simply the complete novelty of the situation I found myself in.

As the surge of acceleration died away, I realised I was now drifting freely in the crash webbing, obscurely grateful that it had been some hours since I'd last eaten. Evidently the automatic systems on board hadn't gone so far as to turn on the gravity for us.[1] Kicking free of the restraints with some difficulty, I took stock of our surroundings.

Our refuge was surprisingly roomy, having been designed, I was later to discover from the instruction slate, to take twenty evacuees under ideal conditions, and two and a half times that number at a pinch. The compartment we'd found ourselves in took up the majority of the available space, lined with storage lockers between metal buttresses of comforting looking solidity, and floored with thick mats which would double up as sleeping space if the pod had taken more than its nominal complement aboard. (Ten of the lockers were later to prove to be fold-out bunks, however, so we never had to trust ourselves to their dubious comfort.) At that moment, most of the interior space was still choked with strands of webbing, stirring fitfully in the current from the recirculators, which gave the whole place an incongruous air of dereliction, as if it had fallen into disrepair and become home to innumerable spiders.

Kicking my way free of the entangling fibres, and slowly recalling the lessons hammered painfully home in the nullgrav room of the schola, I pushed off in the general direction of the hatchway at the opposite end of the chamber. To my vague surprise I missed

---

1. Since escape pods, by their very nature, are inclined to violent acceleration, this is generally left for the occupants to do manually once they've orientated themselves. From his later remarks we can infer that Cain discovered how to activate this system shortly afterwards, although he doesn't specifically mention having done so.

it by less than a metre, and a few seconds of fumbling were enough to get me close enough to trip the latch and push it open.

I wasn't quite sure what I expected to find beyond it, but my first shocked impression was one of open space. My mind remained focused enough for me to realise that that was impossible, however, and as I took in more of my surroundings it rapidly became clear that I was staring at an armourcrys shield, not unlike the one in front of the pilot's station of a conventional shuttle. The cold light of innumerable stars punched into the tiny flight deck, which was no more than a couple of metres across in any direction, whirling across our field of vision with dizzying speed.

'What are those streaks?' Jurgen asked, wallowing through the hatchway behind me like an ungainly skywhale,[1] his odour preceeding him as always, and I found myself hoping that rescuers would be quick to arrive.

'The stars,' I told him shortly. 'We must be tumbling.' I made my way to the control lectern, fastening the straps thoughtfully provided to keep me in the seat, and began trying to work out how to bring our refuge under some kind of control. I presume it was this happy accident, as much as anything else, which led to our survival, as none of the ork gunners seemed

---

1. A species of animal found in the upper atmosphere of Blease's World. It metabolises hydrogen to remain aloft, where it browses on the innumerable plant spores flung out by the thick carpet of vegetation on the equatorial mountain ranges. The natives domesticated several strains millennia ago, harnessing gondolas to these vast, placid creatures, and using them as living dirigibles.

willing to target us, no doubt thinking we were just another piece of debris from the battle.[1]

Fortunately, the pod had evidently been designed in the expectation that whoever found refuge aboard it would be in no condition to deal with any complicated systems, and most of its functions proved to be under the control of the cogitator which had so precipitously flung us out into space. A few moment's browsing through the pictograms, helpfully projected in front of my face as soon as I sat down, was sufficient to give me a rough idea of what I needed to do, and a few cautious experiments with the dials and levers in front of me was enough to steady our progress.

As the streaks of light beyond the armourcrys slowly settled down, reverting to the pinpoints of light I'd grown familiar with from the observation decks of most of the vessels I'd travelled on since my childhood in the underhive had been so abruptly curtailed,[2] we began to get an idea of the scale of the conflict going on around us. Contrary to what you might see in an episode of *Attack Run,*[2] starships in combat seldom approach to within point blank range of one another, exchanging fire at distances of hundreds, if not thousands, of kilometres. There are

---

1. *In all likelihood, none of the enemy vessels had weapons capable of engaging so small a target in any case, orkish ordnance not exactly being noted for its accuracy, and their fighter pilots would have been far more interested in engaging the starships or their opposite numbers from whichever imperial squadrons had managed to scramble before their carrying vessels were hit.*

2. *A popular holodrama of the 930s, about a squadron of fighter pilots in the Gothic War.*

exceptions, of course; you have to get close to your target to launch boarding parties or knock out a fighter screen, for instance, not to mention ramming, which is a favourite ork tactic.[1] Even so, we were able to pick out the positions of the combatants by the sudden flares of light as another lance or torpedo volley struck home, and once by a peculiar sensation of sickness and disorientation as space itself seemed to twist in the middle of my field of vision, sucking some luckless victim into the hell of the warp as its engines exploded.[2]

'We seem to have a couple of options,' I said after a while, as the distant firework display became evermore intermittent. One of the systems I'd found was a locator beacon, which would pinpoint our exact position for anyone who might be listening or looking for survivors. 'We could just fire this up, and wait to be rescued.'

As my finger hovered over the activation rune, I hesitated. There was an auspex screen embedded in the control lectern in front of me, and a positive blizzard of contact icons fogging it up. Some of them might be nothing more threatening than debris, of course, but the vast majority seemed very solid for that, not to mention clearly manoeuvring under power, and far too many of them were noticeably

---

1. *Indeed, the Brute-class vessel referred to earlier is built ('designed' being perhaps too alien a concept for the ork mindset) with precisely this form of attack in mind.*

2. *The ork Ravager* Ardenuff, *according to the final report of the commission previously cited. The name, incidentally, is an ork term most closely translated as 'battleready.'*

closer than the little cluster of Imperial icons clinging on doggedly to one side of the imager.

'Although that might not be such a good idea,' I concluded, withdrawing my hand at last. Clearly, we were heading through the bulk of the ork fleet, and any distress beacon we activated would be far more likely to attract their attention than that of any friends in the vicinity. Besides, they all seemed to have more than enough problems of their own. Jurgen nodded, as if he understood.

'What's the other one?' he asked.

I shrugged. 'Head for the planet, and make contact with our forces there,' I said. According to the instructions I was reading, the cogitator ought to be able to take care of that, and once our course was set, we stood a reasonable chance of slipping through the enemy fleet without attracting too much attention. I hoped. In any event, it seemed like a better chance of survival than trying to hitch a lift with the greenskins.

'How long would that take?' Jurgen asked.

I shrugged again, and retrieved the appropriate information after a little searching through our tiny craft's limited databanks. 'About three weeks,' I concluded.

That didn't sound too bad, it would have taken the troopship a little under half that to coast in from this far out on the fringes of the system, assuming it survived the engagement at all. To my vague surprise I found myself hoping that it did. I'd always been something of an outsider in the command battery, the only friend I had among the officers there being Divas, as I've said before, but most of the others were at least civil to me (my inadvertent reputation for heroism tending to at least balance the instinctive dislike and distrust most of them had for members of the Commissariat, if not actually outweigh it).

As for the common troopers, I'd been careful to give them the impression that I cared about their welfare, so they tended to watch my back when things got sticky rather than start thinking about one of the unfortunate friendly fire accidents which tend to terminate the careers of overly enthusiastic commissars. All in all, I was as comfortable there as I ever expected to be, and the thought of having to establish myself all over again in another posting was unexpectedly disturbing.

As it turned out, of course, it was to be the events of the next few months which were to attract the attention of the senior members of the Commissariat for the first time, marking me down as someone whose career might be worth keeping an eye on, eventually bouncing me into a position at Brigade Headquarters which was to put my life in danger more often than I care to contemplate; but I'm getting ahead of myself.

'Three weeks doesn't sound so bad,' my aide volunteered, leaning closer to read the tiny screen, and giving me the benefit of his halitosis again. At that point it struck me that taking our chances with the greenskins might not be quite such a bad idea after all, but fortunately common sense and my innate survival instinct combined to override the impulse and I nodded. Three weeks in a confined space with Jurgen was not going to be one of the most pleasant experiences of my life, but it certainly seemed preferable to the alternatives. (Just how much preferable I still had no idea, of course, but that blissful state of ignorance was to be dispelled soon enough.)

IN RETROSPECT, THE long, slow fall to Perlia was almost relaxing, although at the time I must confess I didn't think so. Suffice it to say that being cooped up with Jurgen in a volume of space scarcely larger than a cargo module was as trying to the patience and the sensibilities as I'd feared, and the knowledge that every day that passed brought us closer to a desperate and bloody conflict hardly helped to improve my mood. The one bright spot was that the supplies we discovered in the lockers were more than adequate to sustain the pair of us, so at least rationing wasn't an issue. If anything, I put on a little weight, despite the monotony of the diet.

My aide being something less than a sparkling conversationalist, I spent most of the trip practising with my chainsword, running through drills and attack patterns repeatedly for hours at a stretch. I'd always been reasonably competent with the weapon, but such a sustained amount of practice, I was gratified to discover, raised my level of skill with it to an unprecedented degree. A fact I was to become grateful for sooner than I expected.[1] As a result, I had little time to brood about what might be waiting for us when we arrived at our destination, which, given the

---

1. Cain was, I can attest from my own acquaintance with him, an exceptional swordsman; much of that skill undoubtedly came from the sort of combat experience no amount of practice can emulate, but despite the impression he gives here, he was extremely diligent in this regard anyway.

level of apprehension I would no doubt have been experiencing otherwise, was no bad thing. A further advantage of this habit was that Jurgen generally retreated to the cockpit while I was performing these exercises, the space in the main living quarters being uncomfortably cramped for an audience desirous of retaining most of their limbs, where he amused himself as best he could in the absence of his collection of porno slates in some fashion I deemed it best not to enquire about.

All in all I'd settled into something of a routine as the days went by, the unvarying glow of the luminators within our fragile refuge and the star speckled darkness outside combining to almost soporific effect, so when the cogitator chimed one morning and announced in its habitual monotone that we were approaching orbit, I was taken completely by surprise.

'Do you want me to activate the beacon, sir?' Jurgen asked, standing to make way for me in the single seat of the tiny flight deck.

I shook my head. 'Probably unwise at this stage.'

I indicated the rash of contacts blizzarding across the auspex screen. 'We haven't a clue how many of these are hostiles.' No doubt a more sophisticated sensor suite would have been able to tell us, and for all I know save us an inordinate amount of subsequent trouble, but right then the risk seemed just as bad as it had before. Instead, I activated the voxcaster. 'Let's get an idea of the situation before we commit ourselves.'

In the event, my caution was justified. As the limb of the planet rose gently across our viewport, I spun the dial, listening in to as much of the vox traffic as I could pick up. Most of it was scrambled, of course, so that wasn't much help, but I was able to overhear snatches of what sounded like naval orders, and the harsh gutturals of orkish, without making much sense out of either.[1] At length, however, I was able to make out something, which sounded vaguely like a spaceport traffic control and cut into it with my commissarial override code.

'This is Commissar Ciaphas Cain, aboard a lifepod from the *Hand of Vengeance*,' I transmitted. 'Requesting retrieval, or landing instructions.' In truth I hadn't a clue how to land the thing, but the cogitator seemed as capable of doing that for us as everything else it had handled since we first stumbled aboard.

After a short pause, during which I swear I could hear muttered voices in the background, someone answered in clipped feminine tones.

'Unidentified contact, say again.' With a distinct sinking feeling I did so, drinking in the sight of the planet below us as it rose fully into view. Thin wisps of high cloud drifted in its upper atmosphere, setting off the sunlight glittering from the turquoise oceans, while lush greens and deep browns marked the continents below. After three weeks surrounded by drab grey walls and breathing Jurgen's recycled flatulence it seemed almost impossibly beautiful. When the voice responded again it sounded slightly puzzled.

---

1. *Most of the Imperial Guard transmissions on the surface would, of course, have been too weak for the relatively unsophisticated equipment aboard the pod to pick up, leaving Cain with little to monitor other than the chatter between the ships in orbit and the few remaining orbital defence platforms.*

'The *Hand of Vengeance* broke orbit three days ago.' At those words my spirits lifted more than I would have believed possible. 'All survivors of the battle should have been accounted for.'

'We've been busy,' I said, with what I felt was commendable understatement at the time. 'Did the 12th Field Artillery come through all right?'

'You can't seriously expect me to answer that.' The voice took on a faintly suspicious tone. 'Can you give me some positive identification?'

'Emperor's teeth!' I said with some asperity. 'I'm using a commissarial vox code, for warp's sake! How much more positive do you want me to be?'

'A code assigned to a commissar reported killed in action,' the voice shot back. I sighed, keeping my temper with a considerable effort.

'Are you implying I might be an ork?' I asked incredulously.

'You were asking about the disposition of Imperial combat units,' the starport drone replied.

'I was trying to find out if my friends survived!' I retaliated. Well, that was stretching things a bit, but in my experience a bit of emotional blackmail never hurt when you were trying to get the response you wanted out of a woman. This one might just as well have been a servitor for all the good it did me on that occasion, though.

'If you're really a commissar you should know better than to discuss such matters on an open channel,' she snapped back.

'What do you mean *if*?' I responded, outraged. 'Get a recovery shuttle up here and I'll soon show you who I am!'

'Low orbital operations are too hazardous at this time,' the woman said, with an unmistakable air of satisfaction. 'Lock on to the starport locator beam and engage the automatic landing systems. We'll have a reception committee waiting for you.'

'What do you mean too hazardous?' I asked, the palms of my hands beginning to tingle again. But the vox link had gone dead. After a moment or two of inventive profanity, which did nothing practical to help but relieved my feelings a little, I began to ferret through the cogitator systems in search of the appropriate rituals. Long before I could complete the task, however, I was to receive the answer to my question; a series of heavy impacts rang against the hull, alarms began to squark, and the all-too-familiar sound of venting air began roaring through our fragile little craft.

Editorial Note:

This seems as good a point as any to insert a little more background detail about the tactical situation at the time. As before, Kallis gives a commendably concise overview of the prevailing state of affairs, and places the incident Cain is describing into a wider context which perhaps makes things a little clearer than his own unvarnished narrative.

From *Green Skins and Black Hearts: The Ork Invasion of Perlia* by Hismyonie Kallis, 927 M41

Though it was undeniably the greatest tactical surprise of the war in space, and not to be repeated,[1] the Battle of the Halo[2] was to establish unquestionable ork

1. *Presumably because Korbul had run out of weirdboyz.*

2. *A common term for the cloud of comet debris marking the nominal boundary of a stellar system.*

supremacy in this theatre of operations; an advantage they were to cling to grimly for the rest of the conflict. Indeed even to this day isolated pockets of greenskin pirates are said to remain within the Perlia system, picking off the odd freighter, and biding their time to strike again.

Though it only succeeded in destroying five of the relieving ships,[1] and ork losses were, if anything, slightly greater, the ambush succeeded in its primary aim. Forewarned by astropathic messages, subsequent convoys were forced to drop out of the warp far further out than they otherwise would have done for fear of suffering a similar fate, running the gauntlet of sustained attacks for two weeks or more rather than the handful of days they would normally have expected to endure. The resulting attrition to much needed supplies and personnel, not to mention the morale of the merchant crews exposed to these terrifying conditions, was to have the gravest of effects on the fighting ability of the Guard units which had already made it to the surface of the planet, and the sorely pressed survivors of the Planetary Defence Forces. Nevertheless, by the grace of the Emperor, they held on, every drop of aid, which succeeded in making it through the greenskin blockade an incremental step closer to final victory.

By this point, the greenskins had also gained complete air superiority over the territory they'd managed to occupy, their pilots launching hit and run raids against the supply ships in orbit from the landing strips

---

1. *Three freighters and two escorting Sword-class frigates.*

their invading armies had been able to capture. Opposing them were the vessels of the Imperial Navy, which had set up an impregnable defence over the strategically vital starport on the Western continent, and their own fighter wings, which engaged these marauders whenever they appeared above the atmosphere. Unfortunately, not every one could be intercepted before it was able to wreak its damage, and one such opportunistic raider was to come closer than it knew to deciding the whole course of the war...

FIVE

Had we not been in the cockpit, Emperor alone knows what might have happened to us. I for one had no wish to renew our acquaintance with the physiological effects of hard vacuum, and I struggled to get out of the seat, desperate to get to the leak and plug it before it was too late. Jurgen was ahead of me and slammed the connecting hatch to the main compartment, cutting off the scream of escaping air with a resonant clang as the vacuum beyond it all but snatched the handle from his hands.

'Well done,' I said, slumping back into the seat again, my heart hammering, although whether from panic or an automatic response to the thinning of the air I couldn't have said. Jurgen nodded phlegmatically.

'Seemed the best thing,' he said. 'What hit us?'

'Probably that,' I replied, pointing to a fast moving dot on the auspex screen, and keeping my voice steady with considerable effort. 'Some shower of orbital debris, most likely. There must be tons of it left over from the fighting up here.' Then the palms of my hands began to itch again. The blip was changing course, clearly coming round for another pass.

'How's it doing that?' Jurgen asked, ingenuous as a juvie.

'Because someone's steering it,' I said, making a grab for the vox again. This time all I could raise was static; evidently some part of our communications equipment had failed to survive the first encounter with our attacker. There was only one option that I could see. 'We have to get this thing on the ground, now!'

Of course that was a great deal easier said than done. I paged through the pictograms, searching for the right set of instructions, desperation making my hands shake as I did so. Despite the urgency of the task my attention kept coming back to the auspex, and the rapidly closing blip. If it had been any foe but orks we were facing I've no doubt that we'd have been picked off already, but greenskin weapons tend to be short ranged, and even if they're not, their wielders like to get in close enough to enjoy the bang. Just when I thought we weren't going to make it, I found what I was looking for, and turned back to my aide.

'Hang on to something!' I yelled, and entered the code for an immediate emergency re-entry.

'This program entails a significant risk,' the cogitator droned. 'Please confirm instruction.'

'Just do it, you–' Adjectives, perhaps fortunately, failed me at that point, and I slammed the code in again. However significant the risk might have been, being shredded by cannon fire seemed at the time to be a great deal worse. The blip was almost on top of us, and as I glanced up, I caught a glimpse of a small, fast moving shadow beyond the sheet of armourcrys. Pinpoints of light began strobing from it even as I watched.

'Instruction confirmed,' the mechanical voice intoned. 'Passengers are advised to secure themselves.' Faint vibrations began to shake the hull as more cannon rounds pattered against it, but the rear compartment must have been completely depressurised by now, so hardly any of the noise penetrated as far as the cockpit. I just had time to worry that the systems had been too badly damaged to work, when a sudden surge of acceleration thrust me back down in the chair, and the bottom dropped out of the world.

'Hang on!' I yelled to Jurgen, more for the encouragement the words offered than because I believed it to be physically possible. Monotonous cursing and thudding behind me emphasised the point. Jurgen had a distinct aversion to atmospheric flight at the best of times, and this was far from that: perhaps mercifully, he had too much on his mind to think about airsickness, which was probably just as well for the pair of us. After a moment or two, a louder thud than before resonated through the rising scream of air past the battered hull and his voice went silent. Despite my concern, I remained where I was; he'd either be all right or he wouldn't, and trying to get to him now would only end up incapacitating me as well.

Over the years I've made the trip from orbit to ground uncountable times, and in varying degrees of comfort, but I've seldom felt the experience so vividly. Partly, I suppose, that was because I was screaming in uncontrolled panic at the time (the noise of the superheated air rushing past the hull being so great I can't honestly be sure) and partly because I've hardly ever been in a position to observe the experience so closely. The air beyond the armourcrys was a vivid ackenberry red, flickering like the aurora round a titan's void shields, and the ground below was obscured by contrails of boiling air, freezing in our wake. An almost intolerable pressure seemed to be driving the air from my lungs, and the whole pod shook like a twig in a gale.

Despite the impossibility of seeing anything beyond the hellish mist which surrounded us, I kept trying to turn my head in a vain attempt to see if the ork fighter was following us down, intent on finishing the job, but I never caught sight of it again. I can only presume that the pilot, seeing the blazing trail of our re-entry, had assumed that we'd perished and gone to look for another victim.[1]

After what seemed like an eternity of rattling and banging, which sounded like nothing so much as a hivequake in a scrapyard, the buffeting grew less, and I began to discern a blue sky and wisps of white beyond the armourcrys. Gradually, as the reddish glow receded and the clouds below began to part, I was able to make out something of the landscape below us. Dull red desert sands became visible, a far cry from the lush pastures of Keffia which I'd become

---

1. More than likely. Orks aren't exactly noted for the length of their attention span.

so familiar with, dotted here and there with signs of settlement: villages, towns, and once a fair sized city, all surrounded by irrigated fields or linked by vivid blue waterways, the banks of which were verdant strips a kilometre or two wide. These soon petered out, however, as the sand encroached again on the vegetation that the rivers sustained.

Ominously, most of these habitations seemed to have suffered greviously in the fighting. A thick pall of smoke hung over most of them, and whatever life they supported was too far below us to discern. This was probably just as well, or I would have been too terrified for anything even approaching rational thought.

'Warning.' The cogitator chimed in at just the right moment to puncture the first faint stirrings of optimism I'd started to feel since our precipitous descent had begun. 'Repulsor systems severely compromised. Lift capacity reduced to thirty-seven per cent of design specification. Impact will be significantly higher than designated safety margins.'

'Frakking wonderful!' I snarled, so far gone as to vent my frustration verbally. I realised, too late, that relying on the pod's machine spirit was our best chance of survival and that hacking it off was probably not a good idea.

Scanning the horizon, I just made out a patch of blue and green in the middle of the desert surrounding us, the dunes of which were hurtling past uncomfortably close, as we continued to lose altitude; indeed a small, arrow straight sandstorm was beginning to follow our path as the wake of our passage reached the ground. Muttering prayers I was privately sure that the Emperor was too busy to heed, I disengaged the cogitator systems and fiddled with the levers in front of me, hoping I remembered as much as I thought I did about how to control this plummeting death trap manually.

Fortunately, I seemed to have retained enough information to steer the thing, and brought the nose round to point at the oasis I'd spotted a few moments before. It was getting very close, water and trees looming up out of the desert sand and with a jolt, which felt like it had just loosened every tooth in my head, we skimmed the top of one of the largest dunes surrounding it.

'Cut the power, cut the power...' I recited to myself, looking around the lectern for the large red switch I was sure I'd seen there a moment before. Almost at the last minute, I found it, and slammed my hand down on the thing. With a sickening lurch, which would surely have proven too much for Jurgen's tender stomach had he still been conscious to feel it, the repulsor system disengaged entirely and unmodified gravity had us in its grip at last.

My aim was pretty good, even if I do say so myself. We dropped like a white-hot stone almost into the centre of the lake, skipped in an explosion of steam, and ricocheted into the air again, ploughing through the stand of trees fringing the shoreline. As we did so, I thought I saw a gleam of metal somewhere within them, but with the fog we'd created swirling about us, followed almost immediately by splintering wood and thick black smoke as they burst into flame, I had no time to consider the matter. Every muscle and bone in my body seemed to be oscillating in a different direction, and the seat restraints dug into my chest like an eldar wytch's fingernails. My vision began to grey at the edges, and I began to fear that I was on the verge of losing consciousness.

Abruptly, the sensation of pressure began to ease, however, and the notion gradually filtered into my mind that my desperate gamble had worked. The trees had absorbed a fair bit of our momentum, and we seemed to be moving much more slowly now (although that was still something of a relative term). A dune larger than any I'd yet seen, or perhaps I was merely seeing it a good deal closer than the rest, flashed past, jarring our sturdy little craft as we clipped the crest of it, and then we were down, gouging a long trench in the sand, and leaving little patches of glass in our wake as the heat of our hull vitrified the site of every bounce.[1] Eventually the jarring ceased, and to my delighted astonishment I realised that we were down and safe. Well, down and alive, at any rate. As I was shortly to discover, safety was going to be hard to find on Perlia.

For a moment or two, I did nothing but sit, forcing air into my battered lungs, and trying not to feel the little stabs of pain, which shot through every muscle whenever I attempted to move. After a while, when

---

1. *Presumably he means the pod bounced a few times, and gouged out a furrow as it slowed. As so often in the task of editing these anecdotes, I've elected to let his original wording stand, in the interest of preserving their flavour, despite the ambiguity (and in some cases lack of comprehensibility) also being preserved.*

my head had stopped spinning and the white-hot core of agony behind my eyes had receded to a dull, nauseated throbbing, like the most severe hangover imaginable, I fumbled for the harness release. It gave abruptly, and I slid half out of the chair, realising for the first time that our little craft had come to rest canted at a severe angle.

None of the runes on the control lectern were illuminated, and it soon became obvious that the power systems had fused with the impact of our landing. Our gallant little cogitator had become one with the Omnissiah, no doubt starved to death by the lack of energy, so there was no help to be had from that quarter. Barring the intercession of a tech-priest, we weren't going to be able to get the vox up and running, so calling for help didn't look like an option either.

'Jurgen.' Finding my footing with difficulty on the sloping deck, I stumbled around the chair to find my aide sprawled out behind it, an ugly bruise disfiguring his forehead (insofar as it was possible for his appearance to be made appreciably worse). Swift examination in the attenuated sunlight which leaked its way past the mound of sand, all but covering the armourcrys, showed nothing particularly life threatening, his skull apparently too thick to crack by anything short of a bolter round, and as I completed my attempt to determine the extent of his injuries, he began to stir.

'Are we dead?' he asked, cranking his eyes open, and gazing at me with even less comprehension than usual. I shook my head.

'I don't think so,' I said. 'I imagine the Emperor would have put in an appearance by now.' Leaving him to gather what wits he had, I tugged the connecting door open and staggered through into the main compartment.

The first thing which struck me was the smell; burned sand and scorched metal, of course, but overlaid with it, and almost completely masked, the blessed scent of fresh, clean, unrecirculated air. I sucked it in greedily, like an addict taking an obscura hit, almost intoxicated by the rush of oxygen. Clearly, the hull had been breached somewhere, although whether by the cannon fire we'd taken or by the precipitous mode of our arrival, I couldn't be sure. Several of the lockers had burst open, scattering their contents, and I moved through an ankle deep litter of ration packs and other detritus which would no doubt come in handy later. There was no time to think about that now. I stumbled to the exit hatch like a man in a trance, climbing the tilted floor as doggedly, and with as much effort, as if I was clambering over a mountain pass.

At length, I reached my goal, and set to cranking the heavy hatch open using the manual lever thoughtfully provided for just such a contingency. It slid aside surprisingly easily, and I blessed the foresight of the Adeptus Mechanicus in general, and the acolyte who had designed the thing in particular, as I did so. A bright rectangle of warm, clear sunshine poured in on me, and the intoxicating scent of clean air flooded in after it. Hoisting myself up, I staggered out onto the hull, which still felt warm even through the thick soles of my boots, my ears full of the creaks, ticks, and clangs of cooling metal, and shaded my eyes, eager for a sight of our surroundings.

A shadow shifted in the corner of my vision, and I choked reflexively as the smell of the fresh air was abruptly overpowered by a new and foetid odour.

'Jurgen?' I asked, turning to face the source, but even as I did so the rational part of my mind reminded me that it couldn't be him. For one thing he was still back on the flight deck, and for another the stench made his normal bouquet seem like the dew on a bright spring morning. I barely had time to register its presence, looming over me like what seemed at the time to be a small, angry mountain, before the ork let out a bellow of rage and charged.

SIX

In retrospect, I imagine, the greenskin was as surprised to see me as I was to see it, otherwise it would no doubt have finished the matter before my numbed and battered mind had properly registered its presence. As it was, despite the weakness and stiffness in my scarcely better functioning body, instinct cut in and I evaded its rush reflexively, pivoting on one foot and kicking it in the back of the knee with the other as it hurtled past, bellowing like a bull grox catching wind of a rival. I had a moment of panic, wondering if the old trick would work against a slab of insensate muscle fully a head taller and twice as wide as any human opponent I'd ever faced, even the Catachans I'd occasionally sparred with, but it seemed greenskin joints were sufficiently similar to ours after all. It fell to one knee, yelling even more loudly, if that were possible, as the sizzling metal of the hull scorched through the coarse fabric of its trousers. It half rose, to come at me again, and disappeared through the open hatch with an almost comical yelp of astonishment after I kicked it in the face as hard as I could while it was still off-balance. A resounding crash followed, then the unmistakable crack of a lasgun, two single shots in quick succession.

Confident that Jurgen had been able to deal with the problem, I shielded my eyes against the sun and glanced around rapidly, trying to discern where the thing had come from, and, more importantly, whether or not it had been alone.

No such luck, of course. Harsh guttural voices echoed around the dunes, and from my elevated position atop the hull I was able to see two more flashes of green, moving astonishingly fast, closing in on our position. The quick hand-to-hand scuffle with their fellow had been over so fast I hadn't really had time to take in the full ghastliness of the creature I'd faced, but these were sufficiently far away for me to be able to make them out in all their grotesquerie.

I'd be lying if I said I didn't quail inwardly at the sight. Despite my confident assertion to Divas that they didn't sound so tough, and the relative ease with which my first attacker had been dispatched, I was bright enough even then to know a serious threat when I saw one. I'd been lucky in that first encounter, I realised that, only instinct and reflexes honed by years of training enabling me to take advantage of my adversary's impetuosity, and Jurgen's intervention hadn't exactly hurt either (well, it had hurt the ork, and a good thing too if you ask me).

For one thing, the creatures running towards me were big, and bulging with muscle in a fashion I'd only previously seen on ogryns. Even a Catachan would have looked distinctly puny next to one of these monstrosities. Tiny red eyes glared from beneath an exaggerated brow ridge, but unlike the holos I'd seen, they were alive with malevolence, and what, if not exactly intelligence, was the kind of instinctive cunning which quite often made up for its lack. I've got to know a great deal more about these creatures over the last century or so, since that first disconcerting encounter, and one thing I've seen time and again is that dismissing them as simple, unreasoning brutes is a fast route to the graveyard (or more likely their stomachs). Despite their bulk they moved swiftly, and with a kind of grace completely at odds with their appearance, every movement economical and precise.

That, above all else, was the thing, which most struck fear into my heart. Vast as the power of those hulking muscles undoubtedly was, it was contained and directed, focused on a single objective, and that was my demise.

'Commissar!' Jurgen appeared at the hatch, a lasgun from the weapons locker cradled in his arms, and Emperor bless him forever, the chainsword I'd left in the main compartment after completing my practice session what could only have been a couple of hours before, thrust through the motley collection of pouches and webbing he was habitually festooned with. I took it gratefully, thumbed the activator, and drew my laspistol from the holster at my belt, feeling instantly more comfortable for the sensation of weapons in my hands again. My aide turned his head to look at our attackers, his mouth set in a faintly self-satisfied grin. It only occurred to me later that, having dispatched the ork which had stumbled into our pod, his mood was bound to be as cheerful as any Valhallan's would have been under the circumstances. 'Ugly frakkers, aren't they sir?'

'Indeed they are,' I said diplomatically, aware that, as always, the irony of his words would be lost on him. By now, our assailants were close enough to open fire with the crude bolt pistols they carried, but fortunately they proved to be no more accurate with firearms than most of their kind, the explosive projectiles detonating a couple of metres from where we stood. Even so, the noise seemed to excite them, and their pace increased, scrambling up the dunes so fast that for a moment I began to fear that they'd be on us before we could react. Sunlight glittered from the close combat weapons they wielded in their other hands, large stubby axes with short handles, which looked incongruously like something which would have looked more at home in a kitchen than on a battlefield. 'Whenever you're ready.'

I opened fire with my pistol, Jurgen following suit. With relief I saw our las bolts impacting on the torsos of those monstrous assailants, blowing cauterised craters through the dull brown clothing they wore (which blended quite disconcertingly with the desert sands, so that their outlines were blurred, the festering green of their limbs and faces seeming to flicker against the landscape like disembodied parts) and the dense flesh beneath. To my horror, the wounds, which would have dropped a human, barely slowed them, and they charged on blindly: if anything we seemed to have succeeded only in enraging them.

'Waaaaargh!' they yelled, provoked by pain and rage into bellowing the warcry, which no one who has faced these monstrosities can ever forget. I'd never heard it before except through the speakers of a hololith, and although, as I was subsequently to discover, it was nothing compared to the sound produced by hundreds, or even thousands, of ork throats, it was disconcerting enough, let me tell you. It was to save our lives, though. Abruptly I heard it echoed from behind, just in time to turn and face another pair, which had flanked us unnoticed while our attention was fixed on their comrades.

'Frak off!' I parried a downward stroke from one of those large and intimidating axes with my gently humming chainsword, firing four or five las bolts from the pistol in my other hand directly into the creature's exposed belly. To my relief, it staggered back, momentarily blocking the rush of its fellow, which reacted in what I was soon to realise was the typical manner of all its kind. Without hesitation it smashed its own blade down into the skull of its comrade, releasing a gush of foul smelling ichor, and shouldered the falling body aside in its eagerness to get to me. A charnel stench worse than anything I'd ever experienced (and considering I'd just spent three weeks cooped up in a tiny lifepod with Jurgen that was saying something) rolled over me as it opened its jaws astonishingly wide, and bellowed its bone-shaking warcry. For a moment, my entire field of vision was filled with sharp teeth, tusks, and a gullet, which looked quite capable of swallowing me whole.[1]

Almost without thinking, I raised the pistol in my left hand and fired again, a number of shots in rapid succession, straight into that huge and stinking maw. The back of the creature's head exploded, taking whatever brains it had with it. It staggered, staring at me in vapid astonishment for a moment before toppling from the hull to impact against the vitrified sand beneath, with a crack vaguely reminiscent of someone breaking the largest plate in the galaxy.

I whirled round to face our original attackers, to find that Jurgen had switched his lasgun to full auto, and was hosing them down with the same vindictive enthusiasm Valhallans generally displayed while slaughtering their hereditary enemies. Caught in the blizzard of las bolts, the two greenskins staggered at last, dropping to the sand, and rolling down the side of the dunes to leak out the last of their lives in what I expected to be no more than a moment or two of feeble twitching. To my astonishment, however, they began crawling back towards us, the lust for bloodshed still burning in their eyes, until a couple of more carefully placed shots from my imperturbable aide blew their heads apart like overripe melons.

---

1. Cain is exaggerating here. Even a fully-grown warboss (by definition the biggest and most aggressive type of ork) would be incapable of eating an adult human without reducing them first to bite-sized chunks. This, admittedly, wouldn't take it very long under most circumstances.

'Well done, Jurgen...' I began, when my aide's head snapped around, and he began trying to bring his weapon up to bear in my direction.

'Look out, commissar!' he yelled, still trying to find a target, and forewarned by his cry, I was just able to bring my chainsword up in time. With a roar, which left my already abused ears ringing, the ork whose comrade had so casually struck it down charged at me, swinging its cleaver again. Unbelievably, the head wound, which would have proved fatal to a man had, it seemed, barely stunned it, and the belly wounds I'd inflicted hardly slowed it down at all. Ignoring the atavistic voice in the back of my head which gibbered in panic at the creature's seeming invulnerability, I moved instinctively to counter its rush. It wasn't unkillable, we had four pieces of evidence to prove it lying all around us; I just needed to find its weak point. In the meantime, a slash across the torso from my trusty chainblade ought to slow it down a bit... I swung the weapon, ducking under a massive forearm, and was rewarded with another roar of anger as my blade connected.

Ichor continued to pump from the gash in its skull as I danced away, trying to open the distance between us enough to give Jurgen a clear shot at the thing, but it was hellish fast, and closed with me again before I could do so. It blinked, trying to clear its vision, and I took advantage of its momentary distraction to get in under its guard again, striking at its leg. The humming blade struck deep, whining against bone for a moment, and the greenskin staggered, bellowing another challenge. For the first time, it seemed less sure of itself, its movements a little less controlled, and I evaded another desperate swing of its axe with almost contemptuous ease. The blow had been a wild one, and I countered it easily, taking the creature's arm off just above the elbow with a gush of foul smelling fluid that sprayed the surrounding sand and hull, missing me by millimetres.

That ought to have been enough to subdue any opponent, but once again I underestimated the ork capacity for beserker rage and lack of instinct for self-preservation. Instead of collapsing, it surged to its feet, roaring just as loudly as before, staggering slightly as it favoured its wounded leg. That was enough: I sidestepped, striking at its back, and severed the thing's spinal column. It fell at last, rolling down to join its comrades, and twitched for a moment before finally becoming still.

'Nice work, sir,' Jurgen said, lowering his weapon.

I looked around us, breathing hard, not quite daring to believe it was all over at last. 'Is that the last of them?' I asked.

My aide nodded. 'Must be,' he said, with an assurance I quite envied; but then his people had generations of experience fighting these creatures, so I suppose he had good reason for his confidence. 'If there were any more around they'd be all over us by now.'

'Well that's a comfort,' I said, with less sarcasm than I'd intended, then the obvious question struck me. 'But what I want to know is how they found us so fast.'

* * *

As IT TURNED out, the answer to that question lay close at hand, and we were able to find it after a relatively brief search. The task was pretty onerous, however, as both of us were still suffering the effects of our precipitous descent, and the heat of the desert would have been debilitating enough even if we'd both been in the peak of condition to begin with. Not for the first time, I cursed whoever it was who had originally decided that black would be the ideal colour for a commissarial uniform, and discarded the greatcoat (which, in the normal course of events I found extremely welcome, surrounded as I usually was by iceworlders who tended to adjust the temperature in their quarters to levels more usually reserved for the preservation of food). Jurgen, no doubt, found the high temperatures even more onerous than I did, but accepted them as he did everything else with his habitual stoicism.

I'd insisted on resting for a while before commencing our scouting expedition, grabbing some food and water, and was heartily glad I had done so, despite the presence of our uninvited guest inside the pod. The temperature within had risen considerably,[1] and as you can well imagine the scent of baking ork wasn't exactly a spur to the appetite. After a while, and with considerable effort, we were able to lug the cadaver outside, where it joined its comrades on a makeshift charnel heap.

---

1. Presumably the sun was striking down through the open hatch. It would hardly have been able to make much impression on a hull insulated against the heat of re-entry.

'We ought to burn them,' Jurgen said, which I gathered was some sort of superstition among the Valhallans, although since the greenskins were all indisputably dead I couldn't really see the point.[1] It was moot anyway, the arms locker aboard our little craft not having any flamers among its inventory, so we deferred the matter in favour of exploration and set out in the direction from which our attackers had come.

Fortunately, the tracks they'd left were easy to follow, and after some moments of floundering up and down the shifting sands of the endless dune fields, we reached one of the narrow, rocky defiles the Tallarns call wadis. There, the furrows they'd left in their wake died away, although the occasional boot print was still visible in the thin scattering of dust, which coated the ground, and we were able to make reasonable progress. In fact, now we were free of the encumbering sand, in which we had sunk to our ankles with every step, I felt almost invigorated, despite the all-pervasive heat.

By this time, we were both perspiring freely, and I paused for a moment to take a mouthful of water from the canteen I'd slung over one shoulder before we set off. As I did so, I caught sight of a bright flash of reflected sunlight from around the next turn of the defile, and motioned Jurgen to silence. Something metallic was up ahead, that much was certain, although what it was I still had no idea.

---

1. *In the light of current understanding of ork biology this seems remarkably prescient of Jurgen, although it's perfectly reasonable to assume that, over generations of warfare with the greenskins, the Valhallans had noticed that re-infestation rates were significantly lower where ork cadavers were disposed of in this manner and had adopted the practice without fully understanding why this should be the case.*

Readying our weapons, we moved on cautiously, my mouth drier now than it had been before I'd stopped to drink, and the palms of my hands tingling again, although this time it was simply from nerves rather than a warning from my subconscious. Several times during that painstaking advance my eyes registered that telltale flickering again, although what it presaged I still had no idea.

At length we reached the bend in the defile, and, flattening ourselves against the rock walls, peered cautiously around it. My breath hissed involuntarily through my teeth.

'Vehicles,' I said, although in truth that was paying them something of an unwarranted compliment. Had we a tech-priest with us, I'm not sure whether he would have burst out laughing on the spot, or tried to exorcise them as an abomination against the machine spirit. Both, probably; useful as they are on occasion, I have to say most of the cogboys[1] I've come across in my long and discreditable career have been the proverbial Emperor short of a tarot deck.

Jurgen nodded. 'Orkish,' he pronounced, with all the assurance of his heritage, although even I had been able to tell that. There were three of the things parked in a wider canyon, into which the wadi we followed opened out like a tributary joining a river,[2] and I had never seen a more ramshackle collection of

1. *A mildly disparaging nickname for tech-priests and enginFseers common among the Imperial Guard.*

2. *Which, since it was almost certainly carved by flash flooding during the infrequent heavy rains common to desert regions on most worlds, is hardly surprising.*

vehicles in my life. Two were a curious hybrid of tractor and motorcycle, with wide tracks where the rear wheels should have been; one clearly intended for a single rider, while the other had two of the elongated treads side by side, separated by a flatbed on which was mounted a large and intimidating heavy weapon, clearly intended to be fired by a passenger. It was this which had been responsible for the flashing I'd seen. The crude sighting device attached to it had come loose, shifting slightly in the wind, intermittently reflecting the blazing sun up the narrow side canyon we'd been following.

The third member of the convoy looked a little more conventional, being mounted on four sturdy wheels. Like its curious companion, it had a pintle-mounted weapon, which I recognised as an Imperial pattern heavy bolter, no doubt looted and installed by whatever debased equivalent of our own tech-priests these grotesque creatures possessed. Scanning the whole area with an amplivisor from the well-stocked lockers of our lifepod, and detecting no signs of life, I gave the signal to descend.

Close to, the collection of ambulatory scrap we'd chanced across was even less prepossessing. The four-wheeled specimen, which Jurgen kept referring to as a buggy, was well armoured it was true, thick slabs of metal crudely riveted to the chassis, but it had clearly been poorly maintained, if it ever had been at all. Patches of rust and bright silver scoring were scattered equally randomly across its surface, the latter no doubt having been inflicted in combat recently enough not to have oxidised yet, and for reasons I couldn't quite fathom a thick line of red paint had been crudely daubed along both flanks.[1]

'This must have been the boss's,' my aide opined, clambering up on the thing, and poking around cautiously. After a moment, I joined him, keeping a wary eye out for any betraying flash of movement among the scattering of rocks, which surrounded us, and inspected the bolter from force of habit. It seemed fully functional, loaded, and several boxes of ammunition were stacked haphazardly around it.

'How can you tell?' I asked, deferring to his greater knowledge of the creatures we faced without a trace of embarrassment. We'd served together long enough for me to have more confidence in him than anyone else in the regiment, and he knew me well enough not to take a willingness to listen to advice as a sign of weak leadership. (In fact one of the things I go out of my way to try and instil in the young whelps in my charge is to do precisely that; better a moment of embarrassment than a lifetime of ignorance, if you ask me, and on the battlefield, where what you don't know is most definitely going to hurt you, that's liable to be a pretty short span. Besides, there's nothing better calculated to get the Guard officers you'll be serving with to loosen up a bit and establish a tolerable working relationship than showing that you respect their opinions; or at least giving them the impression that you do.)

---

1. It's an article of faith among greenskins that vehicles painted red are inherently faster and more manoeuvrable than others. Where insufficient paint is available to cover one completely, many ork drivers resort to this peculiar striping in an attempt to replicate the effect.

Jurgen shrugged. 'It's got the biggest guns,' he pointed out reasonably. Well that made sense to me, so I prised myself away from the precious bolter and started rummaging through the storage lockers in earnest. Apart from a few crude tools, evidently used to repair whatever damage couldn't be ignored altogether, there didn't seem to be much, although one proved to contain a human arm, dessicated by the desert heat, thoroughly chewed, and smelling to the Golden Throne.

'Somebody's lunch?' I suggested, pitching the foul thing over the side, and trying to quell the incipient rebellion in my stomach.

Jurgen nodded grimly. 'They'll eat anything, even each other.'

'How nice,' I said, with a shudder of revulsion. After that, I opened things a little more circumspectly, as you might expect, but there were no more unpleasant surprises. 'I take it one of the others was carrying the rest of the rations?' Perhaps fortunately, there was no sign of anything an ork might consider food on either of the other vehicles.

'Must have been a foraging party,' Jurgen concluded, and I nodded my agreement.

'The question is,' I said, 'where they were going to forage, and where they'd come from in the first place.' I shivered in a sudden gust of chill wind. We'd taken longer than I'd expected to inspect our find, and the sun was beginning to get close to the horizon. Our short sojourn on Desolatia had familiarised me with desert conditions well enough, so I knew that the temperature was about to drop to levels, which Jurgen would find positively welcome, and I most certainly wouldn't. 'We'd better get back to the pod.' We could shelter there for the night at least, and try to work out what to do next. We could hardly stay there indefinitely, but on the other hand I had no desire to strike out at random across this wilderness of sand, trusting to blind luck and the Emperor that we'd find our own lines before another ork patrol stumbled across us. Of course, I hadn't the faintest idea at the time how far we actually were from the bulk of the Imperial forces on Perlia, or I would probably have been gibbering in panic by now.

My aide nodded. 'Would this help?' he asked, proffering a tattered scrap of parchment he'd found in one of the lockers on the buggy. I took it, finding it unpleasantly greasy to the touch, and examined the spiderwork of crude lines and strange ork sigils spattered across it, apparently at random. 'It looks like a map.'

SEVEN

We returned to our crippled refuge in higher spirits than I'd anticipated, Jurgen lugging a canister of fuel from the smallest of the vehicles we'd found along with us. It still seemed like a waste of effort to me, but if incinerating the corpses of our erstwhile assailants made him happy then good luck to him. For my part, I tucked the scrap of parchment inside my shirt for safekeeping, trying to ignore the way close contact with it made my skin crawl, and watched him ignite his bonfire with a relatively light heart. It certainly looked cheerful enough as the flames took hold, flickering gently against the deep purple of the star flecked sky, and I amused myself for a while, trying to pick out which of the pinpoints of light above us were orbiting starships, until the wind shifted abruptly and the stench of burning meat combined with the deepening chill to drive me back inside the pod.

There, of course, it was almost impossible to see, since the lighting system was as dead as everything else requiring power to function, but once again the well-stocked survival kit came to our aid, and I puzzled at the crude map we'd recovered by the light of a hand luminator balanced on one of the bunks.

It was too canted to sleep on, of course, but I was exhausted enough to feel perfectly comfortable on a nest of rolled-up sleeping bags stuffed into the angle of the bulkhead and floor, and drifted off to sleep as soon as I killed the light. Jurgen, to my unspoken relief, had elected to take a bedroll outside, where he could make the most of the freezing temperature, and his ever-present odour, intensified as always by the daytime heat, had mercifully followed.

Like most Valhallans, Jurgen had a passing familiarity with orkish script,[1] and had been good enough to familiarise me with the basics, or at least their Gothic equivalents, so after a while I was able to work out some of their meaning.

'If I'm reading this right,' I said cautiously, while we enjoyed a leisurely breakfast of reconstituted soylens viridiens on the hull the next morning, 'they were camped at the oasis back there.' I gestured in the direction of the long scar left by the pod as it bounced and slithered to a halt the previous day. Jurgen nodded, leaning in to look more closely at the map I held, and leaving me in no doubt that the rising sun was doing its usual sterling job of bringing out the best of his distinctive bouquet.

---

1. *Or, to be more accurate, pictograms, concepts as sophisticated as writing* per se *being well beyond the grasp of the average greenskin.*

'That's the symbol for a camp,' he agreed, 'and it looks more or less in the right place.' The map had nothing so sophisticated as a scale of distances, but the sigil he pointed to was more or less in the centre of it, and after a bit of thought I'd been able to match a peculiar wavy line along one edge to a stretch of coastline on the eastern continent.[1] I shrugged. We'd descended on the site with the impact of a couple of kilotons of fyceline, so there was no point in going to see if any of the greenskins had survived. More to the point, there wouldn't be much left back there which would help to sustain Jurgen and myself.

'Well, we know where they've come from,' I said. I pointed to a spot a short distance from the flattened oasis, 'and we're about here.' There was only one brutish rune further along in that direction and I tapped it with my fingertip. 'So they must have been heading for this place, whatever that splodge means.'

'Looks like the symbol for fighting,' Jurgen volunteered, 'or lots of enemies.' He shrugged too, and replenished my mug of recaff from the pot, hissing quietly on the portable stove he'd scavenged from the survival kit before I'd woken. I took the drink gratefully. I'd have preferred a pot of tanna,[2] to be honest, but the rations aboard the pod had not been packed

---

1. *From which we can infer that, despite his usual reluctance to immerse himself in the minutiae of the briefing materials provided by the munitorium, he had at least picked up an overview of the planet's geography.*

2. *A kind of tea made from the leaves of a plant native to the ice caverns of Valhalla. Cain spent most of his active service attached to regiments from that world, and acquired a taste for the stuff which was to last for the rest of his life. He only persuaded me to sample it once; the flavour is best described as 'distinctive.'*

with Valhallans in mind, and that particular little luxury would have to wait until we'd rejoined our regiment. Assuming they'd managed to survive the attack on our transport ship unscathed, of course.

'Then that's where we'll head for,' I said decisively. If you've read much of these scribblings, my apparent willingness to go charging off in the general direction of what seemed like a battle zone may strike you as uncharacteristic, to say the least, but to my mind anywhere the orks felt was full of enemies sounded like the right place to be. With any, luck we'd be able to make contact with our own forces, and at the very least we ought to find some PDF trolls to hide behind while we made our way back to the regiment. From which musings you might fairly deduce that I was still blissfully ignorant of just how bad a situation we were actually in.

'That'll be a fair trek,' Jurgen pointed out. 'We'll need to get as much of this stuff stowed in the backpacks as we can.'

I nodded. 'Especially the water,' I said. Under these conditions we'd need as much of it as we could possibly take with us. I hadn't exactly had time to admire the scenery on our way down, but I'd seen enough to realise that pockets of civilisation had been few and far between. It was likely to be more than a week before we got anywhere, even if we were lucky. The irony was that the survival pod contained enough to sustain the pair of us for months if necessary, but remaining where we were would simply mean we starved to death later rather than sooner. Better to set out while we were still strong enough to make the arduous journey. Besides, the fact that we'd undoubtedly annihilated the ork camp when we crashed on it was no guarantee that we'd be spared any more unwanted visitors. If another patrol had set out ahead of the one that had attacked us, they could easily stumble across the abandoned vehicles of their compatriots on the way back and come to investigate…

'Jurgen, I'm an idiot,' I told him. My aide looked at me quizzically, his mouth hanging open just enough to give me rather too good a look at his half-chewed breakfast. 'We might not have to abandon the supplies after all. Do you think you could drive that buggy thing?'

A LITTLE CAUTIOUS experimentation was enough to prove that he could, with almost as much elan as he handled the Salamander I habitually requisitioned, and which he drove in a fashion most people unfortunate enough to find themselves in the vicinity generally considered to verge on the life threatening. The ork vehicles were undeniably crude, but that meant that their controls were correspondingly simple, and my aide was able to work them out without too much difficulty. In truth, there was little more to them than a throttle, a steering column, and a brake. Shortly after we'd begun our examination, Jurgen had managed to fire up the engine, and having spent a few moments getting the feel of the sturdy little vehicle, he opened the throttle and disappeared over the rim of the nearest dune in a flurry of sand and profanity.

I was able to follow his progress by the sound of the engine, and after a few moments he reappeared, a broad grin across his face, and slewed to a halt next to me, raising a miniature sandstorm.

'It'll do,' he conceded, which was about as close as he was likely to come to expressing enthusiasm for anything orkish, and I nodded. Whatever else we'd have to face, we wouldn't have to walk to wherever we were going, after all. I gestured to the other two vehicles.

'We'd better get the fuel cans from those,' I said, beginning to unstrap the nearest. 'Emperor alone knows where we might find some more out here.'

Jurgen nodded. 'Best to be on the safe side,' he conceded.

There was nothing else worth taking on either of them, so once the canisters were safely stowed, I swung myself aboard and directed Jurgen to take us back to the lifepod.

'One more thing,' I said as he jerked us into motion again, and swung the heavy bolter, which I'd been clinging to for support. For a moment, I found myself wondering if it would still function for me, its spirit having been corrupted by its enforced servitude in the hands of our enemies, but it had apparently remained loyal to the Emperor and opened up as readily as if it had still been mounted on the Chimera from which it had evidently been ripped. The hail of shells tore the ork bike things to shreds, which was hardly surprising at this range, cooking off the ammunition in their own weapons and igniting the fuel still in their tanks with a most satisfying roar. 'We don't want the greenies getting these back, do we?' (In case you were wondering, it would have been pointless attempting to salvage either one of them for our own use: having been designed for ork physiology, attempting to ride one would have been somewhere between uncomfortable and impossible.)

'No sir, we don't,' my aide agreed, and opened the throttle fully. Our trip back to the pod was mercifully short, but unpleasant nevertheless. The greenskin who'd built the ramshackle vehicle we rode in had either never heard of the concept of suspension, or considered it something for sissies.

By the time we reached our destination, I was beginning to have severe doubts about the wisdom of this course of action, but we didn't really have much of a choice. Attempting to walk out of the desert would take us far longer, if we even made it out at all, and however uncomfortable the buggy might have been, it was at least well adapted to the terrain. I'd expected us to bog down in the dunes surrounding the crash site, but Jurgen ran us up the treacherous slope as easily as a sump rat up an outfall, and brought us to a halt outside the pod with an air of triumph I had to admit was well merited.

Our next job was to load up as much of the supplies aboard as we reasonably could. Food and water were our first priority, of course, and after that bedding and ancillary equipment. Most of this I left to Jurgen, his expertise in this area being considerably greater than mine, and went to check on the contents of the arms locker. Apart from the lasgun he'd already used on the orks, and which had remained slung across his shoulders ever since, there were eleven other standard issue assault weapons, along with five boxes of powercells for them.[1] Reluctant to leave anything behind which an enemy might find useful, I added them to the stack of equipment to take with us, a fortuitous decision which, although it seemed like a waste of our limited space at the time, was to turn out to be more than vindicated. I had hoped to supplement them with something heavier, but the pod's designers had obviously decided that if you needed support weapons you'd either be able to find them for yourself or you were done for anyway, and devoted the limited storage space aboard to survival gear and comestibles.

The last thing I found was a drawer full of comm-beads, no doubt intended to let the survivors of a crash landing explore their surroundings without losing touch with one another. I seized them gratefully, slipping one into my ear and running rapidly through the frequencies. My commissarial codes were enough to give me full access to any Imperial transmissions in the vicinity, but to my complete lack of surprise all I could find anywhere was static.[2] Nevertheless, the familiar feel of the thing in my ear was obscurely comforting, and I picked one up for Jurgen too, along with a number of spares. We weren't all that likely to run

---

1. *Given the speed with which Jurgen was able to dispatch the ork that fell into the pod we can reasonably infer that the weapons were already loaded, which, assuming a dozen powercells per box, would mean a total of six per gun.*

2. *Hardly surprising, as commbeads are intended for short-range use only, typically between the members of an Imperial Guard squad. The ability to send or receive over greater distances depends on being able to access a wider communications network, such as that of a company or regiment, in order to relay the transmission.*

into a tech-priest out here, and the last thing I wanted was to lose touch with my aide at a critical moment.

By the time we'd finished loading the buggy, leaving barely enough room for the pair of us to squeeze aboard, the morning was well advanced, and I decided to have one more meal before we set off. Despite our best efforts, there was still a considerable quantity of food left aboard the pod, or a fair amount of the basic ration bars at least, and it seemed a shame to waste any more of them than was strictly necessary. (Although for all I know they're still sitting there under a sand dune, as close to edible as they ever were. As the old Guardsman's joke has it, the main reason they last so long is that no one with any possible alternative would actually eat one.)

Despite their usual, and probably fortunate, lack of any clearly identifiable flavour, we ate a couple apiece, and tucked a few more away in our pockets just to be on the safe side. (My greatcoat had been stowed on the buggy, of course, the searing desert temperatures making any other course of action patently ridiculous, but I had a bit of room left in my trousers, and Jurgen, as always, had a motley collection of pouches and webbing pieces hanging off his torso armour like undergrowth clinging to a tomb.)

'Well then,' I said at last, tearing myself away from our refuge with a surprising amount of reluctance, 'I suppose we ought to be going.' I scrambled aboard the buggy, wedging myself as comfortably as I could between the heavy bolter and some crates of survival equipment, and waited while Jurgen fired up the engine, which belched a plume of foul smelling exhaust into the clear desert air. 'Time we saw what's out there.'

Had I known, of course, I'd probably have dug the deepest hole I could in the sand and pulled it in on top of me, but I still thought we were close enough to our own lines to find refuge with little difficulty. So I braced myself as Jurgen kicked our ramshackle vehicle into gear, and with a roar and a bounce, which seemed to loosen the fillings in my teeth, we rattled off to meet our destiny.

EIGHT

THE REST OF the day passed without incident, despite my natural apprehension at the prospect of attracting attention from any enemies in the immediate vicinity. (Not to mention our own forces. If a Guard or PDF unit noticed us before we noticed them, given our mode of transport, they could hardly be blamed for opening fire before we got close enough to identify ourselves as friends.) My fears in this regard were far from unfounded, as any unseen lurkers would have had more than adequate warning of our approach: the roar of our engine echoed from the dunes surrounding us loudly enough to blot out almost any other sound from my ringing ears, and I blessed the foresight which had impelled me to pass one of the commbeads to Jurgen before we set off. Without them, conversation between us would have been impossible.

Not that it was exactly easy even then. We progressed in a series of spine jarring jolts, each one of which drove the breath from my lungs, so that whatever remarks we did manage to exchange were generally interrupted by staccato hesitations every other word. After a while, I discovered that the discomfort was marginally less if I stood at the bolter, or to be more accurate clung on to the thing for dear life, letting my knees flex with the bouncing of our sturdy little vehicle, and that this allowed me a better view of our surroundings. Using an amplivisor would have been impossible under the circumstances, so I had to make do with what I could see with my own unaided eyes, and I have to admit that this wasn't a lot.

This wasn't to say that the landscape was unvaryingly monotonous, however Occasional outcrops of reddish brown rocks broke through the sand, like reefs in an ocean of dust, and thin patches of desiccated scrub clung grimly to whatever crevices they could find. Lichens, too, speckled their surfaces, in an astonishing profusion of colours, although perhaps the eye simply picked them out more easily because of the contrast they made with their surroundings. Of animal life I saw no obvious sign, although I have no doubt that it was there. If there's one thing I've learned on my travels around the galaxy it's that life is incredibly tenacious, and will manage to find a way of getting by even in the most inimical of environments.

At length, with the shadows beginning to stretch and the sky becoming tinged with purple, I decided to call a halt. Jurgen complied with alacrity, which was hardly surprising given that he'd been wrestling those cumbersome controls for most of the afternoon, and coasted us to a halt in the lee of one of the outcrops of rock. I jumped down gratefully, almost stumbling as the sand gave way beneath my boots, and tried to stretch some feeling back into my cramped and knotted limbs.

'How far do you think we've come?' I asked, reaching for the nearest bundle of survival rations and heaving it onto the ground beside me.

Jurgen shrugged. 'About eighty klom,'[1] he said, beginning to set up the stove.

I raised an eyebrow, surprised. 'That far?' I asked, trying not to sound sceptical. Jurgen nodded, taking the rhetorical question as literally as he tended to take everything else.

'That's pretty fast given the conditions, and the way the buggy's loaded down,' he said. I couldn't argue with that, so I left him to set up camp and wandered up the side of the outcrop, searching for some firmer footing where I could try and work some flexibility back into my limbs with a little chainsword practice now that the air was cool enough to make physical exercise feasible again. Fortunately, I found it, and by the time I'd finished running through the familiar routines of attack and defence, I was beginning to feel a great deal calmer and more comfortable.

I returned to the campsite in a mood I can only describe as mellow, to find that Jurgen had been busy in my absence. Darkness was falling in earnest, bringing with it the night time chill, and I retrieved my greatcoat from the buggy. After a hot meal and a mug

---

1. *Kilometres, a common Valhallan colloquialism.*

of recaff, I retreated to the survival bubble he'd erected, rolled myself up in the sleeping bag I found there, and drifted off into the last night of untroubled slumber I was to enjoy for some weeks to come.

NOT THAT THE following morning gave us any presentiment of what was in store. I woke to find Jurgen already abroad, stirring something grey and lumpy in a pan on the portable stove, which, despite its appearance, smelled surprisingly appetising. He glanced up as I stepped carefully over his bedroll, which he'd laid down just outside the bubble, and handed me a mug of recaff.

'Almost ready, sir,' he assured me, and went back to tending his porridge. Emperor alone knows what was in it, but it was packed with enough nutrients to leave me feeling ready for anything (which I suppose is ironic, considering how the day was to turn out). I began whistling cheerfully as I started the job of breaking camp. After I'd stowed some of the equipment and carried a couple of bundles back to the buggy, my aide's silently reproachful look finally succeeded in reminding me that this was supposed to be his department, and I decided I'd better let him get on with it without any further interference. Jurgen was, if nothing else, a stickler for protocol, which normally made my life considerably easier than it otherwise might have been. In the years to come even generals were to find themselves politely but firmly fobbed off when I couldn't be bothered to deal with them.

Knowing that to persist in what he undoubtedly regarded as a menial task far beneath my dignity as a commissar would leave him disgruntled for the rest of the day, I returned to the outcrop I'd climbed the evening before with an amplivisor, and scanned the horizon, hoping to gather some clue as to our whereabouts. From my elevated position, I found I could see a great deal further than I'd expected in the clear desert air, and my attention was drawn to a faint smudge on the horizon, roughly in our direction of travel, (which, naturally enough, had been the first way I'd looked). My curiosity piqued, I magnified the image as much as I could and tried to make out a few more details.

'I think we're approaching a town,' I told Jurgen, the faint rattles and bangs being picked up by his comm-bead telling me he was stowing our equipment in the buggy with his usual efficiency. I tried to bring the image into clearer focus, but the heat haze was already beginning to shimmer over the sands, and it was hard to make anything out other than the vague outline of walls and buildings. Try as I might, I was unable to resolve any details of the inhabitants, if indeed there were any. 'It could be the splodge on the map we've been heading for.'

'That sounds likely,' my aide agreed. 'Orks would mark one of our towns down as lots of enemies all right.' He hesitated, and then went on, a note of caution in his voice. 'Mind you, sir, they'd think that even if it was only civilians there.'

'I see.' I lowered the vision enhancers thoughtfully. That hadn't occurred to me before, and the idea of trotting blithely into an ork infested killing ground (which is what any urban area is to an infantry soldier, and don't let anyone ever try to tell you otherwise), was far from appealing. Nevertheless, I couldn't see any other alternative. We certainly couldn't continue to drive aimlessly around the desert until our supplies ran out. 'We'd best proceed with caution then.'

'Very good, sir,' my aide agreed, barely able to keep a note of relief from his voice. A moment later the roar of our badly tuned engine shattered the stillness of the desert. 'Don't want to attract too much attention, do we?'

WITH THAT IN mind, we approached the town at little more than walking pace, having discovered that the engine was marginally quieter at lower speeds, keeping the ever-present dune fields between us and it for as long as possible to muffle the sound even further. Eventually, we crossed the line of a road, the smooth rockcrete arrowing away from the town towards Emperor knew where, and turned along it. From this point on stealth would be out of the question in any case, and our best bet was simply to make the best time we could into the relative shelter of the outskirts. Assuming no one was waiting in ambush for anyone foolish enough to use the highway, of course...

A quick glance was enough to reassure me that the possibility was remote. Judging by the thin film of wind drifted sand covering the smooth, grey surface nothing had moved along it in a long time, certainly not for several days, and that meant that any defenders would be unlikely to be directing their attention towards it. That didn't mean the carriageway hadn't been mined, of course, but I was pretty sure Jurgen would notice any telltale irregularities in the road surface and react accordingly, so I tried not to think about that.

'I've got a bad feeling about this,' I told him, sweeping the amplivisor across the line of walls, which made up the boundary of the town. On the smooth surface of the highway the ride was much steadier, and I was able keep them trained on the vista ahead with no more effort than if we'd been scooting along in our faithful old Salamander. Signs of fighting were everywhere, none of the structures I could see having been left undamaged, and several had collapsed entirely. The streets ahead were choked with fallen debris, although to my relief none of it seemed to have been rearranged to form barricades or weapon emplacements.

'Looks bad,' Jurgen agreed, slowing to skirt a couple of burnt-out groundcars, which had evidently been hit by heavy weapons of some kind. They looked like civilian models, the thin sheet metal of their bodywork ripped open like ration packs, and I tried not to look too closely at their contents. Whoever the occupants had been they'd piled in regardless of the cars' nominal carrying capacities, their charred bones tumbled together in death, so thoroughly entangled, it would take a genetor magos to tell which bodies they'd originally come from. And the chances of that were negligible; whoever these people were, only the Emperor knew, and probably only He cared. 'Refugees, if you ask me.'

'Seems likely,' I agreed, dismissing the matter from my mind. Whether any of their fellows had made it to safety, shared their fate, or simply fled to perish in the desert, there was no way of telling. All I could infer with any certainty was that the orks had indeed been here, although whether they were still around or had moved on in search of more to defile and destroy I couldn't be certain. The only prudent course of action was to assume that they were still infesting the area, and I instructed Jurgen to proceed with caution. 'Find somewhere we can park this thing out of sight, and let's move in on foot. I want to know what we're getting into.' The palms of my hands were tingling again, and I trusted my subconscious enough to take notice of the presentiment of danger.

'Very good, commissar.' My aide complied with his usual speed and efficiency, coasting us to a halt in the remains of a nearby fabricator unit. What had once been produced here I couldn't tell, the crushed and mangled machinery all around us being half-buried by what remained of the roof, but I nodded approval of his choice. The thick slabs of metal surrounding us would provide excellent cover if we had to conduct a fighting retreat. It would disrupt the outline of our vehicle on any auspex screen (assuming the greenskins had the brains to use such a thing of course[1]), and provide enough concealment for us to make our way deeper into the derelict settlement without attracting any attention... I hoped. I strained my ringing ears as Jurgen killed the engine, but heard nothing beyond the

---

1. Highly unlikely in my experience, although the only thing you can say with any certainty about the species is that you'll always find a surprising exception to any general rule.

thudding of my heart and the faint ticks of the cooling mechanism.

'Better let me go first, sir.' Jurgen unslung his lasgun and scurried to the nearest patch of daylight, squinting slightly as he crouched low and took aim at the street outside. After a moment, he raised a hand to indicate that the coast was clear. 'No sign of life.'

'Good,' I said, with rather more emphasis than I'd intended, and scrambled down from my position at the heavy bolter. I felt a little unsteady on my feet for a moment or two, no doubt as a result of the sudden cessation of the lurching motion I'd grown used to, but by the time I'd crossed the floor to join him the momentary flash of vertigo had faded away as swiftly as it had come. I drew my laspistol and chainsword as I trotted forwards, feeling instantly calmer for having weapons in my hands again, and crouched down next to Jurgen, trying not to breathe too deeply through my nose.

Outside, the midmorning sun struck hard from the face of the building opposite, another industrial structure, which had once housed a power plant of some kind judging by the tendrils of piping emanating from it in all directions. Now, it was a roofless ruin, evidently the result of a massive explosion within; a contingency the architect had obviously allowed for if the metre-thick walls were anything to go by. Even so, the facade had cracked, slumping wearily in several places, and the doors and windows were shattered, lying in pieces across the boulevard, which separated the two structures. I assumed that the power plant itself had gone up, probably as a result of the attendant tech-priests being killed or forced to abandon their posts, as there was relatively little sign of combat damage to be seen.

The consequences had been severe for everything else in the vicinity, however, including the building we had taken refuge in, the rent in the wall through which we were able to observe all this was clearly the result of flying debris from the explosion.

'That made a mess,' my aide commented superfluously. I nodded.

'Let's hope it took most of the greenies with it.'

'As the Emperor wills,' Jurgen agreed, a phrase he tended to trot out as the verbal equivalent of a shrug. Keeping close to the line of the building, we slipped through the hole, and began to move cautiously deeper into the ruined town.

At first, we saw no signs of life, although there was plenty of evidence of its opposite, and I began to hope that I was right after all and the greenskins had abandoned the place.

Bodies lay everywhere, humans mostly, all ages and both sexes, apparently gunned down or hacked to pieces as they tried to flee. The enemy hadn't had it all their own way, though, there were greenskin corpses lying around too, massively muscled brutes like the ones we'd fought off in the desert and a few scrawnier specimens roughly the size of their human victims.

'This happened some time ago,' I concluded, pausing to examine the corpse of a local arbitrator[1] who had apparently died trying to defend a group of civilians.

---

1. See the previous footnote about the distinction between local law enforcers and the Arbites itself. Here Cain is clearly referring to one of the former.

His weapon had gone, of course, looted by the greenie that had killed him, but it had evidently been some sort of high calibre autopistol judging by the wounds it had left in a nearby gretchin.[1] The corpse, like all the others, had become desiccated by the merciless sun, mummified by the constant arid heat, which meant it had been there for some time. Jurgen nodded, staring at the greenskin cadavers, and clearly wishing he had a can of promethium to hand.

'Looks that way,' he agreed.

If anything, the prospect grew even worse as we penetrated deeper into that blighted town, which, ironically, we came to realise from the municipal signage and the business premises we passed, had rejoiced in the name of Prosperity Wells. Everywhere we looked, we saw signs of the savagery of the invaders, death and destruction wrought purely for its own sake, and despite my usual pragmatic temperament, I began to feel angry at the sheer wantonness of it all. What Jurgen felt I can only imagine, and for the first time I began to understand the depth of the hatred the Valhallans felt for these creatures. To see a peaceful community despoiled in this way was hard enough; to know that such things had been done to your homeworld, even generations ago, would be an intolerable affront.

---

1. One of the smaller greenskins Cain referred to a few lines ago, a subspecies used by the larger, more powerful orks as a combination of slave labour, cannon fodder and emergency rations. Whether he learned the orkish term for these creatures from his subsequent encounters with them or the Valhallans he served with we can only conjecture, although he did have a basic working knowledge of the greenskin tongue by the time I made his acquaintance, enough of it to swear fluently, at any rate.

By this time, Jurgen and I had separated by perhaps a score of metres, taking it in turns to cover one another while we moved from one patch of concealment to the next, relying on the commbeads to keep us in touch; although, from habit, we continued to supplement the vox link with hand gestures, keeping transmissions to a minimum. I was just about to leave the shelter of a shop doorway, an apothecary's if I remember right, when he held up a hand to forestall me and slipped into the shadow of a refuse bin.

'Hostiles,' he voxed, readying his weapon. I steadied the laspistol against my other arm, crouching low, and taking aim along the street. I didn't have to wait long for a target. A moment later a mob of gretchin ambled into view, chattering and screeching among themselves in their barbarous tongue, pushing a large handcart. A single ork was with them, clearly in charge, urging them along with inchoate bellows and frequent blows, which the smaller greenskins generally ignored in favour of squabbling among themselves. The cart was loaded with corpses, and remembering the grisly snack I'd discovered in the locker of the buggy we'd acquired, I had a horrible suspicion as to their eventual destination.

'Hold fire,' I replied, as quietly as I could. In the distance, my aide nodded grimly. Tempting as the target was, and consumed as we both undoubtedly were with the righteous anger all subjects of the Emperor would have felt at that moment, there was no point in drawing attention to ourselves by giving way to our emotions. The faint wash of static in my commbead intensified for a moment.

'–ay again?' a tenuous voice enquired, and faded back into inaudibility. I glanced at Jurgen, prepared to repeat the instruction, but he was looking back in my direction, and even at this distance I could make out the expression of puzzlement on his face (which was no great trick, given how familiar I was with it).

'Commissar?' His voice sounded in my ear as clearly as if he were standing right next to me. I glanced back at the cavalcade of greenskins, but they were clearly still unaware of our presence, moving away now at as brisk a pace as their ork overseer could urge them to. I gestured him to silence.

'There's someone else on this frequency,' I told him, and boosted the gain as best I could. Fortunately, he had enough sense to keep quiet after that, and just nodded an acknowledgement before returning his attention to the retreating greenies. I listened hard, trying to make out another voice through the hissing in my earpiece. 'Unidentified contact, respond.'

'–ergeant Tayber, Bravo squa–' filtered through the static. '–who the –ing warp –ou?'

'Commissar Cain, serving with the 12th Valhallan field artillery,' I said. 'What's your position?'

'–ing desperate.'

The greenskins were out of sight by this time, and Jurgen was moving back to join me. Even broken up by static as it was, the voice took on an incredulous edge. '–id you ju –ay Comm –ar?'

'Yes. Where are you?' I repeated, unsure how much of what I was saying was getting through. I was used to Imperial Guard vox nets, but this sounded like a PDF setup, which was liable to be far less sophisticated. For all I knew, we could have been practically on top of him.

'South –ector, hydro –ation. Wha –eft of it.'

'South sector hydro station,' I confirmed. 'We'll find it.'

'If the –nies don't –nd you first,' the voice added encouragingly. '–he whole tow– crawling with the –ing –ds.'

'We'll proceed with caution,' I assured him as my aide returned to my side, and cut the link.

This didn't sound promising. Whoever this Sergeant Tayber was, it seemed he was halfway across this ork-infested killing zone, and joining him would entail a significant risk. Probably the safest thing to do would be to head back to the buggy and resume our journey as best we could. On the other hand, he was the first Imperial soldier we'd been able to contact since we'd landed on this Emperor-forsaken rock, and might know where the bulk of our forces were. All in all, it seemed my best chance of survival was to try to link up with him, and if some of his squad was still around too, so much the better. The more troopers I had standing between the orks and me the happier I'd feel.

'South is that way,' Jurgen said, looking up from the compass he'd extracted from somewhere in his collection of pouches, and pointing helpfully in the direction the foraging party of greenskins had just taken. I sighed deeply.

'It would be,' I said.

NINE

DESPITE MY OBVIOUS apprehension, our journey through the heart of the devastated town passed without incident; which is to say that, to my vague surprise, Jurgen and I made it to the south sector without getting killed. There were a number of narrow squeaks, however. The closer we got to the centre of things, the more greenskins we saw, and other sights too, which even at this remove I'd rather not dwell on. Once we passed a shrine to the Emperor, shattered and desecrated, its offerings looted, now, judging by the stench, being used by the orks as a makeshift latrine.[1] Even that, vile as it had been, was eclipsed by

1. *Highly unlikely: the average greenskin simply answers the call of nature wherever they happen to be, the notion of a specific place being set aside for such activities being too subtle a concept for them to grasp. As, indeed, is the notion of hygiene in general. If Cain is right about the use the building was put to, it was undoubtedly meant as a deliberate insult to His Divine Majesty.*

our first sight of the main Administratum building in the centre of the town.

It had clearly once been an elegant and well proportioned structure, facing a wide, paved square in which fountains had played and artfully sited colonnades had provided shade for the townspeople going about their business. Now it bore a garland of twisted corpses, hanging from windows and statues, no doubt the civic and spiritual leaders of the community judging by the number of Administratum and ecclesiarchy robes I could see. Few had died easily, that much was clear, despite the familiar desiccation of the cadavers.

Jurgen hawked and spat, and I nodded, my own feelings far beyond words. In later years I was to see just as bad, if not worse, on far too many occasions, but at that time I had yet to encounter the minions of the Dark Powers, the necrons, or the infinitely refined sadism of the Chaos-touched eldar, and perhaps for that reason the memories remain so strong. Right then I wanted nothing more than to exterminate every greenskin on the planet, with my bare hands if I had to, but my survival instinct reasserted itself before I could give way to the impulse to avenge these sorry victims on the next of the creatures to cross our path.

There were plenty of them to be seen, large and small, scuttling around on incomprehensible errands of their own, most of which seemed to involve shouting very loudly or hitting one another. On a couple of occasions, we saw weapons drawn to resolve a quarrel, although none of the combatants seemed to take permanent harm from a mere axe wound or bullet hole, and most of the others in the vicinity simply ignored the fracas. Adding to the din was the perpetual roar of their ramshackle vehicles, which hurtled about the place with complete disregard for the safety of either their occupants or any pedestrians in their path. As well as the buggies and bike things we'd seen before, I was able to make out some larger vehicles which looked vaguely like heavily armoured trucks, and once something which might have been intended as a tank, but which looked like nothing so much as a daemon possessed pile of scrap metal rattled past,[1] crewed by whooping orks.

On several occasions, we saw foraging parties like the first we'd encountered, although not all were in search of fresh meat. Some of the carts were piled high with stuff only a tech-priest would recognise, while other groups seemed bent on collecting nothing but scrap metal. To my shock and surprise, in some cases what I'd assumed to be even scrawnier gretchin than usual, proved, on closer inspection through the amplivisor, to be human prisoners. I pointed out the haggard, shuffling figures to Jurgen with an inarticulate sound of revulsion, and he nodded grimly.

'They'll not last long,' he said, and I was forced to agree. Indeed, they must have possessed exceptional fortitude, or faith in the Emperor, to have survived their enslavement for as long as they had. No doubt,

---

1. Probably a battlewagon of some kind. Since the orkish names for most of their vehicles appear to be Gothic loan words mangled sufficiently for their debased larynxes to pronounce, such as 'trukk' for 'truck,' I've elected to let Cain's original wording stand rather than correct the terminology. Interestingly, according to the sisters of the Ordo Dialogus, this also holds true for much of their technical vocabulary, including most of their weaponry.

the atrocity of the Administratum building had been intended to intimidate the survivors into acquiescence, and it looked from here as though it had succeeded in that aim.

'There's nothing we can do for them,' I said, moving a little deeper into the cover of a shattered wall. Trying to liberate the poor wretches would only get us killed, and none of them looked in any condition to make a run for it anyway. Nevertheless, it was in a sober mood that we continued our perilous journey.

At length, we hit a watercourse and took to it gratefully, wading waist high in the blessedly cool liquid. The sun was almost at its zenith, and the relief from the baking heat was more than welcome. I drew the line at drinking it, however, continuing to use the canteen at my waist for that. No telling where it had come from, or what was contaminating it, especially with an army of greenskins in town. If you think that makes it remarkably foolish for us to go paddling in the stuff, you've clearly never experienced desert heat, or tried playing tag with orks, let alone both at the same time.

Despite moving as carefully as we could to avoid betraying our presence by sloshing around too loudly, we made good time. For most of its length, the aqueduct was lined with rockcrete walls, which rose higher than our heads, making it hard to see our surroundings, but by the same token giving us some welcome concealment from the greenskins surrounding us. Jurgen's compass told us we were moving in roughly the right direction still, and after a while, during which time the hubbub of the ork host going about their business had faded away again, I deemed the time was right to stick our heads up and see where we were.

Fortunately, at this point the walls of the aqueduct were sloping, and lined with pre-cast rockcrete slabs, which afforded excellent footing, so we were able to make our way to the top and lie completely concealed below ground level apart from our heads. I raised mine cautiously, seeing no sign of life, and scrambled up, Jurgen at my heels as always. While he dropped into a crouch, lasgun at the ready, I raised the amplivisor.

'We're here,' I said, picking out a sign on a nearby industrial unit informing me that it was the property of South Sector Plumbing Supplies. Like everywhere else we'd so far seen in this stricken community, the buildings bore the scars of fighting or ork vandalism, although there were fewer corpses in the street and more of the structures seemed to have roofs. I activated the commbead. 'Tayber, this is Cain. Respond.'

For a moment nothing happened, and I listened to the familiar hiss of static in my ears with tension winding inexorably at my gut. If this turned out to be a sump rat chase, and we'd come through all those orks for nothing...

'Wait one,' a voice said in my ear, surprisingly clearly. The channel must have remained open, though, because I was able to distinguish a muttering of voices, though not the words. A moment later the voice returned. 'He's on his way.'

'Good,' I said. 'And who are you?'

'Grenbow, sir, commissar, I mean. Sir. Vox specialist second class, sir, I mean commissar...'

'One or the other will do,' I said, hiding my irritation as best I could. PDF without a doubt, probably never seen a scarlet sash in their lives before, and with only the haziest idea of what a commissar actually was. I suppose proper Guardsmen would have been too much to hope for, but if this Grenbow was typical of the locals it sounded as though I'd have been better off following my first impulse and just getting the hell out of Prosperity Wells while I'd had the chance. Oh well, too late to worry about that now, and at least it sounded as though Tayber had a few grunts with him I could hide behind. After all, if they were still on the loose this long after the orks had occupied the town, they must have something going for them. 'How many of you are there?'

'Seven effectives, two walking wounded.' A new voice came on to the vox, calmer, more resolute, and vaguely familiar; obviously whoever it was I'd spoken to before. 'Where are you?'

'We're outside a plumbing supplies warehouse on Oildrum Lane.' I'd been able to read the street sign quite clearly though the amplivisor. 'How do I reach your position?'

'You don't.' Tayber sounded about as trusting as Colonel Mostrue. 'For all I know you're a greenie collaborator with a scavenged vox. We'll come to you.'

'Frak that!' I said heatedly. 'If you think we're going to sit around here in the open waiting to be picked off...'

'Then find some cover.'

The vox went dead. Jurgen and I looked at one another. Clearly this Tayber was as cautious as I was.

Despite the clear breach of protocol, I began to think I'd made the right choice after all, and if it turned out I hadn't, I could always shoot him for insubordination.

'Well you can hardly blame the man for being cautious,' I said, trying not to grin at my aide's outraged expression. I gestured towards the warehouse. 'We might as well wait in there.'

'Very good, sir.' Crouching low, behind a pallet of surprisingly undamaged ceramic sanitary units, we began making our way towards the refuge it offered. We were almost there when Jurgen hesitated, and raised his head. 'Can you hear that, sir?'

'Yes.' The sound drifted towards us on a light breeze, which struck pleasantly cool through the gently steaming fabric of my trousers. I nodded grimly at the unmistakable crack of las bolts, and the harsher bark of crude firearms. 'Gunfire.'

It seemed Sergeant Tayber wouldn't be joining us after all.

'WHAT DO WE do now, sir?' Jurgen asked. I shook my head, regretfully. The way I saw it, prudent retreat would be the most sensible course of action, before the noise of the firefight attracted the attention of every greenskin within earshot. Hard luck on the gallant sergeant, of course, but there didn't seem anything I could do about that now. He'd just have to take his chances with the rest of his men.

'We get the frak out of here,' I said, an instant before the commode beside my head shattered into a thousand pieces. Three orks were charging towards us, blazing away with their crude bolt pistols, fortunately with the complete lack of accuracy common to their kind. That wouldn't be enough to keep us unscathed for long, though, so we returned fire with a will, taking the time to aim our own shots carefully. Time and again I've found that the fraction of a second it takes to make sure each las bolt counts is worth more than all the wild firing in the galaxy. Of course, if you just blaze away in the general direction of the enemy you'll usually persuade him to keep his head down, unless you're dealing with greenskins, necrons, or Khornate loonies of course, but if he's got a cooler head than yours he'll be using that time to make sure he takes it off at the shoulders with his next squeeze of the trigger. Far better in my view to make sure you're the one taking the trouble to aim, and if he's doing the same, do it first.

Anyway, I remembered enough from our skirmish back at the crash site to go for a headshot, taking down the leader with a las bolt to the cranium, while Jurgen did the same for his flankers. Remembering how hard they'd been to kill, I didn't take any chances, running forward as soon as they'd dropped to take what remained of their heads off with the chainsword. I didn't care how resilient they were; they weren't going to get back up after that.

'Right behind you, sir,' Jurgen assured me, his distinctive odour announcing the fact a second or so before his voice did. 'Which way?'

'Down there,' I said, gesturing in the opposite direction to the one our erstwhile assailants had appeared from. If there were any more of them, it was carrots to credits they'd be up that way too. Jurgen nodded, and checked the level of the powercell in his weapon. It seemed satisfactory, and he levelled it, while I took a quick look around. Sure enough, there was a flash of movement, just where I most dreaded it would be, and we started moving, angling away from the approaching reinforcements, keeping our heads down and hoping the warehouse had a sufficiently large stock of commodes to conceal our progress.

No such luck, of course, although we were able to open up a reasonable lead before our pursuers noticed us. Glancing back, I noticed a dozen or so of the hulking creatures jogging forward with that same unexpected fluidity of movement I'd noticed before, expressions of belligerent curiosity on their faces, their heads and shoulders bobbing incongruously above the stacks of sanitary supplies. A couple of them surged forward abruptly, bellowing something incomprehensible in their barbarous tongue, and halted, beckoning the others to join them. Clearly, they'd just found the trio Jurgen and I had dispatched a few moments before.

'Time we were out of here,' I muttered to my aide, and he nodded, not bothering to reply. I indicated the warehouse, now only a few metres away. A blue painted, metal door stood invitingly ajar, seemingly close enough to touch, but across an open space with no sign of cover. Going back the way we'd come wasn't an option, so we'd just have to chance it. A sudden increase in the volume of the ork bellowing behind us drew my eyes in that direction for a moment, just long enough to confirm my guess that a brawl had broken out over the possessions of the ones we'd just killed, and I nodded decisively. We weren't going to get a better chance, that much was certain. 'Now!' I said, in an urgent undertone.

'Right behind you, sir,' my faithful aide responded, and we sprinted for the sanctuary of the portal. We'd almost made it, when a concerted roar of *'Waaargh!'* behind us, punctuated by a spattering of brick dust as a fusillade of badly aimed bolts and heavy slugs gouged their distinctive signatures out of the wall, made it abundantly clear that we'd been spotted.

'Inside!' I suited the action to the word, wondering an instant too late if there were greenskins already inside the building and whether it might have been more prudent to send Jurgen in first, but to my relief the place seemed deserted. A moment later, my aide joined me and we pushed the door closed behind us with a squeal of rusted metal. Clearly it had been hanging ajar ever since the orks had first attacked the town, left unsecured in the general panic, and for a horrified moment I wondered if it had corroded too badly to close. The surge of adrenaline I felt at the thought proved more than enough to overcome any residual resistance, however, and it thudded into place not a moment too soon.

'That won't hold them for long, sir,' Jurgen said helpfully, smacking home a couple of reassuringly solid looking bolts. A moment later, the steel door shivered on its hinges as our pursuers caught up with it, presumably without bothering to slow down first. As usual, Jurgen sounded surprisingly unconcerned, seemingly convinced I had matters well under control, and I found his phlegmatism strangely reassuring.

'Let's hope it doesn't have to,' I said, and activated the commbead again. 'Tayber, what's your position?'

'Reamed,' he responded almost at once. 'We're pinned down and surrounded. How about you?'

'Likewise.' I flinched reflexively as a crude grenade, resembling nothing so much as a ration tin stuck to a length of piping, sailed through a nearby window and rolled under a shelving unit of what looked like air conditioners. Jurgen and I just had time to dive for cover behind a reassuringly solid pallet full of boilers before it detonated, spraying the room with shrapnel which ricocheted off the metal cylinders with a rattle like a Galavan[1] rainstorm. 'Do you have a plan?'

'Take as many of the grox-reamers with us as we can.' The vox went dead, with a suddenness, which would have left me fearing for Grenbow's safety if I'd had any concern to spare from worrying about mine. Either way, it didn't sound like much of a plan to me.

'Are you all right sir?' Jurgen asked, rising cautiously to inspect the damage. I nodded.

'For the moment,' I said as casually as I could, trying to ignore the rhythmic thudding from the door. From the bursts of raucous laughter which accompanied each impact, I deduced that the orks were taking it in

---

1. A world covered for the most part in dense tropical growth, most noted for its exports of timber and pharmaceuticals. Rainstorms are frequent, sudden, and sufficiently heavy to stun an unprotected man out in the open. The joke common on other worlds in the subsector, that the natives are secretly mutants with gills, is merely a piece of heavy-handed humour and utterly without foundation. The Ordo Malleus has, I'm reliably informed, checked.

turns to run at the barrier, hoping to batter it down with their heads, an impression Jurgen confirmed a moment later after a cautious look through another nearby window.

'Why don't they just blow it down?' he asked, honestly puzzled. I shrugged.

'Frak knows,' I said. The longer they kept the game up the better I liked it; it gave us a fighting chance of finding another way out of there. It was only as I began to understand more about what passed for the thought processes of these creatures that the incident began to make sense in retrospect. So far as they were concerned, we weren't going anywhere, and given their tendency to impulsive behaviour and constant jockying for social status it was almost inevitable that trying to get at us would develop into another of their interminable competitions of strength and bravado.

'They're on this side too,' Jurgen reported, somewhat superfluously, as the thudding began to be echoed from the direction of the truck-sized doorway giving access to the loading dock. It didn't look as though there'd be much point in trying to get out that way either, I thought. Shame really, there was a lorry parked in the bay, which would have been a damn sight more comfortable than the ork boneshaker we'd commandeered. If we could have got it to run, that is; a dribble of lubricant ran from somewhere underneath it to vanish down a drainage hole in the corner of the floor.

'Jurgen. Look for an inspection hatch.' I pointed to the drain, which was only about a quarter of a metre across, far too small for either of us to fit. It seemed a pretty fair bet that it led to a sewer or something, though, and that wherever that was it would require periodic maintenance. Prosperity Wells was far too small to have accumulated a proper undercity over the centuries, but there was bound to be a tunnel system of some kind we could access.

Of course there wasn't. Convenient drain covers leading to easily accessible escape routes may be abundant in the cheaper kind of escapist fiction, but if my experience over the years has been anything to go by, they're depressingly rare in real life. (All right, I've found a few on occasion, but nowhere near as many as you'd expect given the number of times I've been stuck in situations like this.) A few moments of frantic searching was enough to convince me of the fact, and I was just beginning to think about firing up one of the torches I'd noticed on a nearby shelf in a futile attempt to burn through the grating over the too-small hole I'd found before, when a rather more practical notion occurred to me. I pointed to the truck.

'See if you can get that thing started,' I ordered, before grabbing an armful of the torches and running back towards the besieged rear entrance. To my relief, the door still held; although it was looking pretty battered now, and the bolts securing the hinges to the wall were beginning to work clear of the brickwork. Judging by the noise outside, the crowd of orks had grown too, considerably, but there was no time to worry about that either.

Fortunately, everything I needed was within easy reach, including the pallet of boilers we'd sheltered from the grenade explosion behind. I selected the nearest, and tipped the pile of brazing torches inside, pausing only to unscrew the nozzle and igniter unit from the last one;

the gas inside the little pressurised cylinder began to hiss out, and I dropped it on top of its fellows hastily, holding my breath as I screwed a metal cover snatched from a nearby shelf over the large hole in the top of the boiler intended for the main outlet pipe. Within seconds the thick metal vessel would be full of flammable vapour, or so I hoped. I stopped up the inlet pipe with the igniter unit, sealing the join with some mastic I'd grabbed on the way, and paused to inspect my handiwork. So far so good; now for the tricky part.

Praying fervently to the Emperor (who I was sure would be far too busy to be listening in any case) not to let me fumble now, I threaded a thin piece of wire through the trigger of the igniter unit and looped it round the handle of the door. As I stepped back, it shifted again on its frame, with a louder thud than hitherto, and a correspondingly loud chorus of approbation from the assembled greenskins outside. My heart skipped as the wire tightened, but my luck held, and the makeshift trigger didn't give enough to detonate the improvised booby trap. Mouth dry, I hurried back to Jurgen, hoping he'd made some progress in the interim.

'It doesn't look good, sir.' My aide shook his head glumly, and indicated the trickle of lubricant beneath the truck. 'The sump's cracked. That's a job for an enginseer, or a tech-priest.' I felt a thick cloud of despair begin to wind itself around me, as though my shroud was already reaching up out of the grave to claim me, as his words sunk in. So much for my brilliant plan, and the last slim chance I could think of to save my neck, and Jurgen's too, of course, probably. 'The engine'll seize up solid within a klom, two at the most.'

'You mean you can get it started anyway?' I asked, relief flooding through me again as he concluded his remarks. My aide looked even more baffled than usual, and nodded.

'For a few minutes, I think. But like I said, sir...'

'A few minutes is all it'll take,' I assured him, beginning to fling the rest of the torches, and anything else I could find which looked potentially flammable, explosive, or both, into the rear cargo compartment. In that respect at least we could hardly have chosen a better refuge; the warehouse was stuffed with such things. Once I'd collected a goodly assortment of solvents and pressurised gas cylinders I taped a small timer unit intended to control a central heating system to a domestic powercell, then added another igniter, and a bottle of cleaning fluid with a gratifyingly large flame logo in a yellow warning triangle helpfully labelled *Flammable: Toxic: Keep away from children and ogryns*. No doubt a tech-priest would have been horrified at such a blatant misuse of the Omnissiah's bounty, and I had no confidence at all that it would work without being properly sanctified, but killing orks was the Emperor's work if anything was and I hoped he might cut us a bit of slack.[1]

---

1. *Cain's apparent familiarity with mysteries generally reserved for the acolytes of the omnissiah may seem a little odd here; but my readers should bear in mind that the equipment he was working with was intended for everyday domestic use by common artisans, and would be both robust and simple as a consequence. Since we can also infer from a number of allusions throughout the archive that he was given to perpetrating practical jokes against the more strait-laced of his fellow commissar cadets at the schola progenium, he may simply have been adapting the lessons learned during these earlier pieces of mischief to rather more serious ends.*

'Very good, sir.' The expression of bafflement never left Jurgen's face, but he fired up the engine nevertheless. It did indeed sound about as well tuned as our purloined buggy, but the revs built up into a howl of protesting metal with gratifying speed.

'Out of the cab.' I wedged the throttle open with a large canister of screws, and gestured to the bolts securing the garage doors against the ork horde outside. I'd set the timer for about two minutes, and hoped that would be enough. The crowning irony would be for us to be immolated by my own cunning plan. 'And undo those, quietly.'

True to form, my aide complied, though looking as confused as ever, sliding the metal rods back against their stoppers before looking back at me for further instructions.

'Get the frak out of the way!' I told him, pushing the truck into gear and jumping for it myself.

I have to admit, even after all this time, the memory of what happened next leaves me with a warm, happy glow. In short, it worked like a charm. As Jurgen dived to one side, the press of orks outside suddenly found the doors they'd been leaning against beginning to give. With another bone rattling yell of *'Waaaaaargh!'* they surged through the widening gap, just in time to meet the truck coming the other way. Engine screaming, the abused vehicle ploughed straight through the middle of them, scattering the lucky ones and flattening the others, who disappeared under its wheels with crunching and squishing noises, uncannily reminiscent of Jurgen eating a bowl of seafood. If any of them screamed, the sound was drowned by the enraged warcry of the rest, who turned as one to race after the fleeing vehicle, firing their weapons wildly as they went.

'Come on,' I called to Jurgen, running in their wake. As I'd hoped, the diversion had worked beautifully; every ork I could see was now chasing the empty lorry. I found myself hoping at least some of them would catch up with it before the timer reached the limit I'd set. 'This isn't going to be a healthy place to be in a moment or two.'

Well, I'd got that right. I led the way at an angle, away from the warehouse, away from the truck and it's wildly yelling escort of greenskins, most of which were continuing to waste ammunition on it with a gratifying lack of success; if I'm honest, just in the general direction of away from there as quickly as possible. We'd just reached the perimeter fence, which a quick slash with my chainsword was sufficient to let us through, and were glancing around trying to decide which direction to take next, when the party of orks at the back door must have finally succeeded in gaining entry. A loud *whump!*, surprisingly flat I thought, although I suppose the walls of the warehouse kept most of the sound in, echoed across the flat space between the building and the large, ruined structure facing us. Slowly, with a cloud of dust rising around it like a shroud, the roof caved in.

'That'll teach 'em to go barging in without an invite,' Jurgen said, with clear satisfaction. The crowd of orks chasing the lorry just had time to mill around in confusion, glancing back and trying to work out what was going on, before that detonated too, spreading its load of burning solvents in a far wider circle than I'd anticipated. The roar of anger and pain intensified, many of the greenskins staggering around drunkenly, turned into briefly living torches, before slumping to the sunbaked rockcrete. Jurgen smiled, his mood turning even lighter. 'We won't need to take the promethium to that lot.'

A fierce elation took hold of me then, and I could hardly prevent myself from punching the air as though I'd just scored the winning goal in a scrumball match; only the reflection that Jurgen would consider such a gesture undignified, and take on the mien of a dyspeptic puppy (which he seemed to think signified longsuffering tolerance), held me back. It was just as well really, as any celebration of our victory would undoubtedly have proven somewhat premature.

'Oh nads,' I said, with considerable feeling. 'You have got to be frakking joking.' Another knot of greenskins was emerging from the ruin ahead of us, weapons at the ready, and as they began to sprint in our direction I heard that all-too-familiar warcry once again. I glanced around, looking for cover, and at that moment an ork rose from a drainage ditch in front of us and swung its oversized cleaver at my head.

TEN

HOW WE'D MISSED the thing I'll never know, it was certainly big and nasty enough, but I suppose our attention had been almost exclusively focused on the carnage we'd wrought in and around the warehouse. I parried its first attack instinctively with my chainsword, which, thank the Emperor, was still activated after carving our way through the wire mesh surrounding the compound. Sparks flew as I deflected the cumbersome weapon and turned aside, keeping the greenskin moving in the direction it had thought it had wanted to go until I'd inconsiderately got out of the way. As it straightened, disengaging its blade and trying to get back on balance, I struck backwards, slicing deep into its chest and eliciting a roar of anger and pain along with a spray of foul smelling ichor. It staggered back a pace, trying to rally, and I shot it with the laspistol in my other hand. After my previous encounter with the things, I was by no means sanguine that even after taking so much damage it wouldn't simply rally and come at me again, but Jurgen was quick to follow my lead, shredding its torso with a burst of automatic fire from his lasgun.

For another instant, the greenskin seemed to sway, an almost comical expression of surprise beginning to curdle on its face, and then it toppled backwards into the rockcrete channel it had so unexpectedly erupted from. I glanced down, half expecting to see it scrabbling back up towards us again, but by the grace of the Emperor it lay still.

There was no time to savour our victory, as a dozen or so of its fellows continued to charge towards us. I dived for cover behind a large metal pipe, crowned with a valve of some kind, and began to take stock of our surroundings. A moment later, the familiar odour of unwashed socks informed me that Jurgen had taken cover too, and not a moment too soon, as the fusillade of badly aimed small-arms fire I'd begun to associate with these creatures began to rattle and ping off our makeshift refuge.

'Where the hell did they come from?' I asked rhetorically, and Jurgen shrugged, switching his weapon back to single shot mode.

'That building over there,' he explained helpfully, beginning to pepper the onrushing horde with his usual commendable accuracy. He scored several hits, downing a couple of our would-be assailants, but just like the ones we'd encountered in the desert, most of the others simply shrugged off wounds which would have disabled a human instantly. At this range, my chances of doing any real damage with the laspistol were virtually nonexistent, although I joined in with alacrity, and at least had the satisfaction of seeing a couple of them stagger.[1]

I stared at the ruin Jurgen had indicated. It was huge, towering over most of the other buildings in the vicinity, and a positive forest of pipe work ran in and out of what remained of the structure. Well, that was good; it seemed the conduit we were hiding behind had connections all over the site, so at least we could remain under relatively solid cover while we were running away. The question was, in which direction? Going back the way we'd come wasn't an option; despite the havoc we'd wrought behind us, I was in no doubt that enough of the orks had survived to make attempting to leave in that direction problematic at best. Straight ahead was out too: apart from the greenskins charging at us, the rockcrete channel that my opponent had erupted from was too wide to jump, and there was no sign of a bridge. I didn't think that little detail would stop the greenskins, from what I'd seen of their musculature they could probably hop across it without breaking stride. Jumping down, hoping to use it for cover as we had the watercourse, would be suicide. It was only a couple of metres deep, but trapped down there we'd have been shot to pieces as soon as the greenskins arrived.

---

1. As ever, Cain tends to understate his abilities. Though the laspistol, like all handguns, is intended for use at relatively close quarters, I saw him take out an enemy well beyond its nominal effective range on more than one occasion.

'This way,' I said, leading my aide along beside the pipe, which continued to ring and reverberate with the slugs and bolts knocking holes in the other side. By my reckoning, we only had seconds to move before the horde was upon us.

'Right behind you sir,' Jurgen assured me, although my nose had already done the job for him, and we sprinted for a small rockcrete blockhouse into which the pipes we were following disappeared. If we could get behind that...

'Oh frak,' I said, as another greenskin appeared round the corner of the structure. I dropped it with a single las bolt, realising in that instant of incredulous relief that it was only a gretchin, but that meant that there was bound to be a whole swarm of them right behind their fellow. I was soon proved to be correct in that assumption, as what seemed at the time to be a positive tide of the little vermin, but in all probability was no more than a dozen or so, boiled around the corner of the blockhouse, squealing and waving firearms which seemed even more primitive than those wielded by their masters. Indeed, at least one exploded in its owner's hands as he attempted to use it. Nevertheless, Jurgen and I swung aside at once, seeking refuge deeper within the tangle of pipe work, which continued to surround us, and just in time too; another ill-aimed volley rattled off the metalwork as we did so.

'I think this is a dead end, sir,' Jurgen said, and with a thrill of bowel clenching horror I realised he was right. On either side of us, the sheltering pipes disappeared into the side of a large storage tank, easily five or six metres high. Climbing to safety wouldn't be an option in the time we had left either. By the time our pursuers reached the end of the narrow gap we'd so incautiously trapped ourselves in, we'd simply be making ourselves a better target.

'Go back,' I said decisively. At least if we tried to engage them just inside the mouth of the metal defile they could only come at us a few at a time, and we might be able to pick them off one by one. It was a slim enough chance, Emperor alone knew, but that was infinitely better than no chance at all. As I turned back, my mouth dry, a sick knot of terror wound itself tighter inside my gut. The deeper, guttural tones drowning out the squeals of the lesser greenskins told me that my earlier fears had been well founded, and that the mob of orks we'd seen before had crossed the drainage channel without any difficulty whatsoever.

Nevertheless, we had no other choice, and turned to face our destiny as best we could. For some reason, the last transmission I'd heard from Sergeant Tayber came back to me at that point: 'Take as many of the grox-reamers with us as we can.' Well it still didn't sound like much of a plan to me, but it would have to do to be going on with. My survival instinct hadn't let me down yet, and I just had to hope that it wouldn't do so today.

I raised my laspistol, taking aim as steadily as I could at the rectangle of sunlight ahead of us. Shadows moved beyond it, and we were abruptly plunged into eclipse as an ork filled the space. I just had time to register the ridiculously large gun in its hand and the inevitable meat cleaver whirling above its head as my finger tightened on the trigger...

Abruptly, the ground shook, and my ears rang to a series of overlapping explosions. The ork disappeared, to be replaced by a cloud of eye-watering dust, which billowed around us for a moment. I shook my head, dazed, and my survival instinct kicked in even more strongly than before. I grabbed Jurgen by the arm.

'Come on,' I shouted, coughing as the dust irritated the back of my throat. 'Move!' The sound of sporadic gunfire forced itself past the ringing in my ears, the harsh bark of ork firearms, and the distinctive *crack* of ionising air, which could only be produced by Imperial lasguns. To his credit, my aide recovered what wits he had, almost at once, and needed no further urging.

We emerged from our refuge into a scene of carnage. Most of the greenskins were down, and in no state to continue the fight; in fact most of them were in no state to continue to live, being scattered around the landscape in a gratifying number of pieces. The few surviving gretchin had clearly had enough, heading for the horizon with as much speed as their stunted little legs could muster, which in all fairness was pretty fast. Only a handful of orks continued to hold their ground, too stupid or belligerent to flee themselves, pouring a hail of slugs and bolts into the surrounding metalwork, from which well-aimed las bolts continued to erupt in reply.

Even as we watched, another couple of orks went down, comprehensively shredded by a neatly executed crossfire, and that seemed to be enough. The remaining trio, all leaking copious amounts of their rancid blood, stared at one another in mutual shock as it finally penetrated their skulls that they were undoubtedly about to go the same way, unless they followed the gretchin. As one they turned, began to flee and then became aware that Jurgen and I were cutting them off from safety. With the inevitable yell of '*Waaaaargh!*' they reacted like all their kind tend to do *in extremis*, lower their heads, and charge.

Needless to say, my immediate reaction was simply to get out of the way, let them go, and good riddance, but, unfortunately, that didn't seem like a viable option. For one thing, Jurgen and I were hemmed in by the blasted pipes, with nowhere to go, and would probably have been trampled in the rush if we'd tried it. For another, there was no guarantee that the orks would simply keep going even if we were able to make room for them. From what I'd seen of the creatures already, it seemed all too likely that now they'd been presented with another target their innate bloodlust would override the impulse to flee again, and they'd simply cut us down on the way past. There were our rescuers to consider too. The initial impression I made on them would have to consolidate the authority of my office.

As I try to impress on the young whelps in my charge these days, it isn't the scarlet sash and the fancy hat that makes you a commissar, it's the way you wear them. The troops you serve with are never going to like you, but if you can get them to respect you that can be almost as good. Remember, you're going to spend most of your career on a battlefield with them, and they've all got guns, so making them think you're a liability is never going to be a very good idea.

Almost without thinking, I stepped to the side, where I'd only have to take on one of the greenies, and lashed out with the chainsword.

'Oh no you don't!' I snarled, with the best impression of martial zeal I could summon up under the circumstances, and ducked under the arm carrying a grotesquely oversized stubber of some kind. Like its fellows, the ork I'd picked on carried a large, heavy axe in the other hand, and I had more sense than to engage it from the side it could swing the thing unhindered. Why none of them shot at us as they charged I had no idea at the time, but I've observed the same thing on innumerable occasions since. Once they get close enough to an enemy they show all the tactical sense of a Khornate cult, so carried away with the prospect of getting into close combat that they seem to forget all about the ranged weapons they're carrying. Anyhow, the only thing this greenie tried to do with his gun was stave my skull in, which I dodged easily, finding as I did so that he'd kindly left himself wide open for a strike to the torso. By luck rather than judgement, my chainblade bit deep, slicing clean through him, and he ran on a few paces before pitching to the ground, coming apart in the middle like a gently sautéed ambull steak.

Jurgen engaged the one on the other flank doggedly, hosing it down with las bolts, his gun on full auto. I only caught a glimpse of the result, but it wasn't pretty, the luckless greenskin coming apart under the relentless hail of point-blank fire, almost as thoroughly as if it had been hit by a necron flayer. That left the one in the middle, which had barrelled on past me while I still had the other one standing between me and it. It lifted the cleaver in its hand, bellowing with rage, and bore down on Jurgen. My aide switched his aim smoothly, hitting it in the chest with a couple of bolts, and then the lasgun went silent. We'd expended a lot of shots between us since leaving the buggy parked in the derelict factory that morning, and full auto will drain a powerpack faster than an ogryn with a beer glass.

Fortunately, I was still turning from the blow, which had bisected the first ork I'd encountered, and even more luckily the enraged greenskin slipped in the mess we'd made of its fellows. As it lost its footing, Jurgen moved with surprising speed, ramming the butt of his lasgun into its nose, with an audible *snap!* It staggered backwards, still trying desperately to regain its balance, and I continued the sweeping motion of my gently humming chainblade, taking it behind the knee. It fell to the ground as its right leg came off, tried to rise with an air of stupefied astonishment, and I swiped its head clear off its shoulders with the backswing. The decapitated corpse swayed slightly, and tumbled to the blood soaked ground.

'Nice move,' I said to Jurgen, glancing around to see if there were any more greenskins in the vicinity. He shrugged, snapping a fresh powercell into his lasgun.

'They have a few vulnerable points,' he said. I nodded. Given the historic antipathy his people had for the greenskins, I supposed he would have been likely to know them. (In fact if I'd bothered to ask before, instead of dismissing the stories I'd heard aboard the *Hand of Vengeance* as pure exaggeration,

I'd have found out that pretty much every Valhallan did.)

'You'll have to run me through them some time,' I said. (Which, of course, being Jurgen he took as an order rather than a pleasantry, presenting me the following day with a datafile detailing a number of ways to take out a greenskin in hand-to-hand combat; something I've had occasion to be grateful for on innumerable occasions in the years since.)

'Very good, sir.' He glanced around, levelling his recharged weapon. 'Was that the last of them?'

'I hope so,' I said. There didn't seem to be any more greenskins in the immediate vicinity, so after a moment I holstered the laspistol and switched off the chainsword, returning it to the scabbard. 'I suppose we ought to find out who to thank for this.' I indicated the chunks of scattered ork littering the rockcrete around us.

'That would be us.' A man emerged from the tangle of piping, his eyes concealed behind a pair of solar-specs which reflected Jurgen and me as large headed mannequins. He wore a vest of flak armour over dusty fatigues, although unlike my aide's khaki ones both were printed in an urban camo pattern. Sergeant's stripes were visible on his sleeves, although the floppy sun hat he wore in place of a helmet, printed like the rest of his uniform in mottled grey, was devoid of insignia. He carried a standard issue lasgun, which he kept casually at rest, not quite pointing at us.

'Neat trick,' I said. The man nodded at the trio of dead orks at our feet.

'I could say the same.' He looked me up and down. 'I'm guessing you're Cain.'

'Unless you know of any other commissars running around the place,' I agreed. 'And you must be Tayber.'

'Guess I must.' He gestured, and a handful of other men began to emerge from the tangle of pipework. 'I see you found us after all.'

Of course. The ruin in front of us must be the hydro station. That would explain all the pipework I supposed. I shrugged, plastering my most insouciant grin on my face.

'It sounded as though you were busy,' I said. 'Under the circumstances it would have been rude to insist on an escort.' Tayber continued to stare at me, and I decided to seize the initiative. 'How's Grenbow? You were cut off pretty abruptly.'

'I'm fine, sir.' A young fellow, scarcely out of his teens if I was any judge, spoke up, a bulky vox set still strapped to his back. It looked as though my guess had been right; it had stopped a round of some kind, but had undoubtedly saved the young trooper's life in the process.

'Pleased to hear it,' I said, and returned my attention to the sergeant. 'We should get moving. There were still some greenskins left back there.' I gestured in the direction of the column of smoke, billowing gently skyward from the point where we'd blown up the truck. Tayber nodded.

'We should. They know where we were hiding out now. Get the rest of your people together, and let's go.'

'We're it,' I said. I gestured towards my companion. 'This is my aide, Gunner Jurgen. Our troopship was hit when we entered the system, and our escape pod crashed in the desert a couple of days ago.'

'Sounds like a fascinating story.' Tayber turned and gestured to his men. 'Come on. We're moving out, although Emperor alone knows where to.'

Editorial Note:

Since, typically, Cain concentrates on his own experiences to the exclusion of anything else, the following extract may shed a little light on some of the preceding section. Alas, like so many other retired military men (and one woman in particular who springs to mind in this context), Sergeant Tayber's memoirs leave something to be desired in matters of style. Nevertheless, they remain perennially popular on his homeworld, as does Cain's own published autobiography To Serve the Emperor: A Commissar's Life. *(Which, incidentally, is far less readable than the more candid private account of his activities; perhaps it's something about the idea of setting their experiences down for posterity, which induces a kind of mental constipation in warriors used to solving problems in a rather more straightforward fashion.)*

From *The March of the Liberator: the Cain I Knew* by Alaric Tayber, 337 M41

It may be some small claim to fame, and certainly pales into insignificance compared to the uncounted thousands who owe their preservation to his inspirational leadership, but mine was the first life to be saved by Cain the Liberator, or, to be a little more accurate, the lives of myself and the remains of my squad.

Since the greenskin plague had descended on our homeworld, we had fought them to the best of our abilities, resorting to hit-and-run tactics, as their overwhelming numbers took their inevitable toll on our gallant defenders. In the previous chapter I set out how, separated from our rapidly disintegrating command structure, we had gone to ground in the remains of the hydro station where Luskins had previously worked, using the tunnels connecting it to the rest of the town to launch guerilla raids on whatever targets we found. By some mischance, we must have betrayed the position of our makeshift citadel on one of these excursions, as we were attacked in our own base by a warband of some considerable size. Ironically, this was on the very day Commissar Cain had made contact with us, the first vox signal we'd managed to receive in almost a month.

Had it not been for this fortuitous coincidence, we would undoubtedly have been caught without warning, and butchered in our lair. However, we had just set out to meet the commissar when the unmistakable sound of ork voices alerted us to the fact that our hiding place had been discovered. We engaged them at once, managing to hold them off, but I could tell that our position was hopeless. To make things even worse, or so it seemed at the time, Commissar Cain had also encountered some elements of the warband surrounding us and was trapped himself, massively outnumbered and facing certain death.

Had I known then what matchless depths of courage and resourcefulness the Liberator possessed I would have worried far less. By a brilliant stratagem, he succeeded not only in overcoming the foes surrounding him, but also in drawing off the bulk of the greenskins besieging us. Fearing, no doubt, from the noise of the carnage this peerless tactician had been able to wreak that they were facing a counterattack, the vast majority of them turned to meet this phantom foe, giving us the opportunity we needed to fight free. By great good fortune, the line of retreat chosen by the enemy took them through an area we had mined in anticipation of an attack from that direction, and for reasons we failed to understand at the time, they had halted right in the middle of the killing zone. One simple detonation sequence was all it took to reduce the bulk of the greenskins opposing us to a handful of stunned survivors.

It was then that we caught our first sight of Cain the Liberator, standing firm in the face of an ork charge, which would undoubtedly have given a lesser man pause. Undaunted, he ran forward to meet them, dispatching his assailants in a flurry of deft strikes and parries, his chainsword hewing greenskin bodies as casually as a woodsman's axe felling trees.

As he sheathed his weapon and strode out to greet us, a self-effacing smile on his face as though embarrassed to have been seen at work, I was struck for the first time how young he was. We had no commissars in the PDF,[1] so all I knew about them were the stories everyone knows, but I was soon to discover that in spite of his apparent youth his maturity and judgement were second to none. Indeed, his first question after we'd exchanged greetings was to enquire after the welfare of our vox operator, who had been hit in the middle of our last exchange of messages, an early indication of the concern we were soon to discover that he felt for all those who had so fortuitously fallen under his care.

It was as we left our former refuge, however, that I first realised the truly inspirational nature of his leadership. To all intents and purposes we had been routed, forced on the run again, but to Commissar Cain this apparently crushing setback was nothing of the kind.

---

1. *Not entirely true, as the Commissariat has overall responsibility for maintaining morale and proper discipline among all branches of the Imperial military, (with the obvious exceptions of the Astartes, the Adepta Sororitas, and the forces maintained directly by the Adeptus Mechanicus). Typically the PDF of a densely populated system, where the number of troopers under arms exceeds twenty or thirty million, will have a single commissar assigned to oversee it, while in most cases the luckless individual in question will have theoretical responsibility for overseeing the PDF assets of an entire subsector. It goes without saying that the majority of these commissars have been selected for the job as a result of disciplinary action, infirmity, or both, and that for the most part the troopers nominally under their jurisdiction can be forgiven for remaining blissfully unaware of their existence.*

Indeed, it was to be the beginning of a victory more complete than any of us could possibly have dreamed at the time.

ELEVEN

RETURNING TO WHERE Jurgen and I had parked our purloined transport was to prove less of an ordeal than I'd anticipated. One of the PDF troopers turned out to have worked in the hydro plant before being conscripted, and knew the network of tunnels and sewers beneath the city well enough to guide us back without fear of running into any more of the greenskins. I hoped. It was becoming increasingly clear to me that brutal and impulsive as they were, the commonly held belief that they were also as thick as sump dregs wasn't exactly true. All right, the average greenskin is pretty stupid compared to a human (or even a ratling for that matter), but then abstract reasoning isn't exactly high on their list of priorities. Something had led them to Tayber's hiding place in the hydro station, and it wouldn't take much for them to realise that we'd taken to the tunnels beneath it. So, even though my old hiver's instincts welcomed the sense of enclosure around us, interpreting it as safe and familiar, my conscious mind was at least partially occupied, the whole time filtering the echoes around us for any sound of pursuit or ambush up ahead.

The further we got from the south sector, the more relaxed I became, and I was able to devote more of my attention to what Tayber was telling me. He and his men had been using these tunnels for some weeks, striking at isolated greenskin patrols and raiding for supplies, and that all in all they'd been making quite a nuisance of themselves. Well, bully for them, it was what they were supposed to be doing, and the more greenskins they took out the happier I was, but it became increasingly obvious to me the more detail he went into, that they were only staving off the inevitable.

'What else do you suggest we do?' Tayber asked once we'd got back to the ruined factory where we'd parked the buggy. He was looking around the place, clearly wondering if it would do as another makeshift base from which to harass the greenskins. 'Just give up?'

'Of course not,' I said. He seemed convinced, now, that we weren't ork collaborators, which was something of an improvement, and was at least inclined to hear me out. How much of that was due to my commissarial authority, how much to my personal charm, which I was exerting as subtly as I could to reinforce the good impression hacking a couple of orks to bits in front of him had evidently made, and how much to the plateful of soylens viridiens he was scarfing down as we spoke, I couldn't be sure. If anything had convinced the PDF troopers of our good intentions it was the pile of survival rations we'd scavenged from the lifepod; it seemed they hadn't had a hot meal in days. 'They know you're out there now. Maybe it's time to move on.'

'Move on where?' Tayber asked, flinching a little as Jurgen leaned across to refill his mug of recaff, which hardly seemed fair to me; after a month or more of living rough he wasn't exactly fragrant either. I shrugged, forking another mouthful of reconstituted glop into my mouth.

'We're hoping to link up with the bulk of our forces,' I said. 'We know our regiment made it down in one piece, and it's our duty to rejoin it as quickly as possible.' So I could get back to sitting quietly, well behind the front line as usual, with nothing more dangerous to look out for than Colonel Mostrue's occasional attempts to see if I was quite as heroic as I was supposed to be, although I didn't think it was advisable to be quite that candid with Tayber. To my surprise he laughed out loud.

'Good luck,' he said. 'You're going to need it.' Something about the way he spoke started my palms tingling again, but I smiled as though we were just exchanging pleasantries.

'What do you mean?' I asked. By way of a reply he drew a map slate out of his pack and showed it to me.

'We're here,' he said, pointing, and to my well-concealed satisfaction I noticed that we were more or less in the position I'd estimated from the crudely scrawled ork map. I nodded, to show I understood. 'And the closest defending forces are here.' He scrolled the image across to the western continent, and tapped the narrow peninsular connecting the two landmasses. 'More or less,' he shrugged, 'apart from the odd group of stragglers like us, of course.'

'Of course,' I said, masking the way my stomach had suddenly seemed to drop clear of my body with the practiced ease of the born dissembler. I shrugged too. 'It seems our tactical information was a little outdated.'

'You might say that,' Tayber agreed. I took another gulp of the recaff, wishing it was tanna.

My head reeled with the implications of this new information. Anyway I looked at it, my original plan looked like the only one with even the slightest chance of ensuring my survival. Remaining hundreds of kilometres behind enemy lines indefinitely was a slow way of committing suicide, nothing more. Sooner or later my luck was bound to run out.

'Nevertheless,' I said slowly, 'I'm going to try it. I have to. My duty to the regiment demands it, my duty to the Commissariat demands it, and besides,' I shrugged, with a faint grin at Jurgen, knowing only he would get the joke, and that I was further from joking about the matter than anyone else would think, 'the nearest mug of tanna is on the next continent somewhere. And I'm just about in the mood to go and get it.'

In the end, I persuaded Tayber to come with me far more easily than I'd expected. I'd been worried that I'd have to exert my commissarial authority, but he was bright enough to realise that the fracas in the south sector would have stirred up the greenskins to the point where sneaking around unnoticed would be far less easy than before. As for the troopers with him, I neither knew nor cared what they thought; once I got Tayber on side they'd follow orders like good little grunts and that was that. If I noticed any signs of reluctance to pull out on his part I simply put it down to the practical difficulties of our intended journey.

'We'll never make it all that way on foot,' Tayber said, shrinking the image to emphasise the point, until where we were and where we needed to get to could just fit onto the pictscreen together. Dusk was falling, which suited me fine; if we were going to sneak out of this firewasp's nest without the orks noticing, it would be far better to do it in the dark. I nodded, conceding the point, and Tayber shrugged, his face wanly illuminated by the tenuous glow of the mapslate.

'Then we'll have to get you some transport,' I said. There was no point even suggesting that they hitch a ride with us. The buggy was so stuffed with supplies from the lifepod, there was barely room for me to cling on to the thing, and even if we ditched them (which wasn't an option given how much ground we had to cover, especially with eight more mouths to feed[1]), there still wouldn't have been enough room for the whole squad to climb aboard it.

Tayber raised an eyebrow. 'And where do you suggest we get it?' he asked.

---

1. *From which we can infer that one of Tayber's squad failed to survive the ork ambush back at the hydro station.*

I indicated the scavenged vehicle with a tilt of the head.

'I'm sure the greenskins wouldn't miss another one of those,' I said. Once again I expected Tayber to argue, but to my surprise he simply nodded, with the first sign of enthusiasm I'd seen since we started this conversation.

'I know where we can get some,' he said.

In later years, I suppose, my innate paranoia would have kicked in at that point, but in those days I was far more naive, and so relieved at his ready acquiescence, it never occurred to me that he might have an ulterior motive.

TWELVE

In the end, the plan we agreed on was simple enough, if more than a little desperate. Tayber and his men knew the town well, which was hardly surprising as most of them had grown up there, and had been keeping a commendably close eye on the greenskins' activities. Tayber called up a street plan on the mapslate, pointing out the local landmarks to Jurgen and me as we leaned over the tiny image. As ever, my innate sense of direction took over as soon as I looked at it, and I was pleased to be able to follow the route we'd taken that morning with little difficulty.

'They keep most of the vehicles here while they're not being used,' Tayber said. Recognising the common map symbol for an Adeptus Mechanicus shrine, I nodded. That made sense, although given the state of repair of our purloined buggy I found it hard to believe that regular maintenance was high on the owners' list of priorities. I said as much, and one of the other troopers, Hascom by name, chipped in diffidently.

'They go there for fuel, mostly,' he said. 'And it's where they build new ones.'

'New ones?' I echoed, and Hascom nodded.

'The greenies have some sort of tech-priests. They build things. Sort of...'

I nodded too, to show I was listening. I'd gathered from Jurgen that a few of the orks had a rudimentary knowledge of technical matters, but the news that the greenskins here were capable of producing new toys to replace the ones that got broken put another face on things entirely. I glanced at Tayber. 'I'd have thought you'd want to take this place out as quickly as possible,' I said. The sergeant looked uneasy.

'It's not quite as simple as that,' he said. I adopted an expression of polite enquiry, and once he realised I wasn't going to push him for details he ended up telling me far more than he'd intended to of his own volition. (Which is a good example of why I try to instil a bit of patience into my cadets, although the little whippersnappers are generally too young and eager to see the point.) 'It's heavily guarded. We'd never have been able to get inside, and even if we did...' He hesitated, and I became aware of a subtle tensing among the troopers, like the first faint presentiment of a distant thunderstorm. 'We couldn't blow it up.'

'Why not?' I asked. 'If it's a refuelling station there must be promethium tanks.' I glanced at Trooper Luskins, the tunnel rat, who carried a missile launcher over his shoulder, and his teammate Jodril, whose pouch of spare rockets was almost but not quite exhausted. 'In fact if you pick your spot, a krak round from outside the compound should do the job nicely.'

'It would,' Luskins agreed quickly, with the air of a man who had argued precisely this point himself on more than one occasion.

'But we'd end up killing our own people,' Grenbow put in. He was still lugging the useless vox set around, although for the life of me I couldn't see why. Perhaps he was just so used to it that he simply didn't notice the weight any more.

Luskins shrugged. 'They're dead already. Just haven't stopped moving around yet.'

Grenbow and a couple of the others flushed angrily, and I stepped in to defuse the situation with the instinctive ease of long practice.

'I'm sorry,' I said, 'I don't quite see what you're getting at.'

Tayber sighed heavily. 'It's where they keep the prisoners,' he said. I thought of the emaciated wretches I'd seen that morning, and privately agreed with Luskins: none of them looked as though they were going to last much longer. Saying so wouldn't get us anywhere, though, so I nodded judiciously as though he had a point.

'We should take whatever precautions we can to protect the civilians,' I said, little dreaming of how that simple platitude was going to come back to haunt me. For the moment, though it had the desired effect, the air of tension around us draining away as swiftly as it had come. 'That goes without saying.' I turned back to the sergeant. 'But the objective has changed from the one you were considering before. We need to get in, obtain some transport, and get out again. How would you do that?'

'We'll need a diversion,' Tayber said. 'But coordinating it will be a problem. Once we split up we'll be out of touch.'

'No we won't,' I assured him, tapping the comm-bead in my ear. 'We've got enough of these to go round.' The sergeant looked surprised for a moment.

'Good,' he said. He glanced at Jodril. 'Got any frag shells left?'

'One,' the loader confirmed, 'and two krak.'

'Sounds like a diversion to me,' I said, turning to the missile team. 'Can you find a spot overlooking the compound?'

Luskins smiled lazily. 'Know just the one,' he said, to my complete lack of surprise.

'Pleased to hear it,' I told him. 'Set up there, wait for our signal, and then drop the fragger on the biggest bunch of greenies you can find.'

'Then head for the rendezvous,' Sergeant Tayber said firmly, clearly worried at the prospect of Luskins's enthusiasm for cooking off the promethium getting the better of him once we were inside. I nodded judiciously, as if I was considering it.

'That might be best,' I conceded, and spun the map-slate towards Luskins. 'Where are you going to be?'

'Here.' He pointed, and I nodded again.

'You can see the main gate from there?'

'Clear as day,' the rocketeer assured me, and his loader nodded a vigorous assent.

'Then I suggest,' I said to Tayber, in a tone of voice calculated to convey that the suggestion was nothing of the kind, 'that they remain in place until we're clear. In case we need covering from pursuit.'

'That might be prudent,' the sergeant agreed, with evident reluctance. I turned back to Luskins, masking my own apprehension at the thought I might just be giving a pyromaniac the biggest box of matches on the planet.

'But don't fire without a specific order from Sergeant Tayber or myself,' I added, as if it were an afterthought. 'Those rockets don't grow on trees.'

'No, sir.' He nodded soberly, and broke into a grin. 'Be good if they did, though, wouldn't it?'

Once the troopers had dispersed to their pre-arranged positions, Jurgen and I had little to do but wait. Night had fallen in earnest, and with it had come the cold, so I fastened my greatcoat with a sense of profound relief. In the darkness, its sombre black was a positive advantage, and one I intended to exploit to the full in the hours to come. As always when waiting for the action to begin, I found myself wondering if I was doing the right thing. Jurgen and I would be running a tremendous risk, and I was by no means sure how much I could rely on my new allies. Perhaps it would be most prudent to simply leave, and head westwards alone, hoping to slip past the orks unobserved.

No. That would be suicidal. My chances of travelling all that distance without backup were virtually nonexistent. If I was going to stand a reasonable chance of making it back to our lines, I'd have to take the troopers with me, which meant getting them some transport. That, in turn, meant I was committed to this ridiculous plan, which now I came to consider it carefully had more holes in it than Jurgen's socks... It was with some relief that I heard the commbead hiss in my ear, followed by Luskins's voice, which sounded breathy and excited.

'Team two. We're in place.'

'Good.' Instinctively, I kept my own voice under control. 'Await signal. Team one, advise.'

'Getting close,' Tayber said, and then went quiet again, maintaining vox discipline like the good NCO he was, at least by PDF standards. I took a deep breath and clambered aboard the buggy, where Jurgen was already waiting, swathed in a blanket.

'All right,' I said, as he fired up the engine and we jerked into motion. 'Let's see if this actually works.'

At first, everything seemed to be going well, Tayber voxing in shortly after we set off to advise us that he and the five troopers with him were waiting in the culvert that Luskins had pointed out would bring them close to the perimeter without exposing them to enemy fire; or, with any luck, sentries, assuming the greenskins were sufficiently organised to have posted some in the first place. It was a fairly safe assumption that they hadn't, at least not there, since the outflow from whatever arcane processes the enginseers had overseen in the depths of their sanctum in happier times was blocked off by a metal grille, rendering entry from that direction impossible without the aid of explosives or other equally conspicuous methods. Explosives were in short supply, of course, and I wouldn't have been too happy in Tayber's shoes at the prospect of setting them off in a confined space in any case, but as usual my aide had proved equal to the challenge, producing a small cutting torch from among the plethora of miscellaneous items he'd scavenged from the wreck of the lifepod.

That would still make a bit of noise, but if everything went according to plan, the greenskins would have a great deal more to worry about by the time the Perlians began burning their way through the barrier. Just so long as their attention wasn't focused on us…

The journey to the former shrine of the tech-priests was nerve-wracking. I crouched behind the bundles of booty encrusting our ramshackle vehicle, hoping that would be sufficient to shield me from view. What little I could see of the night time streets was still more than enough, however, the same bustle of frenetic activity I'd noticed during the day continued unabated throughout the hours of darkness. Here and there, bonfires burned, illuminating the ghastly scene in tones of flickering orange, and once I saw a building ablaze, apparently set on fire purely for the light it afforded.[1] There were fewer vehicles around than before, and most of the ones we saw were heading in the same direction we were, so Tayber's intelligence looked as though it was accurate at least in that respect.

---

1. Probably not. Greenskin night vision seems to be superior to that of humans. In all likelihood it was simply a cooking fire that had got out of hand, or an act of wanton destruction perpetrated purely for its own sake.

Once, to my horror, a gaggle of gretchin tried to scramble aboard, shrieking and babbling at Jurgen, which at least proved that his makeshift disguise was holding from a distance. Expecting trouble, as I was, my weapons were already drawn, and my thumb hovered over the activator of the chainsword. But before I could reveal my presence by starting it, Jurgen punched the nearest one hard and accurately, pitching it over the side, and laughed loudly. It had the desired effect, the other gretchin followed their fallen comrade, and broke into hysterical giggles themselves.

'What was that all about?' I asked quietly.

Jurgen shrugged. 'They wanted a lift. I said no.' A tinge of doubt began to creep into his voice. 'The little ones don't usually drive things.'

'Now you tell me,' I said, a tingle of apprehension beginning to make its way up my spine. If one of the orks noticed something out of the ordinary, we were done for. Too late to back out now, we were committed. I activated the commbead.

'Team two, stand by,' I said. 'On my mark…'

'Already loaded,' Luskins assured me. 'And I've a nice juicy target picked out.'

'I can see you now,' Jodril cut in. With the weapon already loaded and ready to fire, he was observing the scene through a spare amplivisor. Peering round the weapon mount and past my aide's shoulders, I could see we were approaching a pair of wrought iron gates, incorporating the cogwheel sigil of the Adeptus Mechanicus. It was standing ajar in a high, stone wall covered in images of the Omnissiah, which in turn had been largely obscured by vile ork daubs.

'We're going to have to cut this very fine,' I warned Luskins. 'Any second now...'

To my unspoken relief, he didn't bother to reply, evidently concentrating on lining up his shot. Jurgen began to slow us down. A large ork, although in all honesty it was probably no bigger than any of the others, just seeming that way to my terrified mind, detatched itself from the shadows surrounding the gate and ambled forwards, raising a ham-like fist for us to stop. Jurgen began to apply the brake. 'Fire!'

A streak of flame scored the air above our heads, attracting the attention of every greenskin in the vicinity, and disappeared behind the wall. The guard approaching us turned his head with lightning speed to track it, reacting to the threat instinctively, and Jurgen accelerated again while he was momentarily distracted. The meaty sound of the impact as the greenskin disappeared beneath our wheels, making the vehicle shudder slightly, was swallowed up by the sound of an explosion inside the compound, which was followed almost at once by a cacophony of shouts and bellows.

'Go!' I shouted, for the simultaneous benefit of Tayber and Jurgen, and my aide gunned the engine, hurtling through the gates seconds before another sentry slammed them closed, leaping out of our way in the process, with a barrage of language I didn't need to be fluent in orkish to understand.

'Moving in,' the sergeant acknowledged, and Jurgen swung the control yoke again, bringing us around to head towards a gaggle of vehicles parked by a large storage tank, which couldn't be anything other than fuel. Another greenskin turned to watch us pass, its eyes widening with shock and recognition, and pointed a talon tipped finger in our direction.

'Humies!'[1] it bellowed. Before it could do anything about its discovery, its head exploded, and Luskins cackled gleefully in my ear.

'Don't worry, commissar, we'll keep the fleas off your back.'

'Much obliged,' I said, reflecting that at least if he was taking potshots with his lasgun, we were less likely to be immolated by accident, and rose to my feet. There was no point in attempting concealment any more, that much was obvious, so I swung the heavy bolter around and began blazing away at the largest concentration of greenskins I could find.

Just in time, too. No one could accuse them of being organised, but they reacted to the threat almost immediately, every single one of them grabbing a weapon and charging towards us as fast as they could. Fortunately, for the most part, they seemed to be as fixated on getting to grips with us in person as those we'd encountered before, and what return fire we took was sporadic at best, being easily deflected by the thick armour plating riveted to every surface of our vehicle. Even more fortunately, they were clustered so close together that missing them at this range was impossible; all I had to do was hold the trigger down and they fell in droves, most of the casualties being trampled in the rush as the ones behind surged forward to fill the gaps.

---

1. Another Gothic loan word; the closest these debased creatures can come to pronouncing 'humans.'

'Tayber,' I said, keeping my voice even with an effort. 'Where are you?' It shouldn't have taken this long to burn through the barrier in the culvert, surely. 'Are you through yet?'

'On our way,' the sergeant assured me, although the only casualties I could see being inflicted, apart from the damage I was doing myself, was the occasional greenskin going down to sniper fire from Luskins and Jodril. (Or in most cases shrugging it off, but at least staggering a bit and looking round in vague annoyance for the source of the threat.)

'Glad to hear it,' I said, with barely a trace of sarcasm.

Jurgen drew us to a halt with a jerk which almost cost me my grip on the weapon, and I watched him scramble aboard the nearest parked vehicle. It was one of the armoured truck things I'd seen in the street earlier, and looked more than large enough to carry the whole squad. 'Your taxi's waiting.' I disengaged the vox, and glanced at Jurgen. 'If you can get it started.'

'No problem, commissar,' he assured me, and a moment later the truck's engine roared into life, sounding even louder and more badly tuned than our own, if that were possible.

'Good.' I glanced round, finding the greenskins pressing us even more closely than ever. The heavy bolter ceased bucking under my hand, and with a '*Waaaargh!*' I could hear even over the racket of the engines, they began to surge forward. I was out of ammunition.

'Tayber!' I yelled. 'It's now or never! What's keeping you?'

'We had something we needed to do,' the sergeant said. 'How many vehicles have you got started?'

'Just the one.' I dived for the nearest box of ammunition down by my feet, and fumbled a clip into my hands. The greenskin horde was only metres away by now, and for some reason the image of the genestealer hybrids I'd faced on Keffia rose up in my mind. This was even worse, at least then I'd had thick walls to hide behind and allies I could rely on... I slammed the ammunition clip into the bolter with seconds to spare, and opened up again, driving the greenskins back a pace or two, but they were so close now I could make out individual features: a broken tusk, a scar, a missing eye patched with some brutish augmetic...

'We'll need several,' Tayber said. For a moment I failed to understand him, and then the coin dropped. Surely he hadn't...

'You've liberated the civilians, haven't you?' I asked, incredulous horror making my voice rise as I spoke. Overhearing the exchange, Jurgen vaulted into the next truck and fired it up too, then carried on repeating the process despite the number of bolts and bullets slicing the air around him and rattling from the vehicles' armour plate. An ork tried to seize my leg and I slashed down with the chainsword, taking his arm off and opening up his throat on the backswing. Despite my best efforts, the greenskins were under the range of the bolter now, and there was nothing else for it but to engage them hand to hand, at least for the second or two I had before they surely dragged me down and tore me limb from limb.

'You did say we should do everything we could to keep them safe,' Tayber reminded me, and I cursed every overly literal NCO in the galaxy, under my breath.

'Well we could do with a little help here too,' I said, shooting another greenskin in the face with my laspistol. I was suddenly aware of a welcome presence, and surprisingly welcome odour, at my shoulder, and Jurgen began blazing away with his lasgun at point blank range. There was no longer any sense in trying to conserve ammunition, we'd either get out of here or we were dead anyway, so he hosed the greenies down on full auto without another thought of running dry, as he had the day before.

'We're on it,' Tayber assured me, and with a sudden surge of relief I saw the back of the crowd facing us ripple and turn, as a concerted volley of las fire took them from behind. It wasn't just las bolts either, I realised with a start. Several of the orks fell, their torsos exploding into offal, surely the result of a bolter hit. As the line of figures behind them came more into focus, the reason became clear. Many of the prisoners had picked up the guns of the fallen greenskins, and were turning them on their captors with a vengeful enthusiasm I could well understand. How they were even able to lift such clumsy weapons I couldn't say, let alone aim and fire them, debilitated as they were, but no doubt the chance to exact retribution for the privations and cruelty they'd suffered gave them sufficient strength.

That unexpected circumstance was enough to turn the tide. Taken completely by surprise, and probably concluding that they were facing a human army rather than an emaciated rabble with barely enough strength left to stand, the green tide broke at last. With howls of dismay, the orks turned and fled, displaying the same unity of purpose they had while united in bloodlust, leaving Tayber and me to stare at one another across a desolate expanse of feebly twitching ork bodies.

I gestured at the rumbling vehicles behind me. 'Mount them up,' I said, not trusting myself to add anything further, and Tayber nodded, shepherding his charges towards them with touching solicitude. I resumed my post at the bolter, expecting our foes to rally and counterattack at any moment, but to my relief they seemed to have had enough, at least for the time being. I tapped the commbead. 'Luskins, load a krak round.'

'Got one up the pipe already,' the rocketeer said, with undisguised glee, 'just to be on the safe side.' Jurgen scrambled back into the driving seat of our overloaded, and considerably battered, buggy. I was amazed that it could still run at all after the pounding it had taken, but we jerked into motion as easily as before, leading our ramshackle convoy towards the gates with all the speed Jurgen could squeeze out of it. A ragged cheer broke out behind us as the prisoners found themselves on the move too, and I cut in on all the commbeads in the squad.

'Suppressing fire!' I ordered. 'Don't let them regroup or we're done for!' I emphasised the point by hosing down a group of greenskins who seemed to be readying some kind of missile launcher, which despite its cobbled together appearance, I had no doubt was capable of punching through our armour plate, seeing them fall in a welter of ichor and a tangle of shredded metal. By great good fortune, one of our bolts detonated the warhead they were loading as it exploded, extending the radius of the mayhem to a most satisfactory extent.

'We're on it,' Tayber assured me, and the troopers opened up with their lasguns, not bothering to aim, but relying on the blizzard of automatic fire they produced to keep the greenskins hopping. In all honesty, attempting to aim carefully from the back of one of those wildly bucking vehicles would have been completely futile anyway. To my surprised relief, a few of the squaddies, or more likely the liberated prisoners, began popping off the heavy weapons mounted on the comandeered vehicles too, with a complete lack of anything approaching marksmanship, but making a fine mess of things, nevertheless.

'The gate's still closed,' Jurgen reminded me, and I swung the bolter again, targeting the tangle of filigreed metal and the little clump of hysterical greenskins holding their ground in front of it.

'No it's not,' I said, with some satisfaction, as the hail of explosive projectiles shredded the gates and the orks alike. Jurgen rammed us through the gap, bouncing over bodies and striking sparks from the thick steel plate protecting the front of the solid little vehicle, as the remains of the barrier skittered off into the night. He swung us out onto the street, still accelerating, and we barrelled away into the welcoming darkness, our engines howling like the damned as they echoed from the buildings all around us.

'We're clear of the compound,' Tayber voxed, and I activated my commbead again.

'Luskins,' I said. 'Blow the tanks.'

'I thought you'd never ask.' Another streak of fire erupted from the ruined mansion where our missile team was holed up, and disappeared inside the compound. A moment later, the entire world turned bright orange, and my ears were battered by a sound, which went beyond the audible, to be felt as a physical blow. Our hurtling buggy shuddered and skipped for a moment, but Jurgen regained control with his usual air of imperturbability. Looking back, I saw a huge fireball erupting behind us, as though the molten core of the planet had got bored and decided to pop up for a look around.

The rocketeer's voice took on an unmistakable edge of satisfaction. 'That went well.'

'Hascom,' I said, 'pull over and pick them up.' Myself, I didn't intend stopping for anything short of a visitation from the Emperor, and it wasn't until the raging fire behind us had faded to a distant glow that I ordered Jurgen to pull over and wait for the rest of our convoy to catch up.

So far as I could see, we were worse off than ever – instead of a group of trained fighters to hide behind, I'd acquired a train of civilian liabilities that would undoubtedly bring every greenskin on the continent down on our heads. I might just as well have attached myself to a marching band. No point letting any of that show on my face of course, not if I wanted to keep the troopers in line, so I sighed heavily, straightened my cap, and clambered down to the road with as much insouciance as I could manage.

'Come on, Jurgen,' I said. 'Let's go and meet our new guests.'

Editorial Note:

Though he was hardly in a position to appreciate the fact at the time, Cain's actions in Prosperity Wells were to have repercussions more far-reaching than he could ever have imagined. Once again I've turned to Kallis's popular history of the war, since Tayber's own account of the incident inevitably concentrates on Cain's part in it almost as much as Cain does himself. It must be said, however, that where Kallis deals with the specifics of the action he is clearly somewhat wide of the mark; though no more than one might expect, given that he was working from the official version of events.

From *Green Skins and Black Hearts: The Ork Invasion of Perlia* by Hismyonie Kallis, 927 M41

If the war to reclaim Perlia could be said to have had a single turning point, it must surely have been the battle of Prosperity Wells. Much has been written of it since, by many of the surviving participants, so there is no need to examine the incident in exhaustive detail here; but the bare facts are still quite startling enough. Having survived the crash landing of his survival pod, Commissar Cain made his way out of the desert alone and unaided,[1] in itself a feat few men could accomplish.

However, if he hoped to find succour in that ironically named township, later to be rechristened Cainstead once a new community was established on the ashes of the old,[2] he was to be disappointed. The greenskins had made it their own, rampaging brutishly through that once peaceful haven in the desert sands, despoiling all that they touched and enslaving the few demoralised survivors. Fortunately for them, and the future of the entire world, a few brave defenders still fought on, and the heroic commissar lost no time in enlisting their aid in an audacious plan to liberate the greenskins' victims.

Conflagration night, as that night became known, still celebrated throughout Perlia by the lighting of bonfires on the anniversary of that historic victory, took the ork scum completely by surprise. Caught in their lairs, they died in their thousands as their erstwhile captives rose up in rebellion, flocking to the banner of the man who led them: Cain the Liberator.

---

1. *As ever, Jurgen's presence appears to have been overlooked by most subsequent historians; probably because, with the best will in the galaxy, he was hardly the sort of figure you want cluttering up a heroic legend.*

2. *A fact, which to his credit, Cain found hilarious.*

Only after he was sure that everyone else was safe was he finally persuaded to disengage, the last of his gallant band to do so, pausing only to detonate the promethium tanks the greenskins relied on to keep their blasphemous parodies of the tech-priests' holy mysteries in operation. The resulting firestorm swept though the town, obliterating the ork host almost entirely, and showing up as a minor anomaly in the data recorded by the orbiting sensor nets.

At that point, of course, the Imperial High Command had no idea of the significance of the titanic explosion their analysts had noted, but it was enough to persuade them that something unusual was going on in the deserts of the east, and they began to look out for further signs of activity there. They were not to be kept waiting for long.

THIRTEEN

To my mingled surprise and relief, there was no sign of pursuit, the reasons for which became obvious after I'd slogged my way to the top of a sand dune and trained the amplivisor back the way we'd come. The explosion we'd touched off as a parting gift to the greenskins had only been the beginning. The blazing promethium gushing from the ruptured storage tanks had ignited everything flammable within reach, which in turn had spread to other caches of volatile substances, ammunition, and Emperor alone knew what else. Even at this distance, the faint concussion of secondary explosions as something else cooked off or burst into flame rumbled on like distant thunder, making me feel unaccountably nostalgic for the sights and sounds of the 12th's artillery park. Not the least of which would be a nice hot mug of tanna, I thought.

'They won't be coming after us tonight,' Tayber commented, appearing at my shoulder and raising his own amplivisor to check out the inferno in the distance.

I blew on my hands and rubbed them together, the desert chill striking hard even through the weave of my greatcoat, an ironic contrast to the conflagration in the distance.

'I hope not,' I agreed. 'But we'd better post sentries all the same.' Few of the civilians we'd picked up were in any condition to travel far, and I chafed at the delay that imposed on us. So far as I was concerned, the further away we got from the rapidly combusting town the better. Nevertheless, I masked my impatience with the ease of a practiced dissembler. If the worst came to the worst, I could always make a run for it while the greenskins picked off the easy targets. That reminded me, time to keep the good sergeant on my side. 'How are the refugees holding up?'

'About as well as you might expect,' Tayber hedged. 'Better for some food, of course.'

'Glad to hear it,' I said. The first thing I'd done was organise a meal for everyone, or to be a little more accurate about it, got Jurgen to organise one, as it had occurred to me that our guests hadn't been properly fed for weeks, and at least if they were kept occupied filling their faces they weren't likely to wander off or otherwise get in the way. That in itself could be a problem, of course. The supplies we'd packed on the buggy might have lasted Jurgen and me for months on our own, and would have kept Bravo squad fed for a couple of weeks, but now we had almost a hundred extra mouths to feed, and that meant we were in deep trouble. 'The problem's going to be keeping them fed.' I indicated the desert sand surrounding us. 'This is hardly the terrain for living off the land.'

'Not really,' Tayber agreed, looking a little smug. 'But there might be a couple of sandsiders[1] among the civilians. I'll ask around.'

'Good,' I said, wresting the initiative back. 'And while you're at it, see what other skills you can find. Most of these poor devils could do with seeing a medicae, although I don't suppose we'll be that lucky.' Tayber nodded once, briskly, and I carried on. 'Our main priority, apart from supplies, is going to be transport and defence. See if anyone's had any kind of combat training, or failing that been out hunting, anything like that, and arm them. Have a word with Jurgen about the spare lasguns we packed, and make up the numbers with the ork stuff if you have to. If it turns out we really do have enough warm bodies to mount a credible defence, split them into squads and put one of your troopers in charge of each. And we could really do with someone who knows how to keep these piles of junk running.' I looked at the half dozen or so trucks and buggies we'd acquired, parked in a rough circle to form the best defence we could, and shook my head. 'That really would be a miracle.'

'Something the Omnissiah has been known to provide on occasion,' a new voice said, and I turned my head slightly, noticing the young woman standing a

---

1. *Local slang for people who lived or worked away from the townships scattered throughout the Perlian deserts, some of whom had perfected the art of survival in that desolate environment.*

few paces behind Tayber for the first time. Her features were pinched with starvation, like all the other poor wretches we'd saved, but her eyes were still lively and humorous in the flickering light from the burning town. It tinted her hair and complexion, which I was later to discover in daylight were both startlingly fair, a dull orange in colour, a hue which also patinated her stained and grubby robe and flashed from the cogwheel on a chain around her neck. Even though we'd never met before, there was something vaguely familiar about her, and as she took a step closer, holding out a hand, I realised she bore more than a passing resemblance to the sergeant. 'Enginseer Felicia Tayber, at your service.'

'Tayber?' I enquired, raising an eyebrow at the sergeant as I took the hand the woman was proffering. It was cooler than I expected, calloused from the handling of tools, and as far as I could tell completely original. But then tech-priests didn't tend to go in for all that wholesale replacement of organs with augmetics stuff until they'd risen a great deal further up the hierarchy. Tayber looked mildly uncomfortable, although the ruddy light from the inferno in the distance meant I couldn't tell if he was blushing or not.

He coughed. 'My sister.'

'I see,' I said, beginning to suspect that his determination to save the civilians hadn't entirely been motivated by taking my orders too literally. I'd never be able to prove it, and I needed him if I was going to get back to the regiment in one piece, so I decided to let it go. I turned back to the woman. 'It seems we both have a lot to thank your brother for.'

'I'd say that remains to be seen,' she replied, a hint of a smile beginning to form on her face. 'I'll have to take a look at those things first.' She turned her head, taking in the nearest ones, and looked thoughtful for a moment. 'That truck with the yellow skull thing painted on, it's definitely got something wrong with its transmission.'

'You can tell that from here?' I asked, wondering if her eyes were augmetics; although they looked real enough. The few tech-priests I'd encountered up to that point (and most of the ones I've met since, come to that), liked their enhancements to be obvious rather than counterfeiting the natural organs they were replacing, apparently feeling that the less human they looked the closer they were getting to the Machine God.

Felicia shook her head. 'I was riding in it. And my arse is still numb.' A mechadendrite emerged from a fold of her robe, and plucked one of the spare ration bars (which up until then I'd completely forgotten about), from my pocket. She grinned, unwrapping it with her natural hands, and began chewing the thing with relish.

'How long have we got until we move out?'

I shrugged, taken completely aback. 'Dawn, I suppose.' I glanced at Tayber, and he nodded confirmation.

'About six hours,' he said.

'I'd better get started, then.' Felicia waved cheerfully, and started down the dune in a cascade of fire-reddened sand. 'There must be some tools around here somewhere.'

'Ask Jurgen,' I said. If anyone could find what she needed it would be him. I turned to Tayber. 'Your sister,' I said slowly. 'She's not exactly a typical tech-priest, is she?'

The sergeant looked vaguely embarrassed. 'She likes tinkering with things. Always did, that's how we knew she had a vocation. She used to spend all her free time at the Mechanicus shrine meditating on machine parts.' His expression softened, recalling happier times, and I had to remind myself that the two of them were probably all that was left of their entire family. 'We were so proud when she took holy orders. But she didn't do well at the seminary.'

'I find that hard to believe,' I said. I've always been a good judge of character, perhaps because masking my own has made me so adept at reading others, and it had struck me that Felicia would throw herself wholeheartedly into whatever she undertook. That, it turned out, was the problem.

Tayber shook his head. 'She never quite grasped the theological side of things, a bit of a handicap if you want to get on in the Mechanicus. So they told her she'd just have to settle for being an enginseer all her life.'

'There are worse things to be than a good enginseer,' I said. 'The Guard would fall apart without them.'

'I know.' Tayber shook his head regretfully. 'And she seems happy enough. It's just a bit of a shame, that's all.'

'We all serve the Emperor the best we may,' I quoted, as though I thought it was a profound insight rather than something I'd found inside a cracker once,[1] and Tayber nodded.

'Then I guess I should start organising some militia squads,' he said.

To MY VAGUE surprise, I was able to grab a few hours sleep after that, waking to discover that the orks had unaccountably failed to massacre the lot of us during the night, and that things were beginning to look a little more organised. Jurgen pushed a mug of recaff and a slice of salt grox in a bun into my hands, and I ate the hot snack gratefully. The sun was only just above the horizon, and the desert air still felt chill.

'They're waiting for you, sir,' he informed me, as though I had the faintest idea of what he was talking about, and I nodded, sipping the bitter drink, and warming my hands around the mug.

'Good,' I said. 'Who? And why?' Fortunately my aide had seen me through sufficient disorientated mornings, sometimes augmented by hangovers, to take my evident incomprehension in his stride. I accepted a second mug of recaff and tried to chase the cobwebs from the corners of my brain.

'Sergeant Tayber,' he elaborated. 'He's got a report about the defence arrangements. That tech-priest lady. She wants to talk to you about the vehicles. One of them's had it, apparently, and she wants to strip it down for spares. And a couple of the civvies who think they might be useful and want to volunteer for stuff.'

---

1. *Probably in a restaurant on Keffia, where little biscuits containing slips of paper with pious platitudes on are unaccountably popular.*

'I see,' I said, marginally wiser than before. 'And did any of them confide the nature of the stuff they wanted to volunteer for?'

Knowing Jurgen he would have been politely obstructive until they told him, and the fact that he hadn't continued to be so was a fair indication that they could indeed be of use.

'There's a man called Ariott, thinks he might be able to help out on the medical side.' My spirits rose. If true, that was good news indeed. 'And a roadworker, Kolfax, spent a lot of time in the desert before the greenies arrived, says he knows a bit about the conditions out here.'

'That could be useful,' I agreed.

I straightened my cap, and brushed as much sand and macerated ork as I could from my greatcoat. 'Let's see what they have to say.'

IT WAS, BY and large, surprisingly constructive, although getting to meet them was harder than I'd anticipated. I made my way through the swirling crowd of refugees, who for the most part were beginning to stir, with a vague sense of unease. As I passed by, almost without exception, they turned to look, murmuring among themselves, an expression I can only describe as awestruck crossing their pinched and filthy faces. The smell, I'll gloss over, other than to mention that for almost the first time since I'd met him, I had to glance over my shoulder to check if Jurgen was still there.

'Commissar!' A woman of indeterminate age, but probably relatively young given that she'd evidently been healthy enough to survive weeks of captivity by the orks, flung herself at my feet, almost tripping me with what would have been a perfect tackle on the scrumball pitch. 'Emperor bless you forever!'

'Blessed be the name of the Emperor!' a goodly proportion of the idiots chorused in response. I tried to detach her as gently as I could.

'Thank you,' I said, my jaw knotting with embarrassment. 'That's very kind. Bless you too.' I shook her off at last, leaving her sitting on the sand in slack-jawed ecstacy.

'A benediction,' she said. A group of refugees a little less addled than the rest moved in to take care of her. I shook my head.

'I'm just a soldier,' I said. 'If you want one of those you should find a priest.' Luckily the convoy seemed mercifully light on Emperor-botherers, which was the first bright spot I'd been able to find in this whole sorry mess. Unfortunately, this apparent display of modesty was enough to precipitate a chorus of praise and approbation, which seemed to be drawing in every man and woman in the convoy with nothing better to do, which, of course, was just about all of them. In the end, to preserve my sanity, I just raised my hands for silence, more in hope than expectation, if I'm honest. To my surprise, the whole reeking rabble fell silent at once.

'You do me too much honour,' I said, wanting nothing more than to get away somewhere I could finish my recaff in peace and try to work out what to do next. 'If there's any credit to be given, it should be to your own PDF soldiers.' Let them go and bother Tayber; all this was his fault anyway.

Unfortunately, as usual, the more I tried to play down my own part in the previous night's events the more I consolidated them in the minds of my audience. (Something, which I suppose I should have anticipated, having done so many times on purpose. I can only presume that fatigue was dulling my wits at the time.) A cheer went up, which I was only able to silence by raising my hand again. 'I've got to go now, and do, um, military stuff,' I said lamely. 'Enjoy your breakfast.' As I'd hoped, the prospect of food was enough to divert their attention away from me, and I made it to where Tayber and the others were waiting, in the lee of one of the trucks, without further incident.

'Commissar.' The sergeant saluted, more for the benefit of the civilians present than because protocol demanded it I suspect,[1] and I returned the salute crisply. It wouldn't hurt to impress them with the seriousness of the situation, or try to look as though we knew how to deal with it.

'Sergeant.' I nodded too, just for good measure, and sat on a convenient crate. There were several scattered about, drawn into a rough circle, and most of them were occupied. Either Jurgen had been his usual helpful self, arranging them in advance, or the little group had congregated there to make use of them. Tayber sat too, on a box of ration bars (which had already been opened judging by the way the civilians' jaws were

---

1. *As commissars are outside the chain of command, Cain wasn't technically a superior officer. However, some soldiers salute them as a matter of courtesy, or possibly prudence, and it's clear from his memoirs that many of the troopers he served with did so out of respect for his personal qualities.*

working, and I resolved to keep a closer eye on that side of things. All right, they were starving, so they could hardly be blamed for snacking all the time, but things were crucial enough on the food front already, and there was no point in making it worse.) The only one still standing was Felicia, although she looked surprisingly relaxed. It was only after some time that I realised she was leaning back on the mechadendrite, using it as a makeshift seat, something I was to discover over the course of our association that she habitually did. It connected at the base of her spine, like a prehensile tail, so was ideally suited to the purpose.[1] I nodded a greeting, and she grinned at me, clearly in her element after a night spent poking about in the innards of the ork machinery.

'Right,' I said. 'We don't have much time. Sooner or later the greenskin survivors are going to recover enough to pull out, or another group will pass by here on their way into the town. Either way we'll be frakked.'

'If there are any survivors…' a balding man in a tattered Administratum robe put in, and the other civilians nodded.

'There are always survivors,' I told him. 'And even if there aren't, you assume it. Complacency now will get everyone killed.' They all looked suitably chastened, and the Administratum drone nodded again.

'Very prudent,' he said. I glanced round at the other civilians in the group. One was dressed like an artisan, and just had to be Kolfax, while the other wore the

---

1. *How Cain discovered this we can only speculate; perhaps it came up in the course of a casual conversation. Or not.*

tattered remains of a knitted jacket with well-worn leather patches on the elbows. Clearly, captivity among the orks hadn't had quite such a catastrophic effect on his wardrobe as everyone else's. Nevertheless, he exuded an air of dependability and general concern, so I marked him down as the medicae Ariott. Which left the question of whom, precisely, I was talking to. I glanced at Jurgen, raised an enquiring eyebrow, and my aide shrugged, clearly at as much of a loss as I was.

'I wasn't aware that we had any representatives of the Administratum with us,' I said smoothly.

Tayber looked faintly abashed. 'Sorry sir,' he said. 'I should have informed you. But it seemed best to let you sleep.'

'Very considerate,' I said. I turned back to the balding little man in the tattered robe. 'As you've probably gathered,' I said, 'I'm Commissar Cain.'

To his credit, he actually smiled. 'I don't think there's anyone in the convoy who doesn't know that,' he said. 'I'm Scrivener Norbert. Your sergeant seemed to think I could help.'

'Did he?' I asked, allowing the faintest hint of scepticism to enter my voice. Norbert didn't seem to take offence though, which was another point in his favour, just stretching the smile a little wider.

'Whether I actually can has still to be determined.'

'Right.' I nodded, deferring the matter for the time being. 'First things first.' I looked at Tayber. 'Defence.'

'We've got eighteen bodies who know which end of a gun's the front. Three PDF troopers, five tribunes,[1] and

---

1. *Local law enforcers.*

the rest just play with weapons as a hobby.' He frowned, and looked a little dubious. 'Or that's what they claim. At least a couple of them are gangers if you ask me.'

'Good if they are,' I said, to his evident surprise. 'At least they'll know how to fight dirty. How are you deploying them?'

'Three teams.' I nodded slightly at his choice of words. Under the circumstances calling them squads would be wildly optimistic. Even something as cohesive as 'team' would be stretching it a bit. If they could engage the enemy without shooting one another by mistake it'd be a miracle. 'I've put Hascom, Grenbow and Tarvil in charge of one each, with one of the liberated PDF troopers as their number two, for now.'

I nodded again. The trained soldiers would be the natural leaders of a new militia force, and once we'd got the rest up to scratch the members of Bravo squad could be reintegrated back into their own unit (where they'd fight a great deal more effectively). Encouraged, Tayber went on. 'We've distributed the lasguns as evenly as we can between the teams. The ones left without we're hoping can crew the heavy stuff on the vehicles.'

'Good idea,' I said. 'They did enough damage last night.' If we ran into any more patrols the extra punch might make all the difference.

I turned to Felicia. 'Are any of the weapons still usable?'

'Most of them.' She leaned back at what should have been an impossible angle, and shrugged. 'I'll take a closer look before we pull out.'

'Jurgen tells me you want to junk one of the buggies,' I said.

She nodded. 'Junk is right. Half the parts are badly worn. The rest might do for spares, though. Not that the greenies have anything like standardised systems, of course, but I can probably patch and tinker them into place.' She looked positively eager at the prospect.

'How long is that going to take?' I asked.

Felicia shrugged again, seeming even more gravity defying than before. 'I roped in a couple of artisans. They don't know the proper prayers for dismantling a machine, but they can undo a bolt without me breathing down their necks and I don't suppose the orky stuff's exactly consecrated anyway. I'll just do a quick blessing if I have to reuse any of it and hope for the best.'

'So they're taking it to pieces for you now?' I asked. For the first time since we'd met, Felicia looked a little less than completely sure of herself.

'It seemed the best thing to do,' she said, a trifle defensively. 'And you weren't around to ask.'

'You're the expert,' I said. 'I'd just have told you to use your best judgement in any case.' She nodded, seemingly relieved, and I swept my gaze around the rest of the little group. 'And that goes for the rest of you too,' I added. 'Unless you're faced with a decision which will affect our safety as a group, just get on with it.' I was met by a row of nodding heads, which reminded me incongruously of a carnival float I'd once seen.

I returned my attention to the enginseer. 'How much longer is it going to take?'

'We'll be ready to pull out when you are,' Felicia assured me.

'Good.' I nodded myself. Damn, it seemed to be catching. 'That's defence and transport. What about supplies?'

'Barely adequate,' Norbert chipped in helpfully. He held up a data-slate. 'I've spent most of the night taking an inventory of what we have with us. Barring a few items of personal property, I believe this is it.' He leaned forward, proffering the slate, which after a moment I leaned forward to accept. I scanned the list, scrolling down the tiny screen. 'At present rates of consumption, we have food for three days and water for two. I've taken the liberty of outlining some rationing measures which should double that comfortably, or treble it with some degree of difficulty.' I skimmed through to his conclusions. He didn't seem to have missed much.

'This is extremely helpful,' I said, trying to hide the wave of shock and horror, which rolled over me as I assimilated the figures on the little screen. Things were even worse than I'd imagined: if the orks didn't get us, the desert would. Norbert looked appropriately grave.

'The other thing we're critically short of is fuel for the vehicles,' he pointed out. 'Predicting consumption is problematic, given the idiosyncratic design of the individual engines and the conditions prevailing in the desert, but I've tried to err on the side of caution. Assuming the worst case throughout, we can expect to travel no more than two hundred kilometres before running into problems.' A little knot of tension began to wind itself tighter inside my stomach: transmuting the roll I'd eaten into solid lead.

'Then we'll need to find more,' I said, trying to sound confident.

To my relief Tayber was nodding in agreement. 'There should be a supply cache that close,' he said.

'A what?' I asked, trying not to let the sudden flare of hope show in my voice. Apparently it hadn't, because Tayber's tone seemed completely businesslike.

'The PDF maintains a chain of hidden supply dumps all over the continent. Both continents, actually, but that's not important right now. So we'd have something to fight with in the event of an invasion.'

'Seems like a wise precaution under the circumstances,' I said, with barely a trace of irony.

Tayber seemed to take the remark at face value though.

'So long as the greenies haven't found it and looted it,' he agreed. Well that was a problem for later; at least I could deal with some of the more pressing ones now, or palm them off on someone else at any rate. I handed the data-slate back to Norbert.

'Since you've got such a sound grasp of the issue,' I said, 'consider yourself our supply officer.' I gestured to my aide. 'Jurgen will help you make whatever arrangements you feel necessary.' As an afterthought I glanced across at Ariott, who'd said nothing so far, just observing events with an air of mild, polite interest. 'You might as well start by seeing what Medicae Ariott requires.'

'Medicae?' The man's voice was as unassuming as his demeanour. 'I think there's been some mistake. I'm a veterinarian.'

'Well you're the closest we've got,' I told him, masking my feelings with some difficulty. This was just getting better and better. 'If you can treat a grox and a nose vole a medium-sized human being shouldn't be that much of a challenge.' He grinned at that, and hopped off the crate he'd been sitting on.

'I suppose not,' he agreed, and went into a huddle with Norbert and Jurgen. After a few moments of discussion, they wandered away, followed by Felicia who wanted to talk to the bureaucrat about fuel allocations, and I returned my attention to Tayber.

'Right,' I said. 'How far are we from these supplies?'

FOURTEEN

As IT TURNED out, we had a choice of two potential destinations within the two hundred kilometre radius Norbert had specified. Tayber and I looked at the mapslate, comparing their relative positions, while Kolfax hovered around us, clearly uneasy about being in the loop at all. Well, he was the nearest we had to an expert in these conditions, so he'd just have to get used to it.

'This one's the nearest,' Tayber said, indicating a supply dump roughly due south of our present position. I stared at the slate, the palms of my hands tingling in that old, familiar fashion. Something felt wrong about it, apart, of course, from the fact that it would take us almost a hundred kilometres out of our way. (Well, my way at any rate; I still meant to get across the peninsular to the safety of the western continent as quickly as possible.) 'And most of it's on the main highway.'

'Which will probably be crawling with greenskins,' I pointed out, the reason for my disquiet suddenly forcing its way into my consciousness. Tayber nodded, conceding the point, but still prepared to argue his case.

'That's true of any route we take,' he said. I shook my head, becoming more and more convinced that my way was the right one. I indicated the other site, which was a good thirty kilometres further to travel, but more or less westward of where we currently were.

'This one's further away,' I agreed. 'But it's also more isolated. If we head for it instead we should avoid most of the greenskins.' I glanced at Kolfax. 'Isn't that right?'

'It is.' He was a small, wide man, evidently composed mostly of compacted muscle, or at least he had been before captivity among the orks had taken its toll. When he did speak, he was taciturn to the point of rudeness, which might have explained why he'd spent so much time out in the desert. He indicated the mapslate with a stubby thumb. 'There are back trails out here even a greenie'd think twice about taking.'

'Which you know, I presume,' I said. Kolfax nodded once.

'As well as anyone, which isn't much.'

'Then that's how we'll go,' I decided. 'You take the lead vehicle, with one of the militia teams.'

'Right.' Kolfax nodded again. Another thought struck me.

'I don't suppose you know how to find water out here?'

'Take it with you.' Kolfax permitted himself a momentary smirk at his own witticism. 'You'll not find a lot otherwise.'

'Well we'd better hope we find what there is,' I said. 'Or we're going to have a lot of thirsty people on our hands.' Kolfax nodded, his demeanour sobering again.

'We might get lucky,' he conceded. 'If the rains have been good in the mountains you sometimes get seepage from the aquifer, where the rocks are permeable.' He indicated a couple of points on the map. 'I've come across waterholes around there before now. But they're short-lived at best.'

'There's an aquifer under the sand?' I asked. If we could somehow tap that, all our problems would be over. Well, our shortage of water anyway. Tayber nodded.

'About three hundred metres down,' he said. 'Extracting it's what kept the town going.' I remembered the size of the hydro station he'd been hiding out in. There was certainly no chance of drilling down that deep with the equipment we had with us, even if we could have afforded the time it would take.

'Then we'll have to take our chances with the waterholes,' I said. I checked the mapslate again. 'It won't be much of a detour. And if they're dry, we'll just have to ration what we've got.' Tayber looked worried, and I thought I understood why. If that became necessary, some of the weaker refugees probably wouldn't make it. But if the supply dump did turn out to have been looted, we'd all die of thirst before the issue of the fuel shortage had to be faced, whereas replenishing our water would buy us a few more days to deal with that problem if and when it came up. Not for the first time, and far from the last, I found myself reflecting that taking the hard decisions was part of my job, and the aspect of it I could most readily do without. (Well that, and facing innumerable hordes of the Emperor's enemies all intent on killing me, of course.)

'That's going to stretch our fuel reserves,' Tayber commented, but in the tone of a man who knows he's already lost the argument. Feeling magnanimous in victory and quietly relieved not to have needed to exert the full weight of my authority to get my own way, I nodded in agreement.

'It will,' I conceded, 'but there should be plenty more at the supply dump. Once we get our hands on it we'll be well on our way.'

'Where to, exactly?' Kolfax asked, reminding me once more of his existence. I indicated the western continent on the little screen of the mapslate.

'Here, eventually,' I said. He made a short, harsh sound of incredulity deep within his throat, which I ignored easily, Jurgen's periodic expectorations being considerably more explosive. 'But in the short term…' I zoomed in on the image, bringing the area around us into more detail. 'The best route looks like this.' I traced it, hopping from one supply dump to the next. 'Out of the desert here, through the lowlands, and across the mountains.' That was mildly disquieting, as there was only one major pass I could see, and it was bound to be crawling with greenskins. Oh well, we'd just have to face that problem when the time came. 'Then across the coastal plain, hop over the peninsular, and we're home free.' If I said it fast enough, it almost sounded plausible. Kolfax snorted again.

'You left out "through the ork army,"' he said. It was a fair point too. Most of them would be congregating on the coastal plain, pouring into the compacted mass of them trying to flood across the narrow neck of land to the western continent. I shrugged.

'We'll think of something,' I said, trying to sound confident. 'There's no point worrying about that just yet.' The stocky civilian nodded.

'Right,' he agreed. 'We'll probably all be dead by then anyway.'

OLD HABITS ARE surprisingly hard to break. Even though the number of proper troopers in our merry little band was outnumbered almost ten to one by the dead weight, I found myself walking the length of the convoy before we set off, having an encouraging word with random individuals, dispensing pious platitudes, and generally going through the motions of raising morale. To my surprise, it seemed to be working. Spirits seemed pretty high all round, and most of the poor wretches we'd saved had huge grins on their faces as we prepared to set off. Mind you, under the circumstances I suppose they had a lot to smile about, having traded the absolute certainty of imminent death for the merely almost inevitable. (A feeling, which, having experienced it myself on far too many occasions over the last century or so, I can assure you is surprisingly comforting.)

I started at the rear of the convoy, where Grenbow was trying to instil some semblance of order among his ad hoc militia unit, assisted by a hard-faced man in the tattered remains of a PDF uniform, who alone among the recruits looked as if he knew what to do with the lasgun in his hands. The erstwhile vox operator shrugged when I asked him how it was going.

'Well enough,' he said. He'd finally shed the useless backpack communicator, I noticed, leaving it propped up in the back of the truck he was commanding, along with the portion of our precious supplies Norbert had decreed they should take. To my vague surprise, the slate-shuffler had shown enough sense to ensure our food and water travelled with an armed escort, distributing it only among the five vehicles with a military presence aboard them, without making it too obvious that the objective was to reduce pilferage by as much as was feasible. 'They're as ready as they'll ever be.' His tone was enough to tell me how ready he thought that was, and I nodded my understanding.

'I'm sure you'll hold them together if push comes to shove,' I told him.

Grenbow smiled without humour. 'I've told them if the orks attack to switch to full auto,' he said, 'and just hold the trigger down till the powerpack runs dry.' Something of my feelings must have shown on my face, because he shrugged. 'I know. It's a criminal waste of ammo. But at least that way they might keep the greenies off our backs for a short while. And if they don't, lack of ammo will be the least of our worries.'

'We can always recharge them later,' I assured him, 'and there should be plenty more powercells at the supply dump.'

'We'll get you there,' one of his recruits assured me, a wiry young woman with cold eyes and a facial tattoo, no doubt one of the suspected gangers Tayber had mentioned. She was leaning proprietorially against the mounting of the vehicle's heavy weapon, some kind of autocannon by the look of it, and I had the distinct impression that she'd spurned the standard issue small arm in favour of the most destructive piece of ordnance she could get her hands on.

'I don't doubt it,' I assured her.

'Hello commissar.' Felicia approached us, a large sack of something metallic clanking over her shoulder, supported by one arm and her mechanical tail. Tools, I presumed. She had a couple of the civilians in tow, both carrying similar bundles, which she took one by one and slung over the armoured tailgate of the truck with a clangour sufficient to make a few of the more nervy recruits swing their weapons around to cover her for a moment, before relaxing with elaborate pantomimes of unconcern. The two artisans, I assumed, now commandeered as her assistants on a more or less permanent basis. 'Come to see us off?'

'Just checking things,' I assured her. 'I didn't want you missing the bus.'

She laughed as she clambered aboard, followed rather less gracefully a moment or two later by her underlings. In theory, travelling aboard the last vehicle, they'd be able to pull over and come to the assistance of any of the others, which might be having difficulties without the necessity of turning round. Something that Kolfax had assured us would be best avoided on the back trails, and since his job had been to keep them open, I trusted his opinion on that.

'Wouldn't miss this for the galaxy,' she assured me, her attention already claimed by the damaged vox. 'Wow, this has taken a beating.'

'Can you fix it?' I asked, the possibility insinuating itself into my mind for the first time. If she could, we'd be able to use it as a relay, increasing the range of the commbeads, and listening out for any other Imperial stragglers in the vicinity. If there were other PDF units in the area they'd be bound to head for the supply caches too, so it was a fair bet they'd be in range at least part of the time.

'I can try,' Felicia said cheerfully, already beginning to poke about in the interior of the casing with her mechadendrite. 'No promises, mind.'

'Of course not.' I moved on. The next truck held Ariott and the worst medical cases, simply debilitated by their ordeal for the most part, but some exhibiting more serious consequences of their mistreatment by the orks: bone fractures, dislocations, and internal bleeding generally. The amiable vet looked up as I approached.

'Commissar,' he said, as though we'd just been introduced at a formal party. Despite my growing sense of urgency I slowed my pace.

'Doctor,' I responded, making him smile ironically. 'How are your patients?' He shrugged, looking terminally careworn for a moment. Then the air of good humour was back.

'If they were my usual customers I'd have put half of them down by now.' The smile became a little less strained. 'However, under the circumstances, them being middle-sized and all, I'm just having to rely on time and analgesics. A quick word with the Emperor wouldn't hurt either.' He lowered his voice. 'There's very little I can do for the worst cases, to be honest. Just keep them stable until we reach somewhere with the proper facilities.'

'That's a better chance than they'd have without you,' I pointed out, leaving him looking a little more encouraged.

The next couple of buggies were stuffed with civilians. Then I came to the truck commandeered by what remained of Bravo Squad. Tayber I'd briefed already, so I passed them by with only a few words, and a nod to Norbert, who was travelling with them and the most precious of our resources. They were about halfway along the convoy, sandwiching the rest of the civilian vehicles between them and the second militia truck. As I passed the rest of the refugees, a groundswell of cheering seemed to follow me, rippling back and forth along the line, and I wondered for a moment if I should try to quiet them; but once the engines were started, any attempt at stealth would be out of the question anyway. Better to let them blow off a little steam. Things were bound to get bad again soon enough, so they might as well enjoy themselves while they could.

Trooper Tarvil had everything more or less under control among his makeshift command. If anything they seemed overconfident, eager to start taking their revenge against the greenskins, and I took him aside for a quiet word.

'You might have to rein them in a bit,' I told him, and he nodded.

'I know. The mood they're in now they could start taking risks. I'll wait until one of them overreaches himself, and pull him up just before he gets hurt. That way I'll only have to bawl them out once and everyone'll learn from it.'

'Might work,' I conceded. 'But if you'll take my advice, you'll crack down hard once we get on the move. This is a combat patrol, not a pleasure jaunt.'

He was bright enough to listen, I'll give him that. When the shooting started, despite my apprehension, he held them together better than I'd expected.

Our own buggy was next, Jurgen already mounted up and ready to go, which just left the lead truck, containing Hascom's rabble and our native guide, Kolfax. I had a quick word with both, emphasising their vital importance to our enterprise, but not enough to put them under any more pressure than they already felt.

'I'll get you there,' Kolfax said, and climbed aboard the truck, next to the driver.

Hascom watched him go, with a mildly dubious expression. 'Are you sure you wouldn't rather have him with you, sir? I'd have thought your place was at the head of the convoy.'

I shook my head. 'I'd rather hang back a little, so we can help out if anyone gets into trouble,' I told him. Besides, if the tracks were mined, I'd rather not be the one to find out.

Hascom nodded, taking the feeble excuse at face value. 'As you wish, sir.' He saluted smartly. 'We won't let you down, I can promise you that.' As he swung himself aboard the ramshackle vehicle, his ragtag unit cheered as though they were off on a sector wakes[1] rather than about to enter combat, and it belatedly occurred to me that they thought it was an honour to be taking point. Well, good for them, if they were keeping me out of the line of fire they might as well feel good about it.

'Comms check,' I said, returning to my own vehicle, and activating the tiny transceiver in my ear as I scrambled aboard. There seemed a lot more room now the bulk of our supplies had been distributed around the convoy, and I shrugged off my greatcoat as Jurgen, Tayber, Grenbow, Tarvil and Hascom sounded off one by one. It was getting warmer, and I folded the heavy cloth into a makeshift cushion on top of one of the boxes of bolter ammo. I waited a moment, listening to the hiss of static as I re-buckled my weapon belt and sat down, wedging myself into a corner as comfortably as I could. 'Kolfax, can you hear me?'

'Yep.' The artisan's voice was as curt as ever. 'Took me a minute to figure out how you work this thing.'

'Fine.' I hid my irritation easily. 'If everyone's ready then, we might as well go.'

The roar of our engines starting up shattered the silence. The noise building to a series of peaks as each badly tuned vehicle retched into life one after the other. Every time I thought the racket couldn't possibly become any louder or more intolerable it

---

1. A forgeworld tradition, where the production facilities of a sector are closed down for routine maintenance, and the workers relocate en masse to a recreational facility.

redoubled in volume, the ever-present echoes from the sand dunes surrounding us making things ten times worse. After what seemed like an eternity, the truck in front of us lurched into motion. Then, with a jerk, which seemed specifically designed to underline the futility of my coat folding efforts, Jurgen kicked our own transport into gear. There was no more time to wonder if I'd made the right decision. For better or worse we were committed, rolling towards the destiny which has continued to shape the course of my life ever since.

FIFTEEN

THE DAY WORE on in a monotonous haze of dust, noise, heat and boredom, not to mention the spine jarring effects of the buggy's primitive construction. Before long, I felt the urge to take a drink, but held off with a considerable effort of will. Partly because in order to maintain my position among so many desperate and disparate individuals I had to be seen to be leading by example, and partly because I knew from experience that slaking my thirst now would only make me feel twice as parched before very long. If we found water where Kolfax hoped it might be I could give way to the impulse with a clear conscience (or as clear as mine ever was, at least), but if we were to be disappointed in our quest, we'd have no option but to continue with Norbert's rationing scheme, and in that case I'd definitely need my share later on.

The road we followed led away from the main highway, and just in time too. Looking back with the amplivisor, I was able, despite the shaking imparted by our unsteady mode of transport, to make out a number of the ork trucks and bike things scooting along it. Fearing that we'd be noticed and attract pursuit, I alerted Grenbow and his team, but the greenskins ignored us, no doubt taking our ramshackle convoy for one of their own, if they even registered our presence at all. I breathed a quiet sigh of relief, pleased to have my judgement vindicated, and was tactful enough not to remind Tayber of the fact.

'Seems like we've given them the slip,' the sergeant conceded.

I agreed, though allowing a note of caution to enter my voice. 'For the time being at least.'

I brought the others, apart from Kolfax, who didn't need to know the details of what was going on, into the network. 'Let's not get complacent. There could be isolated groups of them wandering about out here.'[1] I was rewarded with a chorus of pledges to remain alert, and sat, cradling the bolter, waiting for the first sign of an attack, which never came.

Shortly after noon we came to a halt, and Kolfax came trotting back down the line to talk to me face to face. Despite the simplicity of its operation, he didn't

---

1. *Quite unlikely in actual fact, as the greenskins' innate tendency towards group action would mean that any isolated stragglers would either be on their way from one known location to another, like the one Cain encountered shortly after landing, or in search of loot, which would be scarce to say the least in the middle of the desert.*

feel comfortable exchanging information over the commbead, especially when he was the bearer of bad news.

'If there's water anywhere around here it should be over that ridge,' he told me without preamble. 'But it doesn't look good.' He gestured with a thumb almost as grimy as Jurgen's; although to be fair I was pretty well caked in the stuff myself. The track we followed had long since ceased to be anything that could possibly be dignified with the name of a road, consisting of little more than a slightly flatter strip of hard packed dirt over which the sand drifted in a thin, choking film which the wind of our passage whipped up into a small localised dust storm. What conditions were like further down the convoy, completely enveloped in that cloud of grit, I could only imagine. (Quite vividly too, which is why I'd selected the second slot for Jurgen and myself, rather than tucking us into the middle where we'd be best screened from incoming fire.)

'How can you tell?' I asked, unwinding the sash from around my face, where it was doing duty as an improvised dust mask. In spite of the protection it afforded, my throat felt lined with the stuff, and I took a carefully graduated mouthful of water from my canteen before continuing. It felt as though I was swallowing a ball of mud, but when I spoke again, fighting the urge to drain the whole bottle as I resealed it, my voice was noticeably clearer. 'It all looks the same to me.'

'That's just the problem,' Kolfax said. I clambered down to join him, grateful for the chance to ease my cramped and aching limbs, Jurgen falling into place at my shoulder as usual. He was carrying his lasgun, and raised a hand to pull the strip of rag he'd tied around his own face clear of his mouth.

'Everything all right, sir?'

'That's what we're going to find out,' I said. I glanced down the line of vehicles, which were gradually becoming visible behind us as the cloud of dust we'd stirred up began to settle, staining them all the colour of the sand. Little terracotta passengers began pointing and gesticulating in our direction, clearly wondering what we were up to. Great, that was all we needed. I activated the commbead. 'Rest stop,' I voxed. 'Pass it down the line. No one's to get out of sight of the vehicle they're riding in.' That ought to damp down any speculation, and keep the curious from following us. But just to make sure... 'And distribute some food. One ration bar apiece, one cup of water.' That was well within Norbert's recommendations, and it was about time we had something to eat. As I'd expected, that was more than enough to keep the civilians' minds occupied, and the troopers busy handing out the rations.

Come to think of it, now that the thought of food had been planted, I felt hungry myself. I pulled a couple of the ration bars from my trouser pocket and handed one to Kolfax, while Jurgen retrieved one of his own from somewhere in the recesses of his uniform. Despite their provenance, they didn't seem to have suffered much, tasting just as good as they ever did, which is to say of nothing particularly identifiable. Nevertheless, they took the edge off, and as we crested the ridge I found myself beginning to feel mildly optimistic.

'I was afraid of that,' Kolfax told me, his voice slightly muffled by the compacted cake of Emperor knows what he was chewing at the time. I surveyed the slight depression in the ground, which had become visible as we came over the rise. It was full of scrubby plants, most of them encrusted with thorns, which looked as though they could poke through ceramite.

'Surely that's good,' I said. 'If there are plants here there must be water.'

Kolfax's face contorted in what appeared to be an ironic grin. 'There was,' he said. 'But it's dried up now.' He bent to examine a large boulder, and pointed into a small cleft beneath it. A tiny, desiccated plant still clung on there, surviving somehow despite the odds. I knew how it felt. 'See that?'

Jurgen nodded. 'It's a plant,' he said, presumably in case no one else had ever seen one before.

'Rock sage,' Kolfax said. 'Last time I came by here the whole area was carpeted with it.' He gestured towards the thorn-choked hollow. 'That was a pool, believe it or not. Never expected to get that lucky this time, you hardly ever find standing water out here. But rock sage means it's close enough to the surface to get at with a spade.'

'What about those?' I asked, pointing at the thorn bushes again. 'They must need water too, mustn't they?' Kolfax shook his head.

'Ripperspikes. The roots go down ten, twenty metres. We've nothing that'll get down that far, right?' My silence was all the answer that he needed. 'And even if we did,' he concluded sourly, 'we'd need to clear the ground first. You don't even want to start thinking about that.'

I stared at the profusion of thorns, and privately agreed.

'Then we'd better get moving,' I said. 'And hope we have better luck at the other hole.'

Kolfax nodded. 'Don't hold your breath,' he counselled.

We returned to the trucks in a sober mood, but I had little time to brood on the matter. Hardly had we crested the rise again, concealing its arid disappointment, than my commbead activated.

'Commissar.' It was Grenbow's voice, sounding agitated. 'We've got a bit of a problem here.'

'What kind of a problem?' I asked, fighting the urge to break into a trot despite the enervating heat. Instead I increased my pace to a brisk, purposeful walk. No point in agitating the civilians unnecessarily. The vox operator hesitated, trying to find the right words.

'A couple of the militia are having an argument,' he said at last.

'Can't you deal with it?' I asked, as Kolfax peeled off to rejoin the lead truck. Jurgen, as usual, stayed with me. 'You're supposed to be in charge.'

'They're not listening to me,' he said.

Great. We'd only been travelling for half a day and things were already falling apart. Loosening the laspistol in my holster, I increased my pace as much as I dared, wondering why in the holy name of Terra I'd ever thought it was a good idea to give these frakwits guns. At least whatever the dispute was about they hadn't started using them on each other. Yet.

That, as I was to discover a moment or two later, was largely because Grenbow had inserted himself between the two antagonists, with more courage than good sense if you asked me, but at least it had prevented things from escalating. The girl with the facial tattoo had a knife out, shifting her weight from foot to foot as though trying to find a way past him, but so far good sense or the lasgun in the vox operator's hands had dissuaded her from making the attempt. She was glaring at a man in the tattered remains of a uniform identical to that of the local arbitrator I'd found lying dead in the street back in Prosperity Wells, who was looking murderously back, his knuckles white on the stock of his own weapon.

'What's going on here?' I asked, striding up to the little tableau with every vestige of authority the schola had endowed me with.

The rest of the militia team parted to let me through, watching the entertainment with every sign of interest, although to my unspoken relief none of them seemed inclined to take sides. At least that would simplify things. Felicia's artisans were watching too, perched on the tailgate of the truck as though waiting for someone to pass the caba nuts. The tech-priest herself was still engrossed in the innards of the damaged vox, merely glancing up to wave a greeting to me before going back to work, humming happily to herself. After a moment, I identified the tune as *The Tracks on the Land Raider Crush the Heretics.*[1]

---

1. *A popular ditty among pre-schola juvies in the sector.*

Grenbow turned to me with evident relief.

'Demara spilled some of Tamworth's water ration.'

'It was an accident!' the girl said. 'Stupid ork-reamer didn't watch where he was going!'

The former enforcer flushed even more deeply, and tried to bring his lasgun up despite Grenbow's presence between them.

'You jogged my arm on purpose and you know it, you lying sack of slith!' Grenbow tried to restrain him, and Tamworth jabbed the young trooper in the stomach with the muzzle of his lasgun. Grenbow folded, riding the blow and allowing his armour to take the brunt of it, rising swiftly to strike the recalcitrant militiaman in the face with the butt of his own weapon. Tamworth staggered backwards and Demara rushed at him, raising the knife to strike.

'That's enough!' I drew my laspistol in one swift motion, planting a single bolt in the sand between them, and the two combatants froze. 'Jurgen, take their weapons.'

My aide moved to comply, plucking the lasgun from Tamworth's hands and shrugging the sling into place across his shoulders.

Demara took a step backwards as he reached for her knife. 'That's mine,' she protested. 'I took it off a greenie myself.'

'Then put it away until you get the chance to use it on one,' I said steadily. I had no doubt that Jurgen could take it from her easily enough if she continued to wave it about, and it was a minor enough concession to let her keep it. Nevertheless, it would begin to take the heat out of the situation, if she was bright enough to see that. Fortunately she was, and sheathed the blade without any further argument.

'Good.' I put my own weapon away. 'What happened?'

Tamworth and Demara both drew breath to renew their accusations, and I raised my hand again. 'Grenbow.'

'We'd just finished handing out the rations to the civilians,' Grenbow said crisply. 'So I gave the order to serve ourselves.'

'About reaming time,' one of the recruits behind me muttered, and I turned, silencing him with a look. Grenbow fixed the man with an almost equally intimidating stare.

'Congratulations,' he said. 'You've just volunteered for double sentry duty.' I nodded approvingly. It seemed Tayber had chosen his team leaders well. The interruption dealt with, he returned to the matter at hand. 'These two were next to one another in line. Demara knocked Tamworth's elbow as she turned, and spilled some of his drink.'

'How much did he lose?' I asked. Grenbow shrugged. 'About half a cup.'

'That's a lie!' Tamworth shouted. 'I dropped the whole thing!'

'You let the cup go when you came at me!' Demara countered, her fists balling, but she showed enough good sense not to go for the knife again. 'If you're going thirsty it's your own stupid fault!'

'That's enough.' I silenced the pair of them again. 'In case you've forgotten, you volunteered to serve in the defence of this convoy, which means you're both subject to military rules and regulations. And that includes military discipline.'

'Oh, I'm scared,' the girl retorted sarcastically. 'What do you think you can possibly do to us that the orks haven't already?'

'I can shoot you, for one thing,' I said mildly. I turned to Tamworth. 'That's the prescribed penalty for striking a superior officer, incidentally.' He went suddenly quiet, the bruise on his face darkening as the blood drained from the rest of it, clearly wondering if I'd make good on the threat. Good, let him stew for a bit.

The rest of them muttered uneasily among themselves for a moment, and then went back to watching us even more intently than before.

'You don't have to do that, do you?' Demara asked, anger gradually giving way to common sense. 'He might be a reamhead, but–'

'I don't need any help from ganger trash!' Tamworth snapped, and I nailed him with my second best commissarial glare. So that was it.

'In case you haven't noticed,' I said mildly, 'things have changed. Whatever differences you used to have are dead and buried. Otherwise, I can make that more than a figure of speech, understood?' Tamworth nodded wordlessly. 'Good.' I turned back to Grenbow. 'Next time we stop for water, he gets half a cup to make up for the portion he wasted. So does she.'

'I told you it was an accident!' Demara protested.

I shrugged. 'I don't care. It's been wasted, that's all that matters. Think of it as an incentive to be more careful next time.'

Both the erstwhile combatants were now glaring at me more than at each other, which I took as a positive sign. I turned to Grenbow. 'I'm not going to shoot this frakhead for hitting you. We need all the fighters we can get right now. If you think further penalties are required, use your own judgement, it's your team.' I jerked a thumb at Demara. 'The same goes for her. I don't want to see either of them brawling again.'

'You won't.' Grenbow assured me.

'Glad to hear it,' I said. I raised my voice a little. 'That goes for the rest of you too. The survival of every single one of us depends on you doing the job you signed up for, and we can't afford any dead weight. The next time a fight breaks out I'm leaving whoever started it behind. Without water or supplies. Pass the word.' Knowing better than to undermine a dramatic exit with any further rhetoric, I turned on my heel and walked away. After a moment, Jurgen handed the lasgun he'd confiscated to Grenbow and hurried after me.

All in all, I thought I'd handled that rather well.

EVEN SO, I made a point of seeking out Grenbow once we'd made camp that night, around a small rockcrete bunker which Kolfax informed me was intended as a way station for people like himself, who in happier times had kept the network of back roads we followed as marginally passable as they still were. The door wasn't locked, which was hardly surprising as there was nothing worth stealing inside, or at least nothing worth going to the trouble of coming all this way from civilisation to take. Nevertheless, I had the place stripped, under Norbert's supervision, adding a few tools, a little bedding, and a frighteningly small box of preserved foodstuffs to our meagre stockpile. The only other thing we found there was a porno slate, apparently left behind by one of Kolfax's colleagues (at least if it was his he didn't bother to claim it), which I surreptitiously diverted in Jurgen's direction. He'd had a lot to put up with in the last few days, and I felt the least I could do was allow him to indulge in his hobby for a while. No sign of any tanna, of course, and I felt a little envious for a moment, wishing my own desires could have been satisfied so easily.

'Any problems?' I asked the young trooper, and he shook his head, sipping at his beaker of water, his face barely visible in the glow of the portable heater we'd scavenged from the workmen's hut. As I pulled my coat tighter, I found myself wishing for a mug of recaff, but hot drinks were out of the question for the foreseeable future. Boiling the precious liquid would have wasted too much of it as steam, a frightening amount according to Norbert's figures, so even that minor solace was denied me. I sipped my own tepid water as he replied, fighting the craving to gulp it straight down. Slow and careful was the only way to ensure that most of it was absorbed by my parched tissues, rather than passing straight through.

'None whatsoever,' he said. 'No one's keen to find out if you were bluffing about leaving any troublemakers behind.'

'I wasn't,' I said, hoping I wouldn't have to prove the point. 'We can't afford to be fighting among ourselves.' I took another sip of the lukewarm fluid, trying to ignore the faintly metallic aftertaste. 'Which reminds me, what did you do about Demara and Tamworth after I left?'

'The worst thing I could think of,' he replied, with a hint of amusement. 'I paired them off, assigned him as loader for her autocannon.'

'That was resourceful,' I conceded. If the members of a heavy weapon team weren't physically joined at the hip they might just as well be.

The young trooper nodded again. 'Now they'll have to get along. Both their lives depend on it once we get into combat.' He shrugged. 'And in case they're still under the impression that they've got off lightly, they're standing double watches every night from now until the stars freeze over. Together.'

'Whoever assigned you to comms wasn't doing their job,' I told him. 'Looks to me like you're a sergeant just waiting to happen.'

To my surprise he laughed. 'Too much like hard work,' he said.

Feeling obscurely cheered by the conversation, I headed off through the makeshift camp, trying not to think too much about the following day. It wasn't all good news: two of Ariott's patients had died during the day, the rigours of the journey proving too much for them, and I found myself wondering how much that would stretch our reserves of food and water. Hardly at all, unfortunately. I checked in with Tayber, confirming the positions of our sentries, and swung the amplivisor around to make sure they were all where they were supposed to be.

To my relief, I was able to discern their faint shapes against the lighter darkness of the star speckled sky, so at least the orks weren't sneaking up on us under cover of night (not that that seemed like their style in any case). Tamworth and Demara were sitting on a sand dune in sullen silence, their backs to one another, but making no move to renew hostilities, so Grenbow's unorthodox solution seemed to be working.

Last of all, I went to find Kolfax, who was still in the depths of the bothy, the faint glow of a low powered luminator filling the space around him. He glanced up as I entered, and went back to prising a ventilator grille off the wall.

'Commissar,' he said, swinging the sheet of perforated metal to the floor. He reached into the cavity behind it and removed something. 'Ah, thought it might still be here.'

'What might?' I asked. By way of reply he uncorked a bottle and took a swig from it with a sigh of satisfaction. The sweet smell of cheap, mass-produced amasec rolled out on his breath as he exhaled, and he lifted the bottle towards me.

'Hid this the last time I was by here, just in case.' He nodded at it. 'Want some?'

Well of course I did, but I had more sense than to take it. In my current desiccated state it would have been like drinking neat alcohol. I shook my head.

'Not now. Save it for when we get to where we're going.'

Kolfax stared at me in astonishment. 'You really believe this slith, don't you?' He tilted the bottle again.

I held out my hand for it. 'The truth is we're going to die out here. Better get used to the idea.'

'You might,' I said. 'But I won't. Give me the bottle, you've had enough.' His eyes locked on mine for a moment. 'I need you sober tomorrow.'

'Ream off.' He took another swallow of the cheap spirit. I drew my pistol.

'Last chance,' I said. Kolfax laughed.

'You can't shoot me. You said it yourself, you need me tomorrow.'

'Yes I can,' I said. 'Just nowhere fatal. You can find water without kneecaps, can't you?' He stared at me, wondering if I'd go through with the threat, which actually made two of us, although he didn't need to know that. After a moment he caved, and handed it over.

'You're a hard man,' he said.

'It's my job.' To his surprise, I handed the bottle back. 'Take this over to Medicae Ariott, will you? I think he can make better use of this than either of us.' The primary aid kit from the survival pod had been pretty well cleaned out by now, and at the very least he could use it as a makeshift counterseptic. Kolfax nodded, any resentment he might have felt neatly undermined by the display of trust I'd just given. If I read the man right, that should be enough to keep him in line, at least for now.

'See you tomorrow,' he said, turning away.

THE NEXT DAY, with the blessed absence of any more fighting in the ranks, turned out to be little more than a repeat of the previous one. Our ramshackle convoy bounced and snarled its way across the desolate landscape, coating us all in dust, until I would cheerfully have killed for a drink of fresh water. Not that I was the only one. When we stopped at noon for a break, Norbert came over for a quiet word.

'Water levels are getting critical,' he warned me. 'How much longer until we reach this supply dump?'

'Day after tomorrow,' I said, 'if Kolfax doesn't get us lost.' He nodded, looking less relieved than I'd hoped.

'It should just last,' he assured me. Then he hesitated. 'Do you want to institute more severe rationing? That should give us another couple of days.'

'I'd rather not.' I indicated the milling mass of cramped and filthy civilians queuing up patiently for their cup of water and handful of food. 'They've got little enough to look forward to as it is. If we take even that away…' I trailed off, unwilling to complete the thought.

Norbert nodded. 'It'll be cutting it fine though,' he warned. 'If we run into any delays…'

'You'll be the first to know,' I assured him. Fortunately we didn't, and the afternoon passed in bone rattling tedium, just as the morning had done.

It was coming on towards the evening before anything changed, the sun dipping close enough to the horizon to force us to squint, and I began to wonder if it was time to make camp. I activated the comm-bead.

'Kolfax,' I said. 'Is there anywhere around here we can stop for the night?'

'I hope so,' he responded. We'd barely exchanged a few words since our conversation in the bothy the previous night, but he seemed a little more open with me now, as if the confrontation over the amasec bottle had increased his confidence in me. Certainly, if he continued to harbour doubts about our chances of success he was keeping them to himself, which was a considerable improvement. 'We should know before long.'

'What's that supposed to mean?' I asked, hoisting myself up on the bolter mount to take a better look at the vehicle in front. Seeing my head appear, Kolfax waved an acknowledgement.

'We've made better time than I thought. Look.' He gestured off to the right, and narrowing my eyes I was barely able to make out a faint discolouration in the shadow of a rock. I just had time to register that it appeared to have a greenish hue before the dust cloud eddied again, obscuring it from view.

'Is that what I think it is?' I asked, hope flaring. Despite his habitual cynicism, Kolfax was unable to keep a note of cautious optimism from his voice.

'I hope so. We'll know as soon as we cross the next ridge.'

Although it could only have been a handful of moments, the wait seemed agonising, stretching out before us like a foretaste of eternity. At last, the truck ahead of us crested the next rise in the trail, and began to be eclipsed by the hummock of rock.

'Well?' I asked, but before Kolfax could reply the entire group accompanying him erupted in cheers.

'We're in luck,' he assured me, somewhat superfluously under the circumstances. I didn't have to wait long to confirm it. Jurgen jolted us over the rise, and I found myself staring at a wide depression in the sand carpeted with tiny leaves, curled tight against the baking sun.

'Rock sage?' I asked.

'You know it.' Kolfax waved from the truck in front, an expansive gesture taking in the whole depression, which must have been over a kilometre across. 'But that's not the best bit.'

The trail widened, and Jurgen was able to pull out a little, allowing me to peer past the tailgate of the truck in front.

For a moment, my mind failed to register the significance of what I was seeing, a dazzling shimmer of blood red radiance reflecting the light of the setting sun, and I thought the plants must be flowering. Then the coin dropped.

'It's water!' I said. 'A whole lake of it!'

'Looks that way,' Kolfax agreed. His voice took on a tinge of awe. 'I've never seen anything like it. Are you always this lucky?'

'So far,' I assured him, wondering how much longer it could possibly hold.

SIXTEEN

THE IMPROVEMENT IN morale that followed our arrival at the temporary oasis was quite remarkable, even to someone as used as I was to tracking its ebb and flow. I suppose that was because for the first time in my career I was being forced to deal with civilians *en masse*. Up until then I'd only encountered them as individuals, usually in some protocol constricted social environment, or bearing self-righteous complaints about some piece of off-duty misbehaviour by one or more of the gunners whose moral welfare I was supposed to give a frak about. (The latter kind seldom getting any closer to me than my outer office, where Jurgen could be relied on to hold the complainers off indefinitely unless the infraction in question was particularly serious or amusing). I must confess, I was agreeably surprised by the resilience our unlooked-for charges had displayed so far, although I suppose the orks had done a pretty good job of winnowing them down to the hardiest of the inhabitants of the unfortunate community they'd come from.

The first thing I did was vox the PDF and militia leaders, ordering them to move up the convoy as soon as the trail had widened enough to permit overtaking, so that by the time the bulk of the civilians arrived there was a cordon of armed men and women standing between them and the lake. I could picture, all too vividly, the lamin rush[1] which would otherwise result, and had no intention of allowing the precious liquid to become so contaminated with churned-up mud from scores of careless feet that we'd be unable to drink it after all. Luckily, that, and the promise of hot food now we had the wherewithal to prepare it, was enough to keep them quiet, for a while at least.

'How much can we take?' I asked Norbert, savouring the mug of recaff Jurgen had thoughtfully provided me with. The Scrivener shrugged, a broad grin on his face for the first time since I'd met him, and juggled some figures on the slate in his hand.

'If we fill every spare container we've got, I think we can forget about rationing,' he told me, something suspiciously close to glee threatening to break through his bureaucratic reserve. 'That'll be more than enough to see us to the supply dump, and a few days beyond that if necessary.'

---

1. A small rodent native to Kengraym Secundus, which migrates across the central continent in kilometre-wide, swarms devouring everything in its path. They breed in coastal inlets, spending the entire summer in the shallows, breaking into a run as they first scent the sea. In the course of this final frenzied rush the smaller and weaker members of the swarm are trampled to death (and then eaten).

'If the place turns out to have been looted, you mean,' Tayber put in. The three of us were sitting slightly apart from the throng, in the lee of one of the trucks, enjoying our meal in as much privacy as the makeshift camp would afford.

Norbert tilted his head in acknowledgement. 'Quite. Even in that unfortunate event, we can worry mainly about food and fuel.' He took another forkful of the salma omelette that Jurgen had prepared for us with every sign of satisfaction.

'We'll do that, then,' I said, 'if you can get your people collecting the water as soon as possible.'

Norbert nodded. 'I'll get right on it.' He seemed almost on the point of abandoning his meal to commence the task, and I urged him to sit down and finish it, which he seemed more than happy to do. 'Anything we should take care of after that?'

'Well I don't know about you,' I said, 'but I could do with a bath. And perhaps it wouldn't hurt to organise a laundry detail while we're about it.' I glanced at Norbert again. 'We won't need to extract any more water tomorrow morning, will we?'

'By no means.' If anything, he looked even happier than before, despite the extra work I'd just dumped on him. 'We'll have more than enough.' He cleaned his plate with a lump of bread, and departed, still chewing.

'Well, that's some good news,' Tayber conceded, not quite managing to conceal the lifting of his own mood now I'd suggested bathing. Emperor knows I felt itchy and foetid enough after only a few days, let alone the weeks of privation he must have endured.

'Glad to hear it,' Felicia said, appearing around the corner of the truck with Grenbow's vox pack dangling casually from her mechadendrite. 'What is? Ooh, salma, haven't tasted that in a while.'

'Help yourself,' I said. I glanced up at Jurgen. 'Can you fix another one of these for the enginseer?'

'Of course.' Jurgen started fussing with his portable stove, and I waved Felicia to the folding chair Norbert had just vacated. She sat gratefully, depositing the vox set on the sand next to me.

'I've managed to fix it,' she said. 'But don't expect too much. I had to take some parts from a power drill we found in the roadmen's hut to make a new flux capacitor, and I ran out of sanctified oil, so I had to bless some lube gel and dab that on instead.' She shrugged. 'It's more or less functioning now, though.'

'More or less is a lot better than not at all,' I assured her. 'What sort of range has it got?'

'Couple of kilometres I should think.' She accepted a plate of food from my aide, glancing up at him with a cheerful smile. 'Thanks, Jurgen, you're a cog.'[1]

'You're welcome, miss.' He flushed uncomfortably, and busied himself with some small task, which seemed to require his urgent and undivided attention.

'Excellent,' I said. It wasn't as much as I'd have liked, which would have been something with enough range and power to call in a shuttle to extract me (along with a fighter escort to be on the safe side), but we

---

1. *A phrase common among enginseers and junior tech-priests, expressing appreciation of a favour or considerate behaviour. The connotation appears to be something generally unnoticed but essential to keeping things running smoothly, which I suppose does sum Jurgen up rather well.*

could relay the commbead signals through it and increase their range dramatically. That meant we could spread out a bit more, and perhaps deploy a few scouts so we weren't moving quite as blindly as before. All in all, our chances of survival had just been materially improved.

'Who's going to operate it?' Tayber asked. 'Grenbow's running one of the militia teams.' An assignment he'd been given purely because, with the vox out of commission, there was no call for his specialised skills, which were suddenly in demand again. On the other hand, removing him from the team now, just when he was turning them into something approaching a cohesive unit, would be catastrophic.

'And from what I've seen we'd be idiots not to leave him there,' I said. 'At least until things have settled down a bit.'

Tayber nodded. 'I agree,' he said, apparently under the happy delusion that hearing his opinion would have made the slightest difference to my own. 'But there's no one else.'

'I could work it,' Felicia said, slightly indistinctly. She nodded at the bulky backpack. 'The principles are simple enough.'

'But you don't know the proper procedures,' Tayber objected. 'Call signs, protocols...'

'She doesn't have to,' I pointed out. 'If the beads are tied in to it anyway to make up a relay net, you or I can respond to any incoming messages.' Tayber nodded, the sudden realisation of the full implications of the little transceiver in his ear finally dawning on him. 'All Felicia has to do is keep the channels open and listen out for any stray signal traffic.'

'I can do that,' the enginseer assured us, swallowing the last mouthful of salma and belching loudly. She grinned, mildly embarrassed, and handed the plate to my aide. 'Sorry about that, I'm not used to having a full stomach again yet. Thanks Jurgen, that was delicious.' Something of an overstatement given my aide's somewhat basic culinary skills, but considering what she'd probably been eating for the last couple of months, understandable all the same. I smiled, intending to dissipate any remaining traces of embarrassment.

'Never thought I'd hear a tech-priest say that,' I said. 'I was under the impression you all considered flavour an irrelevance where food was concerned.'

Felicia grinned back. 'We're supposed to disregard fleshly pleasures in our pursuit of the ideal of the machine,' she agreed cheerfully. 'But some of them are pretty hard to give up.' I nodded in response, beginning to see why her tutors at the seminary had found her so difficult to deal with. 'So what's for dessert?'

THE NEXT MORNING dawned with a palpable air of optimism, which swept the whole convoy. Despite the chill of daybreak, I essayed a final dip in the pool, reflecting ruefully that I'd definitely been hanging around with Valhallans for far too long,[1] and I was far from the only one; it seemed as though half the refugees had had the same idea. I passed Felicia on my

---

1. *Cain was, in fact, to spend most of his career attached to Valhallan units.*

way to the pool, heading in the opposite direction, her hair wet and her robe clinging to her still damp body enough to make it more than clear that she was beginning to fill out nicely now she was getting some proper food again.

'Are you still comfortable with the vox arrangements?' I asked, partly to reassure myself, and partly to enjoy the view for a little longer. Felicia nodded, not fooled for a moment I suspect.

'Fine,' she said. 'Grenbow's in the truck with me, don't forget. I can always ask him for advice if I need it.'

'I'm sure you won't,' I assured her, and resumed my leisurely stroll to the water's edge. A good couple of dozen people had beaten me to it, laughing and splashing as if they were at a resort spa somewhere, instead of deep behind enemy lines. Two of them, I noticed with some surprise, were Demara and Tamworth, chucking handfuls of water at each other like a couple of juvies.

Throwing my towel aside, I plunged in, braced for the invigorating shock, and swam a few strokes beneath the surface, savouring the relative calm. Sound was attenuated, and light filtered dimly through my reflexively closed eyes. For the first time since my abrupt arrival on Perlia, I felt truly at peace.

It was too good to last, of course. By the time I'd dried off, dressed, and collected some breakfast from Jurgen (who had already reacquired his habitual patina of grime, despite bathing for at least as long as I had the evening before), I'd already dealt with half a dozen minor crises, or to be more precise palmed them off on Tayber or Norbert. None of them serious in themselves, but all nagging inconveniences, which I tried to convince myself were not going to set the pattern for the day.

Unfortunately they did. Kolfax continued to guide us as unerringly as before, still basking in the kudos of having led us to water, but the trail was as hard to follow as ever, if not more so. The cobbled together vehicles roared and lurched their way through the barren terrain as if in pain, and the ever-present racket combined with the vertiginous lurching of our progress and the relentless heat of the sun to induce a blinding headache before less than an hour had passed.

'Dehydration,' Ariott diagnosed when I sought him out at our first rest stop. 'Space your drinks, that's all I can suggest.' Hopeless asking for an analgesic, as his patients needed the limited supply far more than I did, and demanding one would be a mortal blow to my fragile leadership in any case. Instead I smiled grimly.

'Easier said than done,' I said. Getting a canteen to your lips without spilling half of it was no mean feat aboard an ork vehicle of any description. I drank a little more under his critical scrutiny, washing the dust out of my mouth for the umpteenth time. By this point, everyone was coated with the stuff again, which was all the more irksome for having so recently been free of it.

Ariott nodded. 'You're telling me,' he agreed, and I belatedly remembered that he had the responsibility for keeping his patients watered as well as himself. I enquired after them, and the makeshift medicae shook his head. 'No more fatalities at any rate, that's something to thank the Emperor for.'

'Indeed it is,' I said, as tactfully as I could, and left him to get on with things.

The afternoon was little better, and culminated in a two-hour delay while Felicia used a couple of her scavenged spares to get one of the civilian transports going again after something in the engine gave way with a catastrophic *crack* that resonated from the dunes around us and had half the armed guards reaching for their weapons. I amused myself by bawling out the rest for inattention, reasoning that if I felt miserable I might as well spread it around, but for some reason it positively encouraged them. Eventually, to everyone's relief, the tech-priest crawled out from under the pile of assorted scrap to pronounce herself satisfied and in need of a cold drink.

'Any joy with the vox?' I asked, joining her in a beaker of lukewarm water, which was the closest we could manage under the circumstances, and she shook her head.

'Not a thing.' Remembering how I'd inadvertently contacted Tayber, I'd asked her to keep scanning for any transmissions on Imperial frequencies. 'I could try broadcasting something, and see who replies.'

I shook my head. 'It could be orks,' I pointed out. 'Best not to let anyone else know we're around until we're sure there are friends out there.'

'Right.' Felicia nodded, and took a swig of water. A glitter of devilment entered her eyes. 'The thing is,' she said slowly, 'what if everyone else out there's thinking the same thing you are?' She grinned and wandered off, her mechanical tail twitching in automatic counterpoint to her hips, leaving me uncharacteristically speechless.

'Oh frak,' I said. I hadn't thought of that.

As IT TURNED out, that was a question the following day was to answer in no uncertain terms, but when we made camp for the night I had no way of knowing that. The headache was still with me, mercifully receding a little as the cool night winds began to blow, but not enough for me to welcome the sight of Kolfax brandishing the mapslate.

'How bad is it?' I asked, and he shrugged, a silhouette of greater darkness against the rich, deep indigo of the sky behind him.

'Not as bad as it might be,' he assured me, dropping into the adjacent folding chair. He held the slate out. 'I'd hoped to make a little more progress today, but we'll still be there by mid afternoon.'

'If nothing else goes wrong,' I finished for him. Nevertheless, the news cheered me. Once we hit the supply dump, things would be a lot easier, at least for a time.

Kolfax nodded. 'One good thing anyway,' he pointed out. 'This is a pretty good spot to set up camp. Better than the one I had in mind, at any rate.' Which I suppose if you were determined to find a positive consequence of the day's delays was some compensation at least. We were in a small side canyon a short distance from the trail, closed off at one end and narrow at the other. We could defend the place indefinitely if we had to.

'There is that,' I agreed, getting rid of him as quickly as possible after a few more questions about tomorrow's leg of our journey. The best cure for my headache, I was sure, would be a good night's sleep. I pulled the closure tab of my sleeping bag up to my head, trying to muffle the sounds around me, and recapture the sense of serenity I'd felt beneath the water of the oasis. I couldn't, but eventually I slept.

Jurgen woke me just before dawn, my nose alerting me to his presence in my tent a moment before a tentative hand shook my shoulder.

'Commissar. Are you awake?'

'I am now,' I assured him, letting go of the laspistol, which I had no conscious memory of having seized. 'What's the problem?'

'Orks,' he said simply. 'Hundreds of 'em.'

As it turned out, that was something of an exaggeration, but it got me moving right enough, grabbing the commbead even ahead of my trousers.

'Tayber,' I snapped. 'What's going on?' As I scrambled out into the open air, Jurgen at my heels, I already had a pretty good idea. The roar of badly tuned engines was echoing down the defile we'd taken the evening before, although whether they were in pursuit of us or heading in the opposite direction was impossible to determine.

'There's a column of vehicles moving up behind us,' Tayber reported. Agitated civilians were milling around in the half light, bleating among themselves, although to my surprise a few of them were grabbing what improvised weapons they could and hurrying to reinforce the militia teams and Bravo squad, who were deploying at the mouth of the canyon. 'Sentries estimate a dozen or so.'

'Acknowledged,' I said, trying to ignore the flutter of apprehension in the pit of my stomach as I translated that into a round number of greenskins. Allowing for the worst possible permutations, that the sentries had underestimated by a vehicle or two and that they were all crowded to capacity, we could be facing anything up to a hundred and fifty fully armed ork warriors. I was under no illusions about our ability to take that many in a stand-up fight, but with the terrain on our side it might not come to that. The mouth of the canyon was a natural choke point, and we should be able to hold them off. I hoped...

Luskins and Jodril dropped into place behind a convenient rock, their single remaining missile poised to punch a hole through the first buggy incautious enough to poke its nose into our refuge, and I drew my chainsword, more by instinct than because I had anything to hand I could use it on. The gesture seemed to calm the crowd a little, though. They pulled back, staring at me, and I gestured towards the parked vehicles.

'Take cover,' I told them, adopting a calm, authoritative voice, and to my relief they began to comply. Good, at least that meant they were less likely to get caught in the crossfire and ruin our sight lines. As they did so, I caught sight of a couple of familiar figures running the opposite way to the rest of the militia, and moved to intercept them. 'Where the hell do you think you're going?'

'To get the truck,' Demara retorted. 'Our gun's bolted to it, remember?' I nodded. It was a fair point.

'Leave it where it is,' I told them. 'If the greenies break through, cover the civilians.' And, more to the point, give me some covering fire while I led the retreat. Tamworth nodded, the urge to serve and protect visibly kicking in at my words.

'You've got it. Come on, Dem.' He resumed his rapid progress towards the truck, the girl jogging a pace or two behind, her voice raised in remonstrance.

'I'm the gunner, you're the loader, I'm the one that says, "come on," all right?' I shook my head and sighed. It seemed their teamwork could still do with a little polish, but there was no time to worry about that now. I turned back to the incipient ambush, and brought Tayber and the three team leaders into the commnet.

'Keep out of sight,' I said, flattening myself behind a convenient boulder, steadying my laspistol against it. After a moment, Jurgen's distinctive odour joined me, followed an instant later by the man himself, who went prone and sighted his lasgun squarely on the gap in the cliff face surrounding us. 'Wait until they've committed themselves before opening fire.'

As ambushes went, I had to concede, it wasn't bad, especially considering the haste with which it had been put together. Once they rounded the edge of the opening, the greenskins would have a clear line of sight to the civilians, which ought to draw them in nicely, intent on slaughter, allowing us to pick them off from the flanks, especially if Luskins was able to stall their lead vehicle, breaking the momentum of the charge.

'Steady...' Tayber encouraged his men, and I heard the tinny echo of Hascom, Tarvil and Grenbow performing the same office for their recruits. My weapons felt glued to the palms of my hands, and the sweat there wasn't entirely due to the heat of the desert.[1] Any moment now...

'They're here,' Tarvil reported, his team having had the dubious honour of being deployed where they'd get the first sight of the enemy. 'Stay sharp.' Superfluous advice if ever I'd heard it, but it seemed to do the trick for his fledgling command, because no one got nervous and betrayed their presence by firing ahead of time. Which was just as well as it turned out. When I heard his voice again, it held an edge of puzzlement. 'Lead vehicle overshooting. And the second... They're not slowing down.'

'They've missed us,' I said, the sudden surge of released tension seeming to liquefy my bones.

'Seems like it.' Tayber's voice was shaded with an unmistakable tint of relief as well. 'But stay alert.'

In the event, his caution was to prove unfounded. The racket of the ork engines died away, and we finally relaxed, feeling a curious sense of anticlimax.

'How could they have missed our tracks?' I asked Kolfax, finding the stocky guide at my shoulder, and he shrugged.

'If they were going as fast as they sounded they'd be whipping up a fair-sized dustcloud,' he pointed out. 'They probably wiped them out for us.'

---

1. *Actually, just after dawn, the air would still be quite chill.*

'Lucky they did,' Tayber agreed, joining my impromptu command group. 'The question is – how long have they been following us?' The palms of my hands began to tingle.

'The question is, have they?' I asked.

Tayber looked at me, unable or unwilling to complete the same chain of reasoning I just had.

'They must have been,' he said, shrugging. 'What else would they be after out here?'

'The supply dump,' I said.

SEVENTEEN

NEEDLESS TO SAY, the thought was a sobering one, and we resumed our journey in a far more subdued mood.

'We can't be certain that's where they were heading,' Tayber said when we stopped for our first break. We were pulled over in a small depression in the landscape, which would have kept the wind off, but not a lot else if we'd camped here the previous night as Kolfax had originally intended, and I shuddered inwardly at the narrowness of our escape. The ork convoy couldn't possibly have missed us, and we'd have been faced with a pitched battle at the very least.

'True,' I agreed, neither of us really believing it, but determined to keep our fears at bay as best we could. There was no other obvious destination out here, but they were greenskins after all, so who knew what they might be after. For all I knew there was an encampment somewhere in the vicinity, like the one Jurgen and I had so fortuitously obliterated with our crash landing, which wasn't exactly a comforting thought, but was marginally more so than the idea that the supplies we so desperately needed were even now disappearing down a few score of greenskin gullets. I turned to Kolfax, who was loitering nearby chewing a ration bar. Emperor preserve me, I was beginning to think he actually liked the things. 'Still no sign of any tracks?'

'None,' he assured me, with a confident nod. 'But then that's hardly surprising.' A gusty wind had been blowing for some hours, rolling successive waves of hot, thick air into my face (along with yet more of the ubiquitous dust), and I'd begun to feel as though I was being followed around by some vast, over friendly animal. 'Apart from the dust we're kicking up ourselves, there's a blow coming.'

'You mean a sandstorm?' I asked, and our guide nodded his head.

'Just a small one, should be over by dawn.' Tayber and I looked at one another, the same thought occurring to both of us simultaneously. Orks or not, unless we found shelter at the supply dump we were in serious trouble. Ariott's patients were unlikely to survive another night in the open even under reasonable conditions, and there was no telling how many of the others would succumb to the effects of bad weather too. More to the point, we needed to get the vehicles under cover. Robust they may have been, but an engine full of sand would cripple them, I had no doubt about that, and I couldn't see Felicia and her artisans being able to fix the whole fleet.

'Better get moving then,' I concluded, draining the last of my water, and beginning to trudge back to the buggy. Tayber nodded.

'Better had,' he agreed.

THE LAST COUPLE of hours before we reached our destination were almost unbearably tense, my nerves winding tighter with every kilometre, like an internal echo of the ominous grey line building moment by moment along the horizon. Kolfax observed it periodically through his amplivisor, responding to my queries with infuriatingly vague predictions like, 'It's building, all right.' So it was something of a shock when we finally crested a ridge, the truck in front of us coasted to a halt, and our guide stood up to point to something on the plain below.

'That's it,' he said, his voice slightly attenuated by the commbead. Jurgen pulled us up too, next to the lead vehicle, and I raised my own amplivisor. 'Looks like the greenies got here first.'

'Not quite,' I said. Our objective was plain enough, a cluster of prefabricated huts crudely camouflaged by having been half buried in the sand (unless of course the wind had taken care of that), protected in turn by a steep sided berm and a chain link fence. Tiny plumes of dust betrayed the presence of the orks who'd passed us that morning, circling the compound at speeds and ranges which both looked reckless in the extreme. Distance, and the ever-present racket of our engines, robbed the little tableau of sound, although occasional flashes of light from the hurtling vehicles and the beleaguered installation were enough to confirm that some kind of battle was going on. 'Someone's defending it.'

'Any idea who?' Tayber asked, cutting in. 'They could just be squabbling over the loot.'

'It doesn't matter,' I said. 'Whoever it is, we're going in.' I glanced back at the ramshackle convoy behind me. 'Disembark the civilians, and tell them to find whatever shelter they can. We'll be back for them later.' I hoped. And if we weren't, they'd definitely have a better chance of survival on foot than riding into a firewasps' nest with us.

At that thought, I paused to consider the wisdom of my order, but I really couldn't see another choice. Moving on to the next supply dump was out of the question. We didn't have enough fuel to get there, even if by some miracle the approaching sandstorm didn't disable our transport first. Our only chance was to drive off the orks and hope that whoever was defending the installation below us would turn out to be on our side. Ignoring the chill of apprehension, which seemed to have settled in the pit of my stomach, I continued to lay out our strategy.

'Once we're over the ridge,' I said, 'Head straight for the main mass of the enemy. Engage at will.' In other words, use their own tactics against them, and hope they were too surprised to respond, at least until we'd taken a few of them out. 'Don't fire until we're right on top of them. With any luck they'll think we're reinforcements until it's too late.' Not exactly the soundest of plans, but no one had any better ideas, or objections (apart from a few of the civilians who seemed less than thrilled at the prospect of being abandoned in the middle of nowhere, but responded well to reason and the threat of execution), so against my better judgement I waved our *ad hoc* attack force forward and ordered the charge.

Truth to tell, the experience was unexpectedly exhilarating. As we accelerated down the slope, raising a huge cloud of dust as we did so, I distinctly heard several of our militia recruits whooping like greenskins themselves, even over the racket of the engines.

I felt a faint flutter of trepidation as I registered the banner of flying grit we were trailing in our wake, which pretty much ruled out any element of surprise we might otherwise have retained. I just had to hope it would even the balance a little by cloaking our identities until we were ready to strike. There was no time to worry about that, though, the greenskins were getting closer by the second, and I voxed the others with a last-minute warning.

'Hold your fire until you're sure of a target,' I reminded them. 'And make it count. We'll only get one chance at this, and if we frak it up things will get messy.' I was rewarded with a chorus of assent and took up my station at the heavy bolter, trying to compensate for the wildly bucking firing platform I was to be stuck with. A buggy with a garish red paint scheme bobbed and weaved through the sights of the weapon, and I swung the mount, trying to keep it centred.

'Commissar.' Felicia's voice echoed tinnily in my commbead. 'I'm picking up some signals. They're very faint...'

'Patch them through,' I told her. A haze of static filled my ear, interwoven with fragments of several voices, none of them intelligible. 'It sounds like another commnet.'

'That's what I thought,' the tech-priest confirmed. Well that was a relief; at least whoever was in the supply dump was human. 'I'm trying to break into it, but this particular blessed gift of the Omnissiah is well and truly fr–.'

'Keep trying,' I said, just as a gout of sand erupted a few metres to the left of our hurtling buggy. Jurgen began swinging us around in an evasive pattern, which I lost no time in urging the rest of our group to emulate.

'Looks like the greenies have spotted us, sir,' he said.

'Greenies be damned,' I replied furiously, spotting a puff of smoke from behind the berm. 'It's our own people!' Who, to be fair, could hardly be blamed for making the same mistake we hoped the orks would. I clung desperately to the bolter mounting as Jurgen side slipped around the burning wreck of something which looked uncomfortably like the vehicle we were riding in, and another piece of the desert erupted, close enough to shower me with debris this time. 'And they've got the range, damn it!' Now it could only be a matter of seconds before the concealed mortars did some real damage to us. 'Felicia, I need that frequency!'

'Working on it,' she said cheerfully, but then I supposed she would be, sitting comfortably back on the ridge enjoying the show.

'Tullock, target the reinforcements,' a new voice suddenly said in my ear, crisp and confident. 'Whittle them down before they can close. Everyone else keep the pressure up on the first wave.' Whoever it was clearly knew their business.

'You got it, LT.'[1] someone responded, presumably Tullock, whoever the hell he was. I cut in immediately, seldom more grateful for my commissarial override.

'This is Commissar Ciaphas Cain, leading the convoy approaching from the east,' I broadcast. Glancing around, I realised with a thrill of horror that it was actually true, Jurgen's habitually robust driving style having drawn us slightly ahead of the others, who were now fanning out across the plain towards the greenskins. 'We're carrying Imperial troops and civilian refugees in commandeered enemy vehicles. Concentrate your fire on the orks between us.'

'Prove it.' The unnamed lieutenant was clearly going to be as hard to convince as Tayber had been, but at least he held back the blizzard of mortar rounds I'd been convinced was about to descend on us.

'We're about to,' I promised him, and targeted the crimson buggy again. If nothing else, Tullock's potshots at us seemed to have convinced the greenskins that we were indeed on their side, an illusion I'd be most gratified to dispel. 'Select your targets.' A chorus of acknowledgement assured me that the rest of our gallant band had already done so, and I squeezed the trigger.

We were close enough for me to make out the crew of the ramshackle vehicle, a couple of brawny greenskins, one driving and the other hanging off the

---

1. A familar form of address often used by a senior NCO to the lieutenant in charge of their platoon, in the same way that their own subordinates might address them as 'sarge.'

mount of a heavy weapon of some kind, directing a stream of un-aimed fire in the general direction of the dug-in defenders. As he turned to face me, noticing us at last, I was able to discern that his entire lower jaw had been replaced by a crude augmetic of riveted metal. I squeezed the trigger, and by luck or the Emperor's guidance, the stream of explosive shells shredded his torso, which bounced to the sand in a welter of offal and gore. The driver reacted instantly, swinging into our path and attempting to ram us.

'Oh no you don't!' Jurgen braked hard, almost knocking me out against the hard surface of the bolter, but years of experience of his driving style had forewarned me of what to expect and I cushioned the impact with the flat of my hand, directing a hail of bolts into the now-unoccupied rear compartment. As I'd hoped, there must have been some spare ammunition or a fuel can in the back, as the whole thing suddenly erupted in a ball of fire. Startled, the driver lost control and spun out, the blazing wreck pinwheeling away until it impacted with a sand dune. Jurgen swung us around in a wider arc, looking for another target.

Our surprise attack had been a stunning success, no fewer than four of the enemy trucks and buggies falling to our initial salvoes, and the rest scattering in shock. To my relief, only a couple of the larger trucks had troops on board, and one of those was disabled, its occupants scrambling away from it, brandishing their small-arms. A few rounds pattered ineffectually off our armour plate, and I ignored them, knowing better than to waste ammunition trying to suppress orks. It was as well I held my fire, though, because an instant later one of our own trucks roared through the middle of the group, squashing a couple of greenskins under its wheels while Grenbow's militia group took potshots at the rest with their own weapons. (This didn't do much beyond confusing them even more, never hard to do with an ork, but at least it kept them from regrouping.)

'Heads up, commissar!' Grenbow called, forgetting in his excitement that the commbead mike was right next to his mouth, and almost deafening me in the process. Fortunately, Jurgen was less easily disconcerted, turning us aside with another spine snapping jerk just as a hail of heavy calibre ammunition began to rattle against the armour plate protecting my firing position. I turned, seeking a target, to find a trio of the bike things bearing down on us, autocannons or something similar strobing as they spat death in our direction.

I opened up at almost the same instant as the heavy weapon on the truck, catching a glimpse of Demara clinging grimly to the wildly bucking cannon as she tried to keep it on aim, Tamworth slamming another belt of ammunition in, and a white, flapping robe apparently anchored firmly to the tailgate.

'Felicia!' I yelled. 'What the hell are you doing here?'

'Keeping the comms open, I thought.' She gave me a cheery wave as the bucking truck moved in to parallel our course, held in place by the mechadendrite, which she'd wrapped around a convenient stanchion. 'How else do you think I got us in range of the other network?'

There was no time to debate the matter further, as the ork bikes were closing fast, their riders hunched low over their handlebars. The leader, who was broad and muscular even for an ork, grinned wildly as we approached, the horns of some large animal strapped to the front of his helmet.[1] An instant later, the grin was gone, along with most of his bike, which seemed to disintegrate under him as Demara finally got her autocannon under control. The open vox relay picked up her voice.

'Wahoo! I got one!'

'Great,' I responded. 'Don't get cocky.' I directed the bolter at the closer of the remaining two, taking out the front wheel. The hurtling contraption buried its forks in the sand, flipping over completely, and crushing its rider under its own weight.

'Mine,' Jurgen said, as though claiming a catch on the grasshopper pitch.[2] Before I could divine his intention, he swung the control yoke again, ramming the remaining bike, and bouncing us over the wreckage of the thing. Driven deep into the sand by the weight of our wheels, its rear tracks continued to spin for a moment, and a pair of legs kicked feebly, waving incongruously in the air as though their owner was

---

1. A common sign of status among greenskins, presumably intended to show that they've overcome something even bigger and nastier than they are.

2. Grasshopper is a game popular on most of the worlds in the Britannicus cluster, presumably so called because of the number of times the players leap into the air in an attempt to intercept the ball after it's been struck by the one with the bat. Its rules are arcane in the extreme, making little sense to anyone not native to one of the worlds where it's played. Matches have been known to last for anything up to a month, not counting stoppages for rain, which are frequent, and even then usually end in a draw.

attempting to run upside down. An instant later the truck followed, reducing what was left to scrap metal and goo.

We weren't getting everything our own way, though. Glancing round I saw one of our own buggies upended, its crew scattered around it unmoving, or twitching feebly. As I watched, one of them tried to rise, only to be bisected by one of the murderous axes being wielded by a greenskin, a stray foot soldier from their wrecked truck by the look of it.

'Help the survivors!' I voxed Grenbow, and the truck peeled off to do what it could. I switched frequencies, getting back to the anonymous lieutenant. 'Convinced yet?'

'Reasonably.'

The other ork truck slewed sideways, a neat hole punched through its side armour, the spray of molten metal spattering its unfortunate crew the unmistakable result of an energy weapon of some kind. I turned, seeing the familiar silhouette of an Imperial Chimera looming over a nearby sand dune, the multi-laser in its turret turning to track its target. 'Thanks for keeping them busy, by the way.' The laser flashed again, cooking off the fuel tank, and the truck erupted in a fireball. Two more Chimeras rolled into view, their multi-lasers stabbing out to pick off targets of their own, and I realised with a sudden surge of relief that all the ork vehicles I could now see were the survivors of our own convoy. Apart from the one I'd seen overturned, we hadn't lost any, and our casualties seemed at first glance to have been astonishingly light.

'Our pleasure,' I said dryly as Jurgen cut the power and coasted us to a halt in front of the command vehicle, easily distinguishable from its fellows by the cluster of vox antennae atop its hull. It came to a halt as well, its engine idling, while its fellows continued to roll forward, their hull-mounted heavy flamers licking out to mop up the scattering greenskin survivors trying to flee on foot. Not many were making it, and so far as I could see our armed civilians, who no doubt welcomed the opportunity for a little payback, were enthusiastically dealing with the ones avoiding the flamers. I climbed down and walked towards the stationary Chimera, straightening my cap and returning my dust encrusted sash to my waist as I did so. 'And you are?'

'Lieutenant Piers.' The turret hatch popped open, and a surprisingly young looking man in a PDF uniform stared down at me. 'I must say, you're not quite what I expected when you said you were a commissar.'

'I've been busy,' I said shortly. I gestured back at the ridge. 'We left our non-combatants a couple of kilometres back that way. Send someone to pick them up, will you?' As I'd expected, a show of concern for the civilians was enough to short-circuit any arguments he might have made. He still looked confused, and who could blame him, but he nodded in agreement.

'I'll see to it,' he promised. His eyes widened as he got his first proper look at the vehicles we'd appropriated and the piratical band of irregulars manning them, and positively boggled as Jurgen hopped down from the buggy to take up his usual position at my shoulder. 'Is there anything else I can do for you?'

'I don't suppose you've got any tanna?' I asked hopefully. Piers shook his head.

'Never heard of it,' he said.

EIGHTEEN

WELL, THEY MIGHT not have had any tanna, but they had pretty much everything else I could have wished for, including showers and air conditioning. I was still basking in the unfamiliar sensation of comfort an hour or so later, feeling clean, cool, and savouring the mug of recaff Jurgen had found for me, as I sat at a table in one of the huts filling Piers in on our journey so far. The faint rattle of the sandstorm against the walls was also quietly soothing in its own way, despite being a tangible reminder that we'd only just reached safety.

'You really think you can make it all the way through?' he asked.

I nodded. 'I wouldn't be doing it otherwise,' I said, skating over the self-evident fact that a large proportion of my impromptu escort wasn't likely to prove so fortunate. I nodded at the mapslate, propped up between us. 'There are two more supply dumps between here and the lowlands. After that, we can live off the land if we have to, although we'll still need to stock up on fuel and ammunition.'

'We will.' Piers nodded, already taking it for granted that he'd be tagging along on our little expedition, a fact which I was more than grateful for. I'd been expecting to have to persuade him, possibly even by exerting my commissarial authority, but for whatever reason, the notion of taking on the bulk of the greenskin army almost single-handed seemed to appeal to him. I didn't question it at the time, just thanked the Emperor for gung-ho idiots, and got on with the practicalities. For some reason, I found myself liking the lad, probably because he reminded me of Divas.

'What have you been doing all this time?' Tayber asked. He was sitting in on the discussion mainly so I didn't have to waste time briefing him later, but he was the ranking trooper in the convoy, so I'd also felt it might be politic to include him. Besides, he hadn't let me down so far (unless you counted landing me with a gaggle of civvies to wet-nurse), and Piers was still something of an unknown quantity; it wouldn't hurt to have the veteran sergeant there to back me up if push came to shove.

'The same as you, by the sound of it,' Piers said. 'After our regiment was overrun, we went to ground, and started hit-and-run strikes against whatever targets we could find.'

Tayber nodded. That had been the last coherent order to get through before the chain of command had collapsed completely, or so he'd told me shortly after we'd met. 'We came by here to rearm and re-supply yesterday, and got caught flat-footed when the greenies found the place.' He manipulated the controls of the mapslate, and the icon marking the supply dump turned red. 'We'll have to blow what's left when we pull out, unfortunately. Now they know where it is, they'll be back.'

I nodded. The reason for his eagerness to join us now abundantly clear: he was evidently as fervent a believer in the notion of safety in numbers as I was. I couldn't fault his reasoning either; I didn't think any greenskin survivors had got away from the skirmish outside, but when they didn't check in, whoever sent them would be bound to send more, and in greater numbers.

'They seemed to know where they were going when they passed us,' Tayber said.

I looked quizzically at Piers. 'Any idea why that would be?'

The young lieutenant shrugged. 'They found a map?' he suggested. 'Perhaps one of the other units that used the place wasn't as lucky as we were.'

'Other units?' I asked.

'This is the third time we've been here,' Piers replied. 'When I booked out what we'd taken, I noticed there'd been some other requisitions in the last month or so.'

Wonderful – their entire society was falling down around their ears, and what was left of the PDF was still filling out forms.

'Show me,' I said.

It took a while, but after a bit of searching and some shouting down the corridor, Piers's sergeant, a large, taciturn man called Vyner, appeared with a slate which he laid on the table between us. Piers fiddled around with it, and called up a screen full of what looked like standard requisition forms.

'There. That was us.' He pointed to a couple of items. 'Looks to me like three more units active in this area.' He glanced up at Tayber appraisingly. 'Four, counting yours.'

'We found all we needed in town,' Tayber replied.

'So I see.' The young lieutenant grinned. 'Very obliging of the greenies to let you borrow it.'

'Any indication of what these units are?' I asked.

Piers shook his head. 'None, it's all encrypted. Security, you see. In case the enemy takes the installation. That way they still won't know what's out there.' I nodded slowly. Maybe Felicia could do something with it, or not. In any case, once the sandstorm subsided there would be a far more direct way of finding out.

'I need to talk to your vox man,' I said.

BY DAWN, THE sandstorm had almost dissipated (just as Kolfax had predicted, much to his ill-concealed satisfaction), and I braved the flurry of stinging grit to inspect the site properly. The largest of the huts contained food and water, which I left Norbert to organise the distribution of, and I moved on to find Felicia and the remaining vehicles with a considerably lighter heart. Even if we were able to supplement our numbers with fresh recruits, we'd still have enough of the essentials to keep us going more or less indefinitely. Assuming there was a supply of fuel around the place too, of course.

'Barrels of the stuff,' the comely tech-priest reassured me. 'Omnissiah alone knows how we'll get it all stowed, but we'll manage.' She led me to a shed with a large door in the side, a strange air of anticipation hovering around her. 'This ought to help.' She flicked the portal aside with a casual wave of her mechadendrite, leaving the weathered timber quivering against its stop. A couple of Piers's troopers popped up like startled sump rats at the noise, lasguns levelled, then relaxed when they saw it was only us. I nodded courteously at them, pleased at their level of alertness, and turned to look at whatever it was in the shed that Felicia was so excited about.

'It's a Sentinel!' I said in astonishment.

The enginseer smiled. 'Better than that,' she said, activating the overhead luminators. 'It's a power lifter.' I'd seen them before of course, many times, but they still seemed faintly odd to me. Instead of weapons, the walker had been equipped with a set of mechanical claws, intended to let it pick up and handle heavy loads, and a massive counterweight hung from its back like a rockcrete rucksack. 'Once I get this up and running we'll have everything stowed in no time.'

There was no point in asking who she expected to pilot the thing, she was gazing at it adoringly and I made a mental note to find urgent business elsewhere in the compound as soon as she started mucking about with it.

'Glad to hear it,' I said. 'How are the vehicles?'

'Good as ever,' she said, whatever that meant considering they were ork junk to begin with. 'We got them under cover just in time. Aldiman and Lyddi are checking them out at the moment.' After a moment's thought I realised she was referring to her artisans, who, it appeared, had progressed a little beyond mere bolt tightening. (Indeed, by the time our journey was over they'd both sprouted cogwheel icons, and seemed to think they were enginseers in all but name.[1])

'What about the Imperial stuff?' I asked.

Felicia shrugged, visibly reluctant to wrest her attention away from her new toy.

'We've got five Chimeras, all of them in pretty good condition considering what they've been through. They could do with some routine maintenance, but that isn't an option right now.' She shrugged, the mechadendrite twitching above her shoulder as she did so. 'I gather time is of the essence.'

'It is,' I assured her. 'We're going to have to pull out of here by tomorrow morning at the latest.'

After some discussion, Piers, Tayber and I had determined that the nearest known concentration of orks could reasonably expect their scouts to be returning by about noon today, and ought to be turning up around dawn if they set out at once to find out what had happened to them. Neither of which was necessarily a correct assumption, of course, but under the circumstances none of us were willing to take any chances. 'Can you get the place gutted by then?'

'Oh yes,' she said, with rather too much enthusiasm for my peace of mind, and I went to find Piers's vox operator before she could get the power lifter started.

---

1. *Both, in fact, becoming lay brothers of the Mechanicus in later life.*

He was a thin, sallow fellow as I recall, waiting for me at the exit ramp of the command Chimera as arranged, clearly wondering if he was supposed to salute a commissar or not. In the end he compromised with a sort of limp wave, which I returned with a parade ground snap and enough of a friendly grin to put him at his ease.

'Everything's ready,' he assured me and ushered me out of the dwindling wind into the welcoming shelter of the APC. It was a little more cramped in there than a standard model, in order to make room for the auspex and the extra communications gear, to which Marquony, the vox man, ushered me. I'd been inside Mostrue's command vehicle on enough occasions to be familiar with the layout of one, although there were a few minor differences of course, and sat next to him with complete assurance. 'Anyone in range ought to be listening out in about two minutes.' Another standing order left over from the invasion, and a pretty handy one for me I have to say. With the full power of a command Chimera's transmitter behind us I should be able to reach any potential allies across a far wider radius than was possible with the portable vox unit Grenbow had carried (which Felicia had now laid to rest, along with the appropriate sacraments).

'Thank you,' I said, inputting my commissarial code as I spoke. Given the scepticism I'd encountered from Tayber and Piers, tagging the message with the full authority of my office from the outset might save us a lot of argument. Marquony glanced at his chronograph, fiddled with some dials and switches, and nodded at me.

'You're on.'

'This is Commissar Ciaphas Cain, for all Imperial units within range,' I said, trying to imbue my voice with the easy expectation of obedience they taught me at the schola. 'Rendezvous at supply post sigma twelve by dawn tomorrow. Message ends.' I nodded at Marquony, who cut the power at once. We listened to the static for a good twenty minutes, but no answer came, not even the odd, 'Did you say commissar?' I half expected.

Marquony grinned at me. 'Good vox discipline,' he said. 'Less for the greenies to pick up.'

'Either that, or there's nobody out there,' I said, trying to sound as if I was joking.

IN THE EVENT, my fears were to prove unfounded. Our first batch of stragglers arrived shortly before noon, adding another pair of Chimeras and over a dozen troopers to our motley band. That gave us almost a full-strength platoon, once you'd added in the survivors of Piers's unit as well, not to mention at least one Chimera we could use almost exclusively for transporting our supplies. I left the sergeant in charge of the newcomers, to sort out the practicalities of integrating the command chains with Piers and Tayber, and went to find another mug of recaff.

In the event, I found Norbert too, who'd evidently had the same idea, and who joined me at my table.

'That was a stroke of luck,' he said, spinning his data slate around so I could see it. 'I've been able to allocate part of our fuel reserves and spare ammunition to an armoured vehicle. Rather less chance of it getting touched off by a stray round that way.'

It was a risky call, one good hit by a krak round or an energy weapon and we'd lose the lot, but the greenskins seemed fairly light on both. It would certainly be safer than putting most of our volatile material into one of the open-topped ork contraptions.

'What about the rest?' I asked.

The scrivener shrugged. 'I'm dividing them up between the trucks and a couple of the buggies. Spread out as much as possible. Even if we lose one or two in the next encounter we won't be crippled.' He didn't sound altogether sanguine at the prospect, but I couldn't really blame him. 'Even so, we'll need to leave some items behind. We still don't have the capacity to transport all of it.'

'I'm sure you have everything under control,' I said.

'I've drawn up a list of priorities,' he said. 'Food, water, and medical supplies, of course, and enough ammunition to keep our weapons functional.' He indicated some items on the inventory he'd compiled. 'Some of the militiamen are asking for new guns, to replace the ork stuff they're carrying.'

'Tell them to take whatever they want,' I said. 'There's enough in the armoury.' And the more we issued, the less we had to pack: I was damned if I was going to leave anything the greenskins could use behind, and it went against the grain to blow up anything we might need later. Besides, the guns we'd taken from the greenskins were likely to be just as lethal to the user as the target.

'I'll do that.' Norbert nodded. 'What about the rest of the civilians?'

I shrugged. 'Why not?' Carrying a weapon would make them feel more secure, I had no doubt about that, and aiming wasn't exactly an option from the back of one of those juddering ork monstrosities in any case. 'Anyone who wants to can arm themselves. Provided they let one of Tayber's men show them how to use their weapon, and are willing to follow orders once the shooting starts.' That should keep most of them from blowing their own feet off, and stick a bit more cannon fodder between the orks and me if things got really desperate.

'Sounds reasonable,' Norbert agreed.

WELL, I SUPPOSE in retrospect I've had better ideas, but it seemed to put fresh heart into the refugees, and in the end almost all of them picked up a lasgun or something similar, cementing their status as part of our growing irregular army. Even Ariott was carrying a laspistol the next time I saw him, although he assured me he had no intention of actually using it. I'd been a little concerned that the regular PDF might look somewhat askance at this development, but it seemed they were all for it. If the civilians could look after themselves, they could concentrate on taking the battle to the enemy without being distracted, or so they seemed to think, and I found more than one trooper offering to give personal shooting lessons to one of the women in our convoy, which I suppose was a sign of improving morale all round.

In fact, the whole encampment soon developed an air of purpose that I found quite surprising, until I had another chat with Piers over a salt grox roll and a mug of recaff shortly before dusk. By that time, a few more stragglers had turned up, bringing with them a couple of heavy trucks, which had Norbert practically rubbing his hands together, a trio of Salamanders (scout-pattern), together with a full set of crewmen, and a Chimera fitted out as a medevac vehicle. I directed that, and the two corpsmen driving it, to Ariott and his casualties, who would be far more comfortable aboard it than in the greenskin rattletrap they'd been condemned to hitherto.

'None of us have felt like this since the greenies arrived,' the young lieutenant said, taking a bite out of his roll. He glanced across at me, chewing furiously for a moment with a peculiar expression on his face. 'We've just been surviving, that's all. But now we have a mission again.'

'The mission's the same as it's always been,' I told him. 'Cleanse this world of the orks.'

'That's easy for you to say.' Piers took a slug of his recaff, recoiling slightly as Jurgen stepped forward to replenish his mug. 'This is just another campaign to you. But the people here have lost everything they ever had.'

'Except for their fighting spirit,' I said, slipping easily into the role the Commissariat had gone to so much trouble to prepare me for. 'And that's what'll win their world back for them.' And keep me in one piece, I sincerely hoped.

Piers nodded, buying it wholesale. 'We will, too,' he said solemnly. 'Or die trying.' He raised his voice, which echoed across the space between the huts, even above the bustle of people, troopers and irregulars alike, hurrying to and fro with boxes and bundles for the vehicles. 'Today's the day we stop running and hiding. Today's the day we stop harassing the enemy, and start to hurt them. Today's the day the greenskins start being afraid of us!' A roar of approbation erupted from threescore throats, echoing from the high-sided structures all around us. I stepped back into the shadows, content to let the Perlians have their little moment. Emperor knew it was going to be hard enough once we resumed our journey.

'Gangway! Oh, it's you. Sorry.' Demara stepped around me, her arms wrapped round a squad support autocannon, which was almost as big as she was. Tamworth was a few paces behind, the tripod and crew shield slung across his back, ammunition boxes in both hands. A strange amalgam of truculence and grudging respect flickered across the girl's face. 'Am I supposed to say "sir"?'

'It's customary,' I said. 'But I'm not exactly a stickler for the formalities.'

'We'd gathered that, sir,' Tamworth said.

Demara nodded. 'Thanks for saying we could take stuff.' A flicker of doubt entered her eyes. 'You didn't just mean the rifles and things, did you?'

'Whatever you're comfortable with,' I assured her.

'Chill.' She glanced up at Tamworth. 'See? I said it would be all right.' She returned her attention to me. 'Tam said we were only supposed to take the little stuff.' She glanced at the heavy weapon in her arms as fondly as if it had been a grynx kitten. 'But I said the moment I saw it, *this* is a gun.'

'Have fun with it,' I said.

The two of them grinned at me, and trotted off into the gathering darkness. A moment later, the power lifter stalked round the side of the nearest building and came to a halt with a hiss of pistons, a box almost as large as I was dangling casually from its claws. Felicia grinned at me, her white robe making her look like a cheerful ghost in the gathering darkness.

'This is just about the last of it,' she told me. 'Everything we can use, anyway.'

'Good.' I nodded. 'What's left?'

'Shells, mostly, but we've nothing to fire them with.' Her grin widened. 'Should make quite a bang when we blow the place, though.'

'Glad to hear it,' I said. 'How are the vehicles?'

'Good enough.' She nodded. 'I'll run some final checks overnight.' Her energy astonished me at the time; it was only later that I discovered, like many tech-priests, she'd had part of her cerebellum replaced with augmetic systems which, among other things, let her go without sleep almost indefinitely. 'And if I can find the time I've got some ideas about this thing.'

'You're taking it with us?' I asked, astonished.

'Oh yes. It might be a glorified shelf-stacker, but it's built on a Sentinel chassis, don't forget.' Her voice took on an unmistakable edge of enthusiasm. 'It'll be a lot faster and more manoeuvrable over rough terrain than a Chimera.' She hoisted the claw in a form of salute, making me flinch as I anticipated the box crashing down at my feet, but it remained in place as she spun the mechanical limb dexterously. 'And this ought to come in handy if anything gets stuck.'

'Good point,' I said, standing aside to let her past. I turned to Jurgen. 'We might as well turn in,' I said.

My aide nodded. 'Busy day ahead tomorrow, sir,' he agreed. Although if I'd known how much of an understatement that was going to turn out to be, I wouldn't have slept a wink.

NINETEEN

DESPITE OUR BEST intentions, it was well past dawn before our motley collection of vehicles was ready to roll, and I hid my impatience as best I could while the civilians sorted themselves out. The last few precious supplies were hung from the sides of Chimeras already so encrusted with external stowage that their anti-personnel lasguns would be all but useless, and Tayber made ready to blow the place halfway to the Golden Throne. We'd placed demo charges in every building, with a couple of extra det packs wired up to the remaining ammunition in the armoury just for luck, and I intended being a long way away before letting him transmit the vox pulse which would touch it all off.

'That's the last of it,' he reported eventually, trotting up to the command Chimera, where Jurgen and I were settling in with Piers and the remains of his command squad. Normally I'd have followed my usual habit and requisitioned one of the Salamanders, but I'd had enough of riding in an open vehicle in these conditions. They were better employed doing the job they'd been designed for: ranging ahead of us and out to our flanks, keeping an eye open for any unpleasant surprises. They'd been doing that since dawn, checking in periodically to assure me that there was still no sign of the greenskins, although I wasn't about to let that lull me into a false sense of security. Since arriving on Perlia I'd learned to trust my paranoid streak more firmly than ever.

Besides, the command vehicle would be right in the middle of our improvised army, as well protected as possible. I hadn't told Piers that was why I was hitching a lift, citing the need to keep on top of any unexpected developments, which the array of specialised vox and auspex equipment aboard would be invaluable with. The fact that I could have done so almost as easily through the commbead, while eating dust in the back of our old ork boneshaker didn't seem to have occurred to him, and if it had he kept the thought to himself.

'Good,' I responded, with a last glance at our ragtag convoy. What with the mixture of ork and Imperial vehicles, all so overloaded with external stowage that their outlines were barely discernible, we looked more like a bunch of scavvies than a military unit.

I was about to give the signal to move out when the familiar hiss of pistons and clanking of camshafts alerted me to the presence of the power lifter. I turned, receiving a typically cheery wave from Felicia as she leaned out of the cockpit, and goggled in astonishment.

'Emperor on Earth,' I expostulated, 'what have you done to that?'

'I told you I had some ideas.' Her voice was conversational, echoing in the commbead in my ear, which was just as well I suppose, as I'd never have heard a word over the roaring of the engines building up around us otherwise. One of the ideas had evidently been the installation of a vox set.

In place of the rockcrete counterweight, she'd mounted a large metal tank, which was full of promethium judging by the tangle of piping which led from it to somewhere within the bowels of the machine. With that much fuel on board she ought to be able to make it to the coast without stopping, although she clearly intended using some of it for other purposes: a heavy flamer had been mounted on the Sentinel's snout, its igniter hissing gently, flavouring the air with a light tang of combustion. How in the galaxy she expected to be able to use it, the panel in the cockpit normally reserved for fire control being devoted to the manipulation of the claws, I had no idea. It was only some time later, when I saw her wading into the middle of a greenskin patrol with every sign of enjoyment, that I realised she'd jury-rigged a manual trigger which she could activate with her mechanical tail.

'Very resourceful,' I told her, keeping my voice as neutral as possible.

Felicia grinned again, and clanked off in search of her artisans, who had commandeered one of the newly arrived trucks for their collection of tools and spare parts (now comfortingly well supplemented by the inventory of the supply dump). I turned to Piers. 'We might as well move out.'

'Outrider two,' a voice said in my ear. 'Contact, south-east quadrant, closing fast.' One of the Salamander teams was doing what it was supposed to. Piers looked grim.

'They were quick off the mark,' he said. I nodded, the dryness of my mouth not entirely due to the desiccating heat and the stink of burned promethium diffusing from the engines of our vehicles like Jurgen's body odour. It seemed our most pessimistic forecast of the ork response to the massacre of their reconnaissance patrol was about to be borne out.

I hurried into the shadowed interior of the command Chimera, a detached corner of my mind still able to welcome the sudden coolness, and stood over the auspex operator.

'Can you give me an estimate of their numbers?' I asked. The man, Orrily by name if I remember right, shook his head.

'They're not in range yet,' he explained, and indicated a blip almost at the edge of the screen, comfortingly tagged with an Imperial icon. 'That's outrider two.'

'This is Cain,' I transmitted, cutting in over Marquony's routine acknowledgement of the incoming message. 'Have you got a visual?'

'No, sir.' The corporal in charge of the four-man scout team responded instantly, no doubt surprised at my intervention and hoping to make a good impression. 'All we can make out so far is the dust they're kicking up.' There was a pause, and I could picture him staring through his amplivisor trying to resolve the image. 'There's a lot of it, though.'

'Let us know as soon as you've got confirmation,' I said. I turned to Piers and Tayber. 'It's decision time. Stay and hope we can defend our position, or pull out now and risk engaging them in the open if they pursue.'

'Pull out,' Piers said. He indicated the auspex screen. 'They're at least twenty minutes away.' Tayber nodded his agreement.

'We were going to blow this place anyway. Pull back to the ridge line while we've still got enough time.'

'Have we, though?' I asked. Our military units could do it, I had no doubt about that, but whether the civilian rabble would be able to get their act together in time was far more debatable. The question was merely rhetorical, however, intended to show some concern for the refugees. I wasn't going to sit around here waiting for the greenskins to arrive, and if some of the civvies ended up acting as a shield for the rest of us I could live with that. So I nodded, as though making a hard decision. 'It's not as if we really have a choice, is it? Let's go.'

To my surprise, the retreat from the supply dump went remarkably well, at least at first. The civilians were able to keep up with the rest of us, despite being mounted on the ork vehicles for the most part, and although the formation dispersed a bit, our Chimeras were able to keep them more or less reined in. My main concern had been the choke point of the main gate, the only way of getting through the berm around the compound, but everything was out on the plain and kicking up dust within little more than ten minutes.

'I've got the contact,' Orrily told me shortly after we'd lurched into motion ourselves. 'One vehicle, medium sized. I can't tell a lot more at this distance.'

'That's good enough,' I told him, trying to hide my relief. Whatever it was, it didn't seem all that much of a threat. A moment later, the Salamander crew chimed in, confirming his estimate.

'It's Imperial,' the corporal told me. 'One Leman Russ.' He paused for a moment, then his voice resumed. 'It's leading some kind of convoy, by the look of things. There's a much bigger dust cloud behind it, trailing by a couple of kilometres.'

'Leading be reamed,' a new voice cut in, crisp, authoritative, and undeniably female. 'We've got greenies up our arse. Whoever's out there, you'd better have some serious firepower or we're flamebread.'

'This is Commissar Cain,' I responded, trying to hide the shiver of unease I felt at those words. 'Identify yourself, please.' The hint of formality would be subtly reassuring, and there was no point in being rude in any case. I've always found you get more out of people by making them feel as though you respect them, and if it doesn't work out you can always shoot them later.

'Sergeant Vivica Sautine, 57th armoured. We're all that's left of it, so far as I know.[1] We're out of ammunition for all our weapon systems. We pulled in to

---

1. In fact a few other survivors of the regiment surfaced later on, having continued their guerilla campaign in the south of the continent. Sautine and her crew had gravitated northwards after becoming separated from their parent company, which had been almost wiped out in the initial ork assault.

re-supply at alpha seven yesterday, and found it crawling with greenskins.'

I shot a glance at Tayber, recognising the designation of the supply dump he'd urged us to make for instead of this one, but had the grace to refrain from saying 'I told you so.'

'We've been running ever since,' Sautine continued. 'I thought we'd shaken them, but they picked up our trail at first light.'

'Bypass the dump,' I told her, hoping the greenskins weren't monitoring our vox channels. 'Rendezvous with us on the ridge.'

'Haven't you been listening?' she responded, with an edge of asperity I could only ascribe to the stress she'd been under and the PDF's usual woeful ignorance of the powers of the Commissariat. 'We're completely dry. If we don't re-arm we're down to harsh language.'

'They're ten minutes behind you,' I pointed out, glancing at Orilly for confirmation of my estimate. He nodded. 'Unless you can get re-equipped that fast, the compound's a death trap,' I concluded, unwilling to spell out the measures we'd taken to keep the remaining ordnance out of ork hands in case our communications were compromised. Sautine was evidently bright enough to join the dots, though.

'Confirm that,' she said. I returned my attention to Orrily, and the luminescent rash speckling his auspex screen. Something about it struck me as subtly awry, although I couldn't quite put my finger on it. After a moment the coin dropped, and I pointed at one of the blips.

'Why's that unit moving the wrong way?' I asked. Whatever it was, it was fast and agile, snaking its way through the mass of vehicles with an ease and speed, which ruled out most of our makeshift company. It had to be the Sentinel, I concluded, an impression, which was borne out a moment later by a cheerful hail over the vox.

'Don't worry, Ciaphas, I'll take care of it.'[1]

'Take care of what?' I asked, already dreading the answer. As ever, Felicia's voice was redolent of the casual optimism I'd come to associate with her.

'I've got plenty of time to get in and out of the armoury,' she assured me. 'We didn't pack any shells, did we?'

'Get back in formation,' I said as authoritatively as I could, while making sure all the other vox links had been cut out of the circuit. I couldn't risk what amounted to a direct challenge to my leadership being noticed by anyone else.

Felicia laughed. 'That's the idea, just as soon as I've picked up some shells for the tank lady. We've already got enough ammo for her bolters, and some lascannon powerpacks.'

The rogue blip was well clear of the rest of the convoy, and closer to the compound than it was to the safety of the ridge. I calculated the timing. If everything kept going at the same speed, she should be in and out by the time the fleeing tank reached the

---

1. *Since this is the first point in the narrative where Cain and Felicia appear to be on first-name terms, we can infer that they spent some time together which he hasn't bothered to record, although Emperor knows how either of them found the time for socialising.*

supply dump, and the two of them could reach safety together. I hoped. We didn't have anything capable of giving them covering fire from this range, and I found myself wishing for an Earthshaker or two. (Or preferably a Basilisk, which could have done the same job and kept up with us as well.)

'Confirm that,' I said, bowing to the inevitable. There was nothing I could do to dissuade her, so I might as well give the impression that I'd sanctioned her actions. That's the trouble with civilians: they keep having ideas of their own instead of doing what they're told. I switched to another channel. 'Tayber,' I said. 'Hold detonation until ordered.'

'Yes, sir.' His voice over the vox link was faintly puzzled, but disciplined for all that. Behind it I could hear the growling of the Chimera that Bravo squad were now riding, and the wind past the mike of his comm-bead, which told me he was standing with his head out of the hatch. 'Is there a problem?'

'Felicia's gone back for something,' I said, confident that he knew his sister well enough to infer the rest.

'I see,' he said, in a tone which told me I was right. 'Any further orders?'

'Form up on the ridge,' I said, 'just as we discussed.' I glanced at Piers, who nodded. If the greenskins bypassed the compound we'd have the advantage of the high ground. Loaded down as we were, we were in no condition for an extended chase, we'd just be picked off one by one, and if we had to stand and fight I wanted all the edge we could get.

'Confirm that. Tayber out.' The link went dead. I glanced back at the auspex screen. Felicia had just reached the compound, and the tank was almost there. Outrider two was making good progress back towards us as well, the highly tuned engine of the scout Salamander keeping them out of weapons range of the orks while they moved around the greenskins in a wide arc, trying to get visual confirmation of the enemy disposition. I drew in my breath. The first blips of the approaching enemy formation had appeared at the edge of Orrily's screen, reflecting from the small round eyeglasses he habitually wore.

'It's going to be tight,' I warned everyone.

'I'm on it,' Felicia assured me. 'I've got two pallets of main gun ammunition stacked up at the gate already. Sautine, can you get them loaded?'

'No,' the tank commander said flatly. 'But we can carry them externally. It'll only take a couple of minutes to get them lashed down.'

'Good enough,' Felicia said, cheerful as ever. 'I'll carry another on the lifter.' That, if I remembered rightly, should give them enough to completely replenish their shot locker and still have a handful to spare.

'You've only got a couple of minutes,' I warned them.

'Outrider two,' our scouts cut in, underlining the point perfectly. 'Confirm eight ork trucks, twelve buggies. They're moving in force.'

'How many infantry?' I asked. If each of those trucks were fully loaded we could be facing more than a hundred greenskins. Even with the advantage of the high ground, we'd have our work cut out.

'Couple of dozen, mainly the small ones,' the scout confirmed, a note of puzzlement in his voice. 'The trucks are mostly empty.'

'They're here for loot,' I said, the pieces suddenly falling into place. While gutting the southern installation, they must have discovered the location of this one, sent scouts to secure it, and followed up with the heavy transport. Crossing Sautine's trail had been an unfortunate coincidence, nothing more, but I was under no illusions that the prospect of combat hadn't fired up their innate bloodlust. Our driver swung us to a halt, and I picked up an amplivisor, intending to assess the situation for myself.

'Looks that way to me,' Piers agreed, lowering the boarding ramp. I trotted outside, Jurgen at my heels as usual, and raised the vision aids. All around me, soldiers were taking up defensive positions, supplemented by the militia, while the rest of the civilians huddled in the rear, clutching their lasguns grimly. This wasn't good; if the greenskins charged us, they were likely to open up in panic, heedless of the troopers in the way, inflicting more casualties on us than on the orks.

'Kolfax.' I beckoned our guide over. 'Get the civilians moving. If the greenskins attack we'll hold them off while you get clear.'

'Right.' He nodded, not bothering with even a token protest, to my unutterable relief, and started herding them back aboard their vehicles.

'Good thinking,' Piers said, looking at me with an expression of sober respect. 'At least we can keep the refugees safe.'

'For the time being,' I said, wondering briefly if I could contrive an excuse to go with them, but overall my chances of survival were better, surrounded by trained troopers. There was a whole continent full of greenskins to get past yet. 'And once we've dealt with this we can catch them up.' I turned, catching sight of Arriot. 'You'd better go too,' I said. To my surprise he shook his head.

'You might be taking casualties,' he pointed out, 'and if you do they'll have a better chance with Kaeti here.'

'Who?' I asked, momentarily confused, and he gestured towards the ambulance, which for the first time I noticed had *Kaeti* crudely painted across its nose: the name of the girlfriend of one of the corpsmen, I assumed.[1] The coin dropping, I nodded. 'What about your patients?' Not that I was particularly concerned, of course, but it was the sort of thing I was expected to say.

Ariott nodded soberly. 'They're stable enough,' he said, meaning the ones most likely to die already had. 'They'll be more comfortable in Kaeti, but they can manage on one of the trucks for an hour or two, and it would free up the stretchers just in case.'

'Good.' I nodded. 'Get it organised, will you? With any luck we won't need them, but it should help.' In more ways than one, knowing there are medical

---

1. *Perhaps wrongly: some medevac units designate each vehicle in the formation with an identifying letter, often expanded into an arbitrarily chosen word for ease of pronunciation over the vox. For some reason, no doubt deeply embedded in the military psyche, feminine names are particularly popular.*

facilities close at hand is always a big morale booster for troopers about to go into combat.

'Leave it to me.' Arriot wandered off to consult with Kolfax, and I raised the amplivisor: with a sudden flare of *déjà vu,* I realised I was in almost exactly the same position I'd been in when I first looked down on the plain below to see the orks besieging the supply dump.

The power lifter was clearly visible by the main gate, a pallet of shells for the Leman Russ's battle cannon already gripped in its manipulator claws, and the tank itself was almost at the compound. As I watched, it slewed to a halt, and the top hatch popped, followed a moment later by the side ones. The crew started scrambling out under the energetic direction of their commander, easily distinguished by the headset she wore, which seemed from this distance to be a cruder and more bulky version of my commbead. They all seemed to be women, which didn't surprise me; mixed-gender units were a rare exception in the Imperial Guard (although I was to serve with one such unit later on, of course[1]), and the PDF tended to follow suit.

Felicia dropped the pallet of shells neatly atop the left-hand sponson, and the tankies started lashing it down, while the power lifter scooped up a replacement and trotted around the hull to repeat the operation on the other side.

I shifted the amplivisor, moving the narrow image to take in the roiling cloud of dust in the distance. It was closing fast, the glint of metal visible behind it, and I was

---

1. The 597th Valhallan. As previously noted, his exploits with them make up the bulk of the material disseminated so far, and need not detain us any further at this juncture.

sure I could make out the dim silhouettes of individual vehicles. As I tried to bring the image into clearer focus, I was able to discern some intermittent muzzle flashes as the first few greenskin gunners gave way to their instinctive aggression, wasting ammunition in a futile gesture of bloodlust long before they could have a hope of finding a target. Nevertheless, it was a sobering sight.

'That's it,' I voxed. 'You're out of time. Get moving!'

'In a moment.' Sautine sounded infuriatingly calm. 'Lina, Belle, grab a can each.' I turned my gaze back to the tank. Two of the crewwomen were breaking shells out of the pallet still lying on the sand. A moment later they began staggering back to their vehicle encumbered by the weights they were carrying.

'You don't have time for this!' I said, my voice rising a little. Felicia scooped up the pallet and began to pilot the Sentinel back towards the ridge, moving in the peculiar jerky run common to such vehicles travelling at speed, which I always find uncannily reminiscent of a startled snowhen.[1]

'I'm not running without something to keep them off our backs!' Sautine snapped back.

I swept the amplivisor towards the onrushing orks, then back to the tank. To my relief, the two crewwomen were disappearing inside, and the tracks were beginning to turn. Sautine scrambled aboard as the tank ground past her, flecks of paint springing from the armour plate as a couple of lucky shots found their mark, and the hatch slammed shut. When I heard her voice again, it was faintly breathless. 'See? Plenty of time.'

---

1. A species of proverbially timid ground-dwelling fowl, indigenous to the deep mountain valleys of equatorial Valhalla.

'Let's hope so,' I said, my eyes glued to the amplivisor. The tank was picking up speed, but the orks were closing fast, taking renewed heart from the closeness of their prey. I swallowed, my mouth dry, and became suddenly aware of Piers standing at my shoulder, equally tense. 'Have we got anything we can cover them with from this range?'

'Nothing,' the young lieutenant said, his voice grim.

'We can take care of ourselves now.' Sautine sounded confident at any rate. The turret of the fleeing tank began to traverse, the cannon, slewing round to point back towards the advancing ork horde. Just when I was beginning to think she'd left it too late, the ork gunners finally beginning to find their mark, a puff of smoke erupted from the barrel, followed a second or two later by the muted thunderclap of the discharge.

The shot was a good one, fully justifying the risk of allowing the enemy to close the distance, detonating against the front armour of a buggy, which appeared to be mounting a rack of crude rockets. The shell penetrated the armour easily, detonating inside the vehicle, which erupted in a fireball. A moment later the warheads of the rockets cooked off too, sending shards of flaming debris pin-wheeling through the air in all directions to disrupt the enemy advance. By great good fortune, the main body of the blazing wreck slewed sideways, ramming a second buggy and overturning it. Locked together, the two piles of scrap started blazing merrily, a single stunned greenskin staggering to its feet after apparently being thrown clear, by a miracle. It just had time to appreciate its good fortune before being mashed flat by another of the ramshackle vehicles, too fixated on engaging the tank to take any notice of stray pedestrians.

'That gave them something to think about,' Piers commented.

I shook my head. 'They're still coming. Get everyone ready. The moment they come into range, I want as much covering fire as we can pour down there.'

The sand around the tank and the power lifter was being churned up by the enemy fire, rippling like water on a beach. Felicia was evading with every scrap of agility the sturdy little walker possessed, but it could only be a matter of time before she took a hit in that massive container of promethium, and when that happened it would all be over. The same thought had evidently occurred to her. To my astonishment she pivoted on the spot, continuing to run the thing backwards almost as fast as she'd been able to go forwards. (Something even a veteran Sentinel pilot would have thought twice about, but Felicia's instinctive rapport with machinery was truly exceptional, even for a tech-priest.) Another of the buggies tried to close, and she hosed it down with the flamer. The wash of fire didn't do any noticeable damage to the vehicle itself, but the driver was immolated on the spot, blazing away merrily like a purgation night effigy.[1] Which, being an ork, wasn't enough to kill him outright of course, before expiring, he tried to

---

1. *A reference to a peculiar annual ritual on several of the Imperial worlds coreward of the Damocles Gulf, in which life-sized dummies representing enemies of the Imperium are ceremonially burned on communal bonfires. After which the local ecclesiarchs lead prayers of thanks for the Emperor's protection, and everyone else indulges in an evening of wild debauchery.*

ram the Sentinel. Fortunately, Felicia was ready for that, pirouetting the clumsy machine neatly out of his way, and the buggy disappeared over the horizon leaving a trail of greasy smoke in its wake.

'All units stand by!' Piers ordered, a ripple of anticipation sweeping along the line of troopers and irregulars, followed almost immediately by an air of deadly intent. Everywhere I looked, in brief snatches, reluctant to tear my gaze away from the drama unfolding in the narrow field of the amplivisor, I saw lasguns being steadied and heavy weapon teams preparing to fire. Luskins had evidently picked a target already, swinging the barrel of his rocket launcher almost infinitesimally as he tracked it, while Jodril was laying out a line of replacement rounds ready to load again the instant his teammate had fired; an alternating sequence of frag and krak rounds, clearly intended to disable a vehicle and take out the crew as they disembarked. Over to my left, I made out Demara lying prone behind her new toy, finger on the trigger, but to my vague and relieved surprise resisting the temptation to fire early, while Tamworth prepared another belt of ammunition.

'Outrider two,' the scout team reported. 'They're bypassing the supply dump.' Hardly a surprise, but disappointing all the same. It looked as though we were going to have to do this the hard way.

Down on the plain, the Leman Russ fired again, taking out one of the trucks, but it was their last shot, and we all knew it. A moment later, Sautine confirmed the fact.

'We're dry,' she said matter-of-factly.

'Keep going,' I said as encouragingly as I could, while Felicia barbequed another buggy incautious enough to get within range. 'You're almost there.' I glanced at Piers, who nodded confirmation.

'Tullock, drop a few rounds behind our friends.'

'You got it, LT.' A second or two later I heard the unmistakable popping of multiple mortar rounds leaving the tubes, and trained my amplivisor back on the tank and the power lifter. The rounds seemed to take an eternity to arrive, but when they did they threw up a cloud of pulverised soil between the fleeing vehicles and their ork pursuers, who seemed gratifyingly disconcerted by the surprise. The leading buggies were almost within the beaten zone, at least a couple of them momentarily losing control as the explosions erupted under their noses, but true to their bestial nature they simply forged on, heedless of the possibility of being hit. Felicia spun the power lifter round again and began bounding up the slope, opening up a slight lead on the tank, which began growling its way up the incline behind her.

'That's it,' I said. 'They're in range. Fire at will, try not to hit our own people.' The last I added in a faintly jocular tone, but the warning was necessary anyway. The militia crews were barely familiar with their new weapons, and couldn't be relied on for anything approaching accuracy.

Fortunately the same couldn't be said for the PDF troopers. They might not have been up to Imperial Guard standards, but months of fighting had more than made up for the deficiencies in their training and standard of discipline. Luskins picked off one of the trucks with a krak rocket, neat as you please, just before the first wave of ork vehicles disappeared under a barrage of mortar shells, which left two of them very definitely out of the fight. The whole of our ragtag army opened up then, although the chances of hitting anything with a lasgun at this range by anything other than sheer dumb luck were minimal (which Jurgen proved almost immediately by picking off the driver of one of the buggies, which obligingly grounded itself in one of the craters left by the mortar bombardment). Rockets, autocannon rounds, bolter shells and lascannon bolts rained down on the greenskins, throwing them into even greater confusion, and slaughtering the crews of the vehicles which had become bogged down or disabled.

'Keep firing!' I yelled, my laspistol out and spitting futile bolts down the slope at nothing in particular, but looking appropriately martial, I hoped. We were taking some return fire, but it was as sporadic and aimless as I'd come to expect from the greenskins, and only a couple of our people went down. 'Drive them back!'

'My pleasure.' The Leman Russ joined us at the crest of the ridge at last; a few forlorn ork rounds spanging disconsolately from the armour plate, and Sautine popped the top hatch as it rolled to a halt. 'Get the rest of those rounds up here!' Felicia obligingly trotted up with the pallet of shells which, against all the odds, she'd kept a firm grip on throughout the chase, and the tankies started handing them off into the bowels of their chariot (which for some reason had been decorated with a crudely-executed cartoon of a red-furred, bushy-tailed creature in flak armour carrying a lasgun, with the word *Vixens* stencilled beneath it.[1]).

'They're breaking,' outrider two reported after a moment.

Jurgen shook his head. 'No they're not. They'll just regroup, and come at us again. It's what they do.' Well, he was the nearest thing we had to an expert on these creatures' behaviour, so I was inclined to listen.

'What can we do to discourage them?' I asked.

My aide shrugged. 'Keep them apart. The smaller a group gets, the more disheartened they are. But if they manage to regroup they'll start to ignore their own casualties again.' An afterthought seemed to strike him. 'And concentrate on the big ones. The little ones will run anyway.' A quick glance through the amplivisor was enough to confirm this much at least, the slighter figures of the gretchin scuttling away from the carnage as fast as their misshapen lower limbs would carry them. They seemed to be heading for the supply dump, no doubt hoping to find refuge behind the solid earthworks protecting it. An attempt, I reflected grimly, which was going to backfire on them badly.

An idea began to coalesce around the information Jurgen had just given me.

'Frag rounds,' I ordered. 'Keep the survivors dispersed.' If anyone wondered what I was playing at they didn't bother to argue. A moment later, my ears were assaulted by the thunderclap of the Leman Russ firing, and another of the ork trucks exploded into scrap.

---

1. *Evidently the nickname of the unit Sautine and her crew were originally attached to.*

'Don't have any of those,' Sautine informed me laconically. 'So if it's all right with you we'll just keep taking the transport out.'

'Feel free,' I assured her. The main thrust of my makeshift plan appeared to be working: as the groups of orks dwindled in numbers, their fighting spirit seemed to drain away too, just as Jurgen had predicted, and they began to pull back in ones and twos, sometimes in groups as large as half a dozen. I directed our fire as best I could under the circumstances, keeping them separated by bursts of autocannon fire or a sudden flurry of mortar rounds, until to my immense relief, I realised the greenskin retreat was turning into a rout. One by one, the surviving vehicles wheeled about and made for the illusory safety of the supply dump, the little clumps of orks on foot following as best they could. A cheer went up all along the ridge line as our makeshift army scented their victory, and the firing finally petered out as even the most enthusiastic irregular eventually realised that the last surviving greenskin was now well outside the effective range of their weapon. I tracked them with the amplivisor until the last hobbling figure made it as far as the berm.

'Tayber,' I voxed. 'Whenever you're ready.'

'No point in hanging about,' the sergeant agreed, clearly determined not to seem any less calm about things than I appeared to be. For a moment nothing seemed to happen, and I was just beginning to wonder if our careful preparations had been discovered and neutralised and if I should ask Sautine to try lobbing a couple of shells into the compound and hope for the best, when the ground shuddered beneath my feet.

'Golden throne!' Demara said, glee and awe intermingling in her voice, and I've no doubt she wasn't the only one to feel that way. The installation was gone, in a flash of eye-stabbing brilliance, transposed in a heartbeat to a thick pall of dust, debris and smoke which rose into the clear desert air like a fart from the bowels of hell.

'Well, that takes care of the orks,' I said, holstering my sidearm with a suitably theatrical flourish, 'at least for today.'

'Oh well.' Demara shrugged, clearly relishing the prospect of repeating the performance. 'Plenty more where they came from.'

'Quite right, miss,' Jurgen agreed, nodding sagely.

Editorial Note:

There now follows one of the many frustrating lacunae in Cain's account of his activities. Typically, these occur where he considers that nothing of particular interest has happened in the interim, picking up his account some hours, days, or, as in this instance, weeks after the previous incident he's described. At least here he does elide the intervening period, but since he does so both briefly and in his habitual offhand manner I felt that a more comprehensive overview of events was warranted at this juncture.

Readers wanting to know more about this stage of Cain's journey are referred to the volume of Sergeant Tayber's memoirs previously cited, which goes into every skirmish in exhaustive detail, along with far more than anyone really needs to know about the minutiae of desert survival, particularly in regard to the processes necessary to recycle urine into potable water.

From *Green Skins and Black Hearts: The Ork Invasion of Perlia* by Hismyonie Kallis, 927 M41

THE DESTRUCTION OF the supply dump was enough to confirm the impression the high command was beginning to form, that something of unexpected significance was occurring in the very heart of the ork held territories, although at that time they had no idea of who might be responsible. If they were even aware of Cain's existence then it would only have been as an unfortunate footnote to the Battle of the Halo, a lone survivor who had almost made it to safety before being killed by an opportunistic marauder.[1] Nevertheless, the explosion was large enough to direct the attention of their orbital sensor nets to the site, from where they were able to track the progress of what was to become the legendary March of the Liberator.

We can only imagine their astonishment at the apparent appearance from nowhere of the first significantly sized fighting force to be sighted on the eastern continent since the greenskins overran the territory. Indeed, initially, they concluded that Cain's convoy

---

1. *In fact Cain's status at this point was still officially 'killed in action.' His brief flurry of communication after making orbit should have changed this to 'missing, believed dead,' but thanks to the usual bureaucratic inertia of the Administratum this adjustment wasn't made until shortly after he rejoined his regiment. The ensuing confusion was to take over a year to sort out; after a few more such incidents the munitorium issued standing instructions that he should be kept on the active roster at all times whatever reports they received to the contrary. (Which accounts for the fact that he's the only person in the history of the galaxy to still be officially regarded as on active service subsequent to being buried with full military honours.)*

consisted of orks, engaged in the usual round of internecine squabbling endemic to the race, and that the Imperial vehicles among the company had been captured by the enemy rather than the other way round.

That impression hardly lasted the first week, however. Analysis of the ensuing engagements showed a tactical sophistication unheard of among the greenskins, with clear evidence of Imperial units acting in accordance with standard battlefield doctrines. From that point on, as the patchwork fighting force swept from victory to victory, its numbers swelling with every civilian liberated and every unit of stragglers absorbed, it could no longer be denied that control of the occupied region was slipping inexorably from the conqueror's grasp.

TWENTY

Jurgen's pessimism notwithstanding, we made pretty good progress over the next few weeks. As we continued to hop from supply dump to supply dump our numbers grew, each stop adding another trickle of isolated units responding to our vox hails, and our scouts ran across the occasional straggler, themselves. It wasn't until after we'd left the desert behind that things really started to improve. Gradually the heat and the sand gave way to cool green vegetation, and the ruins of untended fields replaced the monotony of the unending dunes.

That led to other problems, of course. Now we were entering what had been more civilised climes, we were being funnelled into what remained of the road network, the cultivated ground being far harder for our motley collection of vehicles to plough across than the open desert. Not to mention the walls, fences, and other obstructions, which would have bogged us down if we'd tried to negotiate them. Luckily, Kolfax was still equal to the challenge, having found an official mapslate of the road network at the regional office of his former employers, in a bombed-out township we swept through the morning after leaving the desert for good. (Adding another bunch of civilians to our baggage train in the process, but on the whole I suppose the trade-off was worth it.[1]) With that in hand, we were able to split our forces, spreading them out along several parallel routes, co-ordinating the whole thing over the vox. That kept us moving through the main agricultural zone at a reasonable speed, avoiding too many bottlenecks, and on a wide enough front to reinforce any groups who ran into more greenskins than they could conveniently handle by themselves, without too much difficulty.

'So far so good,' I said one evening, settled comfortably in the kitchen of an isolated farmhouse in the foothills of the mountain range, which just for once had turned out to have its roof still on. We'd reached sufficient altitude for the air to be growing perceptibly chiller, much to Jurgen's evident delight, although everyone else seemed to share my reservations about the fact, keeping as close to the fire he'd kindled in the grate as possible. Kolfax nodded, studying the mapslate.

---

1. The ork garrison in the town of Sandsedge was wiped out in the engagement, the Imperial column having taken them completely by surprise. They took some casualties themselves, of course, but by this time the steady trickle of newly contacted stragglers joining the group more than made up for the losses they sustained.

'You've got us this far,' he acknowledged, in the tone of a man admitting that this was something he'd never expected to see, 'but now it gets really difficult.' The rest of our little group leaned in across the polished wooden tabletop, scarred from generations of use, and heaped with discarded plates, which Jurgen was just beginning to clear.

Piers and Tayber were there, of course, the *de facto* leaders of the military contingent. We'd acquired a few more officers and NCOs of equal rank to both in the course of our travels, but they'd been with me longer than anyone else, and I trusted them accordingly (or, to be a little more accurate, distrusted them less than anyone else in the unit apart from Jurgen). We were up to about company strength,[1] although our patchwork organisational structure was like nothing the authors of the *Tactica Imperialis* would recognise, and I'd granted them battlefield promotions to keep the lines of command relatively clear. Piers was now a captain, at least in theory,[2] and Tayber his CSM.[3] I'd also invited Norbert, who had stayed on top of the increasingly complex logistical problems presented by the steady growth of our merry little band with an ease which astonished me, and Felicia, both as our

1. Probably around three hundred soldiers, if Cain is being literal, although as usual he's infuriatingly vague about specifics.

2. Technically, all such promotions conferred by a commissar would be subject to subsequent ratification by the munitorum, although, since to oppose the decision would be likely to attract commissarial attention to the objector, this would just be a formality in all but the most exceptional of circumstances.

3. Company Sergeant Major, the senior NCO of a company.

technical expert and because she was by far the most congenial company in the bunch, to join us.

'You mean the mountains,' I said, and Kolfax nodded.

'Precisely.' He gestured at the display, zooming in towards the sector we currently occupied. 'At the moment, we're spread out along a two-kilometre wide front, running along these roads, here.' We were roughly in the centre, of course, with the armour spearheading our advance,[1] the mechanised infantry on our flanks, and the scouts ranging ahead to spot any unpleasant surprises. The irregulars and the civilians were with us too, as protected as we could contrive, and, if I'm honest, adding an extra layer of expendable cannon fodder between me and any greenskin formation large enough to threaten us directly. 'The problem is, we're almost into them already, and the higher we go the fewer options we have.' He indicated the network of highways, which were already beginning to narrow towards a single choke point. 'We'll be at the pass in less than a week, and once that happens there's only one way to go.'

'And the greenies will know that,' Tayber put in helpfully, as if I needed his assistance to spot the blindingly obvious. We'd made enough of a nuisance of ourselves on our journey so far for me to be pretty sure that they'd want to shut us down once and for all, and, dim as they were, it should have been pretty evident, even to them, where we were making for. My

1. *By this time Sautine's Leman Russ had been joined by two more tanks of the same type, a Basilisk, and a pair of captured orkish battlewagons apparently based on a looted Chimera chassis.*

palms tingled, anticipating the ambush I was certain would be lying in wait for us as we tried to thread that narrow gorge.

'That would explain the reports we've been getting from the outriders,' Piers added. I nodded soberly. Our scouts had spotted several large formations of greenskins following our trail in the last few days, but hanging back with a patience completely at odds with everything I thought I'd begun to understand about the creatures. No doubt they were waiting for us to begin traversing the pass and engage the ambushing force, before falling on us from behind.

'You're absolutely sure there's no other way through the mountains?' I asked Kolfax, already knowing what his answer was going to be. 'No back trails like there were in the desert?'

He shook his head. 'Nothing the vehicles can manage.' He tapped the screen, just above the pass. 'This is it. Unless we divert around the whole range. If we head north for about eight hundred kilometres we can skirt the edge of it, keeping to the foothills.' His tone was all the indication I needed of what he thought about that idea, and I nodded in agreement. We'd be under attack by the greenskins the whole way, and even if by some miracle we were able to get around the mountains with the bulk of our forces intact, we'd still have the same distance to travel southwards before we reached the peninsular. This time we'd be penned in to a narrow coastal strip, where the orks could mass their forces against us with even greater ease.

'It looks like we're frakked,' I said. I turned to Piers, trying to hide the apprehension churning in my gut.

'We'll have to chance running the pass. If we can punch through whatever they've got waiting for us before the trailing force can get close enough to engage, we might just get away with it.'

'That's a pretty big if,' the young captain said.

I nodded soberly. 'Even so,' I said, 'I think it's the best chance we've got.' The hell of it was, I was right, and everyone knew it; hardly any chance is still better than none at all, a call I would be forced to make innumerable times over the years, and usually in straits far more dire than these. (Like my desperate leap through the necron warp portal on Interitus Prime, or the time I found myself charging a daemon of Khorne with just a rusty bayonet and a vial of holy water, both occasions which still feature strongly in my dreams even after all these years.) I smiled grimly, trying to put heart into the others with a wholly counterfeit display of resolution. 'We can't go over it, we can't go under it, so...'

'Perhaps we can,' Felicia said thoughtfully, looking at the mapslate in a manner I can only describe as speculative. She pointed to a lake, filling a mountain valley not far from the main road though the pass. There was some kind of building on the shoreline, tagged with the sigil of the Adeptus Mechanicus. I looked at her, trying not to get carried away with the sudden surge of hope I'd felt at her words. Despite her impulsiveness and casual optimism, I'd learned in the past few weeks that her judgement could usually be trusted.

'How do you mean?' I asked. By way of reply she zoomed in on the image to its maximum resolution. I studied the topography thus revealed in a state of vague incomprehension. 'It looks like a dead end to me.'

The lake was at the head of a long, narrow valley, which had been dammed at the top end to form a vast artificial reservoir. A thin trail wound up it, following the line of a riverbed in which a trickle of water still flowed, no doubt fed by the sluices, but the banks were a great deal further apart; clearly it had carried far more water in the past. As the road approached the dam, it diverged from the depleted watercourse, rising up the valley side in a series of steep switchbacks, to run across the top of the vast structure, before terminating in front of the building I'd first noticed on the map. This too appeared to be huge, almost large enough to house a titan,[1] and I couldn't imagine what its purpose might be.

Norbert frowned, something obviously striking his innate sense of order as out of place, and indicated the partially dried-up riverbed.

'Where's the rest of the water going?' he asked.

Now he came to point it out, it was obvious that the upper reaches of the river above the lake were feeding far more into it than was appearing through the sluices at the bottom of the dam.

Felicia smiled. 'Under the mountains,' she replied. She reduced the scale of the map again, and indicated another Mechanicus shrine on the lower slopes of the range, this time on the far side from us. I drew in my breath. It was almost on the coastal plain, barely a

---

1. Cain is exaggerating somewhat: even a Warhound would have to kneel down in order to drop below the roofline.

hundred kilometres from the peninsular. If we could somehow reach it without going through the pass we'd outflank the orks, and take the main force no doubt still massing next to the land bridge completely by surprise. For the first time there seemed to be a real chance of getting across it to safety. 'There's a generating station there, powered by the water from this reservoir, and an aqueduct connecting the two.'

'That's all very well,' I said, my head reeling. 'But it would take us days to get everyone that far on foot. And if the greenskins find the tunnel before we get through...'

Felicia laughed, no doubt deducing the image I had in my mind of something akin to the concrete channel Jurgen and I had waded through in Prosperity Wells. 'We'll take the vehicles, silly,' she said. 'The aqueduct's meant to feed a whole temple of turbines, not a couple of kitchen taps. It's ten metres across at least.'

'But isn't it full of water?' Jurgen asked, homing in on the obvious flaw in the plan.

Felicia nodded. 'Of course it is. That's the whole point. But we can drain it.' She pointed to the dam again. 'Once we open the sluices, the water level in the reservoir will drop rapidly. Within a couple of hours the intake vents will be exposed. Getting them off won't be too much of a problem.' She shrugged. 'They're designed that way, so the repair crews can get in for routine maintenance.'

'Sounds good,' I conceded, beginning to feel cautiously optimistic for the first time since this impromptu conference had begun. 'How do we get the vehicles down there?'

'The same way the repair crews do,' Felicia said, with a trace of asperity. 'You don't think they walk all that way, do you?' Well, it was a fair point, so I nodded in agreement.

'I think we've got a plan,' I said.

It still looked good the next morning, despite my paranoid streak worrying away at it all night, trying to find the catch. There was only one that I could see, and I confided it to Felicia over breakfast.

'The valley's a dead end,' I pointed out. 'If the orks find us before we're ready to go, we'll be boxed in.'

'That's true.' She chewed her toast thoughtfully, and plucked another slice from my plate with her mechadendrite. After a couple of months of decent food she'd filled out nicely, and in all the right places, but still hadn't shaken the habit of eating everything she could at every opportunity. 'But we'd only have to hold them off for a short while. And the terrain would be with us.' Like everyone else in the convoy, she'd acquired a thorough grounding in the practicalities of infantry combat. I nodded in agreement.

'That's not what worries me,' I said. 'Suppose they come after us, or just flood the tunnel once we're down there?'

Felicia nodded, and accepted another mug of recaff from the attentively hovering Jurgen, who was barely able to suppress a shudder at the thought of all that water.

'Blow the tunnel behind us,' she said. 'By the time they dig through the rubble we'll be long gone. And if we wreck the sluices before we leave, they won't be able to raise the water level enough to flush us out.'

'That sounds good,' I said. We had enough explosives with us to do the job, neat as you please, so I couldn't see a problem with that. Now my last reservation was gone I was almost looking forward to the venture. 'It's a shame we can't stick around to enjoy the expressions on their faces when they realise we've given them the slip.'

We resumed our journey in something approaching high spirits. True, we'd have to consolidate our scattered forces again, but I could comfortably leave that to Piers and Tayber to sort out. Confident that the closest enemy patrol was some kilometres away, I stuck my head out of the top hatch of the Chimera, enjoying the crisp morning air while I could. Felicia's plan might just get us around the main choke point, but while we were passing through the mountains we'd still be vulnerable to ambushes, and I'd be spending most of the trip behind the comforting solidity of armour plate.

In the event, things went practically without a hitch, unless you count a couple of our foraging parties running into firefights with isolated groups of greenskins, which both ended with gratifying suddenness as soon as Sautine arrived on the scene, and before the week was out I found myself trundling up the narrow valley leading to the dam.

The mountain scenery was even bleaker than I'd envisaged from the topographical display we'd studied, but not without grandeur. High peaks loomed over us, capped by snowfields which Jurgen stared at longingly, but he was to be disappointed on this trip; our destination lay below the snowline, and the opposite end of the aqueduct was a couple of thousand metres below us, almost at sea level. Beside the road, the trickle of water from the sluices in the dam ahead rippled and chuckled in its oversized channel, and thick scrub stained the valley sides with mottled shades of brown, green, and the occasional vivid patch of yellow or purple.

The dam itself loomed over everything, a vast wall of dull, grey rockcrete, which cut across the valley ahead of us like the outer defences of a fortified city, and I tried not to think about the sheer volume of water it held back. Intellectually, I knew that it had held solid for decades, but I couldn't help picturing the scene in my mind of what it would be like if it were to suddenly give way. Shuddering at the image, I turned in the turret of our carrier, and waved to Felicia, who was pacing us easily in her modified Sentinel.

'How do you know so much about this place, anyway?' I asked. When she replied, her voice was as warm as ever, despite the attenuation of the vox link.

'It's one of the great marvels of the planet,' she said. 'Every tech-priest knows about it. We study the systems in the seminary.'

'How very fortunate for us,' I said dryly.

Felicia laughed. 'It's fascinating stuff, even if you ignore all the local superstition about the place.'

'How do you mean?' I asked. 'Surely the shrine is properly sanctified in the name of the Emperor?' I'm not the most pious of men, as I'd be the first to admit, but even in those days I'd seen enough of the malevolence of the galaxy to think twice about tempting fate, and trespassing on unhallowed ground definitely qualified as that in my book. (Of course that was nothing to some of the sights I was to see in later years, the inside of an eldar reiver citadel, a necron tomb world, or a city tainted by the touch of Chaos being far more blasphemous abominations than anything my callow younger self could possibly have envisaged, but I digress.)

'The Omnissiah,' Felicia corrected, her voice amused, 'but yes, of course it is. The stories go back long before the dam was here, though.'

'They do?' Despite its obvious artificiality I found that hard to believe. Somehow, that gigantic wall looked as though it had always been there.

Felicia nodded. 'Thousands of years. How do you think it got its name in the first place?'

'What name is that?' I asked, trying to fight down a growing sense of foreboding.

Felicia's voice took on a familiar sense of mischief. 'The Valley of Daemons,' she said cheerfully.

TWENTY-ONE

DESPITE THE MYRIAD claims on my attention, I couldn't quite shake the sense of foreboding Felicia's casual words had stirred up in me, but there was no time to quiz her further on the matter, as our convoy finally reached the vast citadel looming over the dam and began to spread out around the piazza which fronted it. Fully as large as a parade ground, it was surfaced in tiles the size of my thumbnail, which made up a vast mosaic of images sacred to the cult of the Machine God. I'd have expected work so delicate to be ground to powder under the tracks of our war machines, but to my surprise they weren't even scratched.

'Set up the heavy stuff to cover the road,' I ordered Sautine, who I'd put in charge of our armour detatchment. She nodded.

'Already on it.' She gestured towards the *Vixen*, its turret and lascannon pointing across the valley towards the narrow ribbon of rockcrete clinging to the slope on the other side, flanked by the other Leman Russes. 'And I've got the Basilisk set up to drop some heavy ordnance on the valley mouth if the greenskins try to get through before we're ready to pull out.'

'Good thinking,' I complimented her. The mobile artillery piece would be better employed in that role, where its greater range could be used to its fullest effect. A couple of Earthshaker shells ought to disrupt any ork advance through that narrow choke point very nicely, I thought.

'Shame we can't blow the dam,' Sautine commented, with a regretful look at the causeway running along the top of the two hundred metre-high wall to where we now stood. 'That'd stop them from following right enough.'

'It would,' I agreed, but there was no chance of that;we didn't have enough explosives in the entire convoy to put a dent in that vast expanse of rockcrete. 'You could try mining the causeway.'

'I'll get someone on it,' Sautine agreed, turning away.

Well, that was our defence taken care of. Time to find out whether Felicia was right, and salvation lay a few metres below the surface of the huge and placid expanse of water stretching away into the distance, or whether I'd just led us into a dead-end deathtrap.

I turned and made my way through the throng of soldiers and irregulars, exchanging a word or a joke with a few random faces, dispensing morale boosting platitudes to a handful more, and kept an eye out for a familiar white robe.

The tech-priest was waiting for me at the entrance to the shrine, which loomed over us, votive statuary encrusting its surface, which still seemed somehow to retain a purity of line and form in the best aesthetic traditions of the Mechanicus. Jurgen was with her, a lasgun in his hands, and I have to admit that I was glad to see him. Felicia had made it very clear that the control shrine was consecrated ground, on which only ordained tech-priests were supposed to tread, and that accompanying her was a rare privilege for anyone outside the Adeptus Mechanicus. (To tell the truth I'd have been perfectly happy to leave her to deal with whatever needed doing inside, but she'd pointed out that command decisions might need to be taken, and I could do that most effectively if I was on the spot at the time.)

Her artisans hovered nearby, expressions of envy on their faces, no doubt hoping that their presence would also turn out to be required inside the towering temple of technological marvels.

'Ready?' she asked, glancing in my direction, and I nodded, wondering if that was entirely true. 'Good. We might as well get on with it, then.' It was only at this point I realised that she was a great deal more nervous than she would have liked me to know, and somehow that increased my own confidence again. Leaving Jurgen to fall in at my shoulder as usual, his distinctive aroma assuring me that he'd done so without me having to turn my head to check, I led the way towards the massive bronze portal sealing the entrance to the shrine. After a moment, Felicia joined me, keeping roughly a pace ahead of us, as befitted an excursion onto consecrated ground.

'That's odd.' Her voice held a note of puzzlement rather than alarm, but I found myself loosening my weapons in their holster and scabbard, nevertheless. If push came to shove, I'd use them first and argue about the theological implications later.

'What is?' I asked, noting out of the corner of my eye that Jurgen had followed my lead, flicking off the safety catch of his lasgun. The doors loomed over us, thick slabs of bronze embossed with the cogwheel sigil of the Adeptus, fully four times the height of a man. One of them stood slightly ajar, just wide enough to admit our little party, and Felicia indicated it, frowning in puzzlement.

'That ought to be sealed. Only a consecrated tech-priest should be able to open it.'

'Maybe the staff left it like that when they evacuated,' Jurgen suggested. Felicia shook her head.

'That's just it. They should still be here, carrying out the rituals of operation. This is a sacred site, they wouldn't just abandon it.'

'Then why didn't they come out to meet us?' I asked. I gestured behind us, to the scores of troopers and refugees and our ragtag collection of vehicles. 'They must have noticed us coming.'

'Maybe the greenskins got here first,' Jurgen suggested, looking around warily for something to shoot at. I shook my head.

'Look at the place. It's still intact. The orks would have wrecked it.' There was no sign at all of the wanton destruction an ork assault would have wreaked.

Not so much as a single pockmark in the immaculate white stonework from a stray stubber round. The only creatures that seemed to have left their mark on the building were the local birds. Curiously, however, I found the lack of evidence of foul play even more sinister than its presence might have been. I fought down a rising sense of unease. 'They must just be hiding,' I added, decisively. 'Once they realise we're friends they'll come on out.'

'Unless the daemons have got them,' Jurgen suggested gloomily.

'That's just local superstition,' Felicia snapped, a little too hastily, and my aide subsided.

'Nevertheless,' I said, drawing my laspistol, 'perhaps we should go first.' I was expecting her to object, of course, or I'd never have suggested it, but to my well-concealed surprise she nodded.

'That might be more prudent,' she agreed.

Well, there was no help for it after that, I couldn't risk losing face, so I levelled the weapon and slipped through the gap, my nerves wound up tighter than harp strings. Jurgen followed, his lasgun seeking a target, and a moment later Felicia joined us.

'It's not too late to bring a squad along as escort,' I suggested, taking stock of our surroundings as I did so. Nobody seemed to be shooting at us, but there were plenty of places that might have concealed a sniper, so I kept my gun in my hand in any case.

We were in a wide, high room, artfully lit by concealed luminators, which filled the space with a diffuse glow, no doubt intended to seem both functional and meditative. Arcane mechanisms I couldn't identify were mounted on plinths, for display or veneration, and Felicia stared at them with wide, wondering eyes, although to me they just looked like so much scrap metal.

'No,' she said, her voice hushed. 'We can't profane this place any more than we need to.'

'Fine,' I agreed. 'You're the expert.' Nevertheless, I voxed Tayber. 'Get a couple of kill teams together,' I ordered. 'Ready to come in the moment we call, but not a second before.' I glanced across at the unnaturally subdued tech-priest. 'Is that all right with you?' To my relief she nodded.

'Yes,' she said. 'If we need to call them in, this place will already have been desecrated far more than it would be by their presence.' Which was pragmatic, I suppose, though hardly comforting.

'All right,' I said, trying to get orientated, 'where to?'

'The control chapel should be that way.' She pointed towards a staircase at the far end of the entrance hall. The treads were moving, tending upwards, and we moved towards it as quickly as we could, Jurgen and I remaining alert for any sign of movement among the display cases.

'Commissar.' My aide came to a sudden halt, although an intervening lump of ironmongery prevented me from seeing what had attracted his attention, for a moment. As I rounded the thing and saw what lay on the polished marble floor at his feet, I turned, hoping to block Felicia's view, but it was too late. She was standing right behind me, staring at the dead tech-priest with an expression of slack-jawed horror.

'Do you know him?' I asked, and she shook her head slowly, trying to take in the enormity of it: a member of her own order, slain in the middle of a shrine.

'I've never been here before,' she reminded me. 'Just studied the plans.'

'He's been dead for a couple of weeks,' Jurgen added helpfully. Not killed during the invasion, then. 'Looks like the greenies have been here after all.'

'I don't think Felicia's daemons would have used a bolter,' I agreed. The explosive projectile had detonated inside the man's ribcage, killing him instantly, despite the signs of heavy augmentation packing his chest cavity. 'But the orks would have taken the place apart.'

'They would,' Jurgen agreed. 'And they wouldn't have been so accurate.'

It was only after he spoke that I realised he was right. The tech-priest had been killed with a single shot. Greenskins would have blazed away on full auto, leaving the floor and machine parts surrounding him pitted with impact craters.

'You think humans did this?' Felicia stared from one of us to the other in blank incomprehension. 'But why?'

'I haven't a clue,' I admitted, 'and right now it doesn't matter. We've a job to do here, and a lot of lives depend on us getting it done.'

To her credit, Felicia rallied quickly, no doubt inured to atrocity by her time among the orks and the battles we'd fought since her liberation. She nodded, only the paleness of her face betraying the effort of maintaining her composure.

'Then we'd better get on with it,' she said. 'Whoever's responsible will be long gone by now.'

That was true enough, although I wasn't to become privy to the answer to that particular riddle for more than a decade, and when I did find out what had happened there I can't honestly say that it eased my mind at all.

'Upwards, you said?' I began to lead the way towards the moving staircase, my senses heightened by the sense of imminent danger that the discovery of the corpse had triggered, and it was as well that they were. As I approached it, I noticed a flicker of movement out of the corner of my eye, and threw myself reflexively behind another of the lumps of metal littering the hall. As I did so, the unmistakable chatter of a heavy autocannon echoed through the space, the machine (whatever it was), behind which I was sheltering clanging like a temple bell from the impact.

'Tayber!' I yelled. 'We need backup, *now*! Heavy weapons! Move!'

'On our way,' the veteran sergeant assured me, and I stuck my head up as much as I dared, trying to get a glimpse of whoever was trying to kill us. Felicia had taken cover too, her white robe visible behind a plinth a couple of rows away, and the sudden *crack* of a las bolt ionising the air was enough to let me locate Jurgen (a moment or two before my nose could do the job). The bolt reached its target and expended itself harmlessly against an amalgam of augmetics and flesh, tall and wide as an ogryn and probably twice as smart.

'It's a combat servitor,' I voxed Tayber. No point in letting our backup come charging in blind. 'One autocannon, one chainfist.' I shot at it too, more in hope than expectation, and the thing's head swung slowly in my direction. That was stupid, I thought, I should have let Jurgen draw its fire. Oh well, too late now. 'It's taken some heavy damage,' I added, getting a closer look at the thing. It looked as though someone had hosed it down thoroughly with a heavy bolter, but not nearly thoroughly enough from where I was standing, its carapace pitted and scarred by the explosive detonations. Its close combat weapon seemed to be out of commission entirely, which was something at least, but it could still inflict enough impact damage with its arm alone to pulp an unarmoured human.

'Terminate intruders,' the thing grated through some kind of implanted voxcoder, obsessively repeating the last instruction it had been given in the irritating manner of such devices. 'Protect the sanctum.' It unloaded another burst of autocannon fire in my general direction, and took a heavy step towards me.

For a moment, I thought it was going to charge, but Jurgen shot it again and it halted, with something as close as a mindless automaton could come to an expression of confusion. Then its head turned in his direction and repeated the same phrase: 'Terminate intruders. Protect the sanctum.'

'Keep it busy!' I called to my aide as it fired again, in his direction this time, and turned to take a hesitant step towards him. There was a slim chance, I thought, but once again it was better than none; by the time our kill team arrived, we could all be dead, so there was no point waiting for them to save our necks. Powering up my chainsword, I ran at it as fast as I could, before I had the chance to think about what I was doing and change my mind.

I almost made it, before the thing sensed my approach and turned to face the more immediate threat. My humming blade glanced off the power cables sheathing its back, which a few seconds' rational thought would have told me were bound to be armoured anyway, raising a shower of sparks. It swung its chain fist, which thank the Emperor was still malfunctioning, and I ducked under the punch at the last possible minute, feeling the sudden chill as the wickedly serrated cutting teeth flicked the cap from my head.

I struck upwards with my chainsword, finding a fleshly component more by luck than judgement, and was rewarded with a torrent of foul-smelling ichor, which cascaded down the neck of my shirt. The thing swung back at me, but now its movements were stiff. I seemed to have disabled that arm, at least.

'Back off, commissar! We can't get a clear shot!' The feminine voice sounded vaguely familiar, but there was no time to worry about that now, I was fighting for my life against a machine designed to take it, and attempting to disengage would only give it the perfect chance. It staggered as Jurgen placed another shot squarely into its back, and I took advantage of its momentary distraction to spin round behind it and slash at those power cables again. A move, which had the same lack of success as before, I might add.

'Terminate intruders. Protect the sanctum.' The thing turned towards me again, and I dived for cover as it started to bring the autocannon to bear, knowing even as I did so that I'd never make it, and that there was no way in the galaxy it could possibly miss at this range... I heard a faint, derisory *click*, and rolled behind another pile of scrap, blessing every saint I could think of. The thing was dry. Whatever battle it had been in before must have depleted its ammunition almost completely. A moment later, I thought I must have been mistaken, as the distinctive thudding of an autocannon opened up again, but this time there was no whine of ricochetting bullets in my immediate vicinity, so I stuck my head out to see what was going on.

The servitor was staggering now, taking a hail of autocannon rounds at point-blank range, Demara and Tamworth hosing it down with the assurance of the veterans they'd become. The rest of Grenbow's team was with them, backing up their efforts with lasgun fire, and the former vox operator broke off shooting for a moment to wave a greeting to me. Damaged as the thing was, it couldn't stand up to that sort of sustained abuse for long. Abruptly its knee gave way and it fell heavily to the floor, where it shuddered like a freshly-killed corpse.

'Cease fire.' Felicia stood cautiously, edging out from behind her lump of metal, and after a nod from me the militia team complied. The servitor continued to twitch, attempting to rise, and the young enginseer took a few cautious steps towards it. Its head turned, apparently taking in her presence, and she held up her cogwheel talisman where the thing could see it (or register its presence in whatever manner it normally used).

'Terminate intruders,' it grated again, sounding vaguely confused this time. 'Protect the–'

'Cancel instructions,' Felicia said, slowly and clearly, her mechadendrite flexing behind her like the tail of a nervous cat. 'Power down.' She hesitated, seemingly on the verge of bolting if the thing failed to recognise her as being authorised to be there, but it made no move to attack her.

The moment stretched.

'Powering down,' the thing echoed suddenly. 'Entering standby mode. Some maintenance may be required.' It stopped moving.

'What the hell's something like that doing in a hydro station?' Demara asked.

'A good question,' I said, retrieving my hat, and placing it on my head with as much insouciance as I could muster given that my shirt was now soaking wet and smelling worse than Jurgen. I turned to Felicia. 'Any idea?'

'None whatsoever,' she replied, looking as baffled as I felt.

'Well we haven't got time to debate it,' I said. 'We need to get the sluices open.' I turned to Grenbow. 'You and your people escort her,' I added, 'in case there are any more of these things running around in here.' I had no intention of remaining inside myself, of course. I returned my attention to the vox. 'Piers, I want three more squads in here now. Search this place from top to bottom. If there are any more unwelcome surprises, I want to know about them.' I half expected Felicia to object, but she just nodded, tight-lipped.

'I'll get on it right away,' she said, turning towards the staircase.

'Already sweeping,' Tayber's familiar voice reassured me. 'We're on the lower level now.'

'What lower level?' Felicia's head snapped round. 'According to the plans, this is the ground floor.'

'Well we've found one,' her brother assured her. 'Behind that moving staircase.'

We hurried in the direction he'd indicated, which Felicia needed to do anyway to get to the sluice controls, and sure enough there was a big hole in the wall behind it.

'What could have done that?' Felicia asked. The edges were ragged, the rockcrete seared and scarred by immense heat.

I shrugged. 'A plasma gun, maybe a melta,' I said. At that point, I hadn't seen either used on the battlefield, but I was familiar enough with their effects from the occasional demonstration at the schola to take a reasonable guess at it. 'Whoever did this wanted access, and wasn't taking no for an answer.'

'Access to what, though?' Jurgen asked. There was a stairwell behind the wall, presumably accessed through a hidden doorway of some kind, which had effectively concealed its existence until someone or something had decided to remove the obstacle.

'There's a whole lot of rooms down here,' Tayber reported. 'Full of technical stuff.' He hesitated. 'And dead people. Well armed, most of them.'

'We'd better take a look,' I decided. I couldn't very well avoid whatever trouble this presaged unless I had the best possible idea of what was going on, and it was the sort of thing the people around me expected me to say anyway.

I glanced at Felicia. 'I hate to ask, but you might just spot something the rest of us would miss.'

'I agree.' She nodded. 'The sluices will just have to wait a few more minutes. Let's hope the greenskins do the same.'

'They seem to have ignored this place so far,' I said. The comely tech-priest nodded.

'That was before you led an army here,' she pointed out.

THE MYSTERIOUS LOWER level was pretty much as Tayber had described it. He met the three of us at the bottom of the staircase (Grenbow and the others having been left to guard our rear), with an expression of extreme disquiet. The other members of Bravo squad were with him, glancing around with a mixture of awe and apprehension.

'This is the central point,' he said, indicating corridors branching off in three directions (the fourth would simply have led straight into the reservoir, of course). There were bodies lying at the entrances to all three, ripped apart by bolter fire, but with enough remaining for me to be sure of their identities. Their crimson uniforms, their high proportion of augmetics, and the hellguns they were armed with were all the confirmation I needed.

'Scutarii,' I said. Tayber looked blank. 'Adeptus Mechanicus footsoldiers. They garrison forgeworlds, support the titan legions, that sort of thing. The question is – what were they doing here?' I glanced at Felicia, who looked as baffled as her brother.

'Guarding something, I suppose.' She looked around. 'Are there any tech-priests down here?'

'Yes.' Tayber nodded. 'All dead, mostly in that wing.' He gestured down the left-hand corridor. The chambers along it were large, well lit, and full of arcane devices, which, apart from the ones full of bolter holes, appeared to be fully functional. Most of them also held the corpses of tech-priests, in a similar state of disassembly as their erstwhile bodyguards.

'Any idea what they were doing?' I asked Felicia, as we stepped cautiously into a large room full of the usual collection of technological mysteries, and a couple of dead acolytes of the Omnissiah.

She looked around at the equipment surrounding us, the only parts of which I recognised being hololithic displays and a couple of pict screens.

'They seem to have been studying something,' she said. 'Most of these are analytical engines of one sort or another. I can't tell what they were researching though.'

She padded across to a control lectern, and activated a nearby hololith. The display flickered into life, projecting icons which meant nothing to me, but which left her frowning in consternation. 'Their databanks have been wiped. All the records are missing.'

'Very helpful,' I said dryly.

The enginseer stared at me, her expression grave. 'Perhaps that's just as well. If it was worth killing them to suppress whatever they'd discovered, I don't think I want to know what it was.'

'Neither do I,' I agreed, turning to leave the chamber. 'Let's do what we came here to do.'

'Commissar.' Luskins was waiting outside, Jodril with him as usual, his bulky rocket launcher slung across his shoulder where it continued to get in the way for as long as we were stuck in the narrow corridors. 'We've found something. Looks like a vault.'

That was precisely what it was, the thick impermium doorway leaving little doubt of that. It had clearly been forced. The mark of the energy weapon, which had been used to breach this place was unmistakable, what had evidently once been an elaborate locking mechanism melted to slag by its ravening heat. There was no clue as to what it might have contained, however, just bare metal shelves reflecting the overhead lights.

'We've wasted enough time here,' I decided, after another cursory sweep had turned up nothing more than a handful of additional corpses. 'Let's go get the sluices open and move out as quickly as we can.'

'You won't get any argument from me,' Felicia agreed, and we hurried up the stairs from that charnel pit as quickly as we could.

Once we'd regained the gently lit hall we'd entered by, I felt an undefinable sense of oppression lift from my soul, and we made straight for the moving staircase, our minds now completely focused on our primary mission. The other search teams had failed to find any more combat servitors lurking about the place, so I thought I might as well stick with the tech-priest for the time being, in case my presence was required in the control chapel after all.

My improved sense of well-being wasn't to last much longer, however. Almost as my boots hit the rising treads my commbead hissed into life again.

'Commissar,' Piers reported. 'The orks are here.'

TWENTY-TWO

For a few more moments, I was able to cling to the hope that it was only a scouting party which had found us, but that comforting illusion wasn't to last for long. The control chapel Felicia led us to had a wide, clear window looking out over the valley below, no doubt for proper reverential contemplation of the dam and reservoir, tech-priests in general being too far removed from the realms of the flesh to do anything as human as simply admiring the view (which under less stressful circumstances I would undoubtedly have found quite spectacular). Ignoring the wide banks of brass dials and countless switches inlaid in slabs of age-darkened timber, I hurried to the sheet of armourcrys and looked out and down, my breath stilling in my throat.

'There's thousands of them,' Jurgen said at my elbow, and for once I had to concede that he wasn't exaggerating. The entire valley mouth was choked with lurching vehicles, packed with howling greenskins, beginning to swarm towards us like a tyranid horde. Their sheer numbers were impeding their progress, as they funnelled into that narrow defile, but they were sorting themselves out in their usual brutally efficient fashion, the most aggressive and heavily-armed among them already pulling ahead of the pack. Those on the road were making the best time, but to my horror I noticed that the vast majority were simply not bothering to jostle for position on the highway, fanning out instead across the entire valley floor, trusting to the rugged construction of their vehicles and their hardy constitutions to forge across the relatively open ground at a rate I would scarcely have believed possible.

I was about to order the Basilisk to fire, when the unmistakable thud of an Earthshaker going off told me that Sautine had beaten me to it. Our artillery piece flung three shells in quick succession, all detonating in the heart of the onrushing throng, but we might just as well have been throwing stones into a pond for all the good it did, the tide of howling green death closing as fast as ever.

'How long have we got?' I voxed Piers, wishing I'd headed straight for the command Chimera and its array of instrumentation, instead of coming up here to keep an eye on the tech-priest. Watching this on an auspex screen would have been far less bowel loosening than being faced with the sight of the greenskins themselves.

'The first wave should close with us in about twenty minutes,' the young captain informed me, in surprisingly calm tones. 'They can't get the vehicles up here without coming across the dam, but we'll be vulnerable to their foot troops climbing the slope.'

'Well, that's something,' I said. 'If Sautine can keep the causeway clear, we can pick them off as they disembark.' Even that was a forlorn hope, though, the sheer number of the greenskins was bound to tell in the end. It looked from here as if all the groups trailing us had consolidated into a single formation, outnumbering us by at least eight to one.[1] If they'd had even half that number waiting for us in the pass we'd never have survived an attempt to run it, although I had to admit the alternative wasn't looking all that attractive at the moment either. I turned to Felicia. 'How long until the tunnel's clear of water?'

'I don't know.' Her voice was abstracted as she looked over the control lectern in front of her, ignoring the terrifying sight beyond the window with what seemed to me to be bordering on superhuman self-control.[2] 'It depends on how long it takes me to get the sluices open. The rituals are fairly simple, but it'll take a while before I can get it done on my own.' She glanced around the room, looking vaguely baffled. 'Now if I was an incense burner, where would I be?'

'Tayber,' I voxed, trying hard not to sound too impatient. 'Get the artisans up here. Felicia needs a hand.' I

---

1. *If Cain is being accurate about this, rather than exaggerating for effect, we can infer a horde of anything up to two and a half thousand orks; a formidable prospect to say the least.*

2. *Unless she hadn't even noticed it. Tech-priests do have an unnerving tendency to concentrate on their mysteries to the exclusion of what, to the rest of us, would seem like more pressing concerns.*

glanced at her a trifle apprehensively, wondering if I'd crossed some kind of line, but she simply nodded.

'That might help.'

'Good,' I said, as evenly as I could manage, which was quite an achievement under the circumstances as I'm sure you'll appreciate. 'If it does, how long until the tunnel's clear?'

'About two hours,' Felicia said matter-of-factly. 'That's after we get the sluices open, of course. But that shouldn't take more than an hour or so, if we can perform the rituals cleanly and invoke the Omnissiah's blessing on our first attempt.'

'You've got less than twenty minutes until we're up to the fundament in greenskins,' I pointed out, as patiently as possible, hoping that putting it into words wouldn't make it somehow inevitable. 'In three hours' time we'll all be dead... A lot sooner than that, probably.'

'I can't change the laws of theology,' Felicia snapped back. 'If we open the sluices safely, that's how long it'll take to drain. You'll just have to hold them off until we're done.'

'We'll try,' I said, as resolutely as I could, trying to mask the terror and despair that threatened to overwhelm me even as I spoke. 'Are you sure there isn't anything you can do to speed things up?'

'Positive,' the young tech-priest replied. She gestured towards one of the long boards of instrumentation, full of flickering dials recording information, which meant nothing to me. 'We'll have to move with extreme caution. If this place has been left unattended for weeks all kinds of systems are going to be unstable. A mistake now could be catastrophic.'

'Catastrophic would be infinitely preferable to dead for sure,' I said, a half-formed thought beginning to take root in my mind. 'What exactly is the problem?'

'In terms you can understand?' Felicia's voice was taking on an unmistakable edge of asperity, clearly nettled at my presumption in meddling with things best left to the Omnissiah's annointed. She pointed to a row of indicators, all glowing with a dull, hellish red. 'The power to run this place, and the surrounding villages, is generated by turbines at the base of the dam. When the current isn't being drawn, it's stored in capacitors, and no one's been drawing power since the orks invaded. That means they're fully charged, overloaded in fact, and extremely unstable. If we open the sluices fully, without taking the generators off line and draining off the excess charge first, they'll go up like a bomb. Is that clear enough for you?'

'Very clear, thank you,' I turned and hurried from the chapel, Jurgen at my heels as always, activating my commbead as I went. 'Sautine, how quickly can you retarget the Basilisk?'

'It'll take a few minutes,' the tank vixen said, sounding slightly confused, but trusting my judgement nevertheless. 'What's the new target?'

'The sluice gates at the base of the dam,' I told her. 'Can they depress the barrel that far?'

'If they can't we'll tip the thing over,' Sautine assured me, clearly grasping the point at once. 'Planning to give the greenies a bath?'

'A bit more than that, I hope,' I said, gaining the open air just as Felicia's artisans pelted past in the opposite direction, like over-excited juvies. The mountain chill struck hard as I emerged, reminding me that my shirt was still uncomfortably clammy, but there was no time to worry about that now. I hurried to the edge of the piazza, where Sautine was encouraging the Basilisk crew to slew their ungainly artillery piece, with a steady stream of profanity.

'Almost there, commissar,' she assured me over the grinding of tracks as the driver nudged it round by increments, attempting to line the long barrel up with the plume of water emerging from the foot of the dam.

'So are the orks,' I reminded her. Even as I spoke, a crackle of las fire and the bark of heavy weapons opened up to greet the first greenskin vehicles to reach the other side of the dam. They were bike things for the most part, easy targets even at this distance, and their return fire was predictably inaccurate, downing very few of our own. A couple tried to race across the causeway towards us, the first erupting in a vivid ball of flame as one of Luskins's rockets found its mark. The one behind it hit the wreckage, bounced, and careered over the parapet, its rider clinging grimly to the handlebars all the way down, until he suddenly transmogrified into an unsightly stain on the spillway.

'Block the road,' the tank commander ordered her units, and the Leman Russes opened up almost as one, belching flame and smoke from the barrels of their battle cannons, their las weapons sparking and cracking, so that from where I was standing they seemed to be the centre of a small, but very intense, thunderstorm. The fury of it burst fully on the greenskins packing the narrow road opposite, blowing vehicles and passengers to pieces with equal abandon, no doubt regretting their eagerness to pull ahead of their fellows by taking the highway instead of lurching into combat across the open ground below. That reminded me. I glanced down, finding the whole valley floor seething with greenskins as far as the eye could see, like a bowl of maggots left festering in the sun.

'Open fire!' Piers ordered, as calmly as he could under the circumstances, and troopers and irregulars alike opened up with their small-arms, pouring as much fire as they could down the slope.

A human army would have thought twice at that point, I have no doubt, but true to form it merely seemed to enrage the orks. With that bone-jarring yell of *'Waaaarrgh!'* which I had come to detest so heartily (and still do, come to think of it, even after all these years), they began swarming up the slope, abandoning their vehicles, which had finally reached a degree of inclination they couldn't climb. And a good thing too, or their heavy weapons would have made short work of us, of that I have no doubt. They could still have done us a great deal more damage than they did if the gunners had held their positions and laid down covering fire, but being orks of course they didn't, abandoning their vehicles with the rest of their confederates and joining that hideous, unstoppable charge.

Rank after rank of them fell to our guns, but they just kept coming, trampling their casualties underfoot in their eagerness to close, with a complete disregard for their own safety. No human troops, apart from Astartes I suppose, could have sustained that assault, forging up so steep a slope, but the greenskins charged on as though they were crossing a sporting ground, barely hindered by the incline.

'Keep firing!' I yelled. The Leman Russes swept the road opposite with their heavy bolters, chewing apart the surviving greenskins, while a couple of burning trucks effectively prevented any more of their number from moving up and attempting to assault us across the top of the dam. Unfortunately, they couldn't depress the sponson-mounted weapons enough to engage the green wave slogging so determinedly towards us up the slope, and we were forced to rely on what man-portable heavy weapons could be brought into the fray. The onrushing tide of death was close enough for some of their wild firing to make it over the lip, and I ducked behind the Basilisk, as what seemed like a mixture of bolter and stubber rounds began to whine through the air around me.

'That was a bit close,' Sautine observed, dropping into cover behind me.

Not everyone else was so lucky. A couple of nearby troopers went down hard, and if I was any judge they weren't likely to be getting back up again.

She raised her head cautiously. 'What the hell does he think he's doing?'

'Emperor alone knows,' I said, spotting Ariott at almost the same time she had. The little man was scuttling forwards, crouching low in an attempt to minimise his target profile, clearly intent on tending to the casualties, despite the near certainty of joining them if he did so. I activated my commbead. 'Team Tarvil, cover the vet.' Tarvil waved an acknowledgement, and his militia team switched the focus of their fire, concentrating on wherever the bulk of the rounds continuing to riddle the air around Ariott were coming from. Not that firing to suppress would have any effect on the greenskins of course, but they might get lucky, and tripping over the corpses of the front rank would probably throw the survivors' aim off a bit.

'We're lined up,' the Basilisk commander informed us, and I became aware that the slab of metal I was sheltering behind had stopped moving. The barrel swung down, grating against its rest. 'That's as far as we can depress.'

'Let's hope it's enough,' I said.

The first orks had become visible now, scrambling over the lip of the slope into a wall of las and autocannon fire, falling in droves as they did so, the ranks behind simply hurdling the casualties and rushing forward in their eagerness to engage. They fell too, but far too many of them were getting up again, their staggering resilience keeping them on their feet and on the attack, despite wounds, which would have killed a human three times over.

'Grenades!' Tayber ordered, and fountains of ork viscera erupted behind the front ranks, but even this wasn't enough to stem the tide.

'Then stop reaming about and fire the frakking[1] thing!' Sautine ordered, with remarkable restraint under

---

1. *Presumably she'd picked up the Valhallan oath from Cain or Jurgen at some point during their journey together.*

the circumstances. The artillery crew hardly needed any more encouragement, and the long-barrelled Earth-shaker briefly lived up to its name, the booming of its discharge echoing around the enclosed valley even over the noise of the battle around us. I parried a strike from an axe-wielding ork with my chainsword, taking its arm off at the wrist, and left Jurgen to finish it off with his lasgun while I turned to stare at the dam.

The shot was on target, a testament to the skill of the Basilisk's crew, detonating on the spray-slick wall a hair's breadth above the plume of water jetting out onto the spillway below. A gout of pulverised rock-crete erupted from the surface, and as I raised the amplivisor my aide handed to me, stepping over the corpse of the ork he'd just shot to do so, I thought I could see the volume of the outflow increasing.

'Again,' I ordered, although it was hardly necessary, the hard-pressed gunners already ramming another shell into the breech even as I spoke.

'Ciaphas!' Felicia's voice was shrill in my comm-bead. 'What in the name of the Omnissiah do you think you're doing?'

'Saving you some time,' I riposted, any further comment I might make drowned out by the booming of the Basilisk and the abruptly truncated whine of its shell in flight. With the trajectory so flat, the sound of its detonation was almost instant, rolling into the echoes of its firing, like a double thunderclap.

This time, there could be no doubt that the shot had found its mark. The jet of water from the spillway more than redoubled in the wake of the gout of rubble which erupted from it, and the ork units slogging along the edges of the diminished river found their feet getting wet as the trickle of water they'd been skirting widened to the limits of its banks. Within moments, they were chest deep, a torrent of water sweeping back down the suddenly full watercourse, taking the unwary with it in a rush of flailing limbs and loose equipment.

'That's washed a few of them out of our hair,' Sautine commented with satisfaction, drawing her sidearm to shoot an axe-wielding greenskin in the face as it rounded the corner of the Basilisk, bellowing its monotonous warcry and looking for something to kill. I took its head off with the chainsword as it fell, just to be on the safe side. However tough they were, I'd yet to see one getting up from that.

To my amazement, I noticed Ariott out of the corner of my eye, still not dead, dragging one of the injured troopers to safety with a sublime disregard for the screaming greenskins Tarvil's militia rabble were continuing to drop all around him.

'Didn't you understand what I just told you?' Felicia demanded, sounding remarkably agitated for a member of a sect dedicated to the overcoming of simple human weaknesses like getting over excited about things. 'We haven't even begun to take the generators off-line yet, never mind draining the capacitors–'

'Good,' I said, choking her off in full flow. 'Any idea how big the bang's going to be?'

'Big enough to compromise the integrity of the whole structure,' she said grimly, as though that were a bad thing. 'You'd better just hope...'

I never did find out what I ought to hope, because at that point my most optimistic wishes were well and truly fulfilled. With a low rumble uncannily reminiscent of a hivequake deep in the sump, the outflow of water increased in volume by what seemed like a thousandfold, accompanied by chunks of rockcrete the size of Chimeras, which crashed down into the valley below, squishing a gratifying number of greenskins as they did so.

'Emperor's blood!' Sautine expostulated. 'The whole reaming dam's collapsing!'

She was right too, the blank wall becoming crazed with stress fractures, through which new torrents of water began to jet. With ponderous slowness, the whole edifice began to crumble, the pent-up pressure of the fluid behind it straining for release. Abruptly, an entire section of it seemed to vanish, to be replaced by a solid wall of water, tens of metres high, which began roaring down the valley below us, scouring it clean of the greenskins that infested it. Vehicles and orks alike were engulfed in seconds, with no time to flee even if the press of their fellows behind hadn't made that impossible; picked up and whirled away like specks of refuse in a gutter.

A few of the brighter ones, if that term has any meaning when applied to orks, tried to reach safety on the higher ground, but that meant running into the barrage of fire our defenders were still pouring back down the slope. Though taken as much by surprise at the unexpected deluge as the orks had been, most of our people still had the presence of mind to keep shooting, their morale much improved by the abrupt turn of events in our favour.

'Keep at them!' I yelled, flourishing my chainsword in an appropriately heroic fashion. 'Drive them back!'

The Perlians responded with enthusiasm. Denied reinforcements, the vanguard of greenskins, which had made it through our lines, suddenly found itself outnumbered, cut off, and swiftly annihilated.

With a roar which made everything I'd heard up to this point pale in comparison, a sound so loud that I felt rather than heard it, the rest of the dam finally gave way, torn apart by the torrent ripping its way through the breach. Drenched by the spray, which felt freezing in the chill mountain air, but at least went some way towards diminishing the stench of the servitor's vital fluids still soaking my shirt, I watched in awe as the whole valley filled with tumbling grey water, flecked with foam, and the entire ork army abruptly vanished, swept away as though it had never been. Confident that the few bedraggled survivors that remained would be swiftly mopped up by our exultant host, I turned to Sautine with as much insouciance as I could muster.

'Well,' I said, straightening my cap, 'that went about as well as could be expected.'

Editorial Note:

Cain's impulsive action was to have unexpected consequences for both the course of the war, in the short term, and the entire segmentum in decades to come. A closer examination of the part he was to play in these later events must perforce await the completion of my work on subsequent volumes of the archive, but for a brief and substantially accurate overview of the effect his destruction of the dam in the so-called Valley of Daemons was to have on the campaign to cleanse Perlia I, turn once again to Kallis's popular history of the invasion.

From *Green Skins and Black Hearts: The Ork Invasion of Perlia* by Hismyonie Kallis, 927 M41

As Cain's Heroes[1] continued their unstoppable march towards victory and the Imperial lines, the intelligence analysts watching their progress through their orbital sensors began to appreciate the full magnitude of his achievement. The forces of the Liberator had become such a severe thorn in the side of the enemy that resources, which had previously been used to press the attack on the fiercely-contested land bridge linking the two continents, were being diverted to deal with them. Not, so far, in sufficent numbers to materially weaken the ork onslaught, but enough for their absence to be noticed. That was all to change after the momentous events in the Valley of Daemons.

We can only imagine the anguish the watchers of the high command must have felt at the sight of that gallant band apparently walking into an ambush designed to destroy them, their seemingly suicidal decision to take a last stand in that desolate and ill-named declivity, and their subsequent complete disappearance.

Cain's bold and unexpected decision to destroy the dam was to have wider strategic implications than he could possibly have realised at the time. Believing his followers lost,

---

1. A widespread Perlian nickname for the members of Cain's ad hoc fighting force, first used as the title of a popular holodrama about their exploits, and which subsequently stuck. Cain himself disliked the production intensely, not least because of a wholly invented subplot in which one of the militia recruits has a clandestine love affair with him, and because, almost inevitably, Jurgen fails to appear at all.

killed in the very act which saved them, the Imperial commanders lost no time in taking full advantage of the havoc he'd wrought on the forces occupying the Eastern continent. By the time the flood the Liberator had unleashed had subsided, after scouring its way though the valleys of the foothills, over seven thousand of the greenskin invaders had perished.[1] With the belated arrival in orbit of three Imperial Guard troopships, the Imperial commanders had their first chance since the commencement of the invasion to counter-attack, and they seized it eagerly, deploying their dropships to surround and slaughter the remaining ork strongholds in the occupied zone.

Ironically, by the time the first Guard regiments had arrived on the desecrated soil of Eastern Perlia and begun winning it back corpse by greenskin corpse, Cain and his allies had already embarked on the next stage of their journey, still completely unaware of the fact that they had just tipped the balance of the entire campaign in favour of the forces of the Emperor.

---

1. *Although at first sight this may seem like a gross overestimation, it is quite possibly accurate nevertheless. The network of valleys directed the floodwaters through the remains of several villages in which orkish garrisions were known to have been bivouacked, and the backwash probably accounted for the ambushing force waiting for the convoy further down the pass as well.*

TWENTY-THREE

'You were lucky,' Felicia said shortly, still vacillating between righteous indignation at my cavalier treatment of a Mechanicus shrine and mere human relief at the fact that, thanks to my having done so, she was still alive enough to be annoyed about it. I was standing at the edge of the piazza, looking down a damp and weed-encrusted ramp, wide enough to have taken three of our vehicles abreast (although fortunately no one seemed keen to try the experiment; when we moved out we would do so in single file, keeping as far from the precipitous drop to our right as we decently could), which terminated on a flat platform beneath the towering and somewhat corroded tangle of metalwork masking the tunnel we'd come here to find. Felicia was already mounted up on her power lifter, preparing to remove the massive intake grilles, which blocked the road through the mountains, although since she hadn't started the engine yet we were able to have a relatively normal conversation without needing to go through the vox circuits. 'If we hadn't managed to get the incense lit before you pulled that little stunt of yours, Omnissiah alone knows what might have happened.'

'Well thank the Emperor you were able to invoke its protection in time,' I said, as politely as I could. In my experience, His Divine Majesty tended to be rather too busy keeping the galaxy spinning to waste much time looking out for my welfare, which is why I took care of the matter so conscientiously myself, and I strongly suspected that the same held true for his clockwork counterpart. Nevertheless, it couldn't hurt to be on the safe side. I pointed at the latticework of metal below us, a dozen metres wide and half as high, with as much casualness as I could muster. 'Can you really get that lot down?'

'No problem.' As I'd expected, being faced with a technical challenge focused her mind so much that she forgot she was supposed to be in a snit with me. 'They're sectional. We only need to remove a couple.' She fired up the engine of her modified Sentinel, and clanked down the moisture-slicked slipway to inspect the aqueduct up close. I turned away, content to leave her to it, still trying to assimilate the sudden change in both our fortunes and the landscape surrounding us.

The lake had gone, replaced by a deep gouge in the mountainside where only a short time before the placid waters had lapped almost at our feet. Now it was a scene of utter desolation, the floor and sides of the declivity caked with thick, stinking mud, which ceased abruptly at what had formerly been the waterline. Above this the variegated scrub I'd noticed on our drive up the highway to the dam still grew, a vivid contrast to the stench of decay which now permeated everything around us. A thin, silver trickle was the only thing relieving the monotony of that drab bowl of filth, the river which had been held back to form the reservoir having resumed its former course. It meandered gently down to the tiny pool backed up behind the stunted remains of the dam's foundations, trickled over them, and flowed on through the line of the watercourse the road had paralleled, before we had so peremptorily reordered the landscape.

Nothing much remained of the valley below the site of the dam either, the scouring flood having torn away plants and soil almost down to the bedrock. Stark new outcrops loomed grey and grim over the shattered remains of the roadway by which we'd ascended. Returning the way we'd come clearly wouldn't be an option, even if I'd been inclined to try it. I strongly suspected we'd deterred our pursuers for some time to come, but I'd learned never to underestimate ork tenacity, and turning up somewhere they wouldn't expect still seemed like the best course of action to me.

'Bit of a mess,' Piers said, materialising at my elbow. Lost in the contemplation of the destruction we'd unleashed on the peaceful landscape below, I hadn't heard him approach. I nodded soberly. 'It was the only thing to be done,' I said.

The young captain shrugged. 'I suppose they can always build another one,' he said prophetically, blithely unaware of the hideous consequences that little project was going to have for me a few years further on, and handed me the data-slate he'd been carrying. 'I've got the casualty figures, if you'd like to take a look at them.'

They were better than I'd feared and worse than I'd hoped, as usual, so I adjusted my expression to an appropriately grave one, and praised their noble sacrifice like I was supposed to. I was about to hand it back when one of the names caught my eye.

'We lost Kolfax?' I asked, surprised to find how much that affected me. He'd hardly been the most likable member of our little band, and in all honesty his use as a guide was more or less at an end, but he'd been solid and reliable within his limits.

Piers nodded. 'Took a stubber round through the chest when they rushed us; Ariott did his best, but...'

'Quite,' I said, falling into a matching stride with him. About a dozen shrouded silhouettes were laid out next to the ambulance, in what seemed to me to be a staggeringly insensitive gesture given that that was where our wounded were being patched up, but Ariott and the corpsmen were being rushed off their feet looking after the living. The dead would just have to wait their turn. I gestured to the scoured valley beneath us. 'At least he took one hell of an honour guard with him.'

'I'm sure the Emperor's giving him a pat on the back right now,' Piers said, in the tone of a man who thought no such thing. His platoon sergeant trotted by, bent on some errand of his own, and the young officer called him over, clearly grateful for the distraction. 'Vyner, can you organise a burial detail?'

'No problem, captain.' The stocky sergeant saluted perfunctorily, and began rounding up nearby troopers with the brisk efficiency common to senior NCOs throughout the galaxy. 'I need some volunteers. Tuffley, Bel, Hyland...' Leaving him to it, we turned back to Ariott and his makeshift aid station.

'Commissar.' The little man glanced up as we approached, his habitual demeanour of affability tempered now with evident exhaustion. The two field medics we'd acquired along with the ambulance were still going about their business, patching up fractures and puncture wounds with practiced assurance, and an air of palpable relief which subliminally assured me that the worst was over and they'd moved on to the walking casualties. 'I'm afraid we're a bit busy at the moment.'

'So I see.' I glanced pointedly at the stretcher cases laid out in the back of the ambulance. There were more of them than it had been designed to carry, so a couple of the less severely hurt had been bedded down on the floor. 'I must admit, after seeing you in action this morning I'd half expected to find you hitching a ride in Kaeti yourself.'

'Oh. That.' To my astonishment he actually blushed. 'I couldn't just leave them there, could I?' Well I would have done, at least until the noise had stopped, but admitting as much would hardly have helped morale. Instead I nodded gravely.

'Of course not,' I said. 'If you were a Guardsman I'd put you in for a commmendation. But try to remember you're indispensible next time, will you?' If anything, that only seemed to increase his embarrassment, although for the life of me I couldn't see why.[1] To prevent the entire conversation bogging down in platitudes, I indicated the crowd of wounded troopers and irregulars. 'Any idea how long it'll be before you're ready to move?'

'Another hour or so,' Ariott said, evidently grateful for the change of subject. He indicated the queue of walking wounded, the tail end of the triage process, and shrugged wearily. 'We're on to the superficial stuff now. Most of these will still be able to fight after a hot meal and a bit of rest.' He nodded towards the ambulance. 'We've got twenty severe cases, four of them critical. I'll talk to Norbert about transferring the most stable to another vehicle before we pull out, so we can tend to the worst more effectively.'

'Good man,' I said, running the numbers in my head. With twelve dead, that meant we were down thirty-two effectives. Not a bad trade-off for a whole army of greenskins, but a noticeable dent in our ranks, nevertheless. Fortunately, as always, the irregulars had taken most of the damage, so we hadn't lost that many trained soldiers. I had a sneaking suspicion we'd need all the warriors we could get before this was over.

They wouldn't do us an awful lot of good if they didn't have enough ammunition left to fight with, of

---

1. *According to his autobiography,* All Life Forms Large and Small, *Ariott had acted purely on impulse without even being aware of how much danger he'd been in until afterwards. Ironically, neither of the troopers he'd attempted to save survived.*

course. The thought was sufficiently sobering for me to seek out Norbert as soon as I'd left the makeshift aid station, after a few more encouraging words for our medics, intent on clarifying the issue. The scrivener was right where I'd expected to find him, in the middle of our logistical train, arguing with Sautine about precisely that issue.

'You'll just have to redistribute the remaining shells between the tanks,' he said. 'We've got one more pallet on the ammo hauler we can break up as well, and that's your lot. If it's any consolation, the Earthshaker rounds for the Basilisk are gone completely, apart from what they're carrying themselves.' Overhearing that, my blood ran cold. My time with the 12th Field Artillery had left me familiar with the details of these weapons,[1] and I knew that the artillery crew could only have had a handful of shells left. If my gamble had required any more shots to breach the dam, we might not have made it.

'Right, fine.' Sautine sounded distinctly unhappy about it. 'Looks like we're back to conserving ammo until we can re-supply.'

'That shouldn't be too long,' Norbert assured her. 'If this tunnel comes out where the tech-priest thinks it does, we'll only be about twenty kilometres from another dump.'

---

1. *Presumably he means the Earthshakers themselves, which the 12th deployed on static platforms, relying on Trojan towing vehicles to move them about when required, rather than the self-propelled Basilisk variant which never appeared in their inventory. In either case, the artillery crews would normally have relied on ancillary vehicles to maintain ammunition supplies, the shot locker aboard the Basilisk being too small to contain enough shells for a prolonged battle.*

'In a region crawling with greenies,' Sautine said. 'What do you want to bet that it hasn't been gutted?' So far, we'd been lucky, only a couple of the caches we'd reached turning out to have been looted before we got there, and Norbert's skills had been more than equal to the task of eking out our dwindling resources until the next one. But once we were through the mountains we'd be entering a region where the bulk of the ork forces were concentrated, and the chances of those sorely needed supplies having gone unnoticed in the interstices between mobs would be greatly reduced.

'Then we'll just have to steal it back,' I said, trying to summon the air of calm assurance a commissar was supposed to project at all times.

'Ah well, ream it,' Sautine said, 'we've got this far.' She shrugged, and turned back to Norbert. 'I'll send someone over for whatever you've got.'

'What about fuel?' I asked, as she disappeared. If we weren't able to get the tanks as far as the enemy then lack of ammunition would be the least of our problems.

The bureaucrat smiled thinly. 'We've got enough,' he said, in tones, which warned me I didn't want to know how tight the margin was. I took the hint. After all, he was the expert. 'You heard about the heavy stuff, I suppose?'

I nodded. 'Sautine's voice does tend to carry when she gets excited,' I said dryly. The air reverberated to a loud, metallic clang, which resonated up through the rockcrete beneath my boots. Evidently Felicia had just succeeded in removing the first of the filter covers.

'It does.' Norbert nodded. 'The good news is we've still got plenty of ammunition for the small-arms and the support weapons. If that fails we can always go back to the orkish stuff.' The weapon mounts of our captured vehicles had been refitted with more familiar, reliable and safe Imperial kit, but we'd kept most of the original stuff anyway. Partly because Felicia was fascinated by it, declaring that half of it shouldn't be working at all, and partly as insurance: if we had to fall back on captured ork ammunition in order to fight, it would be just as well if we had something to hand capable of firing it. I nodded in agreement.

'Food?' I asked.

'No problem there,' Norbert assured me, although I hadn't expected there to be. Since leaving the desert, we'd been able to live off the land to some extent, supplementing our rations nicely, and we still had plenty in stock. He smiled, with a trace of good humour. 'You might have let us fill up with fresh water before you gave it all to the greenskins, though.'

'A generous heart is the gift of the Emperor,' I quoted,[1] and he laughed.

'Well, there should be plenty more where we're going,' he said.

THIS WAS A prediction that was to be borne out remarkably quickly. After our painstaking progress of

---

1. *From* The Precepts of Saint Emilia: *rather an unlikely tome for Cain to have taken to heart, given his frequently expressed and somewhat trenchant opinion of the pious, but her keen appreciation of human frailty seems to have struck something of a chord with him, and several quotations from it appear in his commonplace book.*

the last few weeks, the transition through the aqueduct went astonishingly smoothly. The few tens of kilometres we travelled beneath the mountain range passed in a matter of hours rather than the days it would have taken us to scrabble our way over the peaks, even without ork interference, and I began to feel as close to relaxed as seemed possible under the circumstances. The tunnel ran on smoothly beneath our tracks, the beams of our luminators diffused by the tendrils of mist which rose from the moisture permated rockcrete, the echoes of our passage rolling back in on us as we passed.

From time to time, I caught brief glimpses of ancillary pipework, and other equipment which meant nothing to me, embedded in the walls, along with access hatches disturbingly reminiscent of the one Karrie had conducted us through aboard the *Hand of Vengeance*, before the chill and monotony of the surroundings (not to mention the unremitting racket) drove me back inside the Chimera. The mingled odours of Jurgen and recaff greeted me, and I took the mug gratefully, feeling the warmth spreading down my fingers. Happy as I usually was to find myself in an underground environment, at least when no one was shooting at me, I was beginning to find the experience a trifle dull.

'Thank you, Jurgen,' I said, and went to take a look at the auspex display. Orilly shied away from the mug of hot liquid in my hand, not unnaturally given that the Chimera isn't generally noted for the smoothness of its ride, allowing me a clear view of our progress. 'How are we doing?'

'Nearly halfway already, sir.' The bespectacled auspex operator indicated our position on a tactical display, the icons strung out like the beads of a rosary, the command Chimera comfortably near the middle of the formation. Felicia, I wasn't surprised to note, was almost at the front, only the Salamanders ahead of her. The chances of there being any orks in the tunnel ahead of us were remote to say the least, but my paranoid streak was working overtime. The nearer we got to safety, the more concerned I seemed to feel that we wouldn't make it after all, that my luck was running out, and disaster was waiting just around the corner. (A state of mind the next hundred years or so didn't exactly do a lot to alleviate, come to think of it. At least these days the worst I have to worry about is keeping my cadets up to the mark, and the petty-minded idiocy of some of my colleagues.[1])

'Perhaps we should rest up before we go too much further,' Piers suggested, and I nodded, thinking the same thing. 'If we send a scouting party on ahead to clear the way, we should be out the other end before the greenskins even know we're coming.'

'Works for me,' I agreed, leaving it to him to issue the appropriate orders. 'The tech-priest will need some time to get the grilles down anyway.' From what Felicia had told me, I'd half expected the aqueduct to feed us straight into the blades of the generator turbines, which by all accounts were considerably bigger and more impressive than the ones

---

1. *Somewhat ironic given that, as I mentioned in my preliminary remarks, this portion of his memoirs was recorded shortly before he was to be swept up in the momentous events of the Black Crusade.*

we'd blown to bits at the top end, but she'd simply laughed at that.

'There's an access gate upstream of the turbine chapel,' she'd explained, 'so the maintenance crews can get in here from the other end. All we have to do is keep an eye out for it, and crank it open when we get there.'

'And if the greenskins have found it first?' I'd asked. Felicia had simply shrugged.

'Then we'll know about it one way or the other,' she'd assured me. We weren't being assaulted by solid waves of screaming orks, which I took as a good sign, and Orilly's auspex was comfortingly clear of contacts, so, on the whole I thought we were doing rather well. Of course, if I'd known what was waiting for us on the other side of that mountain, I'd have found myself a nice quiet little cleft in the rock, and never come out at all.

TWENTY-FOUR

WE ROLLED TO a halt shortly before dawn, the thin grey light of the dying night seeping through the scroll-work of the ornately wrought entrance gates covering the access ramp that Felicia had mentioned. Like most of our number, I'd passed as many hours of our passage through the mountain as I could in fitful sleep, being a sufficiently seasoned campaigner to do so pretty much anywhere, but I still felt stiff and weary as I hauled myself out of the Chimera and went to join her. To my vague surprise, she was on foot as well, the power lifter idling gently a few paces away.

'This is it,' she confirmed as I approached her, tilting her head to look up at the gates. They were a lot less impressive than the intake grilles at the top end had been, and the ramp was considerably narrower, but it looked tall and wide enough for the tanks and artillery piece to get through unimpeded, so that was one worry I could safely dismiss.[1] 'Get these open and we're home free.' Apart from the army of greenskins standing between us and safety, of course, but I preferred not to think about that.

'Good,' I said, expecting her to hop back aboard the power lifter and simply rip our way clear with the handling claws, but instead, she beckoned her artisans over and started setting up a little brass dish on a tripod. One of them (I never really worked out which was Aldiman and which was Lyddi), tipped some foul smelling powder into it and set fire to the heap (which made it smell a whole lot worse), while the other handed her a little vial of oil. Felicia made the sign of the cogwheel over it and started dabbing it on the gate with the tip of her mechanical tail, in locations which seemed completely random to me, but which no doubt held some arcane significance for the tech-priest, muttering under her breath as she did so. After a moment she looked up at me.

'This is going to take a while,' she said. Fighting down the impulse to simply order up a couple of demo charges, since I supposed the least I could do after blowing up her precious dam was to let her get on with this in her own way without interference, I nodded gravely and returned to the command vehicle.

'The supply dump should be here,' Piers said, indicating its position on the mapslate.

Even enlarged to maximum resolution, the site still fitted on the same screen as our current position,

---

1. *Presumably it had been designed to allow easy access for whatever heavy machinery might be required to effect repairs to the aqueduct.*

though only just. 'We should be there in an hour or so. Maybe less if the going's good.'

'And the greenskins leave us alone,' I added. The young captain nodded.

'Perhaps we should send the scouts out first. If there's no enemy activity we can move on at once. If they're all over the place we can lie low here and assess our options.'

'Cornered like rats in a waste pipe.' I didn't like the thought of that one little bit. Trapped down here we'd be slaughtered if the orks discovered us. Our only chance if it came to combat would be to spread out, where we could bring the full force of our combined firepower to bear.

Piers nodded. 'I appreciate the point you're making, but if they don't know we're here in the first place...'

'If they spot the scouts they'll know someone's about,' I pointed out. 'I think we should be prepared to move out as soon as they report. If it's clear, we'll head for the supplies. If not...' I shrugged. 'We'll just have to make it up as we go along.'

'Well, that seems to have worked so far,' Piers conceded.

In the event, it didn't take Felicia as long as I'd feared to get the gates open. After half an hour or so, they slid smoothly back, opening the way to the surface, and our trio of Salamanders shot up the exit ramp like sump rats up an outfall. Thin yellow sunshine leaked into the tunnel as they cleared it, raising everyone's spirits, and I began to feel an unfamiliar sense of claustrophobia. With Jurgen at my shoulder, his lasgun held ready for use as usual, I walked up the slope, blinking as I finally emerged into the open air. Since we hadn't heard any firing as the scouts set off, I assumed it was safe, an impression confirmed a moment later by their leader.

'Outrider one,' my commbead said crisply. 'No enemy contact. Heading on to the objective.' I let Piers deal with the message, listening to the brisk exchange with half my mind, while the rest of it savoured the sensation of warmth and clean air. Down on the fringes of the coastal plain, the temperature was appreciably warmer, no doubt to Jurgen's well-concealed distaste, and the contrast to the dankness of the tunnel was invigorating.

'Bring them on out,' I ordered, standing aside to let the steady stream of vehicles rumble up out of the bowels of the mountain, fully taking stock of my surroundings for the first time.

We'd emerged onto the roof of a huge building, the size of a modest cathedral, from which a road, uncannily similar to the one by which we'd reached the reservoir, descended, cut into the flanks of the mountain itself until it reached the wider highway leading up to the main entrance dozens of metres below. This in turn led off from a well-paved dual carriageway, clearly a major transport artery in happier times. After a moment's thought, I was able to identify it as one of the main overland routes converging on the peninsular, along which commerce had formerly flowed between the two continents.

Instead of the valleys and surrounding peaks which had encircled us before, we'd begun our descent through the bowels of the earth, the landscape fell away below us in a vista of low, rolling hills, which gave way in turn to the flat, coastal plain. Raising the amplivisor my aide had thoughtfully handed to me, I found I could see beyond even that, to a flat, sparkling expanse of water.

'We've reached the sea,' I said, scarcely able to believe it.

Of course there were a few score kilometres still to go before we actually got our feet wet, not to mention the peninsular to get across, but I'd never really expected to get this far at all, and the sight of open water left me feeling vaguely disorientated. Jurgen nodded, evidently as pleased as I was to be getting close to our goal.

'We'll be there in no time,' he agreed.

WELL THAT WAS something of an underestimate, but by the time our scouts reported in we'd formed up the column again, and Norbert had dispatched a few of the civilians to replenish our water supplies from the pool below the outfall from the turbines. In deference to the fact that we were now in even more hostile territory than before, we'd adopted a defensive formation, but for all the activity we saw we might just as well not have bothered. I briefly considered ordering Tayber to set some demo charges and collapse the tunnel behind us, just to make sure we were safe, but the chances of any greenskins following us seemed as remote as ever, and an explosion that large might have attracted precisely the sort of attention we were hoping to avoid. Besides, I didn't see anything to be gained from hacking Felicia off again. I was standing outside the command Chimera, enjoying another recaff and a hot grox bun Jurgen had somehow been able to find for me, when the call came through.

'Outrider one,' their leader reported. 'We have a visual on the target. Enemy is holding, but it seems lightly defended from this direction.'

'Can you be a bit more specific?' I asked, hurrying inside and across to the tactical display, where Orilly was already busy overlaying the positions of the enemy on the largest scale map of the site we could project.

The scout commander cleared his throat.

'We're transmitting co-ordinates of all the enemy units we can see. They're dug in towards the west, facing outwards.' In other words, they were facing the Imperial lines, evidently braced for a full-scale offensive over the peninsular. No doubt our own forces were mirroring this disposition on the other side; attempting to assault in force across that narrow land bridge would just result in a traki shoot.[1] Since neither side could reasonably expect to get enough troops through that gauntlet of death to fight effectively, both armies had been stalemated there ever since the defenders had pulled back across it.[2] (Although orks being orks they'd tried it a couple of times before getting the message, and were biding their time until they

---

1. A Valhallan colloquialism, one of many, which Cain had picked up from his prolonged association with the natives of that world. The reference is to a species of animal generally too torpid for a hunter to miss, even at long range, and therefore not considered much of a challenge.

2. Cain is clearly writing with hindsight here, as at the time he would have had no knowledge of the prevailing strategic situation.

could build up their forces enough to absorb the losses on their next attempt.) How we were going to manage the trick for ourselves was an issue I preferred to think about later. Perhaps by that time we'd be close enough to the Imperial lines to vox a warning of our approach. Marquony was listening out on all the usual frequencies, but so far hadn't been able to pick up anything intelligible, and none of us felt like chancing a long-range transmission of our own so deep inside enemy held territory. 'In this direction there are only a few outlying pickets.'

'We could take those easily,' Piers said speculatively, and looking at the display, I had to agree. They could hardly have made it any easier for us if they'd tried. The supply dump itself was set back from the road, in a minor depression in the wall of the last valley we'd have to traverse to reach the coastal plain. The mouth of the valley had been closed off by dug in defenders, all their heavy ordnance obligingly pointing in the other direction, out towards the west, while only a few scattered sentry posts held the line in the direction we'd be attacking from. Clearly, the notion that any Imperial units might get behind them, and strike from the east, simply hadn't occurred to the orks. (To be fair, there was no reason why it should: so far as they knew the entire continent was completely under their control.)

'We could.' I followed the line of the highway with my eye. If we moved fast enough we'd be through those flimsy defences and in amongst them before they even knew we were there. Assuming the supplies hadn't been cleaned out already, we could detach a portion of our force to take the compound, while the main body of the formation punched on through to hit the main body of the defenders from behind. With them gone, we might just be able to make it to the land bridge without too much harrying fire from our rear. It was an intoxicating prospect, and I forced myself to remain calm, looking for any obvious flaws in the plan. I pointed to the chain of fortifications cutting off the mouth of the valley. 'These might be a bit harder to crack than they look.'

'Nothing Sautine and the mortar teams can't take care of,' Piers said cheerfully. 'They've enough ammo left for that. And if the greenies aren't still sitting on the stash, why go to so much trouble to guard it?' The palms of my hands tingled a little as I considered that. It seemed an awful lot of trouble to go to just to protect a few huts full of ammunition.

'It looks to me as if they're fortifying the valley mouth for its own sake,' Tayber volunteered. He shrank the scale of the map. 'If a counter-attack from the Westernlands made it across the plain, they could sweep up here towards the pass, flanking the defences they're bound to have in place along the primary routes.'

'Makes sense to me,' I conceded with relief, my doubts receding. It certainly looked plausible on the map, and just how catastrophically wrong he was, we had yet to discover. I stilled my breathing, trying to project an air of calm deliberation. 'Well then, gentlemen, I think we have a plan.'

* * *

It wasn't quite as straightforward as that, of course, the process of ordering our column and hammering out the details taking some time, but the Emperor seemed to be with us for once. Greenskin traffic on the highway below seemed light, even compared to what we'd encountered in the desert (which I suppose should have forewarned me of what we were about to get into, or at least dropped a little hint, but I was so keyed up that it never occurred to me to question our apparent good fortune), and the few ork aircraft which flew over us were either too high to distinguish our true nature or otherwise engaged in dogfights with our own pilots.

The first time we saw a squadron of Thunderbolts in the skies above our heads, a spontaneous cheer erupted, the conviction that we were almost home sweeping the length of the convoy, and buoying our spirits even more than the prospect of victory. No one was taking our success for granted, of course, least of all me, but the sense was growing within us that the battle we were about to join would be, if not the last we'd have to face, the single most decisive encounter of our long trek to safety. In this we were, of course, entirely correct, but in a fashion none of us could possibly have predicted.

Despite all the delays, we were finally ready to pull out just before noon, the armoured spearhead of our advance leading the way, our mechanised infantry following up, and the motley collection of ork scrap crewed by the whooping irregulars buttressing our rear and flanks, forming as much of a protective screen as they could around Kaeti, the supply wagons, and the other non-combatants. After some thought, I'd abandoned the command Chimera, leaving it to Piers to lead the assault on the main defences, and hitched a lift with Tayber and the remains of Bravo squad in a standard pattern vehicle. The supply dump was bound to be more lightly defended, or so I thought, and I'd elected to lead the raid on it in person.

'You don't need me holding your hand,' I told the young captain, who visibly swelled with pride at this expression of confidence (and to tell the truth he wasn't a bad commander for PDF). 'You've been doing this sort of thing since before I got here, and the supply post might yield some useful intelligence.'

Piers nodded. 'Then that's where you should be,' he agreed, with almost indecent haste, clearly relishing the prospect of hogging all the glory. So far as I was concerned, he was welcome to it too. Give me a nice quiet little sideshow where I can keep my head down any time.

I'd begun our journey with my head out of the top hatch, relishing the fresh air (even more so given that Jurgen was riding along with us as usual), only ducking below to finalise things with Tayber as we approached our target. The rest of our *ad hoc* raiding party was clustered around us: one of the ork trucks, almost empty apart from its driver and heavy weapons crew (who to my distinct lack of surprise turned out to be Demara and Tamworth, eager as ever to volunteer for a chance to play with their favourite toy), a buggy containing the rest of Team Grenbow,[1] and Felicia's

---

1. By this point the convention of naming the militia teams after the regulars commanding them seems to have become firmly established.

power lifter, which trotted along next to us like a faithful hound, its white-robed pilot waving cheerfully whenever she caught my eye. I'd tried to dissuade her from joining us, feeling that this was a matter for experienced fighters, but she'd been as adamantly stubborn as before, insisting that she would be more likely to locate the supplies we needed than anyone else, and that loading them once she'd done so would go a great deal faster with the aid of the lifter. Not being able to muster a counter-argument to either point, which convinced even me, I'd eventually acquiesced with as much good grace as I could summon up.

'Everyone clear on the plan?' I asked, glancing around the tense faces in the Chimera's passenger compartment.

Tayber nodded. 'We go in as soon as the shooting starts, suppress all resistance, and grab what we can before they regroup,' he said.

'Sounds good to me,' Felicia's voice over the vox sounded as cheerful as ever. Grenbow chimed in with an acknowledgement too, on behalf of his split forces, and I took a deep breath, despite Jurgen's close proximity.

'Right then,' I said. 'Let's do this.'

TWENTY-FIVE

At first, our plan worked like a charm, the ork picket lines swept away by the speed and ferocity of our advance with almost as much gratifying suddenness as the ones we'd given a swimming lesson to the previous day. As we passed the burned-out hulk of a greenskin battlewagon, the irregulars in the vehicles surrounding us cheered loudly enough to be heard even over the racket of the ill-tuned engines, which drowned out virtually everything else.[1]

'Raiding party stand by,' I ordered over the comm-bead, my head back out of the top hatch again. I'd grown used to following our engagements on the C3[2]

---

1. *A factor, which probably contributed greatly to the element of surprise, the defenders not realising the approaching convoy was anything other than routine ork traffic until it was too late.*

2. *Command, Control and Communication.*

systems in the command vehicle, and felt cut off without them; so despite the marginally greater risk of stopping a stray round, I'd been unable to resist the urge to supplement the clipped reports I'd been getting through the tiny transceiver in my ear with my own eyes. Our driver throttled back, ready to peel off as we approached our objective, and Felicia grinned at me, keeping pace easily aboard her mechanical steed.

'After you, oh fearless leader,' she said cheerfully, with the complete disregard for proper vox protocol I'd come to expect, and demonstrating beyond all possible doubt that tech-priests are lousy judges of character.

'Acknowledged,' Grenbow said, his clipped tones holding more than a hint of reproof.

'Peeling off,' I reported to Piers, or to his vox man at any rate, and Marquony acknowledged at once.

'Confirm that, commissar.' He switched frequencies, co-ordinating the main attack on the defensive positions with Sautine and some of the other unit commanders. The Basilisk had pulled over, ready to drop some long-range ordnance on the targets to divert their attention just before the main armoured wedge started taking them apart, and the mortar teams had hitched a lift in the no doubt uncomfortably overcrowded Salamanders to flank them and start picking off the infantry from the neighbouring high ground.[1]

---

1. *It seems that out of habit, Cain was continuing to use his commissarial clearance to monitor the rest of the battlefield communications, thus getting a more general overview of events; which makes his single-minded concentration on his own experiences to the detriment of the wider picture even more frustrating.*

A moment or two later, the main engagement began, and the walls of the compound were looming up ahead of us. The rest of our ragtag convoy surged past the fortifications, startled greenskin faces appearing over the ramparts as they went by, and I gave the order to go in. As I did so, I noticed a column of greasy black smoke rising in the distance. It seemed our first blow had been successfully struck.

Like the desert installation we'd first discovered, the supply dump had been constructed with local conditions in mind. Instead of a collection of prefabricated huts, we found ourselves facing a compound walled in some locally quarried stone, to a height of around two metres. This alone would have seemed intimidating enough, but the greenskins had reinforced it, piling up an untidy collection of scrap and detritus on top of the solid construction, much of it carved into barbarous totems reminiscent of the glyphs on the map I'd found shortly after crashing in the desert. I suppose Jurgen might have been able to hazard a guess at their meaning if he'd had a chance to see them, and save us no end of trouble as a result, but of course there was only room for me in the top hatch. The original gates had been patched with chunks of scrap metal, no doubt repairing damage wrought in the ork assault to take the place, but that wasn't going to slow us down much either.

'Take the gates,' I ordered our gunner, and the multilaser in the turret crackled furiously, making the hairs on the back of my neck stand on end as it ionised the air around itself. They blew apart in a gratifying display of pyrotechnics, the heavy bolter in the hull mount opening up as well, sending molten fragments spinning away as the explosive projectiles chewed apart the greenskins gathered behind it.

'Sweep the walls!' I commanded, and Demara opened up with her beloved autocannon, scything down the orks trying desperately to bring their own weapons to bear. Some managed it, a ragged volley pinging from our armour plate and making me duck reflexively below the level of the hatch, but they didn't have time to improve their aim. With a roar like a carnifex clearing its throat, Felicia discharged her flamer, sweeping the battlements from end to end with a gout of burning promethium. Much of the makeshift crenellation had apparently been carried out in wood, which continued to burn merrily along with its would-be defenders as we surged on past them to carry the fight to the enemy.

With a crash that reverberated through the sturdy armoured frame of our vehicle, we rammed the remains of the gates off their hinges, and slewed around looking for targets. The hull-mounted lasguns began to crackle too now, echoing the pop and snap of the blaze above, but without the accompanying screams, Tayber and his men evidently feeling that just because they were stuck inside they needn't miss out on all the fun. I looked round, trying to orientate myself, and as I did so the breath left my body in a single horrified gasp. Something had clearly gone very badly wrong.

The layout of the compound was just as Tayber's data-slate had described it: parallel rows of low, slate-roofed buildings constructed of the same grey stone as the walls, ranged about a central quadrangle. There had been nothing in the documentation about the open space being stuffed with ork buggies, however, a couple of dozen of them at least, not to mention the scores of greenskins swarming out to meet our unexpected attack.

'Oh frak,' I said. Felicia bought us a little more time by sweeping another dragonsbreath along the front rank of bawling barbarians, laying down a barrier of burning fuel which even the most aggressive of them would balk at attempting to cross, but there seemed no end to them, and even as she did so, another mob was swarming into our rear. 'Get clear! Get us out!' Our driver attempted to comply, but even as he did so a crude rocket impacted against our right track, shredding it. With a thrill of horror, I heard the grinding of metal as the guide wheels ran free of it, bedding down in the hard-packed dirt as we slewed to a halt.

The buggy, which had been the last vehicle of our detachment to enter the compound, almost made it out again before the driver went down to a hail of typically random small-arms fire. This time, however, it was so dense the greenskins could hardly avoid finding a target. The vehicle spun out of control, mowing down several of its attackers as it did so, before crashing into the grey stone wall of one of the buildings. Grenbow and his team just had time to stagger from the wreckage before a horde of howling, axe-wielding greenskins descended on them.

They gave a good account of themselves, all things considered, managing to get off a few shots as the enemy closed, but they never had a chance against so many. A couple of the onrushing greenskins staggered, las bolts impacting on the crude armour they wore, but that was all the militia team was able to achieve before being overwhelmed. In a frenzied display of bestial savagery, my men were literally hacked apart before my horrified eyes.

'Piers! We need extraction now!' I voxed.

'Sorry commissar, we're a bit bogged down here ourselves,' Piers replied after a moment. 'We'll get someone back there as soon as we can disengage.' By which time I'd be another collection of bloodied chunks, probably. The orks were turning now, and would have swarmed all over us there and then if one of Grenbow's still-twitching subordinates hadn't somehow managed to trigger a grenade he was carrying, in a last desperate act of posthumous vengeance.[1] The sudden explosion took them completely by surprise, blowing a couple off their feet (although I had enough healthy respect for their resilience not to take it for granted that they wouldn't be getting back up again) and sending them turning back to face this sudden and unexpected apparent threat, with the speed of striking serpents.

That brief moment of distraction was my salvation, or so it seemed at the time. Before I even knew I was moving, I was out of the hatch and running, keeping behind the barrier of burning promethium, and heading for the shelter of the nearest wall. It was only as I gained it that I realised I'd put the crippled Chimera,

---

1. *In all likelihood he'd armed it before being struck down, and the timer finally gave out at this point.*

the raging inferno, and the bulk of the ork host between me and the gate.

At least that afforded me some concealment, however. So long as the orks concentrated on the visible targets, I might be able to slip away unobserved. Tayber had evidently decided to remain behind the armour plate, potting away with the hull-mounted lasguns, while the gunner did whatever damage he could with the heavy stuff. Not enough, in my judgement: it could only be a matter of time before the immobilised vehicle was destroyed. Even as I watched, a party of orks ran forward, carrying demo charges little smaller than the cover of the hatch I'd so recently vacated. Just as it looked as though they were going to clamp them to the hull, they went down, the roar of Demara's autocannon audible even over the howling of the greenskins and the crackle of the burning fuel.

Engine screaming, the ungainly ork vehicle we'd commandeered so many weeks before charged towards the stranded Chimera, the two gunners laying down fire all around them, clearly intent on reaching the survivors inside. For a moment I felt sick. It seemed my reflexes had betrayed me, and that I'd impulsively put myself beyond the reach of rescue.

That impression lasted no more than a moment, however. Two more of the crude rockets struck the onrushing truck, and a fusillade of bolter and stubber fire clattered off its roughly welded armour plate. Demara pitched backwards, a bloody crater where the tattoo on her cheek had been, most of her brain following the projectile out through the back of her skull. Tamworth seized the trigger even as she fell, attempting to keep up the rate of fire, only to be cut down in turn, what looked like a bolter shell ripping his ribcage apart. I have no idea what happened to the driver, but I strongly suspect it was nothing good. The abused truck flipped over and rolled, crushing a few greenskins as it did so, but not nearly enough for my liking.

'Look out, sir.' A lasgun cracked behind me, and I turned, my nose already registering a familiar odour. Jurgen stood there, his lasgun raised, and a greenskin with a large hole through its head was lying face down in the dirt a few paces beyond him. 'That one nearly had you.'

'Thank you, Jurgen,' I said, inexpressibly pleased to see him. No doubt seeing my feet disappear through the hatch he'd simply followed, reasoning that his place was at my side, and under the circumstances I wasn't about to argue with that. If you're going to find yourself surrounded by screaming, blood-maddened orks, take my word for it, there's no one better than a Valhallan to have at your shoulder, and there was no Valhallan I'd rather have than that particular one. Jurgen nodded, glancing at the carnage I'd just witnessed with his usual expression of bovine placidity.

'You're welcome, sir. Bit of a mess, isn't it?'

'I'm afraid it is,' I said, drawing my chainsword with as much of an air of resolution as I could muster. My laspistol, I noted absently, was already in my other hand, no doubt drawn by reflex as I sprinted from the doomed APC. I glanced around, but there was no sign of any help. The beleaguered Chimera continued to act as a fire magnet, the only thing, I have no doubt, which prevented the surrounding greenskins from charging forwards and swamping it. As it was, ork marksmanship proving just as much of an oxymoron as ever, they seemed to be doing more damage to one another than to the sturdy armour plate, misses and ricochets taking almost as great a toll among their number as the steady and disciplined fire of the besieged defenders. There was no sign of the modified Sentinel, so I was able to hope that Felicia had made it to safety at least.

As so often when death seems inevitable, I found a curious sense of fatalism beginning to overcome me; something I've noticed on many occasions, and which I'm certain is a facet of the acute survival instinct which, against all odds and expectation, has left me sitting here almost a century later in a quiet study with a glass of amasec and a data-slate to record these memoirs for posterity. (Not that posterity will ever actually read them, of course, Amberley or someone like her will make damn sure of that, so Emperor knows why I'm even bothering; but since I've not been near a confessional since the schola turned me loose on the galaxy all those years ago, and entering one now would probably give Nute[1] an embolism, it's one way of trying to make sense of it all I suppose.[2]) Anyhow, time and again I've noticed that when your chances of living through the next ten minutes seem problematic at best, you tend to shorten your perspective, looking for ways

---

1. *The chaplain of the schola where Cain was appointed tutor of the commissar cadets.*

2. *An uncharacteristically introspective passage, which may point to a side of his character that he seldom acknowledges. Or perhaps it was the amasec.*

to survive the next few seconds, and if that works the few after that. That probably accounts for the fact that my next move might have seemed counter-productive in the wider context of where we were and what was happening around us, but unquestionably bought us the next few seconds of safety in which to look around for another strategy to prolong our lives by another instant or two.

'This way,' I said, heading for the dubious cover of a pile of gutted machine parts, and glancing back at the one-sided battle raging behind us. We scurried along behind the nearest building, and emerged in a relatively quiet space between two more, on the fringes of the open area where the ork vehicles had been parked. Something seemed different about them compared to the examples we'd seen (not to mention blown up or appropriated) in the last few weeks, and I looked a little closer, trying to make out what it was. They were certainly no better maintained than the average, or cleaner, but the armour plate seemed heavier, and most of them had been ornamented in some way. Gaudy banners or grisly trophies hung on poles, or were draped around the weapon mounts, and most of them carried crudely daubed sigils like the ones I'd noticed above the gates. I pointed them out to Jurgen, who, after all, was probably the nearest thing to an expert on these creatures and their customs in the immediate vicinity. 'What do you make of that?'

My aide shrugged. 'Nobs,' he said, as though that explained it. After a moment I recognised the orkish word he'd used before in trying to explain their system of command and organization (which basically boils down to the biggest and nastiest one gives the orders, and everyone else agrees or gets eaten,[1] which I suppose isn't that different to a lot of human institutions when you come to think of it). He pointed to a couple of the banners. 'There seem to be several different ones here.' My bowels clenched as the implications of that seemingly casual remark began to sink in.

'You mean we've blundered into the middle of some kind of command post?' I asked.

My aide nodded. 'Looks that way,' he agreed. Before he could elaborate, the door in the building we were standing next to burst open, violently enough for the wood to split, and the biggest, meanest ork I'd set eyes on since landing on Perlia charged out, bellowing, clearly intent on taking on the humans who had been rash enough to invade his headquarters in person. Fully a head taller than the bodyguards flanking him, who were themselves larger and more muscular than any other greenskins I'd yet seen, he loped forward like the vicious predator he was. A formless sense of recognition flickered in the rear of my terror-numbed cortex for a moment, and then everything fell into place.

'Oh nads,' I said. 'It's bloody Korbul.' Perhaps it was the sound of my voice, or maybe he scented Jurgen, but that huge, tusked head snapped round to glare in our direction, and with a bellow which shook my very bones, the biggest and nastiest ork in the entire sector charged straight at me.

Time slowed, seeming to stretch every second, as it so often seems to when my combat reflexes kick in. Had I

---

1. *Actually just killed, in most cases.*

not got my chainsword already in my hand, he might well have overwhelmed me by the power and ferocity of that rush, but all the practice I'd put in aboard our life-pod and the combats I'd been through since we got here came to my aid, and I evaded that first attack by what seemed at the time to be a miracle. I even had time to put a few shots into his torso with my laspisol, and Jurgen managed to crack off a few as well, but for all the good it did, I might just as well have been throwing rotten fruit. The las bolts expended themselves harmlessly against the grinding plates of scrap metal encasing his limbs and torso, and I just had time to register that however crude the armour he was wearing seemed to be it was undeniably effective, before he was on me, striking out with a mechanical claw apparently grafted to one arm of his metallic carapace.

It was only as I ducked away from it, my counterstrike eliciting nothing more effective than a stream of sparks, that the full implications of that hit home. With a thrill of horror even more acute than those I'd experienced so far, I realised that the armour was powered, like something the astartes or the sororitas might wear, and that the other arm boasted a built-in cannon of some sort with a barrel which looked to my panic-stricken eyes large enough to have poked my head inside.[1]

If Korbul had summoned up the wit to fire at me, it would all have been over in seconds, but perhaps fortuitously he'd been so overwhelmed with rage and bloodlust that the thought had clearly not occurred to

---

1. *Clearly an exaggeration, as examples of this so-called 'mega-armour' in the possession of the ordo xenos, exhibit weaponry roughly equivalent in calibre to an Imperial storm bolter or autocannon.*

him. So I continued to dodge, hewing away futilely with my shrieking chainsword, searching desperately for a vulnerable point, while the metal-clad behemoth darted after me with a speed and precision completely at odds with its bulk, its metallic claw snapping and slicing like a tyranid lictor, bellowing curses and threats in harsh gutturals which made me very glad I didn't speak orkish.

'Jurgen,' I shouted. 'For the Emperor's sake shoot the frakker!' Not that it would have done the slightest bit of damage of course, but I might have been able to take advantage of the momentary distraction to find an opening or an avenue of escape.

'I can't sir.,' My aide had us both in his sights, and I was certain I could put Korbul's bulk between us so he could get a clean shot, but something about the way he spoke forestalled me from repeating the order. He would do so if I did, I was certain, but he knew these beasts, and if he thought it was a bad idea... 'The others will rush us if I do.'

It was only then that I realised the warboss's entire entourage was hanging back, watching the combat like gamblers around an underhive fighting pit instead of piling in as I'd come to expect their kind to do. Clearly they were reluctant to interfere, although for the life of me I couldn't see why.[1] That wasn't really the issue at the

---

1. *By impetuously engaging Cain himself, Korbul had effectively made it a duel between the two of them which his captains would be reluctant to interrupt. To do so would be interpreted as an insult to the warboss, implying that he was too weak to win on his own, which in turn would be taken as a challenge to his leadership. Since they'd normally expect him to kill a pair of humans in short order, followed immediately by any presumptuous challenger, none of them would be willing to risk it.*

time though, the only thing that mattered was winning, and then getting the hell out of there before our audience got bored with passing round the caba nuts and took a hand themselves.

Just about the only thing I could see that wasn't armoured was his face, so I struck at it, aiming a thrust right between his bloodshot little eyes, deflecting my aim at the last possible moment towards the vulnerable point Jurgen had shown me just above the bridge of his nose. Fast as I was, Korbul was faster, his inhuman speed and ferocity boosted even more by the powered armour he wore, and he blocked the strike easily, grabbing the shrieking blade with the claw thing, actually bellowing with laughter as the sparks flew around us as whirling adamantium teeth met whatever alloy the claw was composed of.

Slowly, despite every iota of strength I could pump into my arm, he began to push the blade back towards me. I flinched, as though ducking away reflexively, and he came on, putting his whole weight behind it, enjoying his sadistic little game like the hate-fuelled scumsucker[1] he was. His face leered into mine as he closed the distance, cloacal breath making me gag, thick strands of drool slithering from the corners of his mouth with each bark of merriment. His hangers-on echoed the sound, although whether from genuine amusement or self-preserving sycophancy I couldn't have said.[2]

---

1. *An oath prevalent on the lower levels of many hive worlds, and extremely harsh by Cain's usual standards.*

2. *Probably both.*

'That's right. Get a good close look!' I encouraged him, suddenly slackening my arm and pivoting out of the way of the descending blade, as I'd intended to all along. With my other hand, I rammed the barrel of my laspistol deep into his eye socket as hard as I could, bursting the orbit and spattering myself with mingled blood and goo.

Korbul howled in rage and pain, but before he could even begin to react I pulled the trigger several times. The las bolts ripped through his brain, what there was of it, and burst against the thick metal meant to armour the back of his skull, pureeing the contents in a most satisfactory manner. Not wanting to be crushed to death in the moment of victory, I leapt out of the way, while what felt like a quarter of a tonne of meat and scrap metal subsided to the ground in front of me with the ponderous inevitability of an avalanche.

Silence descended, apart from the crackle of gunfire in the distance, which indicated that, despite all the odds, Tayber was still making a fight of it. If anything, the noise in that direction seemed to have increased. A score of ork faces stared across the handful of metres separating us, all bearing identical expressions of imbecilic astonishment, even by greenskin standards. I began to shuffle backwards.

'Hold your ground, sir,' Jurgen advised, following his own counsel. I retrieved my sidearm with a moist sucking sound, and did so. He knew more about greenskins than I did, and he hadn't steered me wrong yet. 'If we run now they'll be on us like fleas on a hound.'

'And if we stay put?' I asked grimly.

I didn't have to wait long for an answer. One of the onlookers, bigger and meaner than most, but still noticeably less impressive than Korbul had been, bellowed what sounded like a command, and pointed in our direction. My aide never moved, however, so neither did I, just flourishing the chainsword a little to clear the detritus off it, and pointing the laspistol at the shouter, hoping it wasn't too badly gummed up with bits of warboss to fire properly.

'I'm not sure,' Jurgen said, which was far from encouraging. 'But my dad always said–' His voice was drowned out by another bellow, from a different ork, clearly none too keen on taking orders from this upstart. Within seconds, the whole bunch of them were arguing like juvies in the playzone, and being greenskins it didn't take long for the dispute to become physical. The first shot was fired a moment or two after that, and within seconds the squabble had become a vicious free-for-all.

'Ciaphas. Over here!' a familiar voice called, and I suddenly became aware of Felicia's power lifter idling near the corner of the building. One of its handling claws was gone, the other bent, and she was grinning wildly. Hosing down the squabbling greenskins with the flamer just for good measure, she stalked across to us, and waved cheerfully from inside the cockpit. 'That was a pretty good trick with the pistol there. I thought he had you.'

'So did he,' I said, trying not to think about how close I'd cut it. 'That was the whole point.'

'I'll show you the picts later,' she said, the first indication I had that she'd rigged up a data recorder in the cockpit along with the vox, although I suppose being a tech-priest it was pretty much inevitable. And quite handy too when it came to verifying our story, although if I'd known just how far those picts would end up being disseminated, and how much unwelcome attention it would draw to me in the long run, I'd probably have wiped them myself.[1] A thought seemed to occur to her. 'Those flames seem to be getting rather close to the vehicles. Perhaps we should move.'

'Perhaps we should,' I agreed, as the first of the parked buggies detonated behind us. I gestured towards the gate, where the chatter in my commbead suggested Piers had finally arrived with reinforcements and got Tayber out of his box. Despite this welcome intervention, there were still a few stray greenskins wandering around, and the Sentinel was a great deal more bullet-proof than I was. 'Ladies first.'

---

1. Felica's pict recording of the end of Cain's duel with Korbul had two effects: in the short term it provided unequivocal confirmation of the death of the warboss, which shaped Imperial strategy to best take advantage of the ensuing confusion among the greenskins, and in the longer term it made Cain a popular hero throughout the sector, particularly once the Commissariat decided to release it to the newscasts.

Editorial Note:

As is so often the case with these anecdotes, Cain's account of his adventures on Perlia concludes somewhat abruptly. I've therefore inserted a final extract from Kallis's book in order to provide a more satisfactory overview of the outcome, which I trust will fill in most of the blanks.

From *Green Skins and Black Hearts: The Ork Invasion of Perlia* by Hismyonie Kallis, 927 M41

CAIN'S AUDACIOUS RAID on the lair of the monster that had brought so much destruction and suffering to the people of Perlia, was to prove the final nail in the coffin of the ork invasion. With Korbul dead, the coalition of ork tribes he'd led so successfully disintegrated almost at once into the usual maelstrom of internecine feuding, rendering them easy pickings for the Imperial Guard forces which were beginning to arrive in orbit in ever-increasing numbers. Within the year, Perlia had been utterly cleansed of the greenskin taint, only a few scattered starships remaining in system to continue their mischief,[1] and the other worlds touched by their noisome presence had been similarly freed from their loathesome grasp.

It goes without saying that Korbul's whereabouts had always been a matter of great interest to the Imperial high command, and that orbital surveillance of his headquarters had been intense, so the Liberator's attack on it didn't go unnoticed for long. We can only imagine the astonishment with which the news of his intervention was greeted, astonishment which can only have been compounded by the realisation that it had been carried out by the mysterious fighting force which had been thought lost on the other side of the mountains only the day before. Speculation about who these exceptional warriors were, and who led them, must surely have been intense. Both were questions which were to be swiftly answered.

With the ork forces now in total disarray, the high command lost no time in mobilising their forces for the long-awaited offensive across the peninsular. Now that

---

1. The last few raiders are believed to have been tracked back to their base on the fringes of the system and finally eradicated in the early 950s, although, as in so many things where the greenskins are concerned, it's hard to be entirely certain that they've been eliminated for good.

the greenskins were unable to mount an effective defence, the forces of the Imperial Guard and the PDF fell on the barbarous invaders like a hammer blow, sweeping from victory to victory as they went, finally coming within vox range of the returning heroes. And for the first time, the people of Perlia were to learn the name of the man they were to thank for their deliverance, Ciaphas Cain, the Liberator.

TWENTY-SIX

IT WASN'T ALL plain sailing after that of course, we still had the bulk of the ork army to get through before we reached safety, but as the news of their leader's demise began to spread the heart seemed to go out of them. Individually, they were still just as tough and ferocious as before, they were orks after all, but the cracks in their fragile alliance which Korbul had been able to keep welded together with the force of his personality (or whatever an ork warboss has instead), began to assert themselves almost at once.[1] Several times on the last stage of our journey we found ourselves approaching what we thought to be a battlezone, only to find that the combatants were all orks, settling their differences in the time-honoured way of their kind without the slightest regard for the damage they were doing to their own greater cause as a result.

---

1. The loss of so many of his subordinate commanders, who in the normal course of events would have been tribal leaders in their own right, probably hastened this process of disintegration as their would-be heirs fell upon one another in the manner Cain described after Korbul's death.

Not that we were complaining about that. The more of each other they killed, the fewer were left to get in our way. The more organised groups that we couldn't go around we punched straight through, aided in no small measure by the tactical updates we were beginning to get from the Imperial command net, which gave us a far better idea than we'd ever had before of what was lying ahead of us. In the process of accessing it, Marquony had finally managed to get through to someone among the Imperial forces, who bounced us up the chain of command with gratifying speed, until the vox man informed me with an air of faint incredulity that someone called Alcas, who turned out to be the divisional commander of the Westernlands, was waiting to speak to me.

'This is Cain,' I said, raising my voice slightly over the roar of the Chimera's engine, and projecting what I thought was about the right amount of commissarial dignity. 'How can I help you, general?'

'A complete debrief would be a start,' the voice on the other end said, with a faint trace of amusement. Never having spoken to someone of such an exalted rank before, except at the occasional reception, I was pleasantly surprised. 'But that will have to wait. Can you confirm that Korbul is dead?'

'He was when I left him,' I said, realising that the more reticent I seemed now the more credibility I'd have when I managed to work out a story to explain why I'd made a run for it and blundered into him in the first place. The voice on the other end of the vox link faded a little, and I caught enough to gather that he was passing on the confirmation to someone else in the vicinity. When he came back he sounded more genial than ever.

'Your sergeant's report states that you left a covered position to confront him in person.' Well good for Tayber: he must have assumed I bailed out of the Chimera because I'd caught sight of the warlord. I couldn't come up with anything better myself, so I might as well reinforce that impression.

'Once I'd spotted him there wasn't any time to think,' I said, truthfully enough. 'But I suppose on reflection it would have been more sensible to sit tight and wait for the reinforcements to arrive.'

'Lucky you didn't,' Alcas said, sounding gratifyingly impressed. 'I'll look forward to hearing the full story when I see you. Our forward units ought to be linking up with you any time now.'

'If the greenskins are obliging enough to get out of the way,' I responded. I glanced at the updated tactical display. The first wave of Imperial troops was across the peninsular already, the ork defences swept aside by air strikes and a determined armour thrust. They'd lost little time in advancing, and I have to admit I was impressed by how quickly they'd broken through.[1] As I took in the latest dispositions, the palms of my

---

1. *Later analysis shows that the greenskin defences were rather less formidable than Cain's earlier remarks would indicate, having been intended simply to deter an attack while their numbers swelled to a level sufficient to mount a successful invasion of the west. The Imperial forces had adopted a defensive posture at the other end of the peninsular largely because, with the entire eastern continent under orkish control, the effort required to cross the land bridge with the forces remaining to them would have been futile. Once the back of the orkish occupation had been broken, and beachheads established in the east by the newly-arrived Imperial Guard regiments, the strategic picture had changed completely, allowing an advance to take place relatively unimpeded.*

hands began to tingle, in the old familiar and unwelcome fashion. 'There seem to be rather a lot of them heading in our general direction.' Not all of them were routing of course, at least not yet, but the ones who were seemed to be running straight towards us.

'I'm sure after everything else you've had to deal with that won't be much of a problem,' Alcas said cheerily, and I forced my voice to remain neutral as I replied.

'We'll think of something,' I said, acutely conscious that any other reaction would undermine my credibility to a dangerous extent, although inwardly I was cursing about as much as you'd imagine. I glanced up at Piers, who was still basking in the success of our raid on Korbul's headquarters and seemed to think he was the greatest tactician since Macharius as a result. The young captain nodded seriously.

'We will,' he agreed.

In the end, the plan we came up with wasn't much of one at all, but it was the best we could contrive under the circumstances. We were well out on the coastal plain, running as hard and fast as we could directly for the salient occupied by our own forces, which was continuing to expand as they flooded across the peninsular. Fortunately we'd passed through the main concentration of agricultural lands to reach an area of relatively open moorland fringing the coast, over which our vehicles were able to make reasonably good time while maintaining a sound defensive formation (with me as close to the middle of it as I could manage, of course). As the bulk of the retreating greenskins closed with us, we pushed our armour forward, ready to punch our way through the weakest concentration of them that we could find.

The auspex informed me that this was something of a relative term. A positive blizzard of contact icons peppered the screen, and I stuck my head out of the top hatch in order to check with the amplivisor.

I soon wished I hadn't. As the chill coastal wind, redolent of salt and the sharp tang of seaweed, lashed at my face, I raised the vision enhancers, resolving the long, wavering line on the horizon into wave after wave of ork vehicles, packed with greenskin foot soldiers, all heading towards us as fast as they could. Well it was too late to change our minds now, trying to flee ahead of that onrushing torrent would be futile, and there was nowhere in that undulating, bracken-strewn landscape to mount a defence. Speed and power would be our only allies in this, along with the hope that the fear of the forces behind them would outweigh the impulse to stay and slaughter us.

'Break up the line,' I ordered, and our tanks opened fire at optimum range, blowing holes in the larger formations, while our anti-personnel weapons swept the ranks, trying to prevent the disrupted groups from coalescing again. Behind the vehicles, a second line of running figures, orks who'd been unable to hitch a ride, pelted tirelessly after their more fortunate fellows. Shells from our mortars, perilously mounted in the backs of open-topped vehicles, began to detonate among them, provoking the beserker charge I'd expected, and ahead of them the motley collection of trucks and buggies began to accelerate in turn, their gunners firing in our general direction with their usual lack of accuracy.

'Keep them dispersed!' I urged, hoping to overcome the greenskins' instinct to group action as we had in the desert all those weeks before. If we could do that, they might just keep going... One of our captured buggies exploded a few yards away from the hurtling Chimera, the victim of a lucky shot, and I ducked back inside as pieces of debris and its luckless crew pattered down around me. I hurried back to the auspex screen. 'Is it working?'

'Up to a point,' Piers said, indicating the blips. Our attack had thrown the greenskins into disarray, there was no doubt about that, but they seemed to be regrouping in spite of our best efforts, and damnably effectively too. Even as we watched they took out one of the Leman Russes. Any moment now they'd zero in on the main bulk of the convoy, and it would all be over. I felt the bitter taste of bile in my mouth. After all we'd been through, to be baulked here, so close to safety...

'Incoming aircraft,' Orilly reported, pointing to a cluster of fast-moving blips, comfortingly tagged with Imperial icons. A few more friendly symbols were becoming visible on the fringe of the screen too, slower moving, presumably our ground units in pursuit of the greenskins. Perhaps the situation wasn't quite so desperate after all. In spite of my instinctive caution, I peered over the rim of the hatch again, just in time to see the air strike arrive.

Three fast-moving dots, almost too swift for the eye to follow, plummeted earthwards, resolving into the familiar silhouettes of the Thunderbolts we'd seen before (or something pretty much like them). They howled over the ork lines like vengeful daemons, weapon pods sparkling like dew on a fresh summer morning, sowing death and destruction in their wake. A thick pall of smoke began to rise from the centre of the enemy formation, the dazed survivors milling around in abject confusion.

'Head for the gap!' I ordered, as our gunners targeted the survivors, mindful as ever of the necessity of keeping them from regaining a cohesive formation. (Or as cohesive as anything orkish ever got.) Our beserker charge, scarcely less desperate or insane than the ork one facing us, began to wheel, heading for the hole the Navy pilots had so considerately opened up for us. At the time, I just thanked the Emperor for the coincidence, little realising how closely our progress over the last few weeks had been monitored, and how eager the upper echelons were to debrief us.

We continued to take fire as we closed, of course, losing a few more of the militia units and a couple of Chimeras,[1] but the majority of our vehicles kept going regardless, doing at least as much damage as we took, if not more so. I saw an ork dreadnought take a shell from the *Vixen* full in the chest, exploding violently, and taking out a couple of nearby bike things as its ammunition cooked off.

Then sudenly we were among them, and I grabbed the pintle-mounted bolter, blazing away at anything green I could find. It was too late to duck back inside

---

1. The crew of one managing to hold out long enough to be rescued by the approaching Imperial forces.

and let Jurgen take over, the few seconds that would take perhaps allowing the greenies enough of a respite to gather what passed for their wits and start shooting effectively at us again. Whether I actually hit anything, I've no idea, but it seemed to encourage our people, who kept the survivors hopping, and I gradually became aware that the clumps of sporadically shooting greenskins I'd been targeting had been getting fewer and fewer, and that there were no more of their ramshackle vehicles crossing my sights. Our gunner obliterated a final group with a burst from the multi-laser, and I suddenly realised we were clear of them.

'Friendlies approaching from the west,' Orilly reported, with a faint air of disbelief. 'No more enemy units in between.'

'We made it.' Piers patted me on the back as I ducked inside again, and a spontaneous cheer began to ripple around the battered survivors of our convoy. Well over half the troopers and most of the irregulars seemed to have made it,[1] and as we coasted to a halt and Piers dropped the ramp they all seemed to be shouting my name.

'Well done, Ciaphas.' Felicia swung herself down from the cockpit of her Sentinel, which now looked even more battered than ever, and favoured me with the familiar mischievious grin. 'You've finally run out of orks.'

'And not before time,' I said, with some feeling. A familiar odour materialised at my shoulder.

---

1. *All in all about seventy per cent of the group seem to have made it through this final skirmish, quite a remarkable achievement.*

'Recaff, sir?' Jurgen asked, with his usual impeccable timing. I took the drink gratefully, and narrowed my eyes as a squadron of Sentinels came scurrying up to us. Something about the markings seemed familiar, and as they drew closer I breathed thanks to the Emperor. It was a long shot, but...

'Commissar Cain?' the squadron commander asked, clambering down to join us, his accent confirming the conclusion I'd just drawn. I nodded, returning his salute crisply. 'Captain Renkyn, 362nd Valhallan. We've been sent to escort you in.' He gestured towards the west, where the growl of Chimera engines was growing louder. 'Is there anything you need?'

'Medical supplies,' I said at once, playing to my audience with the ease of a lifetime of practice. The captain relaxed a little, no doubt reassured by my display of concern for the troops. He nodded.

'No problem. Anything else?'

I echoed the gesture.

'Got any tanna?' I asked hopefully.

[On which typically self-centred note, this extract from the archive comes to an abrupt conclusion.]

ABOUT THE AUTHOR

Sandy Mitchell is a pseudonym of Alex Stewart, who has been working as a freelance writer for the last couple of decades. He has written science fiction and fantasy in both personae, as well as television scripts, magazine articles, comics, and gaming material. His television credits include the high tech espionage series *Bugs*, for which, as Sandy, he also wrote one of the novelisations.

Apart from both miniatures and roleplaying gaming his hobbies include the martial arts of Aikido and Iaido, rifle shooting, and playing the guitar badly.

He lives in a quiet village in North Essex with a very tolerant wife, their first child, and a small mountain of unpainted figures.

More Warhammer 40,000 from the Black Library:

DARK ADEPTUS

The second novel in the Grey Knights series

by Ben Counter

THE BRIDGE OF the *Tribunicia* was a magnificent cathedral deep inside the heavily armoured prow, with a massive vaulted ceiling and soaring columns of white marble. Scores of crewmen and tech-adepts crowded the pews, working communications consoles or sensorium displays. The command throne of Rear Admiral Horstgeld took up the front pew, just before the grand altar itself, a creation of marble and gold crowned with a golden image of the Emperor as Warmonger. Horstgeld was a religious man and so the ornate pulpit that looked out over the whole bridge was always reserved for the use of the ship's Confessor, who would take to it in times of crisis and bellow devotional texts to steel the souls of the bridge crew.

Horstgeld rose as Justicar Alaric entered. Horstgeld had served with Space Marines before, even if he had probably never quite got used to their presence. The man who sat on the command pew alongside him, however, had no such reservations. He was Inquisitor Nyxos of the Ordo Malleus, a daemonhunter and the man who had requisitioned Horstgeld's ship into the service of the Inquisition.

'Justicar,' grinned Hortsgeld. 'Well met!' Horstgeld strode down the bridge's nave and shook Alaric's hand. He was a huge and bearded man whose heavily brocaded uniform looked like it had been altered significantly to fit him. 'I must admit, I am accustomed to being the biggest man on my bridge. It will take some getting used to you.'

'Rear admiral. I've read of your victory over the *Killfrenzy* at the Battle of Subiaco Diablo. This is a tough ship with a tough captain, I hear.'

'Pshaw, there are plenty of brave men at the Eye of Terror. I was just fortunate enough to have the charge.'

'You would rather be there now?'

Horstgeld shrugged. 'In all honesty, justicar, yes I would. That's where all the Navy wants to be fighting, we're the only ones holding them back. But I don't run my ship according to what I happen to want and when the Inquisition comes calling one does well to answer.'

'Well said,' added Inquisitor Nyxos. He was an ancient, sepulchral man who wore long dark robes over a spindly exoskeleton that kept his withered body standing. Alaric knew that in spite of his immensely frail appearance, he was an exceptionally tough man thanks to the scores of internal augmentations and redundant organs the Inquisition had supplied him with. An encounter with the rogue Inquisitor Valinov would have killed almost anyone, but Nyxos had survived.

It had been Nyxos who had given the order to execute Ligeia. Alaric didn't resent the man for it, it was what had to be done. And now Nyxos was the Ordo Malleus inquisitor with whom Alaric worked most closely. Such were the mysterious ways of the Emperor.

'The reports from this area of space were alarming indeed,' continued Nyxos. 'While we must send everything we can to the Eye of Terror, the consequences will be grave if we take our eyes off the rest of the Imperium. It will do no good to throw the Despoiler back into the warp if the rest of the Emperor's work is undone behind our backs.'

'True, inquisitor, true,' said Horstgeld. 'But do we even know what we are dealing with here? Or if there is anything here at all? All the records the ship has on the Borosis system suggest it is a veritable backwater.'

Nyxos looked at the rear admiral. His large, filmy grey eyes seemed to look straight through him. 'Call it educated guesswork, captain.'

The engines changed pitch again and the whole ship shuddered. Warning klaxons sounded briefly somewhere on the bridge before someone shut them off.

'Entering real space!' came a call from one of the officers in engineering. 'Warp engines offline!'

'Geller field disengaging!' came another cry. The noise on the bridge rose as well-practiced commands were relayed and acknowledged. Down in the bowels of the *Tribunicia* a couple of thousand crewmen would all be labouring to ensure a safe end to the ship's warp jump – engine-gangs redirecting the plasma reactors to power the main engines, weapon crews manning the ready posts for their broadside guns and torpedo tubes, the ship's small complement of tech-adepts calculating the huge numbers involved in making the ship plunge from one reality into another.

The altar in front of Nyxos, Horstgeld and Alaric rose from the floor and Alaric saw that the sculptures of the altar actually crowned the ship's massive main pict-screen. The screen rose up from the floor until it dominated the whole bridge. It was flooded with grainy static until one of the communications officers powered up the ship's main sensorium and the image swam into view.

'Hmmm,' said Nyxos. 'It's bad, then.'

The pict-screen showed a view of the Borosis system from deep orbit, where the *Tribunicia* had emerged into real space. The star Borosis itself was a swollen, livid red, streaked with angry black sunspots, its corona bleeding off into a halo of sickly red light. Borosis should have been a healthy mid-cycle star, similar in type to Terra's own sun.

'Close in on the planets,' said Nyxos. Horstgeld quickly relayed the order to his comms crew and the pict-screen cycled through closer views of the planets that orbited the sickened star.

The light and heat coming from the sun had dropped massively. That meant Borosis Prime, the closest planet in the system to the star, was even bleaker than the burning globe of rock it had been before – it was dying. Borosis Secundus's atmosphere was gone entirely – once covered by a thick blanket of superheated gases, the planet was now naked, the sudden temperature change having thrown its atmosphere into such turmoil that its layers bled off the planet entirely.

There was a long gap to Borosis Cerulean, the most inhabited world, home to seven major colonies with a total population of about one and a half billion. It was cold and dark. The planet's cities were advanced enough to provide shelter from the eternal winter that had now fallen over the world, but their power and supplies would not last forever. Perhaps the world could be evacuated, perhaps not. That wasn't the Ordo Malleus's problem.

The lifeless world of Borosis Minor, almost completely covered in ice, was an inhospitable as ever, as was the gas giant Borosis Quintus where a few thousand workers were probably deciding how they were going to survive on their gas mining platforms when the solar collectors failed. The change in the star had barely affected the outermost planet, Borosis Ultima, a ball of frozen ammonia almost too small to qualify as a planet at all.

The viewscreen cycled to show the last object in the system.

'I cannot claim to be an expert,' said Alaric carefully, 'But I gather that is the reason we are here.'

There was no seventh planet in the Borosis system. There never had been. But there it was.

It was deep charcoal grey streaked with black and studded with thousands of tiny lights. Around the world were thousands upon thousands of asteroids, tiny speckles of light from this distance, like a swarm of insects protecting the planet.

All Grey Knights were psychic to a degree. They had to be for their minds to be so effectively shielded against corruption. Alaric's psychic powers were all internalised, focused around the wards that kept his mind safe – but he was still psychically sensitive and he could still feel the wrongness pulsating from the new world. It was like the echo of a scream, a smell of old death, a slick and unhealthy feeling against his skin.

'We've had astropaths going mad for light years around,' said Nyxos matter-of-factly. 'That would be the reason.'

'Guilliman's rump,' swore Horstgeld. 'I've been in space all my life and I've seen some things, but never a whole world where there shouldn't be.'

'Try not to get too overwhelmed, captain,' said Nyxos. 'I need a full data sermon on that planet, everything you've got. I'll send Interrogator Hawkespur to coordinate. Atmosphere, lifesigns, dimensions, everything the sensoria can find. And what is the arrival time of the rest of the fleet?'

'Within the day,' replied Horstgeld. 'If you could call it a fleet.'

'We'll need it. That's an inhabited world and if they've got ships of their own we might have to go through them to get down there. And we are going down there.'

'Of course, inquisitor.' Horstgeld turned to his crew and started barking orders, sending communications officers and messenger ratings scurrying.

'What do you think?' Nyxos asked Alaric quietly, as the bridge went about its noisy, barely controlled business.

'Me? I think they were right to send us.'

'I agree. What would you do?'

'I would defer to the wisdom of the Inquisition.'

'Come now, Alaric. You know why I had you accompany me, out of all the Grey Knights.'

'Because they are all at the Eye of Terror.'

'Wrong. You showed an unusual level of independence and creative leadership on the Trail of Saint Evisser. The Chapter made you relinquish your acting rank of brother-captain but they all know your qualities. Space Marines are all very well but even Grey Knights are just soldiers. Ligeia thought you could be something more and I am coming round to her point of view. So, think like one of us, just this once. What should we do?'

'Land an army,' said Alaric, without hesitation. 'Take all the Guard we have and send them down. Right away.'

'Risky.'

'Nothing is riskier than indecision, inquisitor.'

'Quite. And as it happens I agree with you. Is your squad ready?'

'Always.' Alaric's squad was under-strength following the costly defeat of the daemon Ghargatuloth on the Trail of Saint Evisser, but it still represented a concentration of firepower and fighting prowess that no Guard being transported by the fleet could hope to match.

'Good. I want you at the data sermon. You'll probably end up the leader on the ground, one way or another.'

'Understood. I shall pray with my men, inquisitor.'

Alaric left the bridge, knowing instinctively that they would find more on the seventh planet than any amount of prayer could really prepare them for.

'THE EQUATORIAL CIRCUMFERENCE of Borosis Septiam is just under thirty-eight thousand kilometres,' began Interrogator Hawkespur, indicating the pict-grab projected onto the screen behind her. 'Rather less than Earth standard. The mass, however, is the same, suggesting super-dense mineral deposits. As you can see, the thick atmosphere and surrounding asteroid field prevents us from probing the surface but we do suspect the planet is without polar caps, perhaps due to deliberate depletion. The atmosphere shows strong indicators of being breathable, but with severe levels of pollutants.'

The ship's auditorium was normally used for tactical sermons, or public dissections of interesting alien specimens and unusual mutations by the sick bay crew. Now it had been set up for Hawkespur's data sermon and the command crew, along with Nyxos and Alaric's squad, sat in rows around the central stage where Hawkespur was speaking. The pict-grab showed the ugly, weeping sore of a world, provisionally named Borosis Septiam, that had so completely mystified everyone on the bridge. Hawkespur's voice was clipped and professional – she was Naval Academy material from the finest aristocratic stock, a brilliant young woman employed by Nyxos who felt certain she would one day take up the mantle of inquisitor herself.

'The asteroids are in unusually low and stable orbits,' continued Hawkespur. 'It is unlikely that anything larger than a single light cruiser could navigate through them and multiple smaller ships would be out of the question. This precludes a large-scale landing.'

Alaric heard Horstgeld swear quietly. Thousands of Imperial Guard were being transported with the fleet – the initial plan to send them down to the planet had failed before it had even begun.

Hawkespur ignored the captain. 'The temperature readings are particularly anomalous. A planet at such a distant orbit from the sun, especially given the current state of the star Borosis, should be extremely cold. Borosis Septiam's climate suggests temperate conditions over almost the entire surface. This can result only from a massive thermal radiation source or climate control on a planetary scale. The indications we have of extremely high power outputs suggest the latter. Finally, there appear to be a great many orbital installations, apparently man-made. The interference from the asteroids means we cannot get a good look at them but they represent a major presence suitable for an orbital dockyard.'

'What are your conclusions, Hawkespur?' asked Nyxos, sitting in the front row of the auditorium.

'Highly industrialised, with a large and long-standing population. All the data we have has been sent to the Adeptus Mechanicus sector librarium to see if any planet matches it.'

'Any idea how it got there?'

'None.'

'Ship's astropaths have done no better,' said Horstgeld. 'They say it's like a blind spot.'

Nyxos looked round to where Alaric and his Marines were sitting. 'Justicar? Any thoughts?'

Alaric thought for a moment. The Imperium had lost planets through administrative error before – all it took was for one scholar to forget to mark down a world's tithes and that world could eventually disappear off the stellar maps, especially in an out of the way system like Borosis. But this world was suspicious enough to warrant Inquisitorial scrutiny, if only to be sure. There was something so wrong with the world that it would be a lapse of duty to leave it be.

'Since no major landing is possible, we should send a small well-equipped mission down to the surface. An investigative team.'

Nyxos smiled. 'Excellent. Hawkespur? How's your trigger finger?'

'Commendation Crimson in pistol marksmanship, sir. Third round winner at the Hydraphur nationals.'

'Then you'll take the team down. I'll co-ordinate from the *Tribunicia*. Alaric, your squad will support on the ground along with as many Imperial Guard special forces as we can get onto an armed insertion craft.'

'Commendation Crimson?' said Horstgeld approvingly. 'Good Throne, girl, is there anything you can't do?'

'I haven't found anything yet, sir,' replied Hawkespur, completely without humour.

THE IMPERIAL NAVY was the only thing holding back the Thirteenth Black Crusade and all the Imperial authorities knew it. Abaddon the Despoiler had shattered the attempt to pen his Chaos-worshipping forces up in the warp storm known as the Eye of Terror and it was only Imperial command of space that had kept his ground forces from taking planet after planet all the way into the Segmentum Solar. Every Imperial warship was on notice that it could be ordered into the Eye at any moment and thousands upon thousands of them had been, from mighty Emperor class battleships to squadrons of escorts and wings of fighter craft.

Rear Admiral Horstgeld, for all his experience and commendations, couldn't tear a handful of good ships away from the Eye for the mission to Borosis, even with the authority of Inquisitor Nyxos and the Ordo Malleus. His own ship, the veteran cruiser *Tribunicia,* was the only ship in the small investigative fleet that he considered ready for a battle. The escort squadron *Ptolemy,* under Captain Vanu, was brand new from the orbital docks of Hydraphur and consisted of three Python class ships of a completely untested configuration.

Nyxos had requisitioned an Imperial Guard regiment, the tough deathworld veterans of the Mortressan Highlanders, along with the transport *Calydon* to carry them. The *Calydon* was a corpulent and inefficient ship with barely enough guns to defend itself and Hortsgeld knew it would do nothing in a battle apart from get in the way.

Along with a handful of supply ships and shuttles, these craft comprised the fleet that exited the warp over the course of a few hours just outside the orbit of Borosis Septiam. Shortly afterwards another craft was detected in the warp which broke through into real space a short distance away, all its weapons powered down in a display of alliance. It was a large ship, easily the size of a cruiser, but of an ugly, blocky design painted a drab rust-red, covered in ornate cog-toothed battlements and training long flexible sensor-spines like the stingers of a sea creature.

The ship immediately hailed the *Tribunicia*. It identified itself as the Adeptus Mechanicus armed explorator ship *Exemplar* under the command of Archmagos Saphentis, who demanded complete jurisdiction over the entire Borosis system.

The story continues in

DARK ADEPTUS

by Ben Counter

ISBN: 1 84416 242 7

DAEMONHUNTERS!

THE EPIC FIRST NOVEL IN THE GREY KNIGHTS SERIES.

Grey Knights
High speed action and adventure with the elite Grey Knights as they battle against the daemons of the warp

ISBN: 1-84416-087-4